BRANDON

TUDOR KNIGHT

TONY RICHES

ALSO BY TONY RICHES

OWEN – BOOK ONE OF THE TUDOR TRILOGY

JASPER – BOOK TWO OF THE TUDOR TRILOGY

HENRY – BOOK THREE OF THE TUDOR TRILOGY

MARY – TUDOR PRINCESS

KATHERINE - TUDOR DUCHESS

THE SECRET DIARY OF ELEANOR COBHAM

WARWICK: THE MAN BEHIND THE WARS OF THE ROSES

QUEEN SACRIFICE

COPYRIGHT

Copyright © Tony Riches 2018
Published by Preseli Press

ISBN-13: 9781790733163

BISAC: Fiction / Historical

Cover Photography by Lisa Lucas LRPS
www.lisalucasphotography.com

ABOUT THE AUTHOR

Tony Riches is a full-time writer and lives with his wife in Pembrokeshire, West Wales, UK. A specialist in the history of the early Tudors, Tony is best known for his Tudor Trilogy. His other international best-sellers include *Mary - Tudor Princess* and *Katherine - Tudor Duchess*.

For more information visit Tony's author website: www.tonyriches.com and his blog at www.tonyriches.co.uk. He can also be found at Tony Riches Author on Facebook and Twitter: @tonyriches.

In memory of my father
Jim Riches

Loyaulte Me Oblige

(Loyalty Binds Me)

Motto of Sir Charles Brandon
Tudor Knight

1

APRIL 1505

He stood before the Lord Steward, his left eye swollen and bruised, his nose possibly broken. The cuts on his knuckles stung after the physician's potion, which made them worse. The charges against him were serious and his whole future now hung by the slender thread of his own defence.

Sir George Talbot, Earl of Shrewsbury, sat behind a grand desk in his oak-panelled office, the white staff, warrant of his authority from the king, used as a paperweight. He peered at Brandon with an appraising stare, as if judging him before he'd even had the chance to speak.

A thickset, powerful man with a well-groomed beard, Sir George was a loyal favourite of the king. Presiding over the royal household was only part of his reward. He studied the parchment on the desk before him, raising an eyebrow at the contents.

'Charles Brandon, I have the duty of administering justice between the domestic servants of the sovereign – and deciding the punishment, where appropriate.'

Brandon groaned inwardly. He'd given no thought to what the punishment might be. Although he'd hoped the escapade would be forgotten, he should have known there would be consequences when he threw the first punch. A heavy fine was likely, and that would increase his mounting debts. He had no money of his own and hadn't yet made any payments to his uncle. He envied the Lord Steward's power and braced himself for what was to come.

'We cannot allow servants of the king to brawl in the street like commoners, Brandon.' Sir George scowled at the thought. 'What do you have to say for yourself?'

'They insulted the memory of my father, my lord.'

Sir George's chair creaked as he sat back in it, and his expression changed from apparent disinterest to one of curiosity. 'I knew your father. He was a good man, to the end.'

Brandon struggled to remain silent. Sir George Talbot was present at Bosworth and might have witnessed his father's death by the sword of King Richard, unable to defend himself while holding the Tudor standard. Brandon's mother once said it was typical of him. To this day, he regretted not asking her to tell him more. He made a judgement to speak.

'They said my father forced himself on a gentlewoman – and her daughter.' He dug his nails into his palms as he battled to control the anger returning to his voice. It pained him to repeat the slur but he had no choice.

'I've heard the story,' Sir George nodded, 'although I've no idea if it's true.' He referred to the papers again and looked up at Brandon. 'You are charged with affray, yet if I find these men set upon you, I can record it as self-defence.' His tone had softened a little.

'I beg your forgiveness, my lord. I do not wish to name those who insulted my father's name.'

'Most noble of you, Master Brandon,' his eyes narrowed, 'although the report before me shows you defended your father somewhat better than he defended himself.' Sir George seemed to reach a decision. 'You hold a position of trust as a servant of the king.' He frowned. 'You should be dismissed, without references.'

'My lord, I confess to acting rashly—'

Sir George Talbot held up a hand to silence him. 'I've decided to reassign you to new duties, in return for your guarantee to show more restraint in the future.'

'You have my word, my lord.'

'Good.' Sir George nodded. 'I've seen your skill at the joust, Brandon. You show much promise. It's a waste of your talents to have you serving the king's table. How old are you now?'

'Twenty-one, my lord.'

'You've served time enough. I could put your name forward for the King's Spears – but I have to be satisfied you are worthy of the task...'

'I am, sir.' He watched Sir George stroke his beard as he made up his mind what to do. 'I won't let you down again, my lord. As you know, my uncle, Sir Thomas, is the king's Master of the Horse. He has taught me well.'

'Then you are fortunate, Brandon, but mark my words: for your father's sake, I'm prepared to show leniency this time – but I shall not be forgiving if you appear before me again. Do you understand?'

'I am grateful to you, my lord,' Brandon gave a brief bow, 'and will not forget your kindness.'

Brandon left Westminster Palace with a new spring in his step, despite the threat of rain from the brooding skies overhead. His uncle would be pleased to hear his news, but first there was someone else he must tell.

The light was fading, yet the narrow London streets were still crowded with noisy market stalls as he made his way to Cheapside. Women wearing shawls haggled over lengths of cloth and Flemish lace. A swarthy man called out, 'Pies, hot pies!' An attractive young girl selling posies of flowers from a basket caught his eye and smiled at him, before looking quickly away as she noticed his battered face.

Brandon quickened his pace as a swift movement ahead attracted his attention. A barefoot boy of about twelve years old reached into an old woman's bag and stole her purse, as quick as a rat down a gutter. The woman had her back to him and seemed unaware she'd been robbed.

He was in a hurry to share his news and could have turned a blind eye to the crime, but his future role as a bodyguard of the king brought new responsibility. He moved with a speed that took the boy by surprise. Reaching out, he grabbed him by the collar of his ragged coat. He held the boy at arm's length, aware that cutpurses carried razor-sharp knives. He also had no wish to share the scruffy thief's fleas.

'You'll return that purse.' His voice carried a stern edge but he kept it low, not wishing to draw attention.

The boy stared at Brandon's bruised face and decided it was useless to struggle. 'Will you let me go if I do, master?'

Brandon grinned at the boy's confident attempt to negotiate, despite his circumstances. He was a survivor, used to living by his wits. Tightening his strong grip to stop the boy escaping, he glanced at the old woman. She was still deep in conversation, wagging a gloved finger at a stallholder. An idea occurred to him. 'See if you can put it back without her knowing.'

He gave the boy an encouraging shove in the woman's direction, keeping a firm grip on his collar, and watched as he dropped the leather purse back into her bag.

The boy turned and looked up at him with wide eyes. 'Let me go now, sir?'

He studied the boy's pale, grimy face. He looked scrawny yet defiant, despite his situation. 'I've had a bit of luck myself today.' Reaching into his leather purse, he fished out a groat. 'Buy yourself some grub.'

The boy looked at the silver coin. 'Thank you, sir.'

Brandon smiled to himself as he watched the boy vanish down a side street. He wished he could have done more for the young rascal but doubted he would ever see him again. The population of London was growing at such a rate that thieves found easy pickings. Even if he'd helped this one boy find honest work, a dozen young urchins waited to take his place.

Cold rain dripped from the brim of Brandon's hat as he waited in the shadows at Anne's back door. He cursed and tried his secret knock again. Candlelight glimmered through the gap between the closed wooden shutters, so he knew she was at home. He was beginning to wonder if she would ever answer when the door opened.

Anne Browne leaned out and glanced down the narrow street, then ushered him inside before anyone could see. She looked beautiful, in a cornflower-blue silk gown, and wore a fine silver necklace with a pearl pendant, his present to her last New Year's Day. Her dark hair, normally plaited under a fashionable French hood, hung loose and lustrous, reaching over her shoulders.

Anne's father, Sir Anthony Browne, had been the king's standard-bearer and an important man at court. He'd found her a position in the Palace of Westminster, which was how she shared her lodging with two ladies of the king's household. As they were away at Richmond Palace, Anne had the lodging to herself – a rare chance to entertain in private.

Brandon, at over six feet tall, had to duck his head under the wooden roof beams in the low-ceilinged room. He glanced around out of habit to make sure they were alone. There was always the risk of being discovered, yet he felt more at home in

Anne's cramped lodgings than in his Uncle Thomas's grand manor house in Southwark.

A welcoming log fire blazed in the stone hearth and beeswax candles lit the room with a soft yellow light. Brandon pulled off his damp coat and hat while Anne poured him a goblet of warmed mead. He sipped it gratefully and felt its sweet heat warm his throat.

She studied his face and frowned. 'The bruising is worse.' She reached out a hand as if to touch his swollen cheek but stopped herself and let it fall to her side. 'My mother used to make a poultice from parsley – or perhaps it was daisies – for the bruising.' She gave him a mischievous look. 'I don't think I'll find either at this time of night though.'

He drained his goblet of mead. 'I'll live.' Taking her in his arms, he gave her the long, slow kiss he'd been looking forward to all day. He liked the soft touch of her hands on his back, holding him close. The delicate scent of lavender aroused memories of their first time together. With reluctance he pulled himself away and gave her a wry grin. 'It might have been worth it, after all. I have news. Good news.'

'You've been spared a flogging?' She raised an eyebrow.

He smiled. 'It seems my luck is changing, for the better. Sir George Talbot has agreed to put my name forward for the King's Spears.'

'His personal bodyguard?'

'The king's yeomen are his bodyguard.' He had to think for a moment, and then decided to be honest with her. 'In truth, the Spears are something of a club for gentlemen adventurers – I've yet to learn what they get up to all day. The important thing is I'll be one of the king's trusted men.' He heard the pride in his voice.

'You already are. You've been serving at his table for how many years?'

Brandon frowned as he tried to remember. 'Three, maybe

four – but this is different. The king takes little enough notice of his servants.' He realised she was teasing him.

Anne looked thoughtful. 'You'll be paid more?'

'Of course.' He grinned.

'Enough to make an honest woman of me?' There was an edge to her voice.

Brandon studied her face, unsure what to say. 'I need the forty pounds' worth of estates which would make me eligible for a knighthood. Then we shall talk of marriage.'

'You talk of being a knight but do you think it will ever happen?' She sounded doubtful.

'I do. My father and my grandfather were both respected knights, and one day I will be too. This chance with the Spears is just the beginning. I'm going to make a name for myself, Anne. The King's Spears are chosen men. If we go to war against the French we'll be made captains and commanders – and I'll be in all the jousts now, not just filling in when everyone else has fallen off.'

It was the most heartfelt speech he'd made in a long time and he believed the truth of his words. He'd somehow won over the Lord Steward and been offered the chance he'd been waiting for since becoming a servant of the king.

She pulled him closer with a look of concern. 'You will take care? I've seen good men horribly wounded and even killed at the king's jousts...'

Brandon kissed her again to silence her. 'I promise to take care. That's how I will become famous – by winning.'

The Lord Steward kept his word and Brandon was summoned to meet the Earl of Essex, Sir Henry Bourchier, Commander of the Spears. He'd been kept waiting outside the earl's study half the morning and passed the time rehearsing what to say.

When he was finally ushered in, his fine words slipped from his mind and he said a silent prayer.

Sir Henry had an abrupt and direct way of speaking. 'My gentlemen are all of noble birth, Brandon. If I had my way, you would serve in the Yeomen of the Guard, so you are going to have to work hard to justify your place in the Spears.'

'I will, my lord.' Brandon wore his best doublet and an old sword on a low-slung belt. He remembered one of the things he'd planned to say. 'You won't find a more loyal man in England.'

The dour earl ignored his reply and continued in the same tone. 'You are expected to provide your own arms and three good horses, as well as your retainers.'

'Retainers, my lord?' This was news to Brandon. He had two horses, and his uncle would lend him a third, but retainers needed paying, for as long as they served.

'Every man in the Spears needs to muster two archers, as well as a squire to carry his shield and lance.'

Brandon nodded, yet his mind was racing. He suspected from the earl's tone that he knew it would be impossible for him to afford to employ three retainers. He could approach the foreign moneylenders in the merchants' quarter but they'd need him to make proper repayments, and he'd promised to settle his debts to his uncle.

'You'll start next week, Brandon.' Sir Henry frowned. 'Wear a doublet. And get your hair cut.' He waved a hand in dismissal. Their meeting was over.

An idea occurred to Brandon as he made his way down the dimly lit narrow corridors of Westminster Palace. If he couldn't borrow the money he needed, he'd have to find a wealthy sponsor, or joining the King's Spears would bankrupt him. He knew just the person. Now all he had to do was find the courage to ask.

Harry hit a fierce practice serve as Brandon arrived. He stopped to watch as the ball cracked against the wall and bounced deep into the court. Brandon enjoyed a game of tennis, but Harry was so competitive, despite the seven-year age difference between them.

Harry was not yet fourteen years old but his height and confident manner made him seem older. He could speak French more fluently than Brandon and had inherited his father's sharp intelligence, often outwitting his tutors.

He played tennis like a boxer in a fight, winning through pure aggression rather than finesse. Once, Brandon rashly agreed a wager on the outcome of a match. That cost him two weeks' pay, but to young Harry the joy of winning was all that mattered.

Brandon inspected his racquet and then took his place on the court, glancing up at the viewing gallery. Courtiers often watched them play, so he was relieved to see the gallery seating was empty. An audience made Harry more determined not to lose. As a point of principle Brandon never deliberately let Harry win, but he needed him in a good mood after their game. He also needed privacy, as no one must know of his request.

Harry called out from the far side of the court. 'Your face is an improvement, Brandon!' His reedy voice echoed provocatively in the vast tennis hall.

'You should see the others!' Brandon swished his racquet in the air as if it were a poleaxe.

'I hear you're joining the Spears.' Harry served without waiting for an answer. It was an old distraction trick.

Brandon knew better. His keen eye followed the ball and he was ready as it bounced once on the roof and fell, returning it over the net as far from Harry as he could. His effort was rewarded by a curse from the far end of the court as Harry stretched to reach, returning the ball with such force Brandon had no chance.

'Mark!' Harry called out for Brandon to note where it bounced.

'Chase six!' He smiled. 'A good enough score.'

He took a new ball from the wicker basket, tossed it in the air and caught it in his hand. While Harry used brute force, Brandon relied on finesse. He'd done some coaching for the nobles and made them laugh by describing his deceptive serve as 'feeling the lady's bottom'.

'You don't have to hit the ball hard,' he would tell them. 'Caress it with your racquet and you can put a little spin on it.'

That was what he did now, skimming the new ball high over the net in a graceful arc to hit the opposite wall just below the play line. Harry had been playing Brandon too long, as he made the return look easy, whacking the ball into the back of the court.

They played until Brandon took the last new ball from the basket. He looked at it in his hand and decided there might not be a better time. 'You were right about me joining the King's Spears – and now I must beg a favour of you.'

Harry flashed him a grin. 'You want me to tell Essex to be easy on you?'

Brandon smiled at the suggestion. 'I need a couple of good archers and a squire. The Earl of Essex said it's a requirement to join the Spears.'

Young Harry swung his racquet back and forth as he thought about it. 'We could hold an archery contest. I know my father will approve. He wants me to take charge of my own household.' He gave Brandon an appraising look. 'Of course, there will be a price for providing your retainers.'

Brandon frowned. 'Thank you, but I can't keep asking my uncle for money. I already owe him a small fortune.'

Harry shook his head. 'Not money, Brandon. I want you to teach me to joust.'

'Your father has forbidden you to take part in a joust...'

Harry grinned. 'Well, we must make it our secret – and be sure he never finds out.' He gestured with his racquet for Brandon to serve. 'Now, let's get on with this game.'

2

FEBRUARY 1506

The Earl of Essex, Sir Henry Bourchier, Commander of the Spears, had been wrong. The men of the King's Spears looked after their own and readily accepted Brandon into their ranks. It helped that he looked the part, with new burnished armour and a fine black destrier – all provided by further loans from his uncle.

His jousting skills won their respect, and now the Spears were commanded by the king to run against all comers in a special tournament at Windsor Castle. They'd made the twenty-mile ride west from London in good time the previous day, despite freezing winter winds.

Brandon's Uncle Thomas had been chosen to escort the king's royal guests, Archduke Philip of Austria, King of Castile and heir to the Holy Roman Empire, and his wife, Joanna, Queen of Castile, daughter of King Ferdinand of Aragon.

His uncle told him that chance, and sudden winter storms, had driven the archduke's fleet off course and he'd been forced to seek refuge in the port of Weymouth, on the Dorset coast. It was an unexpected opportunity for King Henry to impress an important ally.

The tournament was to be followed by a grand banquet, which the victors might attend if they pleased the king. The prospect of such a reward meant more to Brandon than the others. It would be his first time as an invited guest at a royal banquet, instead of a servant in the garish green-and-white Tudor livery.

Samuel checked the tension of the fastenings on Brandon's armour, pulling hard on each of the leather straps, loosening some and tightening others. He stood back to admire his hand-iwork. A bull-necked Londoner, Samuel's head was entirely bald under his battered felt hat. He was a man of few words, yet his sharp eyes missed nothing.

The little finger of his right hand was a blunted stump. When Brandon asked about it he said he'd cut it off with his knife to improve his speed with a bow. Brandon doubted it, but he glanced at the wooden-handled dagger at Samuel's belt. It was the sort archers used to finish off wounded enemies.

Whatever the truth of his story, Samuel had been the outright winner of Harry's archery competition. He impressed them with his ability to fire two sheaves of arrows quicker than Brandon could count, with every one finding its mark on the distant target.

Samuel was now Brandon's squire, groom and all-round valet as his reward and soon learned his duties, from mucking out stables to parading before the king. He took it all in his loping stride, as if he'd never done anything else. Evasive about his past, he'd become a loyal and devoted servant to Brandon.

'A drink, sir?' He held up his own leather bottle of beer.

Brandon reached out and took a swig. It tasted strong and salty. He frowned and handed it back. 'I need to keep a clear head today.' He shivered and glanced up at the slate-grey sky. There had been a light fall of snow in the night and the ground glistened with frost.

Samuel prepared Brandon's black destrier for mounting.

He'd already fitted the saddle, which had a cantle at the back to transfer the force of an impact without pressing on the horse's spine. Now he tied on the flowing blue-and-silver caparison, Brandon's colours for the joust. Finally, he strapped in place the chamfron, a sculpted armoured plate to protect the horse's face, polished until it shone.

'Brandon, you ugly bastard!' A confident young voice echoed across the field.

The shout made them both look round. A grinning William Parr cantered towards them, his horse caparisoned in vermilion and gold and his hapless squire running behind to keep up.

After inheriting his father's fortune, Parr chose to join the King's Spears at the same time as Brandon. They were from different backgrounds but of a similar age, and a bond had formed between them, despite William's bluff northern humour.

'Will!' Brandon was glad to see him. William Parr hadn't been with them on the ride from London or shared their uncomfortable night's sleep on lice-infested straw-filled beds in the old Windsor barracks. 'Where the hell have you been?'

'You missed me?' Will pretended surprise. 'I'm lodged in the state apartments.' He pointed vaguely in the direction of the castle as he brought his horse to a stop. 'I've come with bad news. You're up against Knyvett.'

Brandon cursed. Thomas Knyvett was one of the most accomplished jousters in the country. He'd hoped to face one of Archduke Philip's men but it seemed he would have a fight on his hands.

Will shook his head and tutted in mock sympathy. 'Watch him closely, Charles. Knyvett's not beyond trying a few tricks.'

Brandon nodded to Samuel, who helped him mount his horse. Once safely in the saddle he felt his confidence return-ing. This was his chance to impress the king, prove his worth to

Sir Henry Bourchier, and show his uncle that their long hours of training had been time well spent.

He scratched his horse on the withers and it responded with a friendly snort. Urging it forward, he rode alongside Will to the arena, their squires following behind, carrying their white-plumed helmets and gauntlets.

Brandon was used to the purpose-built lists at Westminster and Richmond, and frowned at the clattering and banging of the workmen still hammering wooden planks into place to create the temporary tournament arena.

The king's canopy of estate, covered with cloth of gold, stood on a raised wooden platform. The purple velvet seats were empty, although a crowd of spectators had already arrived to secure the best vantage points. The colourful standards of Archduke Philip and his nobles hung from flagpoles in the still, frozen air, a garish reminder of the purpose of the day.

A sharp fanfare of trumpets announced the arrival of the king and his royal guests. A ragged cheer from the waiting crowd brought a scowl from King Henry, who wore a heavy cape of black fur. Few would guess he was King of England as he rarely wore a crown, preferring a black felt cap.

As if to reassure the doubters, the winter sun broke through grey clouds and flashed from the magnificent jewelled gold chain around King Henry's neck. He had an escort of yeomen carrying sharp halberds, and the confident figure of Archduke Philip at his side.

Several foreign nobles followed, accompanied by chattering ladies, all wrapped in thick furs against the cold, and Brandon guessed the attractive woman at the side of Princess Catherine might be the archduke's wife, Joanna, Queen of Castile, Catherine's sister.

Fortunately for the competitors the wintry chill meant the time-consuming skill at arms and archery displays were dispensed with. Brandon was still mounted when the Master of the Field called out his name.

Samuel handed him his heavy jousting helm and he pulled it on to his head. Although lined with cotton wadding it had to be a tight fit. The worst thing was the poor visibility; the eye slits were as narrow as possible to prevent splinters of wood hitting him in the face.

Samuel helped Brandon put on his armoured gauntlets. The thick leather gloves were covered with an arrangement of flexible plates, which allowed freedom of movement but would protect his fingers in a clash. Some jousters had studs on the knuckles for close-hand fighting, but Brandon thought these unsporting.

The heavy lance followed and Brandon raised and lowered it to test the balance. Twelve feet long and painted red, it had a white coronal on the blunted tip which was designed to shatter on impact. He couched the long lance under his arm and looked up to where his opponent's squire was preparing Thomas Knyvett.

He remembered William Parr's words of caution. Knyvett was known for his speed and accuracy. Brandon had seen him unhorse good riders by lifting them from the saddle with the sheer force of his charge. He pushed the sense of foreboding from his mind but still found himself muttering a prayer that he might impress the king.

Another trumpet sounded and Brandon rode to his position, raising a gauntlet in salute to the king and his guests. King Henry looked grim-faced. It was said he'd been ill throughout the winter and suffered with aching teeth. The archduke, by contrast, was clearly enjoying himself and grinned as he raised a silver goblet of wine in reply.

Brandon caught a glimpse of a young girl sitting a little behind the king. Princess Mary, the king's daughter, couldn't be more than ten, yet she looked older, dressed in rich furs with a pearl-fringed French hood. In a flash of insight, Brandon remembered hearing that King Henry planned to marry her to Archduke Philip's six-year-old heir, Prince Charles. This would be the perfect opportunity for him to secure their betrothal.

As he lowered his visor he sensed Princess Mary's young eyes were fixed on him with a look that might have been admiration. He'd been so focused on the preparations he hadn't realised how striking he must appear in his newly burnished armour. He held her eyes with his, raising his gauntlet a second time, and was rewarded with a smile from the young princess.

The command he'd been waiting for rang out and he urged his destrier into a gallop. His uncle knew horses and had chosen well; the powerful young stallion took off like a charging bull. There was no time to plan for any of Thomas Knyvett's ploys. Brandon had to rely on his instinct and training.

He heard the roar of approval from the crowd and felt the sharp thump as Knyvett's lance clashed against his shoulder, twisting him in the saddle and making him miss his target. He slowed as he reached the end of the barrier and Samuel leapt forward to grab his horse's halter, bringing them to a stop. He reached up and took the lance from Brandon, inspecting the white-painted tip.

'A miss this time, sir.' He glanced at the scrape on Brandon's shoulder guard. 'You took quite a bash. Do you need to dismount?'

Brandon raised his visor. His shoulder throbbed with a dull ache from the impact. 'I've had worse, Samuel.' He looked back down the list. Knyvett had wheeled his horse round and was already in place. 'Best get ready, they'll be calling for the next pass.'

He caught sight of his uncle approaching and scowled at his bad luck. If he'd faced one of the other riders, his uncle would be coming over to congratulate him, but now his face looked stern. Not for the first time, Brandon reflected on how different his life might have been if his father had stayed away from the fateful battle at Bosworth, as his uncle had done.

Sir Thomas Brandon was a hard man to impress, and treated Charles more like a troublesome squire than his nephew. He wore a gold Garter collar and star, and the dark-blue robes of the Order of the Garter showed under a bearskin cape. The engraved gold-plated hilt of his ceremonial sword glinted at his belt. He took the destrier's halter in his gloved hand and looked up at Charles.

'Use Knyvett's speed against him. Make him come to you.' His gruff voice made it sound like an order.

'I will, Uncle.' Brandon took the lance back from Samuel. 'This horse was eager to run.' He reached up and closed his visor before his uncle could offer more advice. If he won, he wanted it to be on his own terms.

He raised his lance high to show he was ready and waited for the signal. Through the slit in his helmet he glimpsed King Henry deep in conversation with Archduke Philip. He was known by his people as Philip the Handsome, although Brandon thought it a nickname he barely deserved.

When the call came he took his uncle's advice and made his approach at the gallop but with more control. Knyvett's warhorse thundered towards him, hooves digging deep into the frozen turf. Brandon tightened his grip on his lance and thrust it forward. The tip shivered on Knyvett's pauldron with a crack which sent a juddering shock up his right arm.

Shards of wood flew into the air and Brandon heard another cheer, louder this time, as Knyvett dropped his lance to stay in the saddle. Brandon slowed his horse and raised his visor with his left hand. Henry was standing and applauding. He didn't need to hear the score to know he'd pleased the king.

. . .

Brandon found himself seated between Thomas Knyvett and William Parr in the king's grand banqueting hall. They had all ridden another eight courses and shivered many lances against the archduke's best riders. Brandon was declared champion of the day, but Thomas Knyvett was gracious in defeat.

'Well done, Brandon.' He grinned as he raised his silver goblet of wine in salute. 'It was a close-run contest.'

Brandon nodded. 'I thought you had me on that first pass.'

'Each time we joust, we learn something new.'

Brandon raised his glass of wine and smiled. 'To many more victories at the joust.' He liked Thomas Knyvett's easy-going acceptance of him. He was right: it had been close, and they had earned the king's reward.

He tasted the rich wine and glanced across the open dance floor to where King Henry sat in a high-backed gilded chair under his cloth-of-gold canopy. Archduke Philip sat to the king's right with the Spanish ambassador, Don Pedro, and his senior nobles. The king's mother, Lady Margaret Beaufort, sat to his left with Prince Harry, but there was no sign of Princess Catherine, or the archduke's wife, or the young Princess Mary.

William Parr saw him studying the archduke. 'They are saying it was providence that brought the archduke to our shores.'

Brandon grinned and raised his goblet again. 'Well, here's to providence.'

Knyvett glanced across at the archduke and lowered his voice. 'The king hopes to secure a stronger alliance, as well as negotiate the return of Edmund de la Pole.'

Brandon raised an eyebrow. 'The last of the Yorkist plotters?'

Knyvett shook his head. 'Not the last. Don't forget he has a brother, Richard de la Pole, also somewhere in exile. I'll wager King Henry plans to detain Archduke Philip until he agrees terms.'

Brandon also kept his voice low. 'My uncle escorted the archduke from Weymouth. They lost three ships and the rest were taking on water, so they can't leave until their fleet is seaworthy.'

William Parr shook his head. 'They should have waited for the storms to pass. It was foolhardy to set out in midwinter.'

Brandon glanced at Archduke Philip, who was drinking heavily. 'He told my uncle he was on his way to be crowned King of Castile. He wished to claim his wife's inheritance before his father-in-law can turn the Castilians against him.'

Brandon felt tired after a long day and a dozen courses of rich food. He picked at a plate of sugared fruits, preserved in ginger, but wasn't used to so much sugar and exotic spices. He held out his goblet for it to be refilled with the strong red wine. It felt good to be waited on, after so many years as the servant.

He looked up as the king's musicians began to play a few lively bars on fiddles and flutes, creating an air of anticipation. It was time for the evening's entertainment to begin. Heads turned as the king's herald announced the arrival of Princess Catherine of Aragon and Princess Mary.

A year younger than Brandon, Princess Catherine wore a magnificent gown of scarlet silk, with a gold collar studded with glittering diamonds. The princess approached the king and bent in an elegant curtsey.

'Good evening, Your Grace,' she turned her head towards Harry, 'and to you, my lord prince.' Her voice carried an exotic Spanish accent.

Princess Catherine curtseyed to the archduke and addressed him in Spanish. 'It is my great pleasure to meet you at last, Your Grace.'

Archduke Philip replied in Spanish. 'I am pleased we have this chance to become better acquainted, princess.'

She took her place on the dance floor with Princess Mary and one of her Spanish ladies, with the ambassador Don Pedro and two young Spanish nobles as partners. King Henry's minstrels began playing a haunting Spanish dance with an unusual, rhythmic drumbeat.

With their gentlemen partners kneeling on one knee, Catherine, Mary and the Spanish lady danced around them, their colourful silk gowns billowing out as they spun. Brandon watched, impressed to see how well the king's young daughter had learned the formal Spanish dance. He also noticed Harry catch Princess Catherine's eye.

The dancing finished to rapturous applause and a single velvet chair was placed in the middle of the floor, facing the king. William Parr nudged Brandon and gave him a boyish grin.

'Someone's in trouble – not you, I hope?'

Brandon was about to reply when Princess Mary reappeared, carrying a lute. She curtseyed to her father and again to Archduke Philip, and then sat on the stool and began to sing slowly, in perfect Spanish, accompanying herself on her lute. A hush fell over the raucous guests as they listened to the haunting song echo around the banqueting hall in her clear young voice.

Brandon struggled to compare the confident and accomplished young woman in front of him with the shy little sister of Harry he'd teased when no one was watching. He couldn't speak Spanish, yet he could see the meaning of her words was not lost on Archduke Philip.

~

Back in London, alone in the darkness with Anne in her comfortable feather bed, he told her of his adventures at Windsor Castle. She wanted to know all about the king's tournament and the exotic archduke. Anne also insisted on hearing every detail of the banquet, including what the ladies were wearing.

He smiled at her curiosity. 'I not only pleased the king, but my Uncle Thomas also sought me out to offer his congratulations.' He could tell from her silence she didn't understand the significance. 'My uncle has married twice, to rich widows, yet has no heir...'

'So, there is hope you might one day inherit his fortune?' She pulled him closer. 'As well as his manor house in Southwark.'

Brandon kissed her. 'He hinted as much – and all the debts I owe him will never have to be repaid.'

Anne giggled in the darkness at the thought. 'Then it is well you are a patient man, Charles Brandon, as I believe your uncle has a good few years in him yet.'

'I have more important news to tell you, Anne.' He caressed her long hair. 'The day after the tournament, Sir Henry Bourchier promoted me to be his Master of the Horse and the captain of his cavalry. It seems I've finally proved my worth to him.'

Anne rolled on to her side to face him and studied his grey-blue eyes. 'That's a well-paid position, with responsibility.'

'It's a start. The earl is a demanding man, but this will prepare me well to take over from my uncle as the king's Master of the Horse, one day.'

She leaned across to return his kiss. 'Now will you marry me, Charles Brandon?' She spoke softly, as if almost afraid of his reaction.

He pulled her on top of him and was pleased she didn't resist. 'I *will* marry you. All in good time, Anne. I will make an honest woman of you when I can.'

3

MAY 1506

Harry cursed as Brandon shattered another wooden practice lance against his bronze chestplate. They were taking a great risk, defying the king's instruction, but Brandon knew he must keep his word. Harry raised his protective visor and grinned as he wheeled his powerful horse for another run.

'You don't go easy on me!'

Brandon shook his head. 'You'd learn little enough if I did.' He glanced around to ensure no one other than Samuel was within earshot. 'How is your father?'

'He has the quinsy, and can barely speak or swallow his food.' Harry frowned. 'Each time it is worse.'

Brandon felt a twinge of conscience. The king had been keeping Harry too close, his only contact with the world his elderly tutors. To address this, he rewarded Harry's few companions by making them Esquires of the Body. This should have brought Brandon and the others close to the king, attending and watching over him. It was a great honour and would have been a position of considerable influence.

Instead, King Henry's illness confined him to his bedchamber, shut away from all but his doting mother, Lady Margaret, and his ineffective physicians. Harry had been quick to take advantage of his new freedom, and looked happier than he had in a long time.

'Your father will need to show himself soon. Rumours are beginning to spread through London after he didn't turn up for St George's Day. Some are even saying he is dead...'

'He believes his illness is a punishment for his sins.' Harry scowled. 'My grandmother prays for him, and they bleed him every day to balance the humours. There is nothing I can do.' Harry patted his horse. 'I must learn to be a warrior king, like Henry V, and win everlasting glory through feats of arms.'

Brandon smiled. The king's worsening condition inevitably raised the question of the succession. Harry would soon turn fifteen, yet despite being over six feet tall, broad-chested and fluent in four languages, he seemed poorly prepared to rule the country.

In a flash of reminiscence, Brandon recalled his short time as a young servant to Harry's brother. Prince Arthur had been fifteen on the bright November day of his fateful wedding to Princess Catherine. Unlike Harry, Arthur had been diligent in following his father's wishes, taking his new bride to a remote castle at Ludlow to defend the Welsh Marches. Little good it did him, for he was dead by the following April.

Brandon hadn't followed them to Ludlow but he'd heard the stories. Some said young Arthur wore himself out satisfying his demanding Spanish bride. The truth was likely that the sweating sickness took princes as easily as peasants. Arthur Tudor's death affected the whole country, but none more than Harry.

'Let's try another pass.' He gestured for Samuel to hand Harry a new lance. 'This time, lean back a little in the saddle to balance the lance – and don't try to aim as you charge.' He grinned. 'Trust your instinct.'

Harry charged with reckless speed and no concern for his

own safety or Brandon's. They clashed with the violent crack of shattered wood as Harry scored his first good hit. He raised his visor and looked at the shattered end of his wooden lance.

'Mark this day, Master Brandon.' He beamed with satisfaction at his achievement. 'The first of many victories!'

Brandon checked the tip of his own lance had survived the clash without breaking, and gave Harry an appraising look. 'Well done, Your Grace!'

He'd never used such a formal address in private before, but it seemed fitting in that moment. The troubled young boy he'd known was growing up fast. For the first time he'd glimpsed the man who would one day be King of England.

A drunken Will Parr poured foaming ale from a jug into their tankards, laughing as he deliberately overfilled them. Harry wished to celebrate a successful day, so Brandon, Parr and Knyvett joined him in the king's hunting lodge in the grounds of Richmond Palace.

Built after the old palace of Sheen burned down, the lodge was little used; the king rarely hunted due to his worsening gout. Harry had taken the chance to appropriate the comfortable hunting lodge for himself, a sanctuary from the bleak royal chambers.

A good log fire blazed in an iron basket in the hearth, the flickering yellow-orange glow reflecting from the antlers of a stag above the fireplace. One wall featured wooden shutters over small windows and the other walls were hung with Flemish tapestries of hunting scenes. Best of all for Harry, the cellar was well stocked with barrels of ale and casks of good Burgundian wine.

The king remained in his sickbed and the servants were dismissed for the night, so Harry and his companions could enjoy themselves without being overheard. Even this was a rare freedom for Harry, who confessed he could never be sure who was spying for his father, reporting on his every move.

They'd been drinking for some time when Thomas Knyvett produced a well-worn pack of playing cards and shuffled them with practised ease. 'I trust you've all brought plenty of money – I'm feeling lucky tonight!'

Harry patted his purse. 'I'm game,' he glanced at Brandon, 'and if anyone runs out of money I'll help them increase their debts!'

His words were followed by laughter from all but Brandon. His uncle refused to extend his loans until some repayment was made and Brandon's good intentions had been overtaken by his expenses. He had little enough left to last the week but smiled at the possibility of winning at cards.

They took it in turns to cut the pack for the lowest card to deal. Brandon smiled as he turned over a three of diamonds, beating Parr and Knyvett. Harry cut last and laughed as he turned up the king of hearts.

'A good omen!' Harry beamed, despite losing by the greatest margin.

Knyvett raised his tankard, spilling ale on the rush-covered floor. 'Gentlemen. To the king of hearts!'

They all responded to the toast in mock solemnity. 'The king of hearts!'

Brandon, as dealer, took his stake of four groats from his purse and the others added three groats each, making a worth-while pot of thirteen. He dealt them all ten cards each and placed the remaining twelve face up on the table, in three rows of four, so the values could be seen.

He checked his hand of cards. Under the rules a pair could be claimed straight away. 'A pair of tens – and a pair of fours, an encouraging start!' He placed the cards on the table in front of him, already sensing his luck changing for the better.

Harry claimed a pair of threes, and Knyvett gleefully

claimed a pair-royal of three queens, and a pair of twos, and set them down face up on the table with a flourish. 'I'm on a winning streak tonight.'

Will Parr, to Brandon's left, was the first to play. Exchanging the five of diamonds for the seven of clubs, he laid down the pair of sevens, took a deep drink and then turned to Harry. 'They say the king plans to marry the Spanish princess. Is it true?'

Harry looked up sharply from his hand of cards. 'It is not.' He took a deep drink of his ale. 'In fact, I plan to ask his permission to marry Princess Catherine myself.'

'I knew it!' Brandon laughed. 'You couldn't take your eyes off her at the banquet in Windsor.'

Harry grinned, and played a five of clubs for the nine of spades on the table. 'I won't deny it. You know I was betrothed to her once,' he laid down a pair of nines and gave Brandon a wry look, 'but my father tired of arguing over her cursed dowry.'

It was Knyvett's turn to play next and he casually exchanged a ten of diamonds for the five of clubs, as if it was of no real interest to him. 'Take my advice. Princess Catherine is still young and full of spirit. Follow your heart – and don't take no for an answer.'

Parr raised an eyebrow. 'Did *you* follow your heart, Knyvett?' He shook his head. 'I think you followed the money, and snared yourself a rich widow.' He chuckled at his own joke.

Knyvett pretended to look hurt. 'My wife's considerable fortune was of no consequence...'

'Or that her father happens to be Sir Thomas Howard?' Brandon drained his tankard and wiped his mouth on his sleeve. 'Admit it, Knyvett, you're now related by marriage to most of the nobility.'

Instead of replying, Knyvett gave Brandon a withering look

and took the jug, refilling their tankards to the brim. 'I propose another toast, gentlemen. To my son.'

'You have a son by the widow Grey already?' Harry looked surprised.

Knyvett grinned. 'On the way.'

They solemnly raised their tankards again. 'To healthy sons.'

Knyvett looked pleased with himself. 'I also have a step-daughter, Lady Elizabeth Grey. She is only two years old, but has the title Viscountess Lisle, and one day I shall choose a worthy husband for her.'

Brandon laughed. 'It seems you have it all worked out.'

Knyvett sipped his ale and glanced at Harry. 'I'm not heir to the throne of England – and I don't have William's good fortune.' He raised his tankard and nodded to Parr. 'Neither do I envy your debts, Brandon,' he grinned, 'so I must make my own way, using such talents as I have.'

Harry slapped Knyvett on the back. 'You're an example to us all.'

Brandon sipped his ale and looked across at Knyvett. His friend did seem to live a charmed life, but he was right: he'd made his own luck. He realised they were waiting for him to play, and swapped a nine of clubs for the ace of hearts to match the ace of clubs in his hand. He placed the pair on the table next to his two tens and pair of fours.

Parr grinned. 'Don't look so down, Brandon. There are plenty of rich widows for you to charm, if you so wish.' He exchanged a four of diamonds for a two of clubs and laid it down in front of him with the two of spades. 'I could introduce you to Lady Margaret Mortimer, for example.'

Knyvett nodded. 'Now there's a woman of experience for you, Brandon. She's buried two husbands already. I wonder why that is?' He laughed to himself and supped his ale.

Brandon looked puzzled. 'I must confess I've never heard of her.'

Harry switched an eight of clubs for the seven of hearts on the table and laid down a pair of sevens. 'You must have seen her at court?'

William Parr refilled their tankards from the jug. 'You might show more interest if I tell you her maiden name was Neville – and her father was Sir John Neville, Marquess of Montagu, brother to Warwick the Kingmaker, no less.'

Brandon lay awake and alone in the darkness, listening to the strange creaks and groans of the roof timbers in his uncle's old mansion. He frowned to himself as he realised it meant he might have to renew the roof when he inherited the ancient property.

He brightened at the prospect of his inheritance. All he had to do was wait, although his uncle seemed in robust good health. It would help if he could begin repaying the debts, but any wages he earned slipped like sand through his fingers before he could begin to save.

The card game had continued until late in the evening. Despite his early success, he'd lost all his money, to the delight of Thomas Knyvett who, not for the first time, went home with a bulging purse.

William Parr tried to make a wager with him, that he couldn't charm the rich widow Mortimer into marriage. Although he'd been a little drunk, Brandon saw through it as a trick and refused to besmirch the lady's honour with such a bet.

At the same time, the seed of an idea had been planted in his mind and kept returning, like the irritating bite of a bedbug he knew he mustn't scratch. Parr admitted the widow Mortimer was over forty, but added that she was still an attractive woman, and owned wealthy estates all over England.

Thomas Knyvett and William Parr would soon be granted knighthoods – Harry would see to that. It would mark the parting of the ways. Brandon cursed his bad luck and wished his father had lived to become the king's right-hand man. King Henry would have rewarded him with enough land to make sure his son owned the forty pounds' worth of estates to qualify for a knighthood.

Brandon forced all thoughts of rich widows from his mind. He would honour his promise to Anne, and marry her when he could. There was more to life than becoming a knight. One day Harry would become king, and might grant him some land or perhaps even a title.

He returned to listening to the strange noises. It was little wonder he couldn't sleep. A dog began to bark at something in the street outside. A loose shutter at his window rattled in the wind, like the roll of drums at the horrific executions he'd witnessed at Tyburn.

Another thought occurred to him. His uncle, Sir Thomas, had married the wealthy widow of the Marquess of Berkeley and, when she died, promptly married Elizabeth, the widow of Baron FitzWarin. Both marriages considerably expanded his fortune, and he would readily understand someone doing the same.

Lady Margaret blushed at his well-chosen compliments. Despite William Parr's assurances, he'd imagined her to be matronly, with a thick waist, wearing a widow's mourning dress. Instead, she had a slender figure and wore an attractive damask gown, with a gable hood covering her plaited auburn hair.

Her sharp eyes gave him an appraising look, as if he was a

horse for sale. 'I've seen you at the jousting. It seems a dangerous occupation.'

Brandon smiled. 'We put on a show for the crowds, my lady. In truth, it is not so great a risk...'

'You are too modest, Master Brandon. I've heard you take on all comers, and beat them all.'

Brandon suspected William Parr had been trying to help with stories of his bravado. All the same, Lady Margaret sounded impressed. He found his eyes moving to the glittering diamond pendant on a silver chain around her slender neck, and then down to the smooth roundness of her breasts, pushed up by her tightly laced kirtle.

She caught his look and smiled, placing her hand on his arm. 'I'll be frank with you, Master Brandon. William Parr confided that you wish to marry me.'

For a moment Brandon nearly told her that Parr's intentions were honourable but it was all a terrible mistake. Instead, he took her slender hand in his and noticed she wore a large ruby set in a gold ring. 'Is it not too soon to talk of such things?'

'My husband passed away three years ago, Master Brandon. I've mourned him long enough now.' She gave his hand a squeeze. 'I need a good man to manage my estates – and I've been lonely as a widow.' She smiled and her bright eyes sparkled. 'You need me as much as I need you, Charles. It will be, as they say, a marriage of convenience.'

Brandon nodded, aware of the consequences of the decision he was about to make. There was no turning back. She was almost twice his age, yet seemed much younger. He had a sudden vision of their new life together. Parr was right: marriage to Lady Margaret would solve all his problems at a stroke – except for one.

. . .

He'd been expecting the note, yet when it was delivered he studied the scrap of parchment with a growing sense of dread. Sealed with dark-red wax, it bore a terse summons. *Come and see me tonight. A.*

Brandon paced his room, regretting the dilemma he faced as he prepared his short speech. Anne deserved the truth. He loved her deeply, and had no wish to hurt her, yet he'd put his career before all other considerations. Anne knew him well enough to understand he had no choice.

Even as he thought the words, he knew them to be untrue. He did have a choice. Anne would never understand, and no fine words would convince her. He drained another cup of his best wine and pulled on his riding cloak and cap. He must get it over with.

Darkness had fallen by the time he reached Anne's house. Pulling his cap low over his eyes, he gave his secret knock at her door. This time it opened right away, as if she'd been waiting. He stepped in and took off his cap, twisting it in his hands like some street urchin caught red-handed stealing from an apple barrow.

'I'm sorry, Anne.' His over-rehearsed speech was forgotten now she stood in front of him, her eyes red from crying. He fought the urge to take her in his arms and comfort her.

'It is true?' The spark of hope flashed briefly in her eyes. 'Have you really married that awful woman?'

He nodded. Margaret had agreed to his unusual request to marry in secret. A grinning William Parr and Thomas Knyvett were the only witnesses, and he'd paid the priest enough to buy his silence. The problem was that people liked to gossip about things which were none of their business. He'd known his secret would come out soon enough, although he wished there had been time to explain to Anne before she found out.

He realised she was staring at him, waiting for him to speak. 'It's true. I don't feel any affection for her, Anne. It's a business arrangement, a marriage of convenience.' He pictured his new wife saying those words and immediately regretted repeating them.

'I should have told you, Charles...' Anne dabbed at a tear as she struggled to remain composed.

'Told me what?' At the back of his mind he guessed her answer and held his breath.

'I am with child.' She smoothed the front of her gown to reveal a discernible bump. 'And before you insult me by asking, I'm *certain* you are the father.'

4

MARCH 1507

Brandon named his new daughter Anne, after her mother. It was the least he could do. He'd seen little of them, or of Margaret; every spare moment after fulfilling his duties for Sir Henry Bourchier was spent riding up and down the country trying to sort out problems with the tenants of his new-found estates.

Although his wife was wealthy, her income from rents was much less than it should be. Brandon concluded that the land agent she'd appointed to manage them after her husband's death was, at best, inept – and at worst corrupt. He'd yet to prove the latter but the former was evident at each property he visited.

He also learned how generations of Nevilles and Mortimers had carved up once-great estates into smaller holdings, sometimes little more than a few meadows and cottages. Each had different rents and legal agreements to untangle, many operating in favour of the tenants.

His Uncle Thomas was forthright with his advice, having been through the same more than once. 'Hire a good lawyer. Sell off what you can – and pay off your debts.' Brandon's failure to make the promised repayments had become a thorny issue between them.

Brandon frowned. 'Margaret might take objection to that.'

Thomas shook his head. 'You'll be doing the lady a favour. It seems her holdings are in quite a mess.' He gave Brandon a direct look. 'Don't make the mistake of asking her permission. You are her husband now, so act like one. Tell her once it's all sorted out.'

He didn't wish to tell his uncle, but his relationship with Margaret was at a low ebb. They'd consummated their marriage on their wedding night – a mechanical, loveless experience which only served to remind him what he'd thrown away – then she'd somehow found out about baby Anne and confronted him in a stern tone. 'Did you know of this when you agreed to marry me?'

He held up his hands. 'I promise I did not.' A thought occurred to him. Anne had found out about his marriage before he'd been able to tell her and now Margaret seemed to know all about his new daughter.

'Who told you about the baby?' He tried to make the question sound casual, but had to understand how his secrets were getting out.

'You should know, Charles, that Anne Browne is my niece. You've married into the family.' There was a malicious note to her voice which put him on his guard.

'You made sure Anne knew our secret before I could tell her?' His hand formed a fist, although he could never strike her. Margaret's stony-faced silence confirmed his accusation.

The last straw came after Brandon returned from a long ride to York with Sir Henry Bourchier. He found Margaret in an icy mood. She could hardly wait for him to stable his horse before thrusting a folded legal parchment at him.

He recognised it as a formal bill of sale. 'You've been going through my private papers?'

'It is just as well that I did.' She scowled at him. 'You cannot do this to me, Charles. I forbid it.'

Brandon shook his head. 'It is my right, as your husband, to manage your property as I wish. You were being cheated by your tenants—'

'The incomes from those lands are my widow's pension.' Her interruption carried a harsh note.

'I shall see you are always well provided for.'

'And what if you are struck from your horse and die?' She glowered, as if she wished it would happen. 'What would become of me then?'

He didn't want to argue. 'You've survived two husbands, Margaret. I'm sure you'll manage to survive one more.'

She stormed from the room, the thick hem of her damask gown swishing on the rush-covered floor. The door of their bedchamber slammed with a thud. Then came the metallic scrape of the bolt. Her message was clear. He would not be sleeping there that night, and from that day they'd lived separate lives.

After a year of waiting, the royal summons finally came to attend the king as one of his Esquires of the Body. Brandon knew he should have been pleased. It would mean another much-needed income, yet now the opportunity had arrived he worried about finding time to fit in all his commitments.

There were always papers to sign for his lawyer about ongoing land transfers, and his duties for the Earl of Essex had increased. Sir Henry seemed to like his company on their frequent trips to buy and sell breeding stock, and treated Brandon as his right-hand man, allowing him to stay at properties he owned.

Brandon also liked to visit Anne Browne when he could, to

see his lively infant daughter. Although Anne's attitude towards him seemed indifferent, he'd been paying her a generous allowance which she'd accepted for the sake of the child. He'd thought it best not to tell her the money came from the sales of his wife's land.

As he rode with his groom Samuel to Richmond Palace, a familiar shout echoed behind them and he turned in the saddle to see William Parr closing fast. Parr's long-suffering squire followed, leading a heavily loaded packhorse. Brandon slowed his pace to allow William to catch up.

'On your way to the king, Brandon?' William Parr seemed to know the answer before he even spoke.

Brandon smiled, pleased to see his friend again. 'I was beginning to think the day would never come.'

'We have Harry to thank for this. I asked him to propose our names to the king, now his health is restored.'

Brandon wasn't surprised. Yet again, William Parr was managing his life for him, but his intentions were honourable. He could have borne a grudge against his friend for making the past year so complicated. In truth, he'd profited well from the marriage and, to his uncle's amazement, cleared his debts.

'I suppose I should thank you.' He managed to put a note of mock bitterness into his voice.

William Parr grinned across at him. 'So, how is married life?'

Brandon hesitated before replying. 'Like any English rose, the lady has sharp enough thorns.'

Assistants to the Keeper of the Wardrobe had laid out the king's chosen robes, immaculately pressed, brushed and perfumed with lavender, yet only the trusted Esquires of the Body could lay hands on the king. As soon as they entered the king's privy chamber Brandon saw the country had been lied to.

King Henry was said to be recovered from his illness, yet his pale face was riven with deep lines of pain. He sat alone, stooped on a low stool in his nightshirt, looking more like a vagrant than King Henry VII of England. His thinning grey hair hung limp over his ears and a growth of white stubble made him appear older than his fifty years.

The king squinted to see them, a sign that failing eyesight added to his other problems. 'Charles Brandon...' His voice rasped as he spoke, a result of damage done by the quinsy. 'You remind me of your father.' He seemed to withdraw into himself, as if the sight of them had triggered a distant memory. After a few moments he turned back to Brandon. 'A brave and loyal man, Sir William. I've not forgotten his sacrifice. If it were not for his selfless action I might not be here today.'

Brandon bowed. 'I know little of the events of my father's death, Your Grace, only that he carried your standard at the Battle of Bosworth. It has been said he was killed by King Richard.'

The king nodded, still lost in his reminiscence. 'I witnessed your father's death. You know he used my standard to divert the enemy away from me, holding it high and waving it in the air to provoke them.' He paused and took a deep, rasping breath. 'You are right, for none other than King Richard himself took the bait, and charged your father with his lance. He rode with such force his lance pierced Sir William's armour and broke in two. Your father drew his last breath fighting to make me king.'

Brandon felt a frisson of pride. He never imagined he would hear the story of his father's death from an eyewitness who was present at Bosworth, let alone from the king himself. He'd always been a little ashamed of his father's failure to defend himself. Now, at last, he understood.

King Henry turned to William, who also bowed. 'You must be Parr.' He smiled, showing a few browning teeth. 'My son speaks most highly of you both. I am grateful he has the support of such worthy companions.'

'The prince is a great credit to you, Your Grace.' Parr glanced at Brandon, a mischievous twinkle in his eye.

The king gave him a wry look. 'I make it my business to know something of what he gets up to.' He shook his head in disapproval. 'I worry for his safety, so I would ask the two of you to do your best to keep him from the most dangerous occupations.'

Brandon felt the burden of guilt on his broad shoulders. 'We shall do our best, Your Grace, but you must know the prince is not an easy man to divert, once he has set his mind to something.'

The king nodded. 'I don't need to remind you that the stakes could not be higher. The future of the country depends on keeping him safe.'

They helped him out of his nightshirt and into a fresh white linen shirt and hose. A black velvet doublet followed, then an ermine-edged cape. It was said Henry was miserly, yet he spent a fortune on his clothes. As they added each item, Brandon could see why. The effect was completed with a fine pair of polished calfskin boots with gold buckles and the golden chain of the Order of the Garter. In ten short minutes they had transformed him into a king.

The grand May tournament in the grounds of Kennington Palace was one of the most anticipated events of the year, attracting the most influential people in London and attended by the ambassadors of many foreign countries.

Built by King Edward III, who granted it to his eldest son,

Edward of Woodstock, known as 'The Black Prince', the old palace in Lambeth had one of the earliest purpose-built jousting tourneys. Brightly coloured flags and pennants fluttered in the May sunshine, and the air filled with the sound of lively music and the shouts of vendors selling ale and pies to the gathering crowd.

The king sat on a raised throne under a grand golden canopy, high on the royal grandstand. His ageing mother, Lady Margaret Beaufort, sat to one side, wearing a deep vermilion gown, with his youngest daughter, Princess Mary, to the other.

Mary dressed as Queen of the May, in white as a symbol of her purity, and sat on a throne decorated with spring flowers. On her head was a golden tiara and she was surrounded by her young Ladies of the May, all in matching white gowns and throwing rose petals into the air from small wicker baskets. The princess had celebrated her eleventh birthday in March, yet already turned heads with her natural grace and beauty.

Royal heralds in Tudor green-and-white announced the parade of competitors with a fanfare of trumpets. As the challenger, Brandon led the other riders on to the field. In honour of his father's memory he carried the flowing royal standard on a long gilded pole. He wore the royal tabard of the King's Spears over his burnished armour, and his destrier was caparisoned in cloth of gold reaching almost to the ground.

King Henry raised a hand in acknowledgement as he recognised Brandon. It had been true: the honour of being an Esquire of the Body meant he had a personal connection with the king, which significantly increased his status. Brandon held up a gauntleted hand in salute.

He stopped in front of Princess Mary for the traditional favour from the Queen of the May. There was a twinkle in her eyes as the young princess stood and offered him a green silk ribbon from her gown. His groom, Samuel, stepped forward and tied it to Brandon's saddle for good luck.

The archery competition began with a row of men shooting from twenty paces. Arrows swished through the air as they fired at the straw targets. The crowd cheered and applauded as Princess Mary presented the purse of gold to the handsome winning archer, who beamed with pride at the honour and bowed to the king.

Before the jousting, Prince Harry gave an impressive demonstration of riding at the ring. With his black charger caparisoned in the royal colours of red, blue and gold, he raised his lance high in the air and thundered towards the suspended ring. In a show of well-rehearsed bravado, he lowered the heavy lance at the last moment, spearing the ring with apparent ease.

At last it was Brandon's turn, as the Master of the Joust announced the mounted combat with lances. Brandon rode back into the arena and bowed his head before the king. His first ride was against a Burgundian knight in blue-enamelled plate armour. Samuel passed him the heavy lance and Brandon raised it in the air to show he was ready at the far end of the tourney.

The crowd jostled for the best view and shouted as they began to place bets on who would win. At the signal from the tournament master, both horses lurched into a charge and closed in front of the royal grandstand. Hooves pounded, raising clouds of dust from the hard-packed ground.

The crowd gasped as Brandon's lance shattered against his rival's chest and cheered as a section of his lance broke off and spun in the air before thumping to the ground. The Burgundian knight toppled back in the saddle. For a moment it looked as if he would recover, but then he fell from his saddle to the ground with a heavy thud and lay still.

Brandon glanced down at the bright-green ribbon fluttering at his own saddle in the May breeze. As he'd charged, he'd had a sudden recollection of Margaret asking what would become of her if he was killed. For a second it had seemed a bad omen, yet his favour from the young princess had ensured his good luck. He rode back to find her in the royal grandstand and lowered what was left of his lance in a salute of thanks.

He'd decided to spend the night at his uncle's house in Southwark and found his lawyer, Master Gregory, waiting there with a concerned look on his face. A short man with a neat beard, dressed in lawyer's black robes, he'd made short work of sorting out Margaret's complicated legal arrangements.

His lawyer handed him what looked like a court summons, tied with a thin red ribbon. 'I thought you would wish to see this without delay, sir. It is from the Archdeaconry Court of London.'

Brandon raised an eyebrow in surprise. 'What could the Archdeaconry Court possibly wish from me, Master Gregory?' He took the parchment and unfastened the ribbon. He guessed his wife had been trying to interfere with the sale of her properties. He began to read and realised he was wrong, for although the matter did concern his wife, it was an entirely unexpected development.

Anne Browne had been busy while he'd been dealing with Margaret's lands. He'd always felt deep regret for the way he'd treated Anne and could have understood if she wished to have nothing further to do with him. He looked up at his waiting lawyer.

'How are the final land transfers progressing, Master Gregory?'

'It has been complicated work but it's nearly completed, sir.'

'Good.' Brandon smiled. 'The timing is perfect. It seems, Master Gregory, that there is a challenge to my marriage. It

appears likely to be deemed invalid on grounds of consan-
guinity.'

~

Anne looked beautiful in her new wedding dress. Her family
had rallied together to fund the court hearing and force
Brandon to do his duty to her. The Archdeaconry Courts had
taken little time to rule Brandon's marriage annulled, particularly after little Annie was held up in the courtroom as evidence
of his prior relationship.

Margaret threatened to sue Brandon, not only for the
money from the sales of her property but for every penny he
owned. 'She can threaten all she likes,' he'd said, yet in his
heart he worried that she was a determined woman and might
one day persuade a court to make judgement in her favour. He
had his lawyer ensure Margaret was still provided for by her
remaining rents.

A shaft of sunlight lit up the quiet church in Stepney as
they said their solemn wedding vows, watched only by Anne's
brother and two friends of Brandon's co-opted as witnesses.
The young priest seemed unsurprised at the small size of the
congregation, and finally pronounced them husband and wife.

Brandon lifted Anne's veil to kiss her. 'I shall marry you
again in public,' he promised, 'but I think you've waited long
enough for me to keep my word.'

Anne stared deep into his eyes, as if reading his thoughts.
'You are fortunate, Charles Brandon, that I am such a patient
woman.'

That evening, as they lay together in their new marriage bed, a
wedding gift from Brandon's uncle, he could hardly believe his
reversal of fortune. 'We shall have another child, a son...'

Anne laughed at his suggestion. 'We have not yet been married for one day – what will people say?'

'Let them talk, for now we no longer have to meet in the shadows.'

'Well, I shall feel more married once we can rent our own house, rather than live under your uncle's roof.'

'One day you shall have the finest manor house in London, Anne Brandon, with views out over the river and a well-stocked stable.'

'You expect great things now you are close to the king?'

'I do, Anne. I plan to make more than just an honest woman of you. You shall become the lady of the manor, with many servants to care for you – and a grand nursery for our children.'

'And you will be a knight of the Tudor court?' There was a teasing note to her voice, as he'd talked of it so often in the past.

'Not just a knight. The king favours me, Anne. He owes his crown to my father. I will make my name as the king's right-hand man.'

5

APRIL 1509

Brandon's instinct told him something was wrong even before he entered the palace at Richmond. He sensed the tension in the air, like the uneasy calm before a thunderstorm. The Yeomen of the Guard, who usually let him pass with a nod, barred his way and demanded to know his business there.

'What's going on?' He pulled his letter of authority from a pocket in his doublet and waited while the guard checked it with unnecessary care, although he doubted the man could read.

'We've been put on alert.' The guard looked uncomfortable. 'That's all I know. Now, be on your way, if you will, sir.'

Mystified, Brandon used the servants' narrow back staircase to reach the one person who would be able to tell him. There were more men of the king's guard at the door to Harry's chambers, blocking his way with their sharp halberds.

'Will you tell His Grace the prince that Charles Brandon wishes to see him?' His voice sounded more confident than he felt.

His bluff worked; one of the guards opened the door and went inside. He emerged soon after with a nod and Brandon was allowed in. Like the king's tower, the room was octagonal, with tall leaded-glass windows flooding the space with spring sunlight and providing views in all directions.

Harry leaned against the window looking out over the River Thames, a silver goblet of wine in one hand. He turned as Brandon entered, his face grim. 'My father is dead.' The words seemed to take an effort.

Brandon's mind raced with the implications. The old king seemed in good spirits when he saw him last, a few days before. 'I'm sorry. When did it happen?'

'They summoned his confessor to administer the last rites last night...' Harry frowned at the memory. 'He died this morning.' He took a deep drink of his wine. 'They want to keep it secret for as long as they can – pretend he still lives. God knows why.'

Brandon stared at his young friend. Harry's father had been ill for so long he'd had plenty of time to prepare for this day, yet it seemed impossible to imagine him as King of England. Brandon could see why those with power on his council might hesitate. With the death of the old king nothing would ever be quite the same again – not just for him, but for the country.

Harry drained his goblet and looked around for more. He seemed a little unsteady on his feet, as if he'd been drinking for a while. 'I've always known this day would come, ever since my brother died, yet now it has...'

'You can count on me to help in any way I can, Your Grace.' The formal title sounded strange, a sign of how their relationship had already shifted.

Harry shot him a grateful glance. 'My grandmother offered to act as regent until I'm ready, but I must watch my father's old advisors. Given the chance they'd all carry on as if nothing has changed.' He sat down heavily in a chair. 'My father's ministers think I've been poorly prepared for kingship, yet I've had the best education, observing how they lied and cheated behind my father's back. I've seen their greed, Brandon, and how it corrupted my father's court.'

A thought occurred to Brandon. 'Tomorrow is St George's Day – a good day to be announced as the new king.'

Harry brightened. 'You are right, it's a good omen. I shall mark the day by granting a pardon to those persecuted unfairly by my father.' There was a surprising note of bitterness in his voice. 'No one in England can be in any doubt that things are going to change.'

Brandon was one of the ninety-three Esquires of the Body marching with the old king's funeral escort, together with his friends William Parr and Thomas Knyvett. The body of the king was brought the ten miles from Richmond Palace on a gilded carriage draped with the royal standard.

People came out of their houses as the long procession made its winding way down the south bank of the Thames and crossed London Bridge. For once, the rotting heads of criminals and traitors had been removed from their spikes on the bridge parapet.

The slow-moving procession was met at St George's Bar, Southwark, by a civic delegation of the Lord Mayor of London and his aldermen, accompanied by a hundred paid mourners on horseback, all dressed in black. The streets were lined by solemn-faced members of the guilds, many holding flaming torches which gave the scene a surreal light.

The black-garbed clergy, clerks and lawyers, all of whom served the old king, took their place behind the mourners. Next came the ambassadors and merchants of France, Spain, Venice and Florence on horseback and on foot, some carrying the colourful standards of their nations, others with burning torches. The procession gathered more followers as it made its slow progress through the narrow streets.

By the time they reached the great cathedral of St Paul's the line of people following the king's carriage reached too far into the distance for Brandon to see the end. It was hard to guess but it seemed half the population of London accompanied King Henry to his lying in state, all dressed in black.

It had been a long day and Brandon struggled to stay awake as he took his turn with the Esquires of the Body to keep an all-night vigil. All the nobility of England had come to St Paul's. Lords and their ladies, knights and commoners, young and old, all filed past to pay their last respects to their king.

The next day Brandon once again marched at the side of the king's carriage, pulled by seven fine black horses, as his body made the short journey from St Paul's to his final resting place in Westminster Abbey. The old king had planned well, arranging for ten thousand Masses to be said for his soul in all the churches of London, yet his grand tomb in his chapel at the far end was still unfinished after years of haggling about the costs.

Brandon glanced up at the life-sized funeral effigy, cast from the dead king's face. It seemed too faithful a record, with the deep lines of pain there in his face, just as they had been in life. It wobbled as the carriage wheel rode over a cobble stone in the road, making the king seem to shake his head in annoyance.

The late king's chaplain, Bishop John Fisher of Rochester, read the overlong funeral sermon. An unmistakably critical note echoed from the high-vaulted abbey roof as he bemoaned those who would speak ill of the king, now he was no longer able to defend himself.

Brandon looked up at the royal pew and remembered

Harry was absent from the service; it was not fitting for a king, chosen by God, to see the consequences of another king's mortality. Harry's grandmother, Lady Margaret, and his sister, Princess Mary, were in mourning dress. Harry's grandmother had the same cold, fixed expression that he'd seen when he first told Brandon the news. Princess Mary wept as she mourned the passing of her father.

Little Annie was pleased to see him when he returned to their rented house in Southwark. She tottered towards him, holding up her arms for him to sweep her off her feet, and shrieked with delight as he swept her up high to the roof beams.

Anne smiled at the sight of the two of them together, but even as he kissed her he could tell she was concerned about something. She showed him a sheaf of unpaid bills. 'We're living beyond our means, Charles. It can't go on like this much longer.'

He embraced her warmly and tried to reassure her. 'Harry has chosen to move from Richmond to the royal suite at Greenwich Palace, so I'll be home with you both more often now.' He smiled. 'He's also decided to continue the King's Spears under the command of Sir Henry Bourchier – and made me, Thomas Knyvett and William Parr his own Esquires of the Body.'

Anne seemed to relax a little. 'At least we'll have an income. You will be in a privileged position, but the rent...'

He looked around the low-ceilinged room as if seeing it for the first time. They'd rented it in haste after the wedding but it was old, with a smoky fire in the hearth and small shuttered windows overlooking the narrow street. He had to admit it was far from ideal.

'This place is only temporary. When I have my inheritance,

we'll build a fine new manor house by the river, a home worthy of our growing family.'

She gave him a wry look. They'd been trying for the son he longed for, but so far without success. 'Your inheritance seems as far off as ever.' She waved the bundle of bills in the air. 'You need to know that the money I'd saved has all gone, so we will have to seek another favour from your Uncle Thomas.'

'No, I cannot.' He frowned for the first time as the reality of their situation dawned on him. 'I'll not go back to him cap in hand after working so hard to pay back what I owed. It might give him an excuse to be less generous in his will.'

Anne placed her hand softly on his arm. 'We have little choice, Charles. I have to stay at home to look after little Anne and the bills have to be paid.'

'Then I have no choice. I shall have to ask our new king for a loan.'

It seemed strange at first, helping his friend to dress in the mornings, yet it was less intimidating than serving the old king. This particular morning he worked on his own, which meant he was able to explain his financial situation in private. He helped Harry pull on his black woollen hose and an embroidered white linen undershirt.

'I cannot ask my uncle again, and the moneylenders would want repayment more quickly than I can afford.'

Harry shrugged. 'Everywhere we look we find my father had hidden gold and jewels not listed in his accounts.' He smiled to himself. 'They called him a miser, yet I'm grateful for what he's left me, so I'll make you a loan.'

Brandon held up the fine burgundy velvet doublet while Harry put his arms into it. Then he began fastening the pearl buttons at the front. 'I shall repay you as soon as I have my inheritance.' He decided to change the subject. 'I hear you've sent for Princess Catherine, Your Grace.'

'I must marry her without delay, Brandon.' Harry looked pleased with himself. 'Now my father's funeral is over, my first duty as king is to produce an heir and secure the succession.'

He recalled how Harry had spoken of marrying the Spanish princess in the past. She was pretty enough, and talented, yet there might be more suitable brides for the new king than his late brother's widow. He held out a heavy gold chain studded with rubies that Harry had chosen to wear over his doublet.

Harry waited while Brandon fastened the ornate clasp of the chain at the back of his neck. 'It was my father's wish that I marry Princess Catherine and secure our treaty with Spain.' He held out his foot for Brandon to pull on his polished leather boot. 'I started the marriage negotiations right away and Archbishop Warham has issued a marriage licence. I will marry in a private ceremony, here at Greenwich, before people start to interfere and put obstacles in my path.'

Brandon nodded, surprised at how quickly events were progressing. He helped to pull on Harry's other well-fitting boot. 'Will there be a joint coronation?'

'There will – and you will take part as one of my esquires, Brandon. I want it to be a coronation the people of London will remember.'

On Midsummer's Eve a grand mounted procession, led by newly created Knights of the Bath, resplendent in their rich blue gowns, set out from the Tower of London. Sir Thomas Knyvett grinned with pleasure at his new knighthood. He was followed by Henry, wearing a robe of red velvet trimmed with ermine, over a fine doublet of cloth of gold decorated with sparkling diamonds, and a collar of gold set with rubies like overripe cherries.

Henry's destrier was caparisoned with cloth of gold trimmed with ermine and had a gold chamfron over its face. A cloth-of-gold canopy of estate was held over him on long poles by the barons of the Cinque Ports. Unlike his father, no one could doubt they were in the presence of a king.

Brandon's Uncle Thomas rode behind Henry, dressed in his gold-trimmed regalia as a Knight of the Garter and Master of the Horse. Brandon followed his uncle, wearing his jousting armour and leading Henry's caparisoned black charger.

As they passed through streets lined with people desperate for a glimpse of their new king, a cheer went up as Princess Catherine appeared, reclining in a litter covered by a canopy of cloth of gold. She seemed to radiate a new confidence, now Henry had married her in a private ceremony at Greenwich the previous day.

With her long auburn hair loose over her shoulders as a sign of purity, she wore a rich mantle of white silk and ermine, with a gold and pearl circlet on her head. Princess Catherine's eight ladies-in-waiting rode behind, all dressed in matching blue velvet gowns, on pairs of fine grey palfreys.

The people of London lit towering bonfires in celebration of the start of a new era. Midsummer was the day the wheel of the year turned towards a rich new harvest. The ancient traditions of Midsummer's Eve provided the perfect excuse for drinking and revelry. Women danced to groups of musicians at every street corner, and Henry paid for free wine to flow in special culverts.

The distinctive smell of woodsmoke from bonfires still hung in the air early the next morning as Henry and Catherine made their way on foot through the great hall of Westminster towards the abbey. They walked on a carpet of Tudor green-and-white, strewn with herbs and summer flowers. Their route was lined by the yeomen of the king's guard and they were led by twenty-eight bishops and all the Garter knights, in full regalia.

Brandon watched as the dour Archbishop of Canterbury, William Warham, recited a Latin prayer and anointed Henry and Catherine with the sacred holy oil. At last his friend took his place on the throne next to Catherine, wearing his jewelled imperial crown.

The peal of the bells of every church in London failed to drown the raucous cheers from the crowds waiting outside in the bright Westminster sunshine. They called out '*Vivat Rex!*' and applauded their new king, Henry VIII.

Brandon took part in the great procession back to Westminster Hall where rows of tables were set up and covered with white linen for the coronation banquet. After the king and queen took their seats, a fanfare of trumpets announced the arrival of the Earl of Shrewsbury, on horseback, to herald the beginning of the feast. Brandon and the other Esquires of the Body sat at a far table, but were spared the duty of serving.

Instead, Brandon had a starring role at the tournament which followed. The rhythmic beat of a bass drum accompanied the reedy sound of a crumhorn playing a popular tune. Shouts of vendors selling food and ale mixed with the shrieks of excited children.

The lively crowd thronging the barriers around the temporary arena cheered and applauded as the competing knights rode into view to present themselves before their new king and queen. Each had one side of their armour-skirts and horse-trappings of white velvet embroidered with a pattern of gold roses, the other of green velvet embroidered with gold pomegranates, the Spanish emblem of fertility.

As well as the royal pavilion, hung with tapestries and cloth of gold, Henry's carpenters had constructed a white-painted castle, complete with battlements topped by an imperial crown and decorated with roses and pomegranates. Red and white wine ran in endless trickles like a fountain from the mouths of gargoyles into overflowing silver cups.

The only knight in gilded armour, a present from the new king, Brandon rode his powerful black destrier and called out his congratulations to Henry, bowing his head in salute to the queen. The tourney was to be the grand finale of the coronation celebrations, so he had to wait for the endless archery contests and demonstrations of skill at arms and swordplay to finish.

When the moment came at last, an expectant hush fell over the watching crowd. The Master of the Joust made a great play of explaining that a new challenger, a young German knight, would take on Charles Brandon, the king's chosen champion.

Brandon's squire, Samuel, handed him his lance and he lowered the visor of his plumed helmet. Then the order was given and the heavy horses charged towards each other, hooves thumping the hardened earth. The challenger's lance shattered against Brandon's gilded breastplate, sending sharp splinters into the air. He fought to remain in his saddle, and then punched a gauntleted fist in the air to a rousing cheer from his supporters.

He turned and prepared for the next pass, couching his lance tighter under his arm as the Master of the Joust gave his signal. This time his lance struck the German knight with such force the man was lifted from his saddle and slid to the ground.

Uninjured, he sprang to his feet and invoked his right to call out a challenge to Brandon to continue with swords. Samuel held Brandon's horse while he dismounted and drew his sword, holding it high in the air to a cheer from the crowd. Although he'd spent long hours practising the joust and kept his hand in with his longbow, Brandon knew he would be at a disadvantage. He was out of practice with his sword.

The German knight lunged in an attack. Brandon parried the blow and felt a jarring pain in his hand. Before he could recover the German swung his sword again, this time scoring a jagged scar across the gilded pauldron protecting Brandon's shoulder.

In a surge of anger, Brandon realised he would have to act quickly to end the fight or suffer the consequences of a humiliating defeat. Swiftly reversing his sword, he brought the weighted pommel down with as much force as he could on the side of the German's plumed helmet. A metallic clang rang out and the German knight stopped in his tracks. Brandon hit him again, harder this time, and the huge man sank to his knees in surrender.

Brandon raised his visor and walked back to stand in front of King Henry, holding his sword in the air in salute. The crowd erupted into cheering as Henry stood and raised a hand in acknowledgement.

It seemed the coronation celebrations would go on forever, as the jousting and tourneying continued over the next five days. But then came the unexpected death of the king's elderly grandmother, Lady Margaret Beaufort. Henry ordered the bells of London to ring in mourning for six days.

Henry's grandmother had agreed to act as regent while Henry appointed his advisors, but now he was on his own. Her death marked a turning point for the country. Now they had a handsome young new king, enriched by his late father's considerable fortune, with a beautiful Spanish queen at his side.

6

JANUARY 1510

Bright winter sunshine glistened on the fresh dusting of snow covering the tiltyard at Richmond. Brandon had risen early for his last practice with Henry, who was no longer bound by his father's instructions. The king was showing an aptitude for the sport, and wished to ride in disguise at a private tournament.

Their repeated charges dug muddy tracks of hoof prints and turned the pristine snow to mush. Brandon was pleased to see Henry had finally learned to control his brutish gallop and kept his lance steady and true on the approach.

'I shall have to make sure I never ride against you, Your Grace.' Brandon raised his practice lance and shouted across the deserted tiltyard. 'I fear I've shared too many of my secrets.'

'I will unseat you yet, Charles Brandon, mark my words.' Henry grinned and turned his horse for yet another charge. His arrogance had grown since the announcement that Catherine carried his heir. Bells were rung, cannons boomed at the Tower of London and the taverns had never been so busy. King Henry even sent an eloquent letter to Catherine's father, King Ferdinand, to confirm his great joy at the good news.

Full of boyish excitement, Henry arranged a surprise for his pregnant wife. With Thomas Knyvett and others dressed in green as Robin Hood and his band of men, they burst into the queen's private chambers, armed with bows and staves, pretending to be outlaws of the forest. The shock of their prank was not appreciated by Catherine or her ladies.

Brandon, who'd not been invited to take part, failed to understand why Henry would do such a thing. He was also puzzled by the king's plan to remain anonymous at the joust, but had to respect his wishes. To complete his disguise, Henry wore the same plate armour as William Compton, and they were both about the same height and build.

All went well in the early challenges, with Henry shivering his lance twice. Then Sir Edward Neville, an experienced jouster, struck him a low blow on his unprotected leg, causing blood to spurt from a deep wound. There was a collective groan from the onlookers as he fell to the ground and lay injured. One, who knew of Henry's disguise, called out, 'God save the king!'

Henry had no choice other than to reveal his true identity. He pulled off his helmet to show his face. 'I'm safe and well. It's Compton who's been speared!'

His words were greeted by a cheer from the watching courtiers, although Compton's blood turned the snow scarlet where he lay. Brandon was relieved it hadn't been him riding against either of them. Sir Edward Neville's charge had been reckless, but it was fortunate that only William Compton would pay the price.

Brandon stayed on at Richmond Palace with Samuel to check on the earl's horses stabled there. He'd been bitterly disappointed when Henry chose Thomas Knyvett as his new Master of the Horse. Brandon believed himself the obvious replacement for his uncle, and saw it as evidence of how the king favoured his band of knights.

He would have to find a way to secure the land he needed or face a future of being sidelined by more fortunate members of Henry's inner circle.

Brandon waited while Samuel saddled one of the earl's heavy warhorses, then cantered into the vast expanse of the royal park. He'd not ridden far when the rhythmic thump of hooves sounded behind him.

He turned and recognised the slim figure approaching a little too fast on a lively mare. He saw her glance back, and smiled at how easily she'd given her escort and chaperone the slip.

He'd not told anyone of his plan to ride out early to clear his head, so it had to be a chance meeting, although it would be improper to see her unchaperoned. The young princess spurred on her mount as she came closer, so he stopped and turned in the saddle as she approached.

With a jolt he realised Henry's little sister was becoming an attractive young woman. There was an unexpected warmth in her eyes as she smiled at him and he realised this meeting was no accident. There was something she wished to say to him.

He raised a gloved hand in welcome. 'Good morning, Princess Mary.' He glanced back at the distant followers, making a judgement, then ran an expert eye over her horse before resting his gaze on her. 'You ride well – and your horse is quite a beauty.'

Princess Mary's eyes twinkled and she smiled at his compliment, patting her mare on the withers. 'She's descended from Arabians, brought back from the Crusades.' A momentary sadness passed over her young face. 'She was a gift to my late father.'

Brandon looked down at his own mount. 'I doubt I'd be

able to keep up with you on a run. These heavy warhorses are bred to be fast over short distances.'

The princess nodded. 'I heard my brother entered a private joust here, his first one as king.'

Henry's secret was out and Brandon didn't wish to lie to the princess. 'The king jousted in disguise. William Compton was badly wounded in the leg with a broken lance.'

'By my brother's hand?' She frowned with concern.

'It was Sir Edward Neville's lance, although some thought the king had been wounded.' His face became serious. 'Such things are the price we pay for jousting. Fortunately, Compton is as strong as an ox, but I doubt he'll wish to joust again soon.'

Mary's ladies and escort approached before she could reply. They both turned their horses and rode to meet them. He studied the young princess for a moment and sensed there was something else she'd wished to say, but the moment passed.

Henry seemed in a dark mood as Brandon helped him dress. The usually talkative king hardly spoke and his brow furrowed as if he was deep in thought. Brandon fastened a warm fur-lined cloak over Henry's shoulders and stood back to admire his handiwork.

'Something troubles you, Your Grace?'

Henry looked at him with sadness in his eyes. 'Our first-born child was a princess – not the heir I prayed for.'

Brandon didn't miss the past tense and his mind raced with the consequences. 'The child has not survived?'

Henry shook his head. 'Catherine persuaded me to keep the truth from the superstitious people of England. The child was stillborn, a secret known only to a few.'

Brandon understood. Henry trusted him to mention this to no one, yet he struggled to see how the secret could be kept for long, given the public excitement at the announcement of

Catherine's pregnancy. Such secrets seemed to be a feature of Henry's new court.

Henry placed his hand on Brandon's arm and spoke in a pained voice. 'It burdens my conscience to keep up this pretence. Each day that passes there are more lies, more deceptions, yet for what good purpose?' He cursed. 'This is God's displeasure, for marrying my brother's widow.'

Brandon felt it his duty to console him. 'Queen Catherine is young, Your Grace. She will no doubt be with child again soon enough.'

Henry looked up at him with a glimmer of hope in his eyes. 'I pray you are right, Brandon. My grandmother, may God rest her soul, was against the match – and prophesied that some adversity would follow.'

Brandon had heard the same story. Such gossip had a way of passing through the royal household quicker than a plague of fleas. He'd also heard that Lady Margaret choked while eating a cygnet at the coronation banquet, her health failing soon afterwards. It seemed an odd way for such a devout woman to end her long life.

'Let us pray that God provides you with a healthy son and heir, Your Grace.'

Brandon's uncle, Sir Thomas, suffered a mystery illness throughout the long winter that defied the cures of his physicians. When Brandon visited him, he was shocked to see how the once-powerful man had wasted away to become a pale shadow of his former self. Even so, it was a shock to all who knew him when he passed away the following night.

There was another shock waiting for Brandon when he went to the reading of his uncle's will. When he returned home he sat heavily in his favourite chair, pulled off his felt cap and twisted it in his hands before looking up at Anne.

'I never understood my uncle.'

'Not the news we were expecting?' Anne could tell at a glance.

'It defies belief, Anne.' Brandon fought back a curse. 'My uncle has left a considerable sum of money to a woman at court, Lady Jane Guildford.' He frowned. 'It seems she cared for him during his illness – and has profited greatly as a consequence.'

'Has he left you the manor house?'

Brandon shook his head. 'My uncle left his house and the land he owns to Lady Guildford.' He made no attempt to hide his bitterness. 'To add insult to injury, she says she doesn't need it – and will offer it to us at a reasonable rent.'

'We should take up Lady Guildford's offer. Perhaps we'll be able to purchase it when the rest of your inheritance comes through. How long do we need to wait?'

Brandon shrugged. 'I've been left my uncle's gowns, and the wardship of Lord Saye, but the grants of land will have to wait until my uncle's widow follows him to the grave.'

Anne looked shocked. 'You should not wish ill to Lady Elizabeth, Charles. It's no fault of hers.'

He shook his head. 'Don't misunderstand me, Anne. I'm grateful to have the prospect of enough land to be granted a knighthood, even if I have to wait a little longer.'

'The loan from the king bought us some time, but if we move to the manor house we'll be no better off.' Anne didn't try to hide her disappointment.

Brandon placed his hand on hers. 'I am to have a new appointment, Anne. It could be a lucrative one, if I play my cards well.'

'Don't tease me, Charles.' Anne gave him a playful slap on the arm. 'What new position?'

My uncle was Marshal of the King's Bench, and I've been appointed in his place. It will mean regular income from grants of bail – as well as from prisoners who are prepared to pay for better conditions. Most importantly, it will make me a man of some influence.'

Anne smiled. 'You're starting to sound like your uncle.'

'I'm finally becoming my uncle. My time as Master of the Horse to the Earl of Essex has prepared me well to offer that service to the king when the time is right. I must confess to disappointment after learning of my uncle's will, but we will make of it what we can.'

Anne smoothed her gown over her bulging middle and placed his hand there, to feel the child give a healthy kick. 'We must secure our future before your son is born.'

Brandon grinned this time. It was hard to be precise but they calculated that the child she carried would be born in June. It was a mystery to him how a woman might know, but this was the first time she'd said it might be the boy they longed for.

Brandon ignored the tradition to keep out of his wife's confinement chamber. The room was darkened, and scented with lavender and rose water, the only light from a single candle burning at the side of Anne's bed. He placed his hand on her forehead and felt the damp heat. 'You have a fever.'

Anne's eyes narrowed with the pain. 'Have you sent for the midwife?'

He nodded. 'She'll be here soon. Do you know when the child will come?'

She sighed. 'Tonight, with God's grace.'

'I pray it all goes well for you.' He thought of Henry and Catherine's loss and said a silent prayer that all would be well with Anne. He glanced over to the shuttered window. 'Why does it have to be kept so dark?'

'I'm supposed to have no distractions.' There was a wry note in her weakened voice. 'Such as errant husbands asking foolish questions I cannot answer.'

'Forgive me, Anne.' He kissed her. 'I confess I'm worried about you. It wasn't like this when little Annie was born.'

Her eyes widened with sudden concern. 'Who is looking after Annie now?'

He smoothed her brow. 'Don't worry, little Annie's fine. Our new housekeeper cares for our daughter as if she were her own.'

Anne had been against employing a housekeeper due to the cost, but also because that had become her role after they returned to the manor house in Southwark. Brandon insisted, and was proved right when Anne took to her confinement. He didn't know how he would have coped without the housekeeper.

He turned his head at a confident knock on the door. Brandon opened it and stood aside for the elderly midwife to enter. She was followed by a young girl carrying a bundle of linen. The midwife glanced at Anne's feverish brow then gave Brandon a disapproving scowl.

'This bedchamber is no place for a man, sir.' Her London accent carried an insistent note.

Brandon suspected the superstitious old woman believed his presence was a bad omen. Midwives were supposed to be cheerful ... but this one came highly recommended.

He gave Anne one last kiss on the cheek, smoothed her forehead and whispered to her, 'I love you.' He gave a last nod to the surly midwife and left, closing the door behind him.

He sat alone in the room that had once been his uncle's study. Old weapons from long-forgotten battles still graced the walls, together with fading, moth-eaten tapestries. He guessed it must be close to midnight when he heard the first of the screams, muffled by the thick stone walls of the old manor house.

Pouring himself a generous goblet of wine, he felt the warmth in his throat as he took a deep drink. He recalled the first time he'd seen Anne at court. She'd been confident and beautiful, in a satin gown of the deepest vermilion, and had laughed happily at his compliments.

He'd been instantly attracted to her, and only later found out her father was the influential Sir Anthony Browne, Captain of Calais – by coincidence, standard-bearer to the king. Anne's mother Eleanor was the daughter of a wealthy baron, Sir Robert Oughtred.

Brandon never met her, as she'd died at the turn of the century. Sir Anthony promptly married Lady Lucy Neville and Anne's father's fortune was inherited by her half-brother, also named Anthony Browne, when he died six years later.

Anne never suggested she was too good for Brandon, although she teased him about his poor handwriting. She'd been so patient about the way he ran up debts, and she always found the good in people. He closed his eyes and mumbled a prayer for Anne and their child.

He woke to find himself still slumped in his chair and realised someone was knocking at the door. He rubbed his eyes and saw the empty goblet lying on its side. He'd drunk more wine than he'd intended. He crossed to the door and opened it to see the midwife's young assistant.

She bobbed a curtsey. 'The midwife asked me to inform you, sir, that you have a healthy daughter.'

Brandon grinned with relief. 'And my wife?'

The girl hesitated for a moment too long. 'It was not an easy birth, sir, but your wife seems in good spirits.'

They named their second daughter Mary, and her christening

at Southwark Cathedral was attended by several knights of the realm. Anne was ordered to remain in bed until she recovered her health, so she demanded that Brandon describe every detail.

'Little Mary wore the same satin christening robe you made for Annie. She bawled to the rafters,' he smiled at the memory, 'when the priest held her over the font and put cold water on her head.'

'You must bring her to see me, Charles. I cannot allow her to think her wet nurse is her mother.' Anne spoke slowly, as if each word was an effort to her.

Brandon leaned over and kissed her softly on the cheek. 'I will, but for now you must rest. You still feel a little feverish.'

She forced a smile. 'I'll soon be well again, then we shall plan for the son I know you long for.'

Brandon raised an eyebrow. 'All in good time, Anne.'

He took her hand and sat in silence at her bedside. Her slender fingers felt cold in his and her flushed face now looked too pale, as if the blood had drained from it. 'I want to tell you I'm sorry, Anne.' His voice trembled. 'For my marriage to your aunt, when I'd already promised you…'

'I forgive you.' Her voice sounded weak. She closed her eyes and drifted off to a restless sleep.

Brandon kneeled and placed the posy of bright summer flowers on the fresh earth of the grave, then took a step backwards and bowed his head. His mind numbed with loss, he tried to forget the feverish, delirious woman his wife had become.

Instead, he recalled the happiness of their second wedding day, held at Easter with more witnesses than could fit in the church of St Michael's Cornhill. Anne called it their proper wedding, with a mischievous laugh, as if their first, secret wedding in the old church in Stepney had somehow been improper.

She looked beautiful in her wedding gown, the most expensive she'd ever owned, her plaited long hair covered with the latest style of French hood. A diamond necklace glittered at her neck, her only memento of her late mother's fortune. She'd looked at him with a hint of humour in her amber eyes as she promised to love and honour him, for as long as they both shall live.

It took Anne two long weeks to die. At the end she fought for each breath and gripped his hand in hers. He'd allowed her to see their daughters, and she'd wept tears of joy at the sight of them. Little Annie, now four, stared at her mother as if she knew it would be the last time, but Mary gurgled happily at the sight of her.

Brandon looked down at the posy, tied with a silk ribbon, and realised he'd not given her flowers since those first clandestine meetings. He wished he'd told her how much he loved her. The sense of loss and regret overwhelmed him and he finally surrendered to the tears he'd been fighting back.

He'd believed Anne would always be there for him, helping keep his life on track and always encouraging him. Now he would have to bring up his two daughters without her. He wept for his beautiful wife, and had never felt so alone.

7

JANUARY 1511

The bells of every church in London pealed discordantly and the woody smoke of a hundred bonfires filled the crisp winter air. New Year's Day was a time for the people to celebrate, and King Henry provided free wine for all to drink to the health of the newborn prince.

Cheering crowds gathered around the blazing fires, singing and dancing in the streets. The people's joy and a sense of a new beginning seemed even greater than at Henry's coronation. Brandon held his hands over his ears and felt the ground vibrate under his feet as cannons roared another royal salute at Tower Wharf.

It seemed a waste of good gunpowder, but it wasn't every day they had a new heir to the throne. Henry proudly held up his swaddled infant son for the people to see the future King of England. They cheered and called out, 'Long live the king!' and, 'Long live Prince Hal!'

Henry added to Brandon's responsibilities, appointing him as Justice of the Peace for Surrey, and Marshal of the Royal Household. The new posts were some recompense for making Thomas Knyvett the king's Master of the Horse, and had their advantages, as well as good salaries. Most importantly, it meant Brandon's influence at court was growing, despite his lack of a knighthood.

As well as overseeing the arrangements for the royal progress from one palace to another, he had freedom to come and go as he pleased. As Marshal of the Royal Household Brandon also acted as deputy to the Earl Marshal, Thomas Howard, Earl of Surrey. It irked Brandon that his ancestors were once servants to Howard's family, and he knew Thomas Howard would use that to his advantage when it suited him.

At the prince's christening the following Sunday Brandon joined the short procession to the Church of the Observant Friars, built against the walls of Richmond Palace. A gravelled pathway, twenty-four feet wide, was strewn with herbs and rushes, and the church walls were decorated with the old king's priceless collection of Arras tapestries.

Brandon found himself watching Princess Mary to see if she caught his eye. She walked with her coterie of ladies-in-waiting, taller than most, in a fur cloak over a gown glittering with diamonds and pearls, and a French hood covering her hair. She never once looked in his direction.

Behind the young princess followed the queen's thirty maids of honour, then the ambassadors of Spain, Venice and Rome, with their delegations of priests and nobles. The Friars' little church proved too small for them all and Brandon had to shiver outside in the cold with other members of the royal household.

The door was left ajar, so they could hear Archbishop William Warham's dour voice as he read the Latin prayers. It was hard for Brandon to see over the crowds, but there seemed to be confusion about the godparents. The Earl of Arundel was standing in for King Louis of France, and the Countess of

Surrey for the prince's godmother, Margaret, Duchess of Savoy.

The monks' choir sang a *Te Deum* as Archbishop Warham held the infant over the silver font and named him Henry Tudor, Prince of Wales, the next generation of the Tudor line and future king. Brandon smiled as he heard the little child squeal in protest, his shrill cries echoing from the rafters.

He recalled the happiness of his own little Mary's christening the year before and felt a sudden pang of grief at the loss of his wife. Both his daughters were now in the care of Anne's relatives, although he tried to visit them as often as he could.

He needed to prepare his girls to attend Henry's court as soon as they were old enough. He'd sworn an oath to Anne at her graveside that he would find them both noble husbands, worthy of her sacrifice.

Brandon's thoughts returned to the idea of marrying some titled lady, with vast estates and an income of her own. He promised himself that when he did, he would send for his daughters and become a better father to them.

The jousting at Westminster tiltyard to celebrate the christening was planned as the greatest spectacle ever seen in London. The king returned in high spirits from a pilgrimage to the holy shrine of Our Lady at Walsingham, where he gave thanks for his good fortune.

Queen Catherine, safely delivered from the ritual of churching, sat next to Princess Mary with their ladies-in-waiting, swathed in furs against the winter cold. Their purpose-built gallery was lined with purple velvet and covered with the finest cloth of gold, under a grand canopy of estate.

The curious crowd fell silent as a mysterious stranger, dressed in the plain russet-coloured habit of a monk, rode brazenly up to the queen's gallery. He made the sign of the cross in the air with his gloved hand, then threw off his hooded cape to reveal gilded armour and a fine sword at his belt.

Brandon called out, his powerful voice echoing across the tiltyard. 'I request the right to defend the queen's honour, as her champion!'

The crowd cheered and applauded as Queen Catherine accepted. Brandon watched Princess Mary's mischievous French lady-in-waiting, Jane Popincourt, lean across to her. He guessed it was something to do with him, as the princess laughed happily and raised a gold-ringed hand in acknowledgement of his clever charade.

A sharp fanfare of trumpets from green-cloaked foresters announced a pageant of an enormous castle, garlanded with red and white roses, in a wheeled forest of full-sized trees and bushes. Pulled by great warhorses disguised as a golden lion and a silver antelope, complete with gold antlers, the whole pageant was over twenty-five feet long.

When it came to a halt in front of the queen's gallery, the foresters sounded their horns and the golden castle burst open to reveal King Henry with three knights. Dressed in the queen's colours of green satin edged with scarlet, they brandished swords and wore helmets plumed with brightly dyed ostrich feathers.

Sir Thomas Boleyn and Sir Edward Howard bowed to the ladies in the gallery and announced themselves as Sir Good Hope and Sir Good Will. A grinning Sir Thomas Knyvett, wearing an oversized gold codpiece, proclaimed himself Sir Valiant Desire. Henry raised a hand to silence the cheering crowd and announced he was Sir Loyal Heart, with a meaningful bow to Queen Catherine.

Brandon could see Henry was in love with Catherine, despite his bluff capering and bawdy jokes. He remembered how proudly the ten-year-old Henry escorted Catherine on her arrival in London. She'd dressed as a Spanish maiden, her long auburn hair loose over her shoulders.

Henry wore a suit of cloth of gold and carried a sword which looked too big for him. Although Henry insisted it was his father's dying wish, he could have sent her back to Spain. Instead, he'd chosen to marry Catherine as soon as he could.

The pageant of the forest and castle took up so much space in the Westminster courtyard there was hardly room for the tiltyard. When the jousting began, the tilt barriers were so close to where the queen sat she could almost reach out and touch the charging knights. Once she shrieked as a broken shard of lance struck the side of the grandstand in front of her with a hollow crack, too close for comfort.

The twenty-five courses of jousting ended with Brandon, as the queen's champion, meeting the challenge from Sir Loyal Heart, whose warhorse was caparisoned with green satin covered with glittering golden hearts. Queen Catherine raised her hand to her mouth as they clashed in front of her, Henry's lance shattering on Brandon's armoured chest.

Some might have suspected that Brandon contrived to let the king win the highest points. In truth, he'd insisted on the use of lances with tips which shivered more easily. Their long hours of practice had made Henry an accomplished jouster. Most importantly, it allowed him to show his doubting courtiers he could compete against the best.

The christening celebrations continued long after evensong in the White Hall of Westminster Palace. Henry's musicians played dance music and wine flowed like water. Princess Mary and her ladies joined in with the singing but Brandon thought Mary looked relieved she'd resisted Henry's demands to join the dancing.

Henry shouted to the visiting Spanish ambassadors to try their luck against his valiant knights, and they took this as an invitation to start a free-for-all. Some began ripping at each other's clothes, tearing open the gowns of the dancing ladies, and even pulling gold ornaments from Henry's doublet.

Thomas Knyvett was stripped naked after losing his gold codpiece to a Spaniard, and Henry had to call for his guards to restore some order. He'd laughed it off as nothing more than high spirits, but Brandon decided he should escort Princess Mary back to her rooms with her ladies, as he feared for their virtue.

When they reached the princess's chambers she turned and studied his face in the shadowy passageway. 'I am most grateful to you, Master Brandon, for seeing us safe from those rascals.' A smile lit up her face and it looked like she wished to say more.

Brandon felt an unexpected warmth as her gold-ringed fingers rested on his arm, but was aware of her lady-in-waiting, Jane Popincourt, watching them with a glint of amusement in her eyes. He felt sudden anger that they played their games with his feelings.

'I am honoured, Your Grace, and wish you a good night.'

He turned and strode back the way they'd come, his mind a whirl of possibilities. It might not have been a game. He'd not mistaken the look she'd given him, although they had all been drinking and he had no idea what to make of it. From the bawdy singing ahead of him it sounded as if Henry's party would continue until well into the morning.

The shocking news travelled through the long corridors and back stairs of Richmond Palace, touching the lives of everyone who heard. From the humblest servant to the most senior lord, the people could not believe it. Some wept openly, while others clasped their hands in prayer.

Little Henry, the future of the Tudor dynasty, heir to the

king, had been discovered dead in his gilded cot, living for only fifty-two short days.

It was said Queen Catherine believed it was God's judgement on her, and spent long hours weeping and praying on her knees in the cold chapel, refusing to eat or sleep. Henry shut himself away in the high tower, refusing to see anyone. Brandon had been warned not to offer his condolences unless he wished to witness the king's displeasure.

By tradition, neither Henry nor Catherine attended the funeral of the infant prince in Westminster Abbey. Brandon, as Marshal of the Royal Household, helped arrange for the three royal barges, draped in black, which carried the miniature coffin ten miles down the Thames from Richmond Palace.

A wintry breeze lifted the black material from the prince's coffin, making it flap like the beating wings of a giant crow. Brandon would never admit to being superstitious, yet it seemed a bad omen. He pulled his fur-lined cape more tightly around his shoulders and cursed this tragic turn of events.

He followed as the procession made its way from the quay to the abbey, where the child's grandfather, King Henry VII, had been buried less than two years before. He recognised Sir Thomas Boleyn, Sir Edward Howard and Sir Thomas Knyvett among the knights carrying the regal banners, their joyful celebrations now turned to stony-faced mourning.

Behind the knights followed a hundred and eighty black-cloaked paupers, paid by the king to pray for the soul of his child. The light was fading, and candles flickered in lanterns along the entire route to where the bells of Westminster Abbey rang out above the chanting of the monks.

Brandon watched the short service and said a silent prayer for the little prince as his coffin was placed in a stone niche near the entrance to the chapel of St Edward the Confessor. Henry had lost his treasured heir, his Prince of Wales, and it was difficult to imagine life in England could ever be quite the same again.

～

The deer park in the grounds of Greenwich Palace, created by the ill-fated Duke Humphrey of Gloucester some eighty years before, was home to some of the finest stags in England. The problem was that it extended to hundreds of wooded acres, so even with an army of beaters and trackers, hunting there required as much luck as skill.

The king's hunting party included his oldest friends, Sir Thomas Knyvett, Sir Edward Howard, and Sir William Parr, as well as Brandon. No one spoke of it, yet they all knew Henry wished to forget his tragic loss, which had made him seem older than his twenty years.

Dressed in plain hunting clothes, with his bow over his shoulder, Henry looked more like his old self and seemed in surprisingly good spirits. Once they were out of earshot of the gamekeepers he could keep his secret no longer. 'I have good news. We are joining the Holy League.'

'The pope's alliance?' Brandon tried his best to keep up with the politics of state, although he failed to see why Henry was so animated. He'd seen the magnificent golden rose, a gift from Pope Julius to Henry, and now understood its significance. 'The Holy League includes Spain and the Venetians. They are united against King Louis – but we are at peace with France, and King Louis was godparent at the christening.' Brandon immediately regretted mentioning the prince as Henry gave him a scathing look.

Thomas Knyvett urged his horse alongside Brandon's. 'The French would invade us tomorrow if they saw the opportunity, Brandon. The Holy League will keep them at bay,' Knyvett flashed Henry a broad grin, 'particularly now they have the greatest king in Christendom on their side.'

With sudden insight Brandon realised how his friend Thomas Knyvett had progressed so rapidly. If he wished to do the same, he could no longer afford to distance himself from the politics of Henry's court or matters of state. He also noted how Knyvett managed to use humour to compliment Henry without a trace of artifice.

Henry looked pleased with Knyvett's words. 'We shall take the fight to France. We've defeated them before and we can do so again. From this day, I wish you all to prepare for a holy war, as good Christian men. The pope has promised us the Crown of France once King Louis is defeated.' Henry brightened at the thought. 'Now, let's find some venison.' He held up a leather purse for them to see. 'Here's a reward for the first to take a hart.'

They cantered up the grassy slope towards the wooded area where the beaters waited, then slowed their pace. Henry peered ahead. 'My father's illness prevented his hunting. Since then the stags have grown wild and more elusive.'

Thomas Knyvett grinned. 'They'll offer better sport than the tame does at Richmond.' He urged his horse forward, keen to be the first to sight a hart.

Brandon had seen the weight of the purse. He needed the money, although the sight of Knyvett pressing ahead aroused his competitive spirit. His hunting crossbow hung on a leather strap over his shoulder, with a full quiver of deadly bolts.

The beaters worked in a line, combing through the deep undergrowth of the forest, cracking their sticks on tree trunks and calling out, their voices echoing in the overgrown forest glades. Several had running-hounds, straining on leather leashes. Bred to have a good nose for deer, unlike Henry's greyhounds, their hounds remained strangely silent as they hunted.

The occasional rabbit darted into their path, and a fox was

startled from its hiding place, but after half a day the only sign of deer were some dark round droppings at the side of the track. Henry's gamekeeper bent to examine them and held a handful up for Henry to see.

'Still shiny.' He sniffed them. 'A sure sign they're not more than a few hours old.' The man looked pleased with himself, despite their lack of success with the hunt. 'There are prints as well, Your Grace.' He pointed up the narrow track.

Henry cocked his crossbow and turned in the saddle. 'We're close enough now. Be ready.'

Brandon scanned the forest, alert for any sign of movement. He pulled back the powerful cocking lever in readiness but was taken by surprise when the magnificent stag leapt from cover. Thomas Knyvett raised his crossbow and fired a bolt, striking the heavy animal in the rump as it ran. The pain might have made the stag run faster but it faltered and Henry hit it in the flank with a second shot at closer range, causing it to stumble and fall.

Knyvett slid from his saddle and grabbed the stag by the antlers. A bright stream of red blood spurted as he ended the stag's life with a single slash of his knife across the throat. He looked up at Henry. 'Good shot, Your Grace.'

Henry graciously handed him the purse. 'Good work, Knyvett. I trust you'll do as well against the French when the time comes!'

Brandon found himself deep in thought. He'd been distracted from the hunt by Henry's talk of fighting the French. This could be the opportunity he'd been hoping for. The King's Spears would all be given the chance to become commanders if a war was declared.

He had no military experience, but he also had little to lose and everything to gain. At last all the skills he'd learned fighting in tournaments would be put to a real test. If he could distinguish himself as a commander in battle a knighthood was guaranteed, perhaps even a title, and a reputation as a leader of men.

He watched as Henry's gamekeepers lay the stag on its back in a forest clearing. It looked a fine specimen, with massive antlers. One of the men took his knife and made a long, shallow cut down the breast. There was a sharp crack of bone as he forced open the ribcage. His bloodied hand emerged and he held high the fist-sized heart, to a cheer from the hunters.

The men took care to cut out the stag's liver and find the kidneys, setting them aside with the tenderloins, before finishing the disembowelling. One looked up at Brandon. 'This job is best done soon after death – before the belly begins to swell.'

He didn't flinch from the sight of steaming offal spilling on to the forest floor, yet a deep concern at the back of Brandon's mind came into sharp focus. He'd believed himself ready for the battle ahead, and whatever it would demand of him. He knew he'd hesitated a moment too long when he could have killed the stag. He worried that he might not find the courage to take the life of a Frenchman in Henry's holy war – if he hesitated in battle he would pay the ultimate price.

8

JULY 1512

Thomas Wolsey, a round-faced cleric who'd become Henry's trusted secretary, greeted Brandon warmly yet studied him with sharp eyes. 'I believe I owe you thanks, Master Brandon. I hear you've defended my name.'

'It was nothing, Master Wolsey. You must know there are those at court who resent your access to the king.' Brandon returned the smile. 'It bothers them that you come from humble stock.'

Wolsey raised his eyebrows. 'My late father, may God rest his soul, was a respected landowner and innkeeper in Suffolk. He worked hard to pay for me to be educated in Oxford, yet all they remember is that he once worked as a butcher.'

'They call me a stable boy behind my back, because I serve Sir Henry Bourchier as his Master of the Horse.' Brandon grinned. 'I don't let it trouble me.'

'It seems we have much in common.' Wolsey gave him a wry look. 'We serve the same master and ambitions – and share a common adversary.'

'Sir Thomas Howard?' Brandon saw the scowl of distaste

on Wolsey's face and knew he'd guessed correctly. 'I suspect he makes trouble for us both when he can.'

Wolsey's tone became conspiratorial. 'Thomas Howard defends the privileges of nobility. The king rewards him well, but his day of reckoning will come.'

Brandon understood the implied threat and made a mental note never to cross Thomas Wolsey. He needed the cleric to help him understand the politics of court and council, but intuitively knew Wolsey could bear a grudge and make a dangerous enemy.

He glanced around the old king's dusty study, never used by Henry, so ideal for this private meeting with Wolsey. He'd last been there as the late king's esquire and remembered seeing him hunched over his desk, quill in hand, squinting at his ledgers as he initialled each item of expenditure.

Brandon noted the gaps in the bookshelves, like missing teeth. Someone had taken the best of the old king's books, which he'd cherished even when his eyesight faded. Drawers and cupboards had been left half-open, perhaps a sign the study had been searched for valuables after the old king's death.

A parchment mariners' map spread out on the carved oak table before them showed the coastlines of England and France in greater detail than he'd ever seen. Only the cities were marked on the land, but Brandon noted that all the ports and harbours were identified.

Wolsey smoothed out a crease in the map. 'The king wishes to control the Channel.' He tapped a gold-ringed finger on the pale-blue space between England and France. 'His fleet is to make a show of our strength, after the failure of Dorset's expedition.'

Brandon had heard Henry cursing his father-in-law, King Ferdinand of Spain, for leaving Thomas. Grey, Marquess of

Dorset, and his army of twelve thousand men to their fate. The expedition was stricken by disease and over a thousand died. The rest barely returned with their lives.

The devastating fire at Westminster Palace soon after also unsettled Henry. The building was old and in need of renovation, but the people were saying it was a bad omen, a sign of misfortune to come. Henry swore to prove them wrong with a great victory over the French.

Brandon studied the map more closely. The Channel had been illustrated with sea monsters by an imaginative scribe. 'I'm surprised how close Calais is to Dover.'

'Sailors call it the narrow sea, but I caution you not to underestimate it. I've crossed those waters many times, as secretary to the Deputy Governor of Calais and for the late king's diplomatic missions. The Channel has its dangers, particularly in winter when sudden storms can challenge even the most able mariners.' He turned to Brandon. 'Have you been out to sea?'

'I've never been beyond the limits of the Thames.' Brandon waited for a reaction from Wolsey, who looked deep in thought, and wondered if his honesty had cost him. 'I assure you, Master Wolsey, I am ready to take command.'

Wolsey hesitated for a moment, before seeming to make a judgement. 'I shall recommend that you are offered a position on the *Sovereign*. She's a fine ship, with a competent captain and crew.' He fixed Brandon with a steady gaze. 'In return, I wish you to be my eyes and ears. I must remain at the side of the king, but when you return I'll need your full report.'

It seemed a small enough price to pay for such a consideration. 'Of course, and I am grateful for your support.'

Wolsey nodded. 'Our job is to do whatever the king wishes to be done. We must work together, Master Brandon, to protect King Henry from those who would hope to influence him for their own ends.'

. . .

Late that night Brandon reflected on those words as he lay awake and alone in his comfortable bed. One of the challenges for Henry, now he was king, was that everyone sought to profit from him in some way or other, including himself.

Wolsey was a complex man, with many secrets. Brandon knew the cleric kept a mistress – Joan Lark, in Fleet Street – and heard that, like him, he had two small children by her whom he could visit only rarely. It was also said that Wolsey had connections with the pope in Rome and hoped one day to become a cardinal.

It seemed Henry trusted him with decisions about the most important matters. As well as being Dean of Lincoln, he was also the king's almoner, a canon of Windsor, and elected by the Knights of the Garter as their registrar. Thomas Wolsey would be a most useful ally as he learned to master the politics of court, not only in England, but on the continent too.

Brandon contrived to see Princess Mary before he left for Portsmouth. Their liaisons had become more frequent over the past few months and he enjoyed her attention. One of the advantages of his position meant he could see her in an official capacity without attracting much attention.

Mary spotted something was going on as soon as she saw him. 'You look pleased with yourself, Charles Brandon.' She studied his face, waiting for an explanation.

'I'm off to fight the French.' Brandon couldn't help the pride in his voice. Henry had chosen his most trusted men as commanders, although Thomas Howard's younger brother Edward had been made Admiral of the Fleet, which suggested Wolsey had not had it all his own way.

Mary stared at him with wide eyes. 'Are we at war with

France?' The mischievous note in her voice suggested she knew the answer.

'Pope Julius promised your brother the Crown of France, once King Louis is defeated.'

She frowned. 'It will take time to assemble another army. How is it that you are leaving so soon?'

'I've been given command of your father's old flagship, the *Sovereign*, and my good friend Thomas Knyvett has the *Regent*.'

'Do you know how to command a warship?' She looked as if she doubted it.

'It's my duty. The king would wish to take command, but he's chosen those he knows he can depend upon, so I consider it an honour.' He smiled at her. 'In truth, I shall be relying a great deal on her experienced captain.'

Mary seemed reassured. 'I know the *Sovereign*.' She smiled. 'The French would probably run at the sight of her fine cannons.'

Brandon thought he saw a look of longing in her eyes, despite her flippant manner, and he found himself wishing Mary wasn't a princess and Henry's younger sister. Once she'd talked of her betrothal to Prince Charles, heir to the House of Valois-Burgundy and the Holy Roman Empire. Wolsey seemed to think there was a good reason for the young prince's delay. Brandon decided to find out more when he returned.

He had plenty of time to think about his future on the hundred-mile ride from Greenwich to Portsmouth. His groom, Samuel, rode at his side, followed by a wagon loaded with supplies and their retainers. Henry's solution to raising the money for his holy war was to require each commander to meet his own costs.

Samuel glanced behind at the retainers, some riding on the wagon, others on horseback. 'They will have to pick up the pace, sir, or the king's war will be over before we reach Portsmouth.'

Brandon agreed. 'They've yet to receive any pay. I recruited them in Southwark and trust their loyalty will make up for their lack of military experience.'

He glanced back at his twenty retainers. Ten were competent archers, the rest carried halberds and wore swords at their belts. He had no idea how he would pay them if the holy war lasted longer than a few months, but if they captured a French ship they would all have a share of the spoils.

The salt in the air carried with it a sense of excitement as they finally reached Portsmouth harbour. Brandon counted seven high-masted warships at the quayside and another dozen or so sitting at anchor. Some, like the *Sovereign* and the *Regent,* had been the old king's ships. Other ships were converted merchantmen, commandeered in the name of the king to carry soldiers, horses and supplies for the warships.

Henry's royal standard and banners flew from the topmast of his magnificent new flagship, the *Mary Rose*. A floating fortress, she bristled with the latest guns. Henry boasted that over six hundred oak trees were used in her construction, making the *Mary Rose* the most expensive warship ever built.

Brandon watched as sailors clambered high in the rigging to prepare the huge canvas sails. Teams of men sang as they hauled on ropes and used great wooden cranes to load supplies. Crates and casks littered the quay and a pig squealed in distress as it was hoisted into the air and lowered into the dark hold of a ship.

The crowds who'd gathered to see the fleet sail cheered and shouted as fighting men queued at gangplanks, the sun glinting off new armour and weapons as they waited to embark. The atmosphere seemed like a celebration and proved Henry right. The people wanted a victory against the French.

Samuel found a longboat and helped two sailors load Brandon's baggage. His groom had a new role, for as well as acting as Brandon's steward for the sea voyage, he carried his longbow and quiver of thirty arrows with sharpened iron tips. He would fight with the archers if they encountered hostile ships.

The longboat rocked in the swell as they pulled away from the stone steps of the quay. The iron-grey sea looked threatening, and white-crested waves crashed in the distance. Brandon tasted the sharp tang of salt on his lips and nervously gripped the gunwale as a wave slapped hard against the side of the longboat.

'Can you swim, Samuel?'

'I cannot, sir.' He looked doubtfully back to the quay. 'I never planned to go to sea.'

Brandon shaded his eyes against the sun and peered towards the dark outline of the *Sovereign*, sitting at anchor. 'Neither can I, so we'll have to trust in the Lord – and our captain.'

As they came close he could see Wolsey had chosen well. The *Sovereign* was a great carrack, with four towering masts and a long bowsprit. A two-deck forecastle rose high at the bow and a four-deck aftcastle, painted in Tudor green-and-white, at the stern. The square canvas sails were furled but the mizzenmast carried a triangular lateen sail, which cracked like a whip as it flapped in the light breeze.

They pulled alongside and climbed the rope ladder. Brandon looked around as he heard his name called out. Sir Henry Guildford, wearing a shining silver breastplate over his doublet, strode to greet him. He felt a stab of annoyance as he realised he wasn't to be trusted with his own command after all.

'Master Brandon!' Henry Guildford grinned. 'You are to be

my second in command. If you follow me, I'll show you around the ship.'

They picked their way through to the aftcastle accommodation and climbed steep wooden steps. Brandon turned and looked out over the ship. Men worked in every available space, securing stores and preparing weapons.

'She's grander than I expected.'

'You are fortunate, Brandon. The *Mary Rose* is newer and the *Regent* more powerful, but *Sovereign* is the best of the older ships in the fleet.' He surveyed the busy deck. 'The king ordered her to be fitted with fourteen new cannons,' he pointed to the iron barrels jutting from open gun ports, 'although we'll no doubt have more use of the swivel guns. They fire across the decks of an enemy warship and cut the crew to pieces without doing too much damage to the structure.'

Brandon breathed refreshing sea air as the fleet finally set sail and cleared the headland of the Isle of Wight. He raised a hand to his friend Thomas Knyvett, sailing alongside on the *Regent*. Like the *Sovereign*, she was a floating symbol of England's power, heavily armed with over two hundred swivel guns.

Knyvett cupped his hands around his mouth and shouted across to Brandon. 'I'll wager fifty ducats we capture a French ship before you!'

Brandon laughed at the bet. Thomas Knyvett looked like a pirate, with a fine sword at his belt and a sailor's cap on his head. He shouted back. 'I wish you the best of luck with that, Sir Thomas!'

The next two weeks were a new experience for Brandon as he learned his way around the ship. He got on well with the captain, a cheerful Cornishman with a long grey beard, who agreed to teach him all the nautical terms. Henry Guildford also proved to be a good choice of companion. He respected Brandon's willingness to learn and showed him how to navigate by the stars.

The seas were calm enough and the winds in their favour, although they could change with surprising speed, forcing the fleet to tack up the Channel. Brandon found command of the night watch a challenge and fell asleep on duty more than once. He'd imagined they'd be fortunate to capture any foreign ships, but Admiral Howard pursued everything in sight.

Only three of the ships they apprehended proved to be French, and all surrendered without a fight, so when they next came alongside their sister ship, the *Regent*, Brandon wasn't surprised to see Knyvett looking pleased with himself.

Knyvett leaned over the rail and called out. 'Twelve ships boarded!'

Brandon grinned and called back, cupping his hands to be better heard. 'I'll be expecting you to honour your bet!'

The rocky point of the Saint-Mathieu peninsula marked the entrance to the sheltered waters leading to the port of Brest. Saint-Mathieu was also the northern limit of their patrol area, so it was the second week of August before they sailed within range of the enemy guns.

Henry Guildford called for Brandon and pointed into the distance. 'The French and Breton fleet.' He frowned. 'Now we'll be put to the test.'

Brandon peered towards the horizon at the forest of distant masts. As they sailed closer he could make out some ships flying unfamiliar pennants, and others that were heavy with guns. There were more ships in the French fleet than he could count.

'Watch and learn, Brandon.' Henry Guildford studied the French fleet with an expert eye. 'They are at anchor, with no sign of sail yet. It seems we've taken the French by surprise, but we won't have the advantage for long. They'll cut their anchor cables when they sight us.'

Two of the largest French warships set their sails and headed towards them, like silent ghosts. Not for the first time Brandon felt a sense of misgiving. There was a difference between picking off a lone ship and confronting the entire French and Breton fleet in their home waters.

He'd settled down well to the daily routine of the *Sovereign*, yet lay awake in his narrow wooden bunk worrying about what he'd do if their ship started to sink. He stared at the cold, green-grey sea and shivered at the thought of how it would fill his lungs as he sank into its murky depths.

Henry Guildford broke through his reverie with a loud curse. 'Those are the flagships, *Marie la Cordelière* and *Petite Louise*. The *Cordelière* is at least a thousand tons, the size of the *Regent* and *Sovereign* together, and heavily armed.' He scowled. 'They're going to keep us busy while the rest of the fleet escape to the safety of Brest.' He turned to the men. 'Stand to!'

Brandon recognised Samuel among the archers lining up along the side of the ship. Other men prepared heavy iron grappling hooks on thick ropes. They aimed to capture one of the French flagships as a prize to take home to King Henry. The new cannons would do too much damage, so they would manoeuvre alongside and seize the enemy ship with the grappling hooks. The men at the swivel guns would hold their fire while their archers picked off the enemy at close range.

Henry Guildford swore as the *Regent* broke formation, heeling over as it sped towards the French flagship. He bellowed to the captain, 'Steer a course for the *Regent*.' He muttered under his breath. 'What does he think he's doing?'

Brandon knew the answer. He'd seen Thomas Knyvett in

action many times before. Whether gambling at cards or in the joust, he was a risk-taker, relying on his legendary luck. He would win the credit for the capture of the *Marie la Cordelière*, even if it meant endangering his crew and ship.

The sails of the *Sovereign* strained in the wind as they turned to follow the *Regent*, with another of Henry's warships, the *Mary James*, keeping close on their starboard side. Brandon turned at the sound of a thundering boom and guessed from the rising plume of gun smoke that the *Mary Rose* had fired her cannons. A jagged hole appeared above the waterline of the second French warship, the *Petite Louise*.

Henry Guildford shook his head in annoyance. 'That's one prize we'll not be taking home – but at least it's shifted the balance in our favour.' His eyes narrowed as he stared at the French warship. 'Let's hope the captain of the *Cordelière* has the good sense to surrender before any more damage is done.'

A second boom of cannons, closer this time, made Brandon flinch and he heard shouts of alarm. He turned in time to see the main mast of the *Mary James* topple into the sea in a tangle of ropes and sails. Several of the crewmen were thrown overboard by the blast, thrashing the water in panic before disappearing into the waves.

The air filled with the booming of cannons, the sulphurous smell of gunpowder and the yells of injured men as the battle turned against them. Brandon felt powerless to do anything other than watch as the *Cordelière's* cannons fired again and again, this time at the *Sovereign*.

A cannonball crashed into the water at their bows, sending a shower of seawater over the foredeck. The archers began firing at the approaching French warship as it came within range. There was a ragged cheer as one of their arrows met its mark, striking one of the French gunners in the chest. It was a small victory, as another stepped in to take his place.

Another cannonball shattered the mast in front of Brandon

and he felt a sharp sting as a splinter of wood slashed his cheek. He held his hand to the wound and warm blood seeped through his fingers. Too late, he remembered he'd meant to wear a breastplate and helmet when the fighting started.

The towering mast shuddered and fell backwards towards him, stopping at a rakish angle, the sail flapping, held only by the straining rigging. Men began the dangerous task of cutting the thick ropes and the mast crashed to the deck like a fallen tree, smashing the corner of the gilded aftcastle.

Henry Guildford shouted the command the *Sovereign's* swivel-gunners had been waiting for. 'Open fire!'

Brandon felt the deck vibrate under his feet as the gunners began their deadly work, raking the deck of the *Cordelière*. The French warship turned to present her bows as a smaller target, but not before several of her crew had been killed or wounded.

The men of the *Regent* saw their chance and closed on the *Cordelière*. Grappling hooks flew in an arc and cheers rang out as the great French ship was pulled close. Brandon saw armed Frenchmen leaping across the narrow gap. The practice boarding they'd done hadn't prepared them for the enemy attacking first. With surprise on their side, the French were rapidly taking control of the *Regent*.

The *Margaret of Topsham*, commanded by Thomas Knyvett's younger brother James, turned towards the two ships and pulled alongside the *Regent* to reinforce the beleaguered crew. A few dozen armed men boarded before a smaller French ship appeared from nowhere and began firing at close range, forcing the *Margaret* to turn back into open water.

It seemed the reinforcements from the *Margaret* had turned the tide of the battle in their favour when the roar of a massive explosion lit up the sky and made Brandon's ears ring. It took him a moment to realise it had come from deep inside the hull of the *Cordelière*.

Bright orange flames and black smoke billowed into the sky

as a fire caught hold. Another explosion thundered and flames leapt across to the *Regent*, finding the tarred rigging and tinder-dry canvas sails. They watched as the fire became a raging inferno. Acrid smoke drifted across the water, with the inhuman screams of men being burned alive.

The sea seemed to boil as English and French men plunged into it, many with their clothing on fire. Some floated face down in the water, already past saving. Others could swim, and set out towards the English ships. Brandon called to the men nearest him.

'Launch the longboat. If we don't get to them soon those men won't have a chance.'

He should have stayed aboard the *Sovereign* but found himself climbing down the long rope ladder into the rocking longboat, his fear of drowning and the deep gash on his cheek forgotten. The oarsmen pulled hard as Brandon shouted directions, taking them to the nearest survivor and hauling him aboard.

The two blazing ships parted as the ropes burned through. More men dived into the water as the *Marie la Cordelière* began to list heavily to port. Waves soon lapped over the rail and sluiced the burning deck with a hiss of steam.

The bows of the French flagship began to tilt upwards and reared into the air like a dying beast as the stern filled with water. The pride of the French fleet sank in moments, leaving only scattered timbers, a man clinging to a barrel and a dark slick of ashes.

One of the men rowing the longboat called out. 'My God, the *Regent*!'

The *Regent* also sank with amazing speed, the fierce flames extinguished as she vanished beneath the waves. Brandon and his men were too busy helping a man with terrible burns to his face and hands into the longboat to watch. He would not last long, but at least he would have a Christian burial.

The fighting over, Brandon began the gruesome task of searching the corpses and the injured for his friend. After an hour he had to accept the painful truth. The swirling debris of burned timbers was the only sign that Thomas Knyvett or his fine ship had ever been there.

9

JANUARY 1513

Wolsey's London house was surprisingly grand for a cleric, with vivid Flemish tapestries and expensive leaded-glass windows. Brandon was served fine wine in a gilded cup and wondered how the king's secretary could afford to live so well.

Thomas Wolsey frowned at the scar on Brandon's cheek. 'You are fortunate it was not a little higher. You could have been blinded.'

'It has healed well enough, but I shall have to grow a thick beard to conceal it.'

Wolsey looked at him with a new respect. 'It's an honourable wound. I've heard good accounts of your conduct.'

'I did what I could for the survivors.' Brandon took a drink of his wine as he forced horrific images of burned and drowning men from his mind. 'We were unlucky, as the fight was turning in our favour.'

Wolsey leaned forward in his chair. 'Conflicting rumours have been circulating since you've returned. I must silence those who would make trouble for the king.' He scowled at the thought. 'In truth, how many men were lost?'

'We saved sixty of the crew of the *Regent*. At least four hundred men went down with her or died from their injuries.'

Wolsey's face looked grim. 'A great loss, may God have mercy on their souls.'

'Although my ship the *Sovereign* was dismasted, our fleet captured thirty-two French warships before we returned.'

Wolsey nodded. 'The king will take some comfort that the French losses were much greater than ours.'

'We pulled twenty French and Breton sailors from the water alive, many with terrible burns. They told me the *Marie la Cordelière* had over a thousand men on board, as well as some three hundred guests, including women.'

'Women?' Wolsey raised an eyebrow.

'They were the wives of guests visiting the *Cordelière* when we encountered the French fleet. I'm afraid none survived – they were kept below decks when the fighting started.'

'I pray their end was swift.' Wolsey stared at the floor for a moment, and then turned to Brandon. 'The king is pleased with you, Master Brandon. I shall recommend you to lead his next expedition to France.'

Henry took aim with his powerful longbow and fired. The arrow thudded into the centre of the distant target and the small group of watching courtiers applauded politely. Henry turned to Brandon and smiled. 'A beard suits you. I knew sending you to sea would make a man of you.'

'I've learned a great deal, Your Grace.' Brandon chose an arrow from his quiver and raised his bow. He pulled back the powerful bowstring and took steady aim before letting it slide through his fingers. The arrow struck the target a little wider than Henry's but was still an excellent shot.

Henry flashed him a curious look. 'Some are saying the explosion on the *Cordelière* was no accident.'

'I doubt we'll ever know what caused the French flagship to catch fire, Your Grace, or how it reached the stores of gunpowder.'

Henry nocked another arrow into his bowstring. 'I miss that rascal Knyvett. He owed me money.' He fired again, another perfect shot.

Brandon guessed the moment was as good as any and decided to ask a question that had been on his mind since his return. 'One consequence of the death of Thomas Knyvett is that you have no Master of the Horse, a position formerly held by my late uncle.'

Henry grinned. 'I've been wondering how I should reward you for your service, Brandon. You will make an excellent Master of the Horse – and I must also grant you a knighthood, now you've won your spurs.'

'Thank you, Your Grace.' Brandon always believed the position of the king's Master of the Horse should have been transferred to him on his uncle's death, but a knighthood was more than he could have hoped for. He suspected Wolsey's hand was behind the offer and decided to risk one more request. 'There is another consequence, Your Grace. I understand Thomas Knyvett's stepdaughter, Elizabeth Grey, is orphaned, without a guardian.'

'You wish me to grant you her wardship?'

'The girl would be good company for my two daughters, Your Grace.' Brandon nocked another arrow, as if the matter was of little concern, although his mind focused on the king's answer.

Henry looked thoughtful. 'Lady Elizabeth is heiress to a great fortune and has the title Viscountess Lisle.' He gave Brandon an appraising look. 'I shall sell you her wardship. I'm sure Knyvett would have approved – and you can pay me in instalments, for I'll wager you don't have any money.'

Brandon wore a white silk doublet and breeches, with shoes of white doeskin and a silver sword-belt with his new sword, a gift from the king. He'd spent the last few days being lectured on the traditions of knighthood. Much to the annoyance of the nobility, he was to be made one of the most important knights in England and invested into the Most Noble Order of the Garter.

A mantle of deep-blue velvet was draped around his shoulders, with the shield of St George's cross, encircled by the garter, on the left breast. A red velvet hood and surcoat was placed on his right shoulder and his cap was black velvet, decorated with the badge of St George and a plume of ostrich and heron feathers.

He followed a procession through Windsor Castle to St George's Chapel in the castle grounds. The knights of the order took their places in the quire stalls and watched as Brandon was presented with a collar of golden knots and Tudor roses, with the pendant of St George slaying a green dragon.

Henry was dressed in his Garter robes, with a cap of crimson velvet in the French fashion, decorated with jewels. His doublet was striped with white and crimson satin and his scarlet hose was fashionably slashed from the knee. His cloak of rich purple velvet reached to the ground, and over it he wore a solid gold collar of the order, glittering with diamonds.

Brandon bent on one knee before King Henry. 'I swear that I shall well and faithfully observe, to the utmost of my power, all the statutes of the great and noble Order of the

Garter.' His voice echoed in the silence of the high-ceilinged chapel.

Henry allowed himself a smile as he knighted Brandon with his sword on both shoulders.

'Arise, Sir Charles Brandon, and take your place with your fellow knights.'

As he listened to the Archbishop's dedication, Brandon marvelled at his change of fortune. In one short year he'd been transformed from a commoner to a holder of the highest order in the land, become the king's Master of the Horse and a commander of his army.

Brandon's ward, Elizabeth Grey, seemed wiser than her eight years. He thought her intelligent enough to understand the significance of their betrothal, although she stiffened for a moment as he took her small hand in his and placed a gold ring on her slender finger.

In truth they were strangers; he'd hardly spent a moment with her or his daughters, due to the demands of court and his new positions. A studious girl, with good French and Latin, Elizabeth had the noble bearing of a lady. She would make a good wife once she reached the age of fourteen.

Brandon's brush with death in the Channel had made him realise it was time to put the memory of Anne behind him and remarry. The six-year wait before he could marry Elizabeth didn't trouble him, as he planned to spend the time building his reputation as a military commander.

Elizabeth had never known her father, John, Viscount Lisle, as he'd died before she was born. Her mother, Muriel, had been the younger sister of Thomas Howard and had also died two years before. Brandon hoped it might be to his future advantage to be related to the Howards through marriage.

In the meantime, Henry consented to Brandon acquiring

the income from Elizabeth's lands, her fortune, and her late father's title of Viscount Lisle through their betrothal. Together with the income from his new positions, he'd become a wealthy man, although he knew the old noble families resented his good fortune.

Brandon placed a soft kiss on Elizabeth's forehead. 'You must learn the ways of court, and trust no one other than me. Do you understand?'

Elizabeth nodded, although she eyed him warily. Brandon suspected her Howard blood had already poisoned her mind against him. He could imagine her uncle, Thomas Howard, would have made sure she knew the Brandons had once been their servants.

Sir Richard Wingfield, Brandon's cousin, recently appointed Lord Deputy of Calais, waited for him as he climbed the stone steps from the harbour. Sir Richard wore a gold chain of office and had the handsome charm and warm smile of an experienced ambassador.

'Welcome to Calais, Charles.' He gestured towards the bustling town. 'I'd like to invite you to stay at my house, if you will.'

'I'd be honoured.' Brandon glanced back at the ship. 'I've had a rough crossing, with the wind against us. It's good to feel the land under my feet again.'

Richard Wingfield led him through narrow, cobbled streets past curious crowds already gathering for a sight of the king. 'My men will bring your baggage.' He turned and looked out to sea. 'The king will be here soon, so let's have something to eat and you can tell me the news from court.' He shook his head. 'It's impossible to distinguish the truth from rumour these days.'

Brandon followed Richard to his house, a fine mansion with views out to sea. A serving girl brought trenchers of bread and a platter of salted beef, filling a large goblet with dark-red wine.

'I don't claim to understand the politics of the king's council.' Brandon tasted the wine and nodded in approval. 'It seems Sir Thomas Howard has the whip hand there.'

Richard nodded. 'I spoke to his brother, Admiral Howard, last week. He was taking on supplies.'

'He's still pursuing the French fleet?'

'The admiral vowed he will not see the king until he's avenged the death of Sir Thomas Knyvett.'

'I served as second in command on the *Sovereign*. It was a sad day for the English – and the French.' Brandon loaded his bread with thick slices of beef. The fresh sea air had given him an appetite.

'Now you are High Marshal of the King's Army.' Richard grinned. 'I must congratulate you, Charles, you've done well.'

Brandon smiled. 'Well, you are Governor of Calais, an appointment I'd like to have one day. I'm honoured to command the king's vanguard, some three thousand men, but our army is ten times that – and we have a further twenty thousand from Emperor Maximilian.'

Richard raised his goblet in a toast. 'To our king – and victory against the French.'

Brandon raised his goblet. 'To King Henry.' As he sipped the sweet wine he said a silent prayer that their victory would not be at too great a cost. Leading the vanguard meant he would be first to confront the enemy. He still didn't know if he would be able to kill a man face-to-face, and hoped he wouldn't hesitate too long.

Brandon peered through the morning mist at the walled town

of Thérouanne in Artois. Thirty miles inland from Calais, it was chosen as an easy target, yet they'd held the town to siege for three days and the men grew restless. One of the older soldiers told him such sieges could go on for months. The summer sunshine made waiting more tolerable but Henry wanted a victory before the autumn. He smiled to himself as he recalled the king's grand arrival at Calais.

Henry rode a white charger in the grand procession through the town. Dressed in gilded armour, he was preceded by heralds and trumpeters, and followed by six hundred archers and yeomen in Tudor green-and-white livery. It had seemed he was already a conquering hero, before the fighting even started.

In the harbour, some three hundred servants had unloaded tents and colourful pavilions, horses and weapons, as well as the king's gilded bed of estate. It was quite an achievement for Thomas Wolsey, who'd had the task of seeing Henry's army was properly equipped and supplied.

Three days of feasting and celebration followed. Only the arrival of Emperor Maximilian's army brought a reminder of their purpose in Calais, and they'd marched into France with over fifty thousand men to lay siege to the closest town, Thérouanne.

The campaign began with a stroke of good luck, as Henry Percy's cavalry routed the French who'd intended to relieve Thérouanne. They captured valuable prisoners, including the Duke of Longueville and the Vice Admiral of France. Henry hadn't been present but was already busy writing letters describing his victory.

Brandon called for Samuel. It was time to test the resolve of the people of Thérouanne. He fastened his black-plumed helmet and stepped from his tent. His retainers waited, tense and grim-faced. They were all mounted and wearing armour, but unarmed, although one carried a trumpet. Samuel helped

Brandon mount his destrier and handed him the hastily made white flag. It hung limply in the still air but would serve his purpose.

'Watch for archers.' Brandon peered towards the town walls. 'We're not the only ones who've learned how to make steel tips which can pierce armour.'

The bright sunshine had lifted the mist and glinted from their armour as they rode the short distance to the town gate. Several heads appeared at the top of the wall and Brandon fought off his nerves as they came within range of the enemy.

He thumped on the iron-studded wooden door with his gloved fist and stood back, holding the flag of truce high. The door creaked open and a deputation of French officials stepped out. They wore dark robes with wide-brimmed black felt caps, and seemed nervous.

Brandon was relieved to see they were unarmed. 'I am Sir Charles Brandon. I have the authority to ask for your surrender to King Henry of England.' He spoke in French. 'If you do not, we will bombard the town with our cannons.'

Their leader, a distinguished-looking man with a well-trimmed beard, studied Brandon and his small band of retainers and replied in French. 'I am Anthoine de Crequy, and agree surrender, in return for your word that our people will not be harmed.'

Brandon realised he'd been holding his breath. 'You have my word. Those who wish to leave may do so, and any who swear loyalty to the King of England will be treated as his subjects.' His trumpeter sounded a single sharp blast – the all-clear for the army. The siege of Thérouanne was over, without a single casualty.

Henry rode at Brandon's side as they entered the city of Lille to visit the court of Duchess Margaret of Savoy, daughter of

Emperor Maximilian and Regent of the Netherlands. They travelled with courtiers and heralds, two hundred men-at-arms, and the king's musicians to entertain the duchess.

Henry turned in his saddle. 'Duchess Margaret would make a fine wife for you, Brandon – but it's said she carries her late husband's heart with her at all times in a velvet purse.' He laughed heartily. 'She has vowed never to remarry!'

Brandon grinned. 'Well, you know how I enjoy a challenge, Your Grace.'

Henry laughed louder. 'Tread carefully. Margaret of Savoy is a most powerful and influential woman.'

Brandon smiled at Henry's meaningful glance when they were introduced to the duchess at the welcoming banquet. He'd expected her to be much older, in widows' mourning dress, but Margaret of Savoy wore a shimmering gown of cloth of gold with a Burgundian hood ringed with pearls. He wouldn't describe her as beautiful, yet she had an aura of nobility that outshone Henry's boisterous arrogance.

'I congratulate you on your victory at Thérouanne, Your Grace.' She spoke in French, her words meant for Henry yet her sharp eyes studied Brandon's as if reading his thoughts.

Henry kissed her outstretched hand, more like an awkward boy than a conquering hero. 'The first of many, duchess. We have God on our side in this holy war.'

Duchess Margaret's eyes focused on the king. 'Pope Leo wishes for a universal peace to the honour and profit of Your Grace, my father the emperor, and the King of Aragon.' She spoke softly, yet somehow managed to offer Henry a mild rebuke.

Henry didn't seem to notice. He could hardly wait to show off his prowess jousting in the temporary tiltyard constructed in the palace grounds. Although he broke many lances, his energy was undiminished. At the evening entertainments he played the lute and harp and sang and danced until dawn with an attractive young maid of honour.

Brandon realised they'd both had too much to drink and decided it was time to somehow persuade Henry to leave. He bowed to Duchess Margaret, intending to explain he had a long journey the following day. Instead, she thought he wished to dance, and took his arm.

The dance required him to take her by the hand and place his arm around her waist. As he did so, he was entranced by her rich perfume. It might have been the effects of too much wine but he found himself drawn to her, like a moth to a flickering candle.

A year ago, he could never have considered marrying a duchess, but now he saw an opportunity. An idea occurred to him, a way to bind them closer, so he would have an excuse to return. 'I have a daughter, Anne, who would greatly benefit from time at your court.'

She smiled at his suggestion. 'Send her to me. I will enjoy completing her education.'

The dance ended and he bent on one knee and took her hand in his. He touched his lips to her hand in a kiss, then removed one of her gold rings and placed it on his little finger. He played the game of courtly love, and she played her part, pretending to be shocked at his boldness.

'Does the King of England keep a thief as a companion?' Margaret teased him and tried to pull it from his finger, but he was too strong for her. 'I must have it back, Sir Charles, it is too well known.'

Brandon saw the look in Margaret's eyes and knew she was enjoying their flirtation. He pretended not to understand her. He liked the idea of wearing the gold ring of the emperor's daughter, a trophy of his conquest. He had no idea this simple act would have such far-reaching consequences.

Henry's victorious army returned to cheering crowds as they paraded through London with a fanfare of trumpets. As well as the capture of Thérouanne, the ancient city of Tournai, a further sixty miles into the heart of France, had surrendered after eight days of siege.

Brandon broke the siege when he seized one of the gate-houses. It was an act of reckless bravado, yet Henry rewarded him by presenting him with the keys to the city. He also made Thomas Wolsey Bishop of Tournai for his service in keeping the army well supplied.

The only real casualty of the war was Admiral Edward Howard, who'd been killed while boarding a French ship, his body thrown into the sea. Henry's army captured some thirty more French nobles, brought to England, like the Duke of Longueville, to be held to ransom.

The bells of every church in London rang in celebration. Musicians played and banners welcomed the returning victors. Throngs of people lined the narrow streets, straining for a view, cheering and calling out, 'God save the king!' and, 'Long live King Henry!'

10

JANUARY 1514

An ominous air of brooding hung over Greenwich Palace, like a black thundercloud. King Henry was ill with a sweating fever and had taken to his bed. Rumours spread through the taverns of London that his physicians suspected smallpox, an often deadly disease with no known cure, and feared for his life.

Brandon was surprised to be summoned to the king's chambers. The terse message from Thomas Wolsey said the matter was urgent and he was to come straight away. Although pleased to be needed, he'd found excuses to avoid Greenwich since Henry developed a temperature after Christmas.

The rambling palace seemed eerily silent and deserted; even the most loyal courtiers stayed away. A servant took Brandon's winter fur coat and led him to Henry's bedchamber. The windows were shuttered and the room felt cold. A grim-faced Wolsey stood as he entered, and Brandon immediately sensed something was wrong.

Wolsey kept his distance from the king, no doubt for fear of infection, and Brandon did the same. With a nod to Wolsey, he then bowed to Henry, who lay propped up in bed on silk cushions, his face red and glistening with sweat. Brandon looked for signs of the pox but there were none, at least not on Henry's face and hands.

'You took your time getting here.' Henry sounded in a sour mood. He gestured to Wolsey who handed Brandon a folded parchment with a large, broken seal.

'From Emperor Maximilian, delivered by the emperor's ambassador.' Wolsey grimaced. 'It seems your escapade has upset our noble ally.'

Brandon struggled to read the elaborate handwriting, which made little sense to him. 'He says Duchess Margaret claims I offended her...'

Henry cursed. 'It's a ploy by her father, to embarrass us – and it seems he is succeeding. I've been informed they are taking bets in London that you will marry her. There are also rumours on the continent that I encouraged you.' He managed to sound incredulous, although he knew it was the truth.

Brandon folded the letter and handed it back to Wolsey. He felt a deep misgiving as he realised Henry would have to distance himself from the incident. He'd also heard rumours about his proposal of marriage to Margaret of Savoy and laughed, thinking them of no consequence.

Pulling the innocent-looking gold ring from his little finger, he held it up for Henry to see. 'I will return this, with my personal apology.' He studied the ring that had caused so much trouble, as if seeing it for the first time. Set with three small rubies, it was distinctive enough to be recognised but of no great value. Henry was right. The whole business was being used by Margaret's father to seek advantage.

Brandon looked across at Henry. 'My daughter Anne is to travel to Margaret's court. With your permission, I will escort her.'

Henry raised a hand. 'I've sent the duchess a fine ring with a large diamond, as a peace offering.' He frowned. 'As for your daughter, I shall provide an escort. You must stay away from the Duchess of Savoy, Brandon – *et ne nos inducas in tentationem.*'

And lead us not into temptation... Brandon agreed with Henry; he should not allow himself to be led a second time. 'I've tried to recall the events of that night.' He bowed his head. 'I was the worse for drink, but I remember Margaret saying the ring was too well known.' He handed the small gold ring to Wolsey. 'It has to be this one.'

Henry scowled and shifted position in his bed, groaning with the effort. 'I've not forgotten how we were tricked by Emperor Maximilian. He made us pay for his army in France – and they did little enough to help us.'

'What are you planning to do?'

Brandon braced himself for bad news. The simplest solution would be for Henry to punish him, in some public way. The old king would have levied a crippling fine, but Henry was more likely to make him marry his ward, Elizabeth. It would help secure her lands, but she was still too young.

Thomas Wolsey looked at Brandon with shrewd eyes. 'Emperor Maximilian's main objection to your courting his noble daughter is your low status.'

Brandon barely controlled his anger. 'I am a viscount—'

Henry interrupted from his sickbed. 'Then I shall make you a duke, Brandon. That should send a clear enough message to the so-called Emperor of Rome.'

After Mass on Candlemas Eve, the great chamber of Archbishop Warham's palace in Lambeth was filled with the nobles of Henry's court. Henry's fever had broken, yet he looked tired and lacked his usual boisterous energy. Brandon guessed the illness had been something of a shock for Henry, particularly as he had yet to produce an heir.

Queen Catherine had lost another stillborn child while

they'd been in France. Her loss was overshadowed by the invasion of the north by King James of Scotland, who thought to take advantage of Henry's absence. Catherine sent an army to defeat him and sent his bloodstained coat to Henry in France as proof of her victory, to be used as a war banner.

She watched with Princess Mary, who caught Brandon's eye and smiled when he entered. He felt a jolt of envy as he recognised the princess's escort as the suave Louis of Orléans, Duke of Longueville. Henry claimed it was his chivalric duty to show the duke favour and enjoyed his risqué stories about the goings on at the French court.

The archbishop gave his blessing and Henry rewarded those who had served him well. Brandon was made Duke of Suffolk and granted the manor and castle of Donnington, in Berkshire. A crimson robe was placed over his black velvet doublet and a golden coronet on his head. He carried a rod of gold, the sign of becoming one of the highest-ranking men in the country.

He watched as Sir Thomas Howard was made Lord High Admiral of the King's Fleet, in his late brother's place, Earl Marshal of the King's Army, and restored to the wealthy dukedom of Norfolk. Brandon took the trouble to congratulate him but noted he didn't reciprocate.

He wondered what he would have to do to prove himself worthy to the old noble families. Behind his back they called him an upstart, and worse. He needed to be on his guard. Men like Thomas Howard were waiting for their chance to bring him down.

~

The magnificent new flagship *Henry Grace à Dieu*, already nicknamed the *Great Harry*, was to be launched by the king at the royal dockyard, ten miles downriver from Greenwich Palace.

The royal standard flew proudly from the topmast, along with smaller pennants of countries represented by visiting ambassadors. Henry intended to send a clear message with his costly investment.

Two years in the making, the *Great Harry* even dwarfed the *Mary Rose*. Her captain, the grey-bearded Vice Admiral Thomas Wyndham, served with Brandon on the *Sovereign* and greeted him warmly as he joined the guests on board.

'Welcome, my lord.' He bowed in deference to Brandon's new status as a premier noble.

Brandon shook his hand. He wasn't used to such formality from old friends. 'A fine flagship, admiral.'

'She's the largest and most powerful in Europe, my lord, and weighs in at fifteen thousand tons.'

Brandon peered up at the forecastle, towering over their heads, four decks high. 'I hope that doesn't make her unstable?'

Admiral Wyndham lowered his voice so only Brandon could hear. 'I suspect she'll roll like a whale in rough seas, but it means she can accommodate nine hundred men – a thousand if we have to.'

Brandon smiled. 'A floating army … and you have the new bronze cannons.'

'Twenty of them, in proper gun ports.' He frowned. 'Too many ships have guns added at refits. It's asking for trouble.'

The dour Archbishop of Canterbury, William Warham, conducted a long-winded blessing of the ship. Brandon grew bored and spotted Princess Mary looking in his direction. He gave her a brief nod and Mary raised a white-gloved hand and smiled. Now she'd turned eighteen the princess was truly beautiful. Brandon had heard stories about how Mary's mother, the late Queen Elizabeth, turned heads wherever she went. Now he saw the princess was doing the same.

It frustrated him that she was tantalisingly out of his reach, betrothed to the hapless Prince of Castile. Brandon had met the prince briefly during the fateful stay in Lisle with Margaret of Savoy. He'd thought him cold and underserving of such a prize as Princess Mary, even if he was heir to an empire.

Henry's hand formed a fist as he spoke. 'King Ferdinand of Aragon has betrayed us again. He and Maximilian have gone behind my back and agreed a truce with the French.' He spat out the words and his eyes burned with anger.

Brandon cursed, but it was not unexpected. The compromise negotiated with Margaret of Savoy was to cancel their plans for a second invasion of France.

'This news changes everything.'

'There will be consequences, mark my words. We shall *not* allow my sister's marriage to their grandson.' Henry banged his fist on the table, causing an empty silver goblet to topple and fall to the floor with a hollow clang.

Brandon retrieved the goblet and placed it back on the table. 'The preparations for Princess Mary's wedding are well advanced. All her new household in place...'

Henry glowered. 'A reversal at this late stage will suitably insult both Ferdinand and Maximilian.'

There was an edge to his voice and Brandon knew better than to argue.

Thomas Wolsey, now Bishop of Lincoln, tried to calm him. 'We must renounce her engagement, Your Grace. Shall I make the arrangements?'

Henry nodded. 'They will regret their treachery.'

Wolsey bowed and left Henry alone with Brandon.

'Do you have another suitor planned for her, Your Grace?' Brandon held his breath as he waited for the answer.

'I do.' Henry's chair scraped on the tiled floor as he prepared to leave. 'My youngest sister is the ace up my sleeve in forming a new alliance with the French. How can King Louis resist such an offer?'

Brandon's spirits sank. The Duke of Longueville told them the King of France was ravaged by disease and treated his mistresses with cruel disdain. Henry was unconcerned that Louis was old enough to be Princess Mary's grandfather. It seemed a harsh use of his favourite sister.

The thought troubled him as he rode back to his house. He lay awake for some time, running over his conversation with Henry, before he realised this could be the opportunity he'd hardly dared wish for. Brandon sat up in the darkness, his pulse racing at his audacious idea.

Archbishop Warham read the Latin address at Princess Mary's wedding ceremony in the great banqueting hall of Greenwich Palace. The princess officially obtained Henry's permission to renounce her engagement with Charles, although the truth of the matter was a little different.

Brandon was surprised when Wolsey told him she'd agreed to Henry's plan without complaint. He guessed Wolsey gave her no choice – or she saw it as her duty to continue her father's ambition to ensure peace with France. Either way, King Louis could hardly believe his luck and sent Mary a valuable diamond as a token of his love.

The Duke of Longueville, standing in for King Louis, wore a glittering suit of cloth of gold and purple satin. He'd been recognised as the official ambassador of France, and was now a member of Henry's privileged inner circle.

Mary said her vows in perfect French. Then the duke took her right hand and placed a gold ring on her finger before kissing her. Queen Catherine stepped forward to congratulate Princess Mary. To Henry's delight she'd survived her father's disloyalty by becoming pregnant for the fourth time. He was, it seemed, prepared to overlook anything if it meant he might yet have a healthy son and heir.

Brandon glanced at the watching crowd of guests and caught the eye of Thomas Wolsey. He doubted many knew that Wolsey was the man behind this scheme, not through any love of France but hatred of Ferdinand and Maximilian. The new treaty with France included reparation of a million gold crowns, more than compensating for Princess Mary's dowry.

Wolsey's reward was to be made Archbishop of York, as well as Bishop of Tournai. He'd already taken ownership of York Place as his London residence and begun improvements. Brandon was tempted to ask where the money had come from but thought better of it. Wolsey also confided that Henry had written to the pope, asking for him to be made a cardinal.

A herald called for the guests who were to act as witnesses as the princess was led to the richly decorated bedchamber. Brandon followed several bishops and ambassadors, knights and nobles, and even a papal envoy to watch the strange ritual.

Mary's ladies unlaced the kirtle of her cloth-of-gold wedding gown and dressed her in a nightdress of shimmering white satin. They unpinned her French headdress, combing her long red-gold hair so it flowed over her shoulders, a sign of purity.

Brandon felt a strange mixture of arousal and concern as Mary crossed her hands protectively over her breasts. He'd never seen her with her hair down and was transfixed by her beauty. She avoided looking at anyone, keeping her eyes to the floor as her handmaidens led her to the richly carved bed.

She lay back and stared up the ornate ceiling as the Duke of Longueville removed his scarlet hose, lifted the hem of her nightdress and then placed his bared leg against hers. The symbolic act of intimacy drew a cheer from some of the witnesses, and a blush to Mary's face.

Brandon turned away and left, glad to have some fresh air yet feeling a bleak emptiness. He couldn't bear to watch the celebration and stayed away from the Mass in the palace chapel, the lavish banquet, and the dancing which followed.

As he rode home he recalled the look he'd often seen in her eyes. There was a special bond, a mutual attraction between them, and he found himself dreaming of life with Princess Mary. If what the Duke of Longueville said was true, King Louis of France would not live for long, and Mary would be left a wealthy, widowed dowager queen.

He'd heard tales of how Mary's great-grandfather, Owen Tudor, was a servant who'd secretly married the young widowed queen of King Henry V. Brandon smiled as he remembered what Knyvett once said when he'd accused him of being lucky. He'd raised a goblet of wine and quoted Seneca: luck doesn't exist; there is only the moment when talent meets opportunity. He missed Thomas Knyvett.

A stiff October breeze carried Brandon and his cohort of jousters to Calais. Chosen to lead the celebrations for Mary's coronation as Queen of France, he also had a secret mission. Henry wished him to ensure the heir to the French throne, Duke Francis, son-in-law of the king, would agree a peace treaty with England if anything happened to King Louis.

Brandon stayed with his cousin, Sir Richard Wingfield, in Calais before riding to Paris. Dressed like an ambassador, in rich furs with a gold chain, he'd arranged to meet Wolsey's man, John Palsgrave, an ordained Cambridge scholar who'd been appointed as Mary's secretary.

Palsgrave had been chosen well. Engaging and efficient, he persuaded Mary to take an early morning walk in the palace gardens. Although her ladies were in attendance, Mary ensured they kept their distance when Brandon contrived his chance meeting.

He smiled as he approached her. 'You look well, my lady. This new life in France must suit you.'

'It's good to see a friend from England.' She returned his smile. 'I've missed you.' She moved closer and her white-gloved hand touched his arm.

The subtle sign was all he needed. 'You've been always in my thoughts.' He kept his voice low. He had to ask the question that had been in his mind since she'd sailed from Dover. 'Did Henry agree?'

'He did. He promised.' Mary studied his face. 'You were right. I chose my moment well. But let us not discuss this again while Louis lives.' She glanced back at her ladies. 'He sent away my household. I only have my secretary, Palsgrave, and my physician, with these few ladies.'

'I heard. Henry is not pleased and told me to ensure you are being well treated.'

'I was saddened when my household left, but Louis shows me great kindness.' She seemed to struggle to compose herself for a moment, but then brightened. 'Are you taking part in my coronation joust?'

'Someone has to represent England.' He looked back at her ladies, to make sure they weren't listening. 'Henry is concerned about what will happen to you if King Louis dies.' His voice became serious. 'I haven't come here alone. We stand ready to return you to England – if the worst happens.'

Duke Francis made no secret of the fact he saw the celebratory joust as an opportunity to make his name. Handsome and athletic, the king's cousin was everything the frail King Louis was not. A Valois noble, he was the son of Duchess Louise of Savoy.

The spectacle of the tournament seemed to have attracted most of the population of Paris, as well as many of the outlying districts. Brandon had never seen so many people and realised the city must be many times the size of London.

Duke Francis wore gleaming silver armour with a gold fleur-de-lis on the breastplate, a helmet plumed with red feathers, and a flowing blue cape. He raised a gauntleted hand in the air as he drew level with the royal podium where King Louis sat with Mary.

Next came the English knights, led by Brandon in gilded armour, carrying Henry's royal standard. Mary gave a nod of acknowledgement to Brandon, and then frowned as someone in the crowd called out something about the English, to laughter and cheering from the French, who had been mortal enemies only six months before.

A fanfare of trumpets announced the start of the contest, with a flamboyant French knight promptly being unhorsed and crashing to the ground. Time and again the English proved to be superior, much to the increasing disappointment of the crowd.

Brandon unseated several French knights, scoring the highest number of points. Then the brother-in-law of Duke Francis, the Duke of Alençon, struck him a sharp blow on the helmet, winning a roar of approval from the nobles. Brandon felt his ears ring and struggled to recover before raising a hand to show he could continue.

After many clashes between French and English, the time came for the ultimate confrontation: Brandon and Duke Francis. Their armour glinted as they charged, both shattering their lances with great force. On the second pass Duke Francis sprained his hand and the Master of the Joust declared the contest a draw.

The jousting continued for the rest of the afternoon, with Brandon emerging as equal champion with his sparring partner, Sir Thomas Grey. A heavy shower of rain turned the tournament arena to mud, yet Brandon managed a grin as he rode to salute the king. Louis called out his congratulations in French, loud enough for everyone within earshot to hear.

On the second day of the tournament the Master of the Joust announced that Brandon and Thomas Grey, as joint champions, would take on all comers on foot. A Frenchman had died fighting on foot the previous day and many more had been injured, including Duke Francis, who decided to withdraw – but not before taking his revenge on Brandon.

Brandon and Thomas drew their heavy swords and stood back to back, like gladiators of Rome. There was a cheer as a dozen Frenchmen marched into the arena and surrounded the two English knights. With surprising swiftness, Brandon swung his sword in a vicious arc, causing the nearest Frenchmen to spring back in alarm.

Reversing the weapon in a fluid motion, he used the heavy pommel as a club to fell one of the men with a crushing blow to the helmet. Another took the opportunity to try to push him off balance. Brandon seized his arm and twisted it so hard the man fell into the slippery mud.

Another of the Frenchmen aimed a savage two-handed swing at Brandon's helmet. Thomas Grey sprang forward and parried the blow, forcing the man back with the blunted tip of his sword. They stood their ground, defending each other and defeating their attackers one by one.

The French nobles called out to rally their countrymen and cheered and shouted '*Géant Allemande!*' as a thickset brute of a man, even taller than Brandon, entered the arena. He wore a suit of heavy chain mail, with an old-fashioned open helmet. Duke Francis had been keeping the huge German mercenary back for his grand finale.

Brandon didn't hesitate. Sidestepping the German's swinging blade, he smashed his gauntleted fist into the man's face, breaking his nose. With a groan, the large man dropped his sword and collapsed to his knees. The French court rose as one and applauded as Brandon raised his sword high in victory.

11

JANUARY 1515

Brandon lit a new tallow candle from the flickering stub of the old one as he worked in his study. Since he'd become Duke of Suffolk the pile of letters to read and papers to sign grew daily. His lawyer, Master Gregory, had taken on an assistant to help him deal with all the land transfers and tenant disputes.

He lay down his quill and rubbed his eyes, about to retire for the night when his servant tapped on the door. He had a visitor from France, who asked to see him urgently and in private. Intrigued, Brandon asked for him to be shown in.

John Palsgrave looked tired and unshaven. His dark cloak was spattered with mud and he carried the distinctive musky odour of horse sweat. He clutched a leather saddlebag and held it tightly, as if it contained something of importance.

'Thank you for seeing me at such a late hour, my lord. I regret it is my duty to tell you the King of France passed away on the first day of this year. I came as soon as I could.'

Brandon gestured for him to take a seat. 'We expected this day would come, but not so soon.'

Palsgrave nodded. 'King Louis had suffered with poor

health for the past ten years, and took to his bed a week before Christmas.'

'How is Princess Mary?'

'The Queen Dowager of France, as we should call her now, is in mourning. Her Grace wishes you to return to Paris, to escort her back to England.' He patted the saddlebag. 'I must deliver her letter to the king, but first… She asked me to give you this.' He unfastened the buckle on his saddlebag and produced a silk purse. He took out a gold ring and handed it to Brandon.

Holding the ring in the candlelight, Brandon turned it in his hand and read Mary's motto engraved around the inside: *La volenté de Dieu me suffit.* The will of God is sufficient for me. Brandon looked up at Palsgrave. 'I shall ride with you to the king in the morning.' He called for his servant. 'You are welcome to stay at my house tonight – and thank you, John, for coming here first.'

Henry and Wolsey listened to Palsgrave's report and studied Mary's letter, firing questions at him. Brandon watched, noting how Henry now relied on Wolsey in such matters and had not sent for his other counsellors.

'Has Duke Francis taken over?' Henry looked up from the letter.

'His mother, Duchess Louise, acts as Regent of France, Your Grace.' Palsgrave looked more his old self now he'd had a good night's sleep. 'When I left, they were already making plans for the duke's coronation.'

Wolsey leaned forward. 'When is that to be, Master Palsgrave?'

'One month, or perhaps two. As soon as it is known there is no child…'

'A child?' Henry sounded surprised. 'Are you saying my sister could be pregnant?'

'If I may speak frankly about the Dowager Queen Mary, Your Grace … she has assured me she is not, although Duchess Louise keeps her at Cluny Palace, until it can be proven.'

Wolsey held up a hand before Henry could reply. 'It is their custom, Your Grace, and suits our purposes.'

Henry frowned. 'How do you mean?'

Wolsey gave Brandon a knowing look. 'Once he has the Crown, I predict Francis will marry your sister to one of his relatives – or even marry her himself. We must return her to England before he can do so.'

Henry turned to Brandon. 'You will lead the mission. You are to go to Paris and see if you can do a better job of winning over Duke Francis than you did last time. Bring my sister back – with as much of her jewellery and plate as you can. I didn't go to such great expense to see her married off to some French squire.'

Brandon rode with Richard Wingfield through the snow-dusted streets of Paris to the coronation banquet. With them rode Dean Nicholas West. He wore a cleric's robes, yet their poor quality suggested his legal expertise did not pay well. Like John Palsgrave, West was another of Wolsey's men, and travelled with them in repayment of his debt to Brandon.

Their journey from Calais took a week in the icy conditions, so Brandon had time to reflect on Henry's words. Before he left for Dover, Henry asked to see him in private. He'd made it sound like a joke, but his eyes were serious as he spoke.

'I know you care for Mary, Brandon, but don't think about using your roguish charm on her.'

Taken off guard by Henry's frankness, he'd given his word. Too late, Brandon realised he might have thrown away the greatest opportunity of his life. Henry was no doubt already planning a profitable new marriage for Mary. To go back on his word and risk the king's anger would be too great a test of their friendship.

Duke Francis sat proudly in the late king's golden throne with his mother, Duchess Louise of Savoy, on one side and his sister on the other, a sign of what was to come. Although she was now Queen Consort of France, his long-suffering wife, Claude, Duchess of Brittany, sat some distance away with Mary and her ladies.

Brandon arrived late and took his seat with the other ambassadors on the opposite side of the banqueting hall to Mary. She was deep in conversation with Queen Claude, yet seemed to sense his eyes on her. She looked across at him and raised her silver goblet in welcome.

He raised his own in reply. No one, even his cousin sitting at his side, would have thought anything of the gesture, yet Brandon felt his heart race. Mary looked even more beautiful than in the dreams he'd had so often since she left for France.

The banquet seemed to take an eternity, with long speeches in French. He'd been hungry after the long journey, yet he wished the platters of glazed suckling pig, exotic fishes, and spiced birds would come to an end. He also took care not to drink too much wine; he needed a clear head.

At last, the time came for the ambassadors to line up and congratulate the new King of France. When it came to Brandon's turn he was pleased to see Francis grin in recognition.

'Duke Charles, we have some unfinished business.'

Brandon bowed his head and looked up at King Francis. 'Indeed, Your Grace, and I bring congratulations from King Henry of England.' He wondered if Francis referred to the need to renew the peace treaty or a wish to ride against him in a joust. It would be good if he could accomplish both before he returned to England.

As soon as he could he made his way through the throng of guests and bowed to Mary. 'How are you, Your Grace?'

'My time to mourn is over.' She glanced towards the top table, where Francis played a noisy drinking game with his young courtiers. 'I confess I'm ready to leave France – and pray to see England and my brother again soon.'

Her face looked pale and she had dark shadows under her eyes. Brandon gestured to the men at each side of him. 'Your Grace will remember Sir Richard Wingfield, Lord Deputy of Calais and our ambassador to France, and Dean Nicholas West.'

Mary gave Sir Richard a wistful look, as if an old memory had returned. 'You arranged my betrothal to Prince Charles of Castile.' She shook her head. 'How different my life might have been if I had married him.'

Sir Richard bowed. 'At your service, Your Grace. Please accept our condolences on the loss of your husband. King Louis was a good friend to our country.'

'Thank you, Sir Richard.' Mary turned to Nicholas West. 'Dean West, you've drawn up the papers for my betrothal twice now.'

Dean West bowed his head. 'Indeed, Your Grace.'

Mary smiled. 'It's a comfort to me to see such loyal friends come to speak on my behalf.'

Richard Wingfield glanced towards the new king, who laughed at some joke made by his fawning courtiers. 'We also have to broker a new peace with your ... stepson.' He smiled at the thought; Francis was two years older than Mary.

'King Francis will continue the alliance, Sir Richard. My late father spent his life working for peace with France, so while I still have some influence, I regard it as my duty to see it preserved.'

She turned to Brandon. 'You must visit me in the morning and tell me the news from England.'

'Of course, Your Grace.' He felt a frisson of anticipation as he bowed one last time and turned to leave.

Brandon was led to Mary's chambers by a servant in the livery of the late king. Mary signalled to her ladies to withdraw and showed him into the next room, where he warmed his hands at the fire which blazed in the ornate marble hearth.

He removed his heavy winter coat and sat in the chair she offered, close to hers. 'At last, we can speak freely.' He smiled at Mary, who looked beautiful in an azure-blue gown and seemed more at ease than she'd been at the coronation banquet. 'I must tell you we suspect the French plan to keep you here, to strengthen their hand in peace negotiations.'

'I'm not their prisoner. Can you not take me with you when you leave?'

Brandon's pulse raced at the suggestion in her voice. 'Dean West cautions against it, at least until we've secured a new treaty with King Francis.'

Mary leaned closer. 'Francis plans to arrange another marriage for me. He warned me not to tell anyone, or there would be consequences.'

'Wolsey predicted as much. King Francis thinks he can play us for fools and delay agreement while he arranges a match for you.' Brandon scowled. 'Did he say who he intends as your suitor?'

'He mentioned his uncle, the Duke of Savoy.'

'How did you reply?'

'I told him I would take myself to a convent.'

He remained silent as he saw her studying him. For a

moment he wondered if she was playing a game of courtly love, then realised she spoke the truth.

She placed her hand on his arm. 'There is one way to prevent Francis. He could do nothing if I were already remarried.' Her suggestion was almost a whisper, but he heard the tenderness and longing in her voice.

Brandon stared at her without answering for a moment. 'Henry knows I have feelings for you. He made me promise not to try to charm you, and his meaning was clear.'

'And your intention, Charles? Is it your intention to obey your king or the Queen Dowager of France?'

'Henry will never agree. He will wish another marriage for you – but one which brings him wealth and political advantage. I don't think you have any idea—'

'I do, which is why I extracted that promise from my brother before I left for France. He gave me his word he will allow me to choose my next husband.' She smiled. 'I choose you, Charles Brandon, if you will have me.'

Brandon stared into her eyes. She offered him the greatest prize of his life, yet the stakes were so high even Thomas Knyvett might have hesitated. He took a deep breath. 'I must be mad.' He placed his free hand over hers. 'I am risking everything – my reputation, my liberty, and possibly my life – but I *will* marry you, Mary Tudor.'

He took her hand in his, her fingers as small and pale as a child's, then leaned across and gave her a slow, lingering, lover's kiss. He felt a long-forgotten excitement and arousal, yet the risk they were taking put him on his guard.

'We should be mindful of your servants, Mary. This must be kept secret until we are ready. Any one of the servants could start rumours that would spread through this place like a lit taper on dry kindling.'

She looked at him for a moment then nodded. 'You are

right. The French courtiers love to gossip even more than the English.'

Brandon stroked his dark beard as he considered what they should do. 'We must take Dean West into our confidence, Mary. We need his help.'

'Can we trust him, Charles?'

'Nicholas West is Wolsey's man, and Henry listens to Thomas Wolsey's counsel more than any other.' Brandon leaned forward for one last kiss before he left.

He returned the next day with Dean West. More snow had turned Paris white, and frozen overnight. The roads looked unsafe for horses, so they had to walk to the palace on foot. They waited for Mary's servant to take their coats and watched her leave, closing the door behind her.

Brandon was pleased to see a fire in the hearth, and placed three chairs closer to the warmth, gesturing for them to be seated. 'Nicholas has devised a plan.'

Dean West nodded. 'We have a number of difficulties to remedy.' He ticked off the points on his fingers. 'We must secure a new peace treaty, which means we have to win over King Francis. We will have to somehow placate King Henry and,' he looked across at Brandon, 'not compromise the promise you made before you left England.'

Brandon leaned forward in his chair and looked into Mary's eyes. 'Is it true your mourning has left you in a state of some distress?'

'I felt I was being punished. They banished me to that dreadful Cluny Palace, although I'd done nothing wrong.'

'Then it will not be too difficult to convince Henry of your vulnerable state, and appeal to his sense of brotherly duty.'

Mary nodded. 'I will write again to my brother.'

Dean West turned to her. 'It is fortunate the king agreed to permit your choice of husband. You could beseech him to honour his word – but you must convince him this is your own initiative.'

'Yes.' Mary brightened. 'I'll also write to Thomas Wolsey. Henry listens to him.'

Brandon's face became serious. 'There is another problem. We understand that Queen Catherine has been delivered of another stillborn son.'

Mary raised her hand to her mouth. 'No...'

Brandon shook his head. 'Queen Catherine was out of favour because of her troublesome father, so the loss of this son is a bitter blow.'

Mary frowned in concern. 'We must pray for her, and for my brother ... but we cannot afford to wait until they've finished grieving.'

Dean West agreed. 'Which is why you must ask King Francis to assist you.'

'He's the last person I would confide in.' Mary's voice sounded doubtful.

Brandon leaned forward in his chair. 'King Francis likes to think he has a sense of chivalry. Ask for his help. He might surprise you.'

Mary looked doubtful. 'What about your oath to Henry?'

'I will also write to him, after you have made it clear this was your own doing.' He grinned. 'How could any man refuse you?'

Brandon received a summons from Mary as soon as she returned from her meeting with King Francis. He arrived with Dean West and listened intently as she recounted what happened.

'He said it amuses him to rob Henry of the opportunity to choose my husband.'

'We have his support?' Brandon was surprised it could be so easy.

She frowned at Brandon. 'He told me you were planning to marry Margaret of Savoy. Is that true?'

'The idea of my marrying Margaret of Savoy was a joke, started by your brother, and one which I have had much cause to regret.'

'Then will you marry me now, here in France?'

'Of course,' he smiled at her, a twinkle in his eye, 'if that is your wish.'

Dean West had watched them in silence. 'You must be aware you both risk King Henry's displeasure—'

Brandon stroked his beard as he thought for a moment. 'We can win his favour with a token of our goodwill.'

'What do you have in mind, my lord?'

'You shall deliver my letter of explanation in person, together with Mary's magnificent jewel, the Mirror of Naples – a wedding gift from King Louis – which the king knows is valued at more than sixty thousand crowns.'

Dean West turned to Mary. 'Do you have the jewel, my lady?'

'I do – and will gladly surrender it as the price of my brother's favour.' Mary turned to Brandon. 'We must marry before Henry receives your letter, or he will forbid you to do so. It must be done in secret but with witnesses.'

Dean West looked doubtful. 'King Henry can still order such a marriage annulled.'

Brandon gave him a wry smile. 'He can – but I doubt he will if the marriage is consummated.'

Mary blushed at his suggestion, yet Brandon knew it was the truth. It would be even better if she was with child before Henry could prevent them.

. . .

Their wedding required little arrangement. Brandon escorted Mary and her ladies, who were dressed as if for any other Paris day in winter, with riding capes and furs over thick gowns instead of fine silk wedding dresses. They rode through snowy backstreets and aroused no interest from passers-by.

He saw Mary shiver in the chill air as the priest began the service, uninterrupted by any music or singing for fear of drawing attention. Her voice echoed in the emptiness of the old chapel when she said her vows, and Brandon smiled at her as he placed the gold ring on Mary's finger. It was the one inscribed with her motto: *La volenté de Dieu me suffit.*

Brandon stared into her adoring eyes and struggled to remain composed as he swore to love and honour her, then kissed her. He bent close to her ear and whispered, so only she could hear.

'I love you, Mary, with all my heart.'

A light flickered briefly in the high window, the signal it was safe for Brandon to enter Mary's apartments by the servants' stairs. He enjoyed the subterfuge, and entered like a silent thief, dressed in black to conceal himself in the shadows.

Mary wore a nightgown of shimmering lilac silk, her unplaited red-gold hair combed loose over her shoulders. She beckoned him into her room. 'I've dismissed my servants for the night. We are alone.'

Brandon stared at her. 'You look beautiful, Mary.' He glanced back at the entrance to the servants' passageway. 'We shall have to declare our marriage soon. There are too many eyes on us to keep our secret for long.'

'Only until our letters arrive in England.'

Brandon gave her a look of concern. 'That might be longer than we would wish. I'm struggling to find the right words. It's no easy thing to tell the King of England I have disobeyed his wishes.'

'My secretary, John Palsgrave, will help you – but we needn't talk of such things now.'

She took his hand and led him to the sanctuary of her bedchamber. The tall windows were shuttered and draped with thick curtains against the cold. Beeswax candles and a log fire gave the room a warm glow. Mary closed the door behind them and slid across the bolt.

Brandon embraced her, feeling her respond to his passionate kiss. When he spoke, it was in a whisper, as if they might be overheard. 'We are alone together at last.'

'As husband and wife.' She smiled, her eyes reflecting the candlelight.

'Yes.' He kissed her again. 'As husband and wife.'

Mary pulled the end of the thin ribbon securing her silk gown and it fell to her feet. Brandon's pulse raced as she stood naked before him. This time she made no effort to cover her bare breasts with her hands.

He lifted her in his arms and lay her down on the canopied bed, then began pulling off his clothes. Tearing a button off in his haste, he smiled as she giggled. He lay naked at her side and felt her soft hands caress his body, exploring hidden scars.

Brandon stroked a strand of her long hair from her face with his hand and looked into her eyes. 'I dreamed of this day, although I never believed that dream would come true so soon.'

'You dreamed of me?' There was a note of pretended surprise in her voice.

'You were always close, yet so far from my reach.'

'I believe it's our destiny to be together, Charles. Nothing can stand in our way.'

'Not even his royal majesty, the King of England?'

'Or the King of France.' Her eyes shone in the firelight.

'What will you do, now you have me in your spell, my lord of Suffolk?'

His answer left him breathless. Of all the women he'd known, none seemed so perfectly aware of his desires. She could read his mind, taking him to the edge again and again before finally surrendering to him in a shuddering wave of ecstasy. Afterwards, he lay on his back, his chest glistening with sweat and his pulse racing. He finally understood why people were prepared to risk everything for love.

12

MARCH 1515

Brandon pulled off his cap, ran his fingers through his unruly hair, and frowned at the folded parchment he held in his hand. He regretted reading the letter he'd been waiting for from Wolsey. The last thing he needed was more bad news.

Mary crossed the room, her emerald-green gown swishing on the marble floor tiles. She leaned down and kissed him. 'What's happened?'

'King Francis demands the return of your jewel.'

'It's not unexpected. He told me many of the jewels Louis gave me are the Crown jewels of France, so they now belong to Queen Claude.'

'He insists we return the Mirror of Naples.' Brandon scowled. 'It was a mistake to send it to England.'

'I have other jewels. You can give them all back to Francis, if it means we can return home.'

Brandon shook his head. 'Henry told me to return with as many of your jewels as I can. I've told Francis I'll do my best to retrieve the jewel but he knows Henry will never send it back.' His hand formed a fist in frustration. 'He plays games with us and, to make matters worse, my enemies accuse me of being lenient in my negotiations with the French.'

'Your enemies?'

'The old families of England resent my title and look for any chance to ruin my reputation. There have always been whispers behind my back at council. Now they could turn the king's mind against me.' He frowned. 'Against *us*, Mary.'

'I've made it worse for you.' Mary placed her hand on his arm. 'I will meet again with Francis, tell him about our secret marriage, and that it was me who sent the jewel back to Henry.'

'You should read this letter.' Brandon handed her the folded parchment. 'Thomas Wolsey says I must discontinue my ambassadorial duties, and there seems no prospect of the king's forgiveness.'

Mary unfolded the letter and began to read. She stared at Brandon. 'Even if you restore the agreement of King Francis, others will take credit for any peace treaty.'

'Wolsey's tone has changed. If he sets himself against us we are ruined.'

'Then we shall have to make sure he does not.' Her eyes narrowed. 'Whatever it takes.'

'He hints at a remedy, although there is no promise of success and it will cost us dearly.'

'The price of my brother's forgiveness is that we must return my dowry in full?'

'Two hundred thousand crowns, as well as all your gold and silver plate and every one of your jewels. It's impossible, Mary. Everything we have will not be enough to satisfy him. Could you live without all this?' He gestured at the grand furnishings that graced the luxurious royal apartments.

Brandon watched Mary refold the parchment and guessed her answer, although he doubted she would admit it. All her life as a princess of royal blood, surrounded by servants, would have shielded her.

'When my father was my age he had nothing, yet he confessed to me once that his years in exile were some of the happiest of his life.' She smiled at him. 'You've risked everything for me – and I will happily sacrifice everything for you, Charles Brandon.'

Another letter finally arrived from Thomas Wolsey setting out in detail the cost of their return. He proposed payment of the money by instalments of two thousand pounds a year, and for Mary to sign everything she owned over to Henry.

Brandon cursed. 'He knows that's beyond our means. The de la Pole estates Henry gifted with my title are worthless until they transfer – and your French incomes are at the whim of King Francis.'

Mary looked unsurprised. 'Thomas Wolsey needs to silence our critics with a substantial sum. We must play his games. We'll agree in good faith, then negotiate a smaller annual charge when we can't afford the payments.'

'I could sell my wardship of Lady Elizabeth Lisle. She's ten now, and her wardship must be worth a good sum.'

Mary glowered at him. 'I trust you're not still betrothed to the girl?'

He grinned at her jealousy, his mood already improving. 'I never was. I began to use the title in presumption of marriage and no one challenged it.' He kissed her to hide his lie, as Mary's servant entered to tell them their escort was ready to take them to Calais.

King Francis surprised them by escorting them the seven miles to Saint Denis, on the outskirts of Paris, with fifty mounted knights. He embraced Brandon, wishing him luck, and then kissed Mary's hand and promised to ensure she would receive the income from her dower lands.

After he'd gone Brandon looked across at Mary, riding at his side. 'Do you think he'll keep his word after we're in England?'

'We must make certain of it. The income is worth several thousand marks, so I shall write to Queen Claude as often as I can. We can never be free of the French court, so it will be useful to have at least one friend there we can rely on.'

Brandon agreed. 'Once we've been accepted back at court I'll arrange a joust to honour King Francis and will persuade Henry to meet him in France – without an invading army. If Francis sees we support his interests he'll be less likely to withhold your income.'

It took five days of riding on rutted and muddy French roads, stopping overnight in modest inns, before the welcome sight of Calais appeared on the horizon. Brandon was pleased to see Richard Wingfield, who raised a gloved hand in greeting.

'Welcome to Calais, my lord,' he bowed his head to Mary, 'my lady.'

Brandon slid from his saddle and embraced his cousin. 'Good to see you again, Richard. Is there news of our passage to England?'

'I sent Sir William Sidney with your message to the king. We should have his reply any day now.'

As they followed him through the busy, cobbled streets of Calais, Richard announced he'd arranged a private supper as he had important news to share with them. He waited until they were alone then turned to Brandon.

'I must ask you to keep to my apartments while we wait for your passage to be approved.'

'Why is that?' Brandon gave him a puzzled look.

'I postponed a delegation to England, which has caused a bad feeling among the merchants of the Staple.' He frowned. 'I wished a good welcome for you but instead it seems I've stirred up resentment.'

Brandon was dismissive. 'I'll take care of myself, although I'll keep my head down, if that's what you wish.'

Sir Richard looked relieved. 'You must wonder how the treaty discussions progressed in your absence.' He tore a chunk from his bread and used it to mop the sauce from his plate.

'I trust you found it easier once the king wasn't distracted by my haggling over my wife's jewellery?' Brandon glanced at Mary and grinned as he refilled his goblet from the jug of red wine, his mood improving.

Sir Richard smiled. 'The treaty is agreed in principle, which is not unexpected,' he looked from Brandon to Mary, 'and I have good news, my lady. King Francis has agreed to repay your dowry.'

'The full two hundred thousand?' Brandon was surprised.

'It took some persuasion, but King Henry might feel better disposed towards you.'

Mary raised her goblet of wine. 'We are truly grateful to you, Sir Richard.'

'I had a modest part in the negotiations, my lady. It seems Dean West spoke frankly to King Francis and persuaded him to understand your circumstances.'

'He rode with us all the way from Paris and didn't mention it.' Brandon gave Richard a questioning look.

'We received confirmation after you left Paris. All the same, Dean West is the one who deserves your thanks.'

After they retired to bed Mary shared her concern with Brandon. 'Sir Richard's messenger has had time to bring news from England, yet Henry has still not consented to our return.'

He put his arm around her. 'Let us look on the bright side, Mary. He hasn't refused us.' He kissed her.

'Do you think our punishment is to languish here in Calais forever?'

'I can think of worse things. I could be banished from court, lose all my titles, be locked up in a dungeon at the Tower of London, executed at Tower Hill—'

'Don't jest about such things.' She gave him a stern look. 'We will both write to Henry in the morning, advising him of the dowry settlement and signing over my jewels and gold plate. You should take some credit for the peace treaty. You won over Francis before they even started the negotiations.'

He pulled her close. 'Sir Richard told me they are saying I conceded Tournai in return for Francis supporting our marriage.'

'You must tell Henry the truth.'

'In good time.'

Mary frowned. 'If he believes these stories it will count against us.'

He used a kiss to silence her. There would be time enough to worry about what Henry might do to punish them or how they would ever repay Wolsey. He felt her hands caress him and forgot about the world.

Brandon breathed the fresh, salty air and watched as Calais slipped into the sea mists behind them. Henry's letter, summoning them to England, triggered a flurry of packing and goodbyes, and they'd sailed on a merchant ship leaving with the early tide.

He put his arm around Mary's waist to steady her as the ship rolled in the light swell. 'It feels good to be heading home.'

'It's been seven months since I last saw England, although it feels like a lifetime.'

'You'll find England much the same as when you left, although *you've* changed.' He smiled at her. 'You left as a girl and return as a woman.'

'You are right. I was innocent of the world outside London, let alone the French court.'

'It's good you've lived a little.' Brandon looked into her eyes. 'You know it will be a struggle, until Henry shows his forgiveness?'

'Where will we live?'

Brandon pulled his warm cloak over her shoulders as a chill sea breeze blew across the deck. 'I have a house by the Thames, close to Greenwich and Westminster. It needs work, but if I can raise the money it could be made fit for a queen.'

'I've never had my own house. Richmond Palace belongs to Henry, and I never felt at home in France.'

'We shall name it Suffolk Place, and once we are established I'll build us another house in the country, somewhere we can escape to.'

At last, the shadow of Dover loomed in the distance. Brandon's misgivings returned now that England was in sight. Wolsey's letters had warned there would be consequences for their actions and he'd lain awake at night worrying about what they might be. He'd seen Henry's displeasure in the past. He was not a man to cross.

A delegation of nobles rode to greet them, banners flying in the breeze. Twenty mounted Yeomen of the Guard rode behind them in the king's livery, and Brandon wondered if they'd come to take him to the Tower.

Mary brought her horse to a halt and looked across at him. 'You can't let them arrest you.'

He stopped at her side, shading his eyes from the sun with his hand as he studied the approaching men, trying to judge their mood. 'I'll have to take my chances. I trust your brother will allow me to explain.'

'What will we do if he locks you in the Tower?'

'Then you'll have to speak on my behalf.' He turned to her. 'Have faith. Henry gave his word you could marry of your own choosing. He can't have forgotten – you've reminded him often enough.'

Brandon watched the guards ride closer. 'That's Thomas Howard, Duke of Norfolk, riding at the front with his sons.' He scowled. 'I'll wager he's been looking forward to this moment.'

Mary pointed. 'Thomas Wolsey rides behind them. Do you think it's a good omen that he's come in person?'

Brandon continued to study the approaching riders. 'We are about to find out.' He turned to look at her. 'If they arrest me, I want you to know I regret nothing. I would gladly do it all again.'

Wolsey remained in his saddle as he bowed his head to Mary. 'We thank God to see you safe back in England, my lady.' He gave a curt nod of acknowledgement to Brandon. 'The king waits to greet you at Sir George Neville's manor of Birling.' He lowered his voice. 'He wishes you to wed at Green-wich without undue delay.'

King Henry, accompanied by Queen Catherine and most of the royal court, processed in silence to the Church of the Observant Friars, a short walk from Greenwich Palace. He had grown a thick ginger beard and wore cloth of gold, an acknowledgement that this was a royal wedding.

Henry had few words for Brandon, who knew he must show proper deference. Most of the royal court were listening and watching his every move, waiting for anything to fuel the inevitable gossip.

Wolsey confided that Brandon's enemies had encouraged

the king to have him imprisoned in the Tower. Others had wished him to suffer the full punishment for treason. Brandon frowned as he recalled how Wolsey said he should be thankful to be spared with only the exorbitant fines.

He knew he would never be able to repay them, and found little comfort in the stern face of John Fisher, Bishop of Rochester, who presided over the service as they repeated their marriage vows. As Brandon did so, he felt a stab of conscience at the sight of Mary's pale face and the troubled look in her eyes.

Late that night Brandon lay awake in the darkness and realised Mary was also restless and unable to sleep after such a day. 'I think our friend Wolsey exaggerated your brother's anger for his own profit.'

Mary turned towards him. 'I forgot to tell you, Charles. I pleaded with Wolsey. He has agreed to halve the sum to be repaid each month, although it will still be difficult to repay even twenty-four thousand pounds.'

Brandon was silent for a moment. He was well used to being in debt, but it would be a new experience for Mary. He changed the subject. 'I've rarely seen Henry looking more pleased with himself – or Catherine looking so sad.'

'Catherine confided to me that he's taken a mistress. One of her maids of honour, Elizabeth Blount.'

Brandon remembered Bessie Blount. Young and full of fun, she was one of Catherine's most attractive ladies. 'There is nothing Catherine can do?'

'She prays each day that she will give him a son.'

Brandon's riverside mansion at Suffolk Place looked like an abandoned soldiers' barracks. The wood-panelled walls were decorated with the antlers of long-dead stags, ancient weapons, and faded tapestries of hunting scenes. The rambling property enclosed a large courtyard and the formal gardens, now overrun with weeds, led to a private jetty on the Thames.

Brandon had grand plans for their home, despite their lack of funds. Inspired by what he'd seen in Paris, he commissioned a grand new entrance and the courtyard soon rang to the clink of masons' chisels on stone and carpenters sawing wood.

The work had hardly begun when he had to travel north to oversee the transfer of his estates. There were over forty manor houses in different ownership, and tenancies to resolve. It was work Brandon needed to do in person but Mary remained at Suffolk Place to make their house fit for a family.

Before he left, he ran his hand over the bulge, growing larger each week, under her gown. After the baby was born he planned to send for his daughters, to complete their family. Little Annie, now eight, had been sent to the court of Margaret of Austria the year before. Little Mary, only five years old, remained in the care of her mother's relatives.

The leaves on the avenue of trees at Suffolk Place had turned an autumnal golden brown by the time the invitation finally came. Brandon broke the royal seal and studied the contents. 'Thomas Wolsey has achieved his ambition – he's been made a cardinal, and I am chosen as one of those to escort him to a celebratory banquet.' He grinned and passed it to Mary to read.

Mary scanned the royal summons. 'Is this the forgiveness we've been waiting for?'

Brandon shrugged. 'Let us hope so. It bears Wolsey's signature, so there is no mystery about whose hand is at work. We are also invited to the launch of the king's latest warship. A good omen, although her name might cause some comment.' He watched for her reaction as Mary studied the invitation.

'The *Virgin Mary*? I hardly think my brother named her after me.'

'I've heard they are already referring to her as the *Princess Mary*.' He grinned. 'She's a full-bodied ship, you see, broad at the waterline.' He placed his hands on her hips.

Mary laughed and gave him a playful jab in the ribs. 'I shall take it as a compliment from my brother. He loves his ships more than anything he owns.'

The *Virgin Mary* towered over the buildings on the banks of the Thames, the latest symbol of Henry's power. With four great masts and over two hundred guns she was a floating fortress and, like the Venetian galleys, the massive sails were supplemented by sixty pairs of long oars.

The curious crowds which had gathered cheered as King Henry waved from the deck. Dressed in a sailor's costume of cloth of gold, he wore a diamond-studded sailor's whistle on a chain around his neck. He called out to Mary and Brandon as he spotted them.

'Dear sister!' Henry beckoned them to join him on the deck. He turned to Brandon. 'Is she not the most beautiful ship?'

'She is a credit to you, Your Grace.'

The chill wind did nothing to spoil the cheery mood as Queen Catherine named the ship, giving a meaningful look to Mary as she did so. Catherine was with child again and her eyes sparkled with happiness.

Brandon thought her lost children must have tested her faith, yet she seemed confident this time she would provide Henry with the heir he so desperately wished for. If all did not go well, he doubted she would have another chance.

13

FEBRUARY 1516

Brandon returned to the peace of Butley Priory in good spirits after visiting the king at Greenwich Palace. Mary found sanctuary at Butley as her time drew closer. They were guests of the prior, Augustine Rivers, a shrewd, grey-bearded man, who wore the black habit and wide belt of the Augustinian order, a silver crucifix around his neck the only sign of his rank.

The elderly prior had welcomed Brandon as the new Duke of Suffolk. Hidden in the sandy heathlands of Suffolk, the priory was more like a self-contained village, with an ancient stone wall enclosing twenty acres of good farmland, complete with barns and cottages, as well as the old abbey and its many outbuildings.

The prior provided them with substantial apartments built of local stone, adjacent to the abbey. The furniture was rustic, the walls whitewashed, the only ornament some faded tapestries of the life of Saint Augustine. The floors were covered with old rushes, which crackled underfoot. The contrast with Mary's chambers in Paris couldn't have been greater, yet the simple piety of the Augustinian order made it a tranquil place where they both felt at peace.

Part of the reason was that they were far from the ears of gossiping courtiers. Most of their army of over a hundred and fifty servants remained at Suffolk Place in London. Only a handful of the most trusted had travelled north with them, and knew to leave them in peace, so for once they could talk freely.

Pulling off his leather riding boots, Brandon warmed his feet in front of the blazing log fire before sharing his news. 'Queen Catherine's child is a girl, born at four in the morning.' His eyes twinkled with amusement as he watched Mary's face to see her reaction.

'Are they both well?' Mary's hand went to the rapidly growing bulge of their own child.

'With God's grace.' Brandon grinned. 'Henry has chosen to name her Mary, in your honour. First his new warship and now his daughter.' He laughed at the thought. 'It shows his affection for you is not diminished.'

'I'm pleased for Catherine – but we both know how much Henry longs for a son.' Mary looked serious as she counted on her fingers. 'Three lost sons and two daughters. Enough to test even Catherine's faith.'

Brandon looked up at her. 'It's little wonder Henry grows impatient, although now King Ferdinand is dead we need no longer worry about where Catherine's loyalty lies.'

'It has been difficult for her, yet she cannot be held responsible for her father's scheming. Catherine has always been a good loyal wife to Henry, and a healthy child will give them both hope.'

'He certainly seems in a better mood. I must return for the christening. Henry plans to make quite an event of it.' Brandon took off his black felt cap, straightening the gilded badge before running his fingers through his hair, grown longer since their return from Paris. 'He kept the news of her father's death from Catherine until the child was delivered. I understand she has remained in her bed ever since.'

'I wish I could see her. We were close, but something has changed since I came back from France.'

'Everything has changed, Mary, and you'll soon be entering your own confinement. Our good benefactor, Thomas Wolsey, has offered his own mansion for the purpose.'

Mary pulled a face. 'I suppose I'm obliged to accept, although it's another reminder of how he controls our lives.'

'Since becoming a cardinal Wolsey's been even more full of his own importance. He's taken to sitting on a cushion of cloth of gold, like a scarlet-robed king. We're fortunate to have his support yet, as always, there is a price to be paid.'

Brandon wore his heavy black bearskin fur coat to ward off the cold, yet he shivered at the sight of the icy River Thames, frozen over again. A bitter wind blew from the river, threatening to take his cap, like some mischievous spirit, a portent of even colder weather to come.

He scanned the faces of the congregation and realised that, apart from the officers of the household with their gold rods of office, only Henry's favourites were invited. It was just as well, as the Church of the Observant Friars at Greenwich was barely large enough to hold them all.

They'd braved the wintry breeze in a grand procession, led by the king's heralds in cloth-of-gold livery. The wide pathway from the court gate to the church was newly gravelled and strewn with rushes and fresh herbs for good luck. Magnificent Arras tapestries, decorated with precious gems and pearls, brightened the church doors, and the inside glowed with the light of countless tall candles.

Henry, following the tradition established by his grandmother, Lady Margaret Beaufort, waited in Queen Catherine's presence chamber. After the christening, the congregation would make their way back to join them for the royal blessing by the archbishop.

King Francis had been invited to be little Princess Mary's godfather, yet refused to attend. Rumour said it was because Henry hadn't personally signed the invitation, but Brandon knew better. Instead, Wolsey found himself taking the role and dressed in new crimson robes with his wide-brimmed crimson cardinal's hat.

Brandon entered the crowded church where the friars sang as Henry's three-day-old daughter was carried to the silver font by Lady Elizabeth Howard, the Countess of Surrey. Named Princess Mary, in honour of his sister and Queen Catherine's companion, the child looked impossibly small and frail to Brandon.

A canopy of cloth of gold was held over her head by four knights – the king's great-uncle, Sir David Owen; Sir Nicholas Vaux and Sir Thomas Aparre, loyal supporters of the late king; and Sir Thomas Boleyn. Married to Howard's daughter Elizabeth, Boleyn's presence reminded Brandon of the risk he took. By staying away from court, he was leaving the way open for the Howard affinity to take his place.

Thomas Howard gave Brandon a nod as their eyes met, a sign he was becoming accepted at last. There was no question that his status had increased significantly through his marriage to Mary, yet he'd not forgotten Wolsey's warning. Howard and his supporters in the king's council had called for him to be locked up in the Tower for treason.

The friars, led by the king's chaplain, interrupted his thoughts with a haunting descant *Te Deum* to give thanks to God. Before Brandon left the ancient church, he raised his eyes to the tortured figure of Christ and said a silent prayer for the new princess. Henry and Catherine had suffered enough loss. *Miserére nostri, Dómine.* Lord have mercy upon us.

Wolsey's mansion had been transformed out of recognition. As he was led down the long oak-panelled corridors Brandon realised his costly work at Suffolk Place was quite modest by comparison. He'd respected the tradition not to visit Mary in her confinement. The time passed quickly enough, yet she'd been on his mind every waking moment.

His worry about Mary and the child she carried had nagged at the back of his mind like a rat gnawing at an old crust. He'd sent his physician, Master Leonard, to check on Mary, and braced himself for bad news when his servant announced the physician's return.

Master Leonard, a frank-speaking Yorkshireman with a neatly trimmed beard, had a way of looking askance at people, as if he doubted their word. Brandon had grown used to his physician's bluff manner and, as usual, his reply to Brandon's questioning look was direct.

'Her Grace is in good health, my lord, and she asks me to convey her best wishes.'

Brandon studied the physician's face for a moment. 'Her time is close?'

'The midwife says a day or so, God willing.'

'And you are certain there is no sign of fever?'

'None, my lord.' Leonard's tone softened a little. 'I see no reason to be concerned. Lady Mary is young and in good care.'

'So was my last wife.' A note of bitterness sounded in Brandon's voice. He had no one to confide in, least of all his dour physician, but he'd been plagued by troubled dreams. More than once he'd woken up bathed in sweat at the thought of losing Mary or their child.

At last he was shown into the darkened bedchamber which had been Mary's home during their long weeks of separation.

She looked up as Brandon entered. Her eyes had dark shadows underneath but her smile was radiant as she held their baby for him to see.

'Our prayers are answered, Charles. We have a strong and healthy boy, as my physicians predicted. He's perfect, thanks be to God.'

Brandon kissed her on the cheek and studied the newborn baby, wrapped in linen swaddling. Unexpected tears filled his eyes to see them both looking so well. 'I prayed it would be a son.' His voice wavered. 'We must name him Henry, in honour of the king.'

Mary smiled. 'My little Henry Brandon. It seems strange to think one day he will be my lord of Suffolk – or even King of England.'

Brandon gave her a puzzled look, then realised she was right. Little Henry was in the direct line of succession if Catherine failed to provide the king with a son. 'We must take care who hears you say that, Mary, even though it's the truth.'

She gave him a knowing look. 'We shall invite my brother to be godfather. He will be pleased enough.'

'Of course – and Cardinal Wolsey as well.' Brandon looked around the richly tapestried room and glanced up at the ornate decoration on the high ceiling. 'In thanks for his kindness in accommodating you in this modest house.'

'Perhaps he will overlook the fact we've yet to make any payment on the money we owe.'

The years had not been kind to Mary's elder sister Margaret, the widow of King James IV and mother of the three-year-old James V. Her body had suffered after seven children. Her face was marked with the scars of the pox and her uneven, browned teeth reminded Brandon of her father, the late king.

She should be living in a castle as Regent of Scotland, yet

her choice of marriage to Archibald Douglas, Earl of Angus, had forced her exile to England. With little more than what she could carry, she'd thrown herself on her brother's mercy.

Mary confessed to Brandon that she thought she might never see her sister again. Sent off as a fourteen-year-old girl to marry King James IV of Scotland, Margaret had finally returned. Henry had welcomed her, despite her marrying for love. Her new husband, the Earl of Angus, was on the wrong side of the civil war in Scotland, and they already had a daughter named Margaret.

Margaret stepped forward and embraced Mary. 'Dearest sister,' her voice had the accent of the Scots, 'I've prayed for this day for so long.' Margaret still held Mary by both arms. 'I must congratulate you on the birth of little Henry.'

Brandon noticed Mary's sister glance at Queen Catherine, who watched their reunion surrounded by the ladies of the court, and realised Margaret was already making trouble. The two of them had been on opposing sides while she'd been in France. Catherine had celebrated the slaughter of King James after his disastrous border raid. Reconciliation would take time. Brandon could see Mary's smile was forced.

'You must see him, and I can't wait to see your daughter Margaret.'

Margaret returned Mary's smile, apparently unconcerned by her bad teeth. 'We have so much catching up to do.' Her sharp eyes studied Brandon with open curiosity as she held out a gold-ringed hand for him to kiss. 'Duke Charles. I have heard so much about you.'

He gave her a bow. 'Welcome back to England, my lady. Do you intend to stay?'

Margaret flashed a glance at Henry, who was enjoying a joke with a group of noisy young courtiers. 'For as long as my good brother allows.'

Brandon heard the determination in her voice. He knew

Henry had paid for her lodgings, her servants and even the fine gown she now wore. He'd found it hard to believe she was the sister of either Henry or Mary – she looked so different. Now he caught a glimpse of how she'd retained her fierce pride despite great hardship. Margaret might sound like a Scot, but she had the heart of a Tudor.

Henry joked to Brandon that he now had three queens to contend with, each with a baby. The novelty drew crowds of the curious to the celebratory tournament at Greenwich. Queen Catherine sat in the centre of the royal grandstand, with Mary to her left and Margaret to her right, as Henry led the competitors in a flamboyant procession.

Brandon rode his black destrier at Henry's side and wore his gilded armour with a blue ostrich plume on his helmet, matching the king's. No one watching could doubt he'd finally become the most privileged of Henry's companions.

The crowds cheered as, one by one, Brandon defeated thirty-four knights. As the last threw up both hands in surrender, he knew only Henry remained unbeaten. He would have to ride against the king. The thought of what could happen troubled him. If he unhorsed or defeated Henry it could undo the progress they'd made since returning from France, yet if he dropped his guard to let Henry win he could be injured.

Trumpets blasted a fanfare and the Master of the Joust announced the final tournament of the day. The two champions would meet in a grand finale. Henry raised a hand to a cheer from the watching crowd, then lowered the visor of his helmet.

Brandon took his heavy lance from Samuel. These were proper jousting spears, not the fragile practice lances he'd insisted on using in the past. A weapon of war – a direct hit from such a lance could unhorse even the most skilled rider.

He dropped his visor and watched for the sign that both were ready. He said a silent prayer as he urged his horse into a charge. They closed with a violent crack of shattering lances. The air crackled with tension and the crowd gasped as the Master of the Joust declared the first pass for Brandon.

On the second run Henry's lance crashed into Brandon's breastplate, forcing him back in the saddle. The crowd cheered and called out, 'Long live the king!' This time the points were awarded to Henry, so the winner would be decided by a final joust.

Brandon raised and lowered his new lance then charged with a heavy thump of hooves on the hard-packed ground. They closed again with a deafening clash and both shattered their lances. Dropping the broken lance, he grimaced as he pulled off his right gauntlet, throwing it to the ground. He gestured to Henry, who understood his signal of defeat and seemed happy to accept victory.

Brandon cursed his luck. 'It hurt like hell, Mary.' He held up his bandaged hand for her to see, like a badge of honour. 'I'm told it will heal well enough – but I won't be riding at the joust for a while.'

'Henry told me he will only ride against you. He says the younger men like Sir Nicholas Carew go too easy on him.'

'He's given Carew his own tiltyard to practise at Greenwich.' He frowned. 'Wolsey confided he thinks Nicholas Carew is a bad influence on the king, yet I'm happy to take a rest for a while. The younger ones must learn their craft.'

Mary threw back the brocade bedcovers, inviting him to join her. 'That might not be such a bad thing. I'd like to see more of you – and it could have been worse for us if my brother were injured.'

Brandon struggled to undress with his good hand. 'Are you suggesting I meant it to happen?'

Mary smiled. 'You handled it well, Charles. I was proud of you.'

He climbed into their bed and pulled her into his arms. 'And I was proud of you, Mary.' He kissed her. 'Your sister looks old enough to be your mother. You'd never guess she's only seven years older.'

'Margaret's been through much hardship. She lost her son, Alexander, and would have been wealthy if she'd not married so rashly.'

Brandon stroked Mary's long hair, which had been freed from its restraining plaits and brushed until it shone in her nightly ritual. 'It seems to run in your family. Your sister seems determined to exploit the advantages of her visit to her brother's court as much as possible.' A note of disapproval sounded in his voice.

'She confided to me that she suffers from pains in her back which keep her awake at night.' Mary frowned. 'She has no money of her own and plans to stay at least a year.'

'Henry will tire of her before then, mark my words.'

Mary took his injured hand in hers. 'This is an omen, a sign we need a change. Will you take me back to Suffolk? You can spend more time with your son and daughters and learn to be a better father to them.'

Her words struck their mark like a well-aimed arrow. She was right. He'd not been much of a father to his girls and must do better for his son. Brandon agreed it was time for a change. 'We shall make Westhorpe Hall our country home. It will be less costly to live in Suffolk than at your brother's court, at least until your money arrives from France.'

'I shall sell more of my jewels to help make Westhorpe a home fit for our family. It will be good to raise little Henry away from the mud and filth of London. You must send for little Mary and write to Margaret of Savoy for Annie to return to us.'

Brandon nodded. 'I shall. It's time we all lived together as a family, not as the Queen Dowager of France and the king's stable boy,' he grinned, 'but as the Duke and Duchess of Suffolk, lord and lady of the manor.'

14

APRIL 1517

Samuel glanced back at their long convoy of hastily packed wagons, stretching down the winding lane behind them. The first and finest carried Mary and little Henry, with his two nursemaids. Those behind were loaded with furniture and tapestries, servants and supplies. He turned to Brandon, riding at his side.

'Did you hear talk of the sweating sickness in Suffolk, my lord?'

'I did not, Samuel, and I'm relieved to be out of London. It's the worst the city has seen for a good many years.'

'They say a man can be merry at dinner and dead at supper, my lord. Starts with a headache, then the sweats and shivers. Most are beyond all hope in a few hours.'

Brandon frowned at the truth of Samuel's words. 'May God have mercy on them.' He recalled Henry's rash plans to leave the relative safety of Richmond to inspect a Venetian galley at Greenwich. This was no time to take unnecessary risks, and for once he'd declined the invitation.

Their move to Suffolk was timely, although he'd have liked to have seen the work at Westhorpe finished before he returned for them. He didn't tell Mary, but he'd covered the seventy-five miles back to London with reckless haste, riding from dawn until dusk.

As he rode, he'd prayed he'd find Mary and little Henry safe and well at Richmond. He'd been right to return in person, as Mary seemed in little hurry to leave – but then, she hadn't seen what the sweating sickness could do. No one knew how it spread and there was no cure once the fever took hold.

At last the impressive red-brick towers of Westhorpe Hall showed above the trees. The old manor house had been abandoned in a sorry state of disrepair by the disgraced de la Poles. Brandon had to rebuild most of it, despite their rising debts. He hoped Mary would appreciate his investment in their future.

They rode over the bridge, the stone pillars decorated with newly carved Tudor roses, into the gravelled courtyard in front of the house. Brandon looked up at the octagonal towers, topped with turrets and pinnacles. Inspired by those at Richmond Palace, they'd caused the builders unexpected problems and cost double the estimate.

He'd also spent a small fortune on the new mullioned windows, each crafted from countless diamonds of leaded glass to fit the irregular window openings. Like the towers, they added expense but transformed the once-dingy mansion, allowing the sunlight to flood in.

Brandon dismounted and stretched his aching back as he handed his reins to Samuel. He strode across to Mary's carriage, waiting while she was helped down by her young groom.

She smoothed the creases from her gown before she looked up at him. 'I don't mind if I never ride in a carriage again. We felt every bump all the way from London, although little Henry slept for most of the journey.'

He glanced at the iron-rimmed carriage wheels. 'Next time

you must ride your palfrey.' He took her hand in his. 'Come, I want you to see what I've done with our new home.' He gestured to where a line of servants waited to greet them.

'I didn't know we already had such a household here. They seem to be expecting us.'

Brandon nodded. 'I sent a rider ahead, Mary. I have a surprise for you inside.'

He led her through the heavy oak doors into the great hall and was disappointed to see the work hadn't been finished in his absence. One wall was covered with a fine tapestry depicting a victorious King Henry VII at the Battle of Bosworth, one of the few things of value he'd inherited from his uncle.

The other walls and ceiling were rendered in whitewashed plaster, with a motif of the letters C and M intertwined and alternating with Tudor roses. Brandon frowned at the sight of old rushes still covering the floor, instead of the tiles he'd imported at great expense from Calais.

The tang of soot and woodsmoke suggested the new chimneys weren't drawing properly, but the smell of new paint and freshly sawn timber told him the workmen had not long gone. Mary took her time to look round the hall before turning to him.

'We shall make this one of the finest houses in Suffolk soon enough. All it needs is a woman's touch.'

He felt a stab of irritation at her tone, then recalled she'd said the same about their London home at Suffolk Place. 'I hoped you would like it.'

'I do.' She placed her hand on his arm. 'I'm just tired after the journey.'

He nodded in understanding and led her into the side chamber, where a polished oak dining table was set ready for a meal. Shining silver goblets, knives and spoons waited at each place, and a pair of high-backed, gilded chairs with crimson velvet cushions sat at the head of the table.

She smiled at him. 'Are we expecting guests?'

'I want you to have a little of the finery you've been used to – and we must be ready for a visit from the king.' He grinned. 'I've suggested a royal progress of the north.'

She gave him a quizzical look. 'You said you had a surprise for me?'

Brandon signalled to a waiting maidservant, who opened a side door. Two young ladies entered, the eldest in a fashionable gown of deep-red satin, the younger one in a gown of corn-flower-blue edged with lace. Both wore pearl-fringed head-dresses in the latest French style, with long veils of shimmering silk at the back. The taller of the two gave Mary an elegant curtsey.

'Good day, Lady Mary. Welcome to Westhorpe Hall.'

Although Mary had suggested that Brandon's daughters should join them, she seemed amazed to see them both so soon. 'You must be Annie. It seems you've learned much at the court of Margaret of Savoy. How old are you now?'

'Ten years old, my lady.' She spoke with a cultured French accent and there was a twinkle in her eye as she replied. 'My time with the Duchess of Savoy has been quite an education.'

Brandon felt an unexpected pang of grief, mixed with pride, at his daughter's confidence. Annie was the image of her mother, with her natural grace and beauty, and even shared her mischievous sense of humour. Her mother would have been so proud to see her daughters now.

Duchess Margaret of Savoy had sent a short and cryptic message in French, saying how she would greatly miss his daughter, who had been a credit to him. He'd read it several times, but if there was a hidden message it was too subtle for him. Although Annie's time at Margaret's court had been shorter than he'd intended, it seemed to have prepared her well for the noble marriage he would arrange for her soon enough.

He gave a nod to his youngest daughter, Mary, who took a hesitant step forward and curtseyed with less confidence than Annie. She'd inherited his grey-blue eyes and heavier build, and confessed she'd not enjoyed her time being passed from one distant relative to another.

'My lady. It is my pleasure to meet you.'

Mary smiled. 'How old are you now, Mary?'

'I shall be seven this year, my lady.' Her well-educated young voice echoed in the chamber.

'I welcome you both to our new home. I shall be glad of your company, as I expect your father will be away with the king quite often.'

Brandon heard the note of criticism. He should not have to explain that their future depended on retaining his influence at court. Again, he made an allowance for her tone, as she'd had a long journey, and smiled at his daughters. 'You must meet little Henry. He will be tired from travelling but it's good to have our growing family together at last.'

They continued their tour of the house, visiting the freshly limewashed kitchens, where their cooks were busy preparing a welcoming meal. He showed her a well-stocked pantry hung with rabbits, pheasants and a young doe, then cavernous cellars lined with wine barrels, giving off a richly sweet aroma. He'd been evasive when she'd asked him how much he'd spent but he'd calculated it must be over twelve thousand pounds.

He led her out through a door and across the cobblestoned courtyard, dominated by a tall, white-painted dovecot. Startled doves fluttered into the air as they crossed to the arched doorway of the private chapel. Brandon pushed the oak door and was pleased to see Mary gasp at the magnificent stained-glass windows, a final surprise he'd been saving for her.

The high centre window featured a serene depiction of the

Madonna and Child which seemed to glow with the sunlight filtering through. In the window to the left was Mary's golden fleur-de-lis and crown as Queen Dowager of France. To the right shone Brandon's gold-crowned arms and Order of the Garter.

'They are so beautiful.'

He smiled as Mary took his hand in hers. 'A craftsman from York has spent months working on them, but the design was my own.' He led her back out into the courtyard. 'You must be tired. Let me show you our apartments.'

A narrow gallery led to a winding stone staircase. The floorboards creaked underfoot, reminding Brandon of his time at sea, and the unfashionable furniture was mostly what had been left behind by the fleeing de la Pole family. At least the canopied bed was new, with velvet hangings trimmed with gold tassels and a brocade coverlet embroidered with red-and-white Tudor roses.

Brandon watched Mary lie back on the bed, and decided to join her. The thick new ropes supporting the mattress creaked as they tensioned under his weight. She turned to him with the now familiar questioning look in her eyes.

'We came here to make economies, Charles, but I see you've spent a fortune, and there is still much to do.'

He turned and studied her face for a moment before replying. 'You are a Tudor princess. I can't ask you to live like a commoner.' He expected her to laugh at the thought, but instead her forehead creased in a frown of concern.

'I would rather live within our means than place ourselves at the mercy of men like Wolsey...'

'Don't concern yourself with Wolsey. He is our benefactor.' Brandon grinned. 'I've been in debt all my life, and it seems neither your brother nor Thomas Wolsey are in any hurry to be repaid.'

'We must owe him a small fortune...'

'You could offer him some of your jewels to keep him from demanding what is owed.'

Mary looked thoughtful. 'I'm supposed to have given all my jewels to Henry.'

Brandon pulled her closer to him and put his arm around her slender waist. 'You can rely on Wolsey not to be troubled by such details.'

'What will we do if King Francis withholds my dower payments?'

'I shall sell my estates in the south. It always was my plan to make the most of our holdings in the north.'

She smiled. 'I hope you are right – we have a larger family to care for now.'

He raised himself on one elbow to see her face. 'What do you think of my daughters?'

'They have both grown into beautiful young ladies. Annie is much like her mother, but little Mary has your eyes.'

Brandon smiled at the thought. 'They will be good company for you when I'm away.'

'Do you have to return to court?'

'You know your brother, Mary. I'll have no choice if I am summoned.'

Mary relaxed back on the soft bed. 'This country air will be good for our children.'

'And the new baby.' His hand slid to the growing bulge in her silk gown. 'A girl this time?'

Mary smiled. 'God willing. I shall be happy if it's a girl or another boy, so long as the child is healthy.'

The summons came sooner than they expected, but not from the king, and it was for Mary, not Brandon. The letter, delivered by a royal herald, came from Queen Catherine, recalling

Mary to court as her sister Margaret was soon to return to Scotland.

Brandon gave her a look of concern. 'I've heard talk of riots in London. I'd prefer you to remain safe here with the girls and little Henry.'

'This might be the last time I'll be able to see my sister.' Mary frowned. 'It's most unusual for Catherine to summon me like this.' Brandon watched her hand fall unconsciously to her bulging middle. 'She is also with child again. I hope this doesn't mean there is a problem.'

Brandon doubted it. 'I told you Henry would grow tired of your scheming sister soon enough. He wants rid of her, and you are to help make sure she leaves.'

Mary turned on him, a rare flash of anger in her eyes. 'Do not forget she is my sister and has been through great hardship. My father confessed to me on his deathbed that his advisors told him her marriage would ensure peace with Scotland, yet he wept when she left.'

Brandon took her in his arms and held her, seeing she was close to tears. 'I'm sorry, Mary. I meant no insult to your sister.'

Mary spoke in a whisper as she remembered. 'Father told me Margaret was barely thirteen, and my grandmother was concerned Margaret was too young. She had been only a year older herself and nearly died when Father was born.' Mary brushed away a tear. 'She tried to persuade him to wait until Margaret was sixteen but it was too late. He understood her concern, but had to let Margaret go. He told me he watched her carriage disappear into the distance and knew he might never see her again.'

The hooves of four hundred horses clattered on cobblestones, like rolling thunder, the sound echoing in the narrow London streets. Trumpets blared and crowds cheered as Henry's extravagant reception parade for his new allies made its way to Greenwich Palace.

Brandon led the richly dressed escort of the senior nobles of court, riding his fine black destrier at the side of the Duke of Norfolk. He wore a long flowing cape and his ceremonial sword. His chain of the Order of the Garter flashed gold in the sunshine as he rode.

The King of Aragon's ambassadors were followed by Spanish Knights of the *Toisón*, the Order of the Golden Fleece, their mounts caparisoned with gaudy chequered patterns and black, double-headed dragons. Then came the elderly Bishop of Spain, Cardinal Francisco de Cisneros, riding alongside George de Theimseke, Provost of Cassel, and Nicholas Sagudino, the Venetian ambassador.

Although Brandon welcomed the Spanish and Venetian delegation, he worried Henry's new peace treaty might alienate King Francis. Despite his promises, none of Mary's French revenues had been paid on time. He found it hard to keep up with Henry's changes of foreign policy, although he understood why an alliance with Spain and Pope Leo was important in the delicate balance of power.

The new King of Spain was the same young Charles who was to have married Mary, and now ruled Castile, Aragon, Sicily and Naples. The old king, Henry VII, had shown vision in his first choice of husband for Mary. It was expected that Charles would also soon replace the ailing Emperor Maximilian. It was rumoured that the emperor carried an ornate coffin with him wherever he went and was not expected to live much longer.

It seemed half of London thronged to see their king joust. First came the joust marshal, in a surcoat of cloth of gold, surrounded by thirty footmen in yellow-and-blue livery. Then came the king's drummers and trumpeters in white damask, followed by twenty young mounted knights dressed in white, with doublets of cloth of silver, and white velvet. Their horses were barbed with silver chains from which silver bells tinkled tunefully as they rode. Next followed thirteen royal pages, on horses with trappings of purple velvet embroidered with gold stars.

The king and fifteen jousters wore matching armour of shining silver, and alongside each rode a squire, carrying his master's lance and helmet. Brandon rode with Samuel, now resplendent in the blue-and-yellow Suffolk livery. The grand procession was followed by thirty gentlemen courtiers marching on foot and dressed in velvet and white satin.

Henry proclaimed he would take on all comers, but Brandon persuaded him against it. They'd met many times at the joust yet it was never any easier, and Brandon flinched as their lances clashed, sending shattered splinters high into the air. They ran eight courses, both shivering their lances every time, to rousing cheers and applause from the spectators. The jousts lasted four hours, with Henry and Brandon being declared joint champions.

At the banquet which followed, Henry sat at the head of the hall with Queen Catherine on one side and Mary on the other. Dressed in matching cloth of gold, they wore coronets glittering with diamonds. Henry managed to outshine them all with a heavy golden collar studded with rubies the size of grapes.

After the banquet, musicians on a raised stage in the centre of the hall sang and played the king's favourite melodies on flute, five-stringed rebeck, and harpsichord while the queen's ladies danced. Henry out-danced them all, jumping and carousing until dawn with such energy the ambassadors could not fail to be impressed.

. . .

Brandon woke with a curse at the sound of sharp knocking at his door. He'd decided to stay at Suffolk Place while Mary accompanied Queen Catherine on a pilgrimage to the shrine of Our Lady at Walsingham. He opened the door to see his servant with a lit candlestick in one hand and a folded parchment in the other.

'A rider has arrived with a message from Her Grace, Lady Mary, my lord.'

Brandon felt a shiver of worry at the man's words. It would not be good news. He'd been against the idea of Mary making the long journey of over a hundred and twenty miles in such a late stage of pregnancy, but she'd been insistent. He understood Catherine's wish to provide Henry with a healthy son. At the same time, he worried about the risk to Mary and their unborn child. He dismissed his servant and took the candle and parchment over to his desk, where he broke the red wax seal, his lips moving in a silent prayer as he began to read her familiar handwriting.

Mary had felt faint and stopped to rest at the manor house in Hatfield of their old friend Nicholas West, now Bishop of Ely. Mary claimed it was God's plan for their child to be born earlier than expected and had been delivered of a healthy girl on St Francis' Day. She wrote that Bishop West had christened their new daughter Frances Brandon.

Brandon smiled. He was glad he hadn't known what Mary had been going through. It seemed so long ago, but he recalled a snowy day in Paris when he'd loaned money to his old friend Nicholas West. Now that favour was repaid in full, with interest. He closed his eyes and gave thanks to God.

15

JUNE 1519

Brandon sensed at once that something had changed. He cursed to himself as he realised he'd stayed away in Suffolk too long. Courtiers gossiped in corners and neither Henry nor Queen Catherine were anywhere to be seen. Greenwich Palace buzzed with a great secret, and he was determined to discover it.

He spotted Thomas Wolsey, in his distinctive scarlet hat and cloak, talking to two finely dressed Venetian ambassadors on the far side of the great hall. Wolsey was the one man who would be sure to know what was going on. Although it seemed his influence over the king was waning, he still made it his business to protect Henry.

The previous year the palace had been on high alert, with armed guards at every entrance, after rumours of a plot against the king. Even Brandon came under suspicion because of his close connections with the French. Wolsey confided that he'd been told to keep a close watch on him, as well as Buckingham and any others he might suspect.

His warning was yet another sign of the shift in the balance of power. It had been a worrying time, as Henry stopped inviting Brandon to come hunting and cancelled his planned progress of the north. Brandon heard rumours that he'd been sent away to the north to keep him in his place.

Henry gathered his young favourites around him, an irreverent, rowdy band he called 'the gentlemen of the privy chamber'. Brandon found himself excluded from the king's company in favour of younger, more fun-loving and carefree men such as Nicholas Carew, Francis Bryan and Henry Guildford.

Then Wolsey negotiated a new peace treaty with the French, and Henry's daughter, Princess Mary, was betrothed to King Francis' heir, the dauphin. Brandon's ties to the French court were no longer frowned upon, yet he suspected his enemies awaited their chance, like carrion crows watching over a dying sheep.

He hoped the sweating sickness had not returned and afflicted the king or queen. The previous year it took Henry's trusted Latin secretary, Andrea Ammonio, as well as Lord Grey and several servants of the royal household. Wolsey himself had succumbed to the fever, one of the few to survive. He claimed to have been spared by the goodwill of God, but Brandon suspected it was simply Wolsey's legendary luck.

As he waited for Wolsey to finish his discussion with the ambassadors, a more likely possibility crossed his mind. The nation had mourned when the queen lost yet another daughter the previous November, her baby so frail she died before she could be christened. Henry did not mourn his loss, but instead caused a scandal by his open and public affection for Elizabeth Blount.

Brandon had been quite taken by young Elizabeth. She was lively and vivacious, with blonde hair and entrancing blue eyes. Her father was Sir John Blount, who'd served at Brandon's side as Captain of the Guard at the successful siege of

Tournai. Now seventeen years old, Elizabeth was one of Catherine's most attractive ladies-in-waiting.

Henry called her 'his Bessie', paid for her beautiful gowns and chose her for his dances and masques more often than any other. Elizabeth had also taken Mary's place as an ornament of Henry's court, singing in her melodious voice to overenthusiastic applause from the king.

Brandon realised he hadn't seen Elizabeth Blount at court since the previous October, and Henry had taken to disappearing, as he had today, for days on end. There was one explanation which occurred to Brandon. One which might explain the need for secrecy about the mysterious sense of excitement at the palace.

Wolsey beckoned him into a private alcove and fixed him with a knowing look before he'd even asked his question. 'Yes, it's true. The king has been delivered of a son.'

'The young Blount girl?'

Wolsey nodded. 'I recommended that the king's mistress was moved to Jericho House, the former Priory of St Lawrence near Ingatestone, which is where she is now.'

Brandon frowned. 'I've heard Jericho called a house of ill repute. That must be what they were referring to. Either way this does not bode well for Queen Catherine.'

'A lesson to us all, Charles.' Wolsey glanced across the room to check they were not being overheard. 'The king asked me how God could grant him a son out of wedlock – yet deny him such a blessing in a lawful marriage.'

'How did you reply?'

'That the will of God is beyond the understanding of a mortal such as me.' Wolsey frowned. 'I fear he will ask for my help to prove his marriage to Queen Catherine ill-founded.'

Brandon studied Wolsey's grim face as he considered the implications of this news. 'Mary has always been loyal to

Catherine. She might even confront her brother if he tries to have his marriage annulled.'

'We might all find our loyalty to the queen is tested soon enough.'

'I'm not minded to cross the king a second time.' He gave Wolsey a wry look. 'It was only through your good grace that I was spared the last time. I might find myself again in need of your support, if your prediction is correct.'

'And I yours, Charles. I confess the king keeps me at arm's length of late.' He gave Brandon a rare smile. 'I'm pleased you are back in his favour. I might need you to tell me how the wind blows.'

Brandon grinned. 'You can rely on me. I think we might have a blustery time ahead of us both.'

The household had retired for the night by the time Brandon returned to Westhorpe, but Mary was awake, her perfumed beeswax candles, imported from Paris, burning low. Pulling off his cap, he ran his fingers through his hair before kissing her on the cheek.

'You didn't have to stay up for me.'

Mary wore her long nightgown, with an embroidered white linen coif covering her hair. 'I wanted to.' Her eyes twinkled with excitement.

'What's happened?' He held her close. 'I know you too well, Mary Tudor. You have something to tell me?'

'I have good news, Charles.' She smiled. 'I'm with child again. We're going to have another little Brandon in our growing family.'

He grinned and held her close. 'Let us pray it is another boy.' He looked thoughtful. 'We should name him William Brandon, to honour my good father.' He unbuckled his sword, placing it in the corner of their chamber, then sat on the bed and pulled off his riding boots. 'This time you must take more care. No more foolish pilgrimages to Walsingham when the baby is due.' He wagged a finger at her in mock seriousness.

'Of course, my lord.' She curtseyed to him, like a servant.

He poured water from the heavy earthenware jug into the bowl they kept in their bedchamber, then turned to her. 'When is the child due?'

'I wanted to be certain.' She counted on her fingers. 'Our baby will be born before the end of this year, by Christmas time.'

He splashed cold water in his face and dried it with a soft cloth. All the way from London he'd been rehearsing the best way to tell her about Henry's son and hoped she would not react badly. He led her to their comfortable, canopied bed before blowing out the last of the candles.

The ropes supporting the mattress creaked with his weight as he lay at her side. He put his arm around her and pulled her closer. Her hair had the delicate scent of rose water, reminding him of their first time together in Paris. Brandon kissed her on the cheek.

'I've missed you, Mary, and our children. How have you all been while I was away?'

'Little Harry asks for you all the time. He makes good progress with his French. I teach him a few words each day, and a little Latin. Annie has become a talented seamstress. She's sewn a new gown for herself from the blue silk from Paris I'd been keeping for a special occasion.'

'I must ask to see her in it in the morning.' A thought occurred to him. 'Annie is twelve now, old enough to be introduced at court. I must find a husband worthy of her. How is little Mary?'

'She takes after her father.' Mary laughed at his frown. 'She's named the fattest of our pigs Cardinal Wolsey.'

'That reminds me. I heard important news from our good

friend the cardinal when I visited him at Greenwich.' He took a deep breath. 'He told me the king has a healthy son at last.'

He felt Mary tense in his arms and her hand went to the swelling at her own middle. She remained silent for a moment, and when she spoke it was a whisper, as if to even say the words would make it true.

'Bessie Blount?'

'You know?'

'Catherine confided to me that she suspected this might happen. She was distraught at the possibility...'

Brandon pulled her closer, his arm embracing her protectively. 'I'm afraid your brother makes no effort to keep the boy a secret. Wolsey was his godfather, and he's been named Henry Fitzroy, son of the king.'

'I can't imagine how Catherine must feel now.' A new sadness carried in her voice.

'They already use it as an excuse for celebration in the taverns of London – but the child is a bastard and will never inherit.'

Mary stroked his chest. 'I fear I shall have to choose between my best friend and my brother. Catherine has always been so good to me.'

It was hard to tell in the dim light but Brandon thought a tear glistened on her cheek. He tried to change the subject. 'I also have news of your Charles.'

She turned to face him. 'I've told you before, you are not to call him *my* Charles.' Her voice sounded serious.

He lay back in the darkness. She'd confessed to him once how, as a girl, she'd dreamed of life with the young prince. She had kept his miniature gold-framed portrait by her bedside so that it would be the last thing she saw before she went to sleep and the first when she woke.

Brandon recalled the sallow-faced, humourless young man he'd met briefly at the court of Margaret of Savoy. Mary would never have found happiness with him, despite his numerous titles and great wealth. At the same time, he felt an unexpected envy, even a stab of irrational jealousy.

'It's no surprise to anyone, but he has been chosen as emperor. Henry has already invited him to visit in the new year to discuss a peace treaty.'

'Do you think my brother will invite us?'

'He will. We are back in favour, Mary. Henry gave me the present of a fine black horse, and we are both to accompany the entire court as honoured guests at a meeting in France with King Francis in the spring.'

'The entire court?'

'Wolsey has been put in charge of making the arrangements. Including servants and workmen, he's planning to take five thousand across the Channel.'

'That sounds more like an invasion than a diplomatic meeting – and where will they all stay?'

'The meeting is to be just outside Calais, near Guines, so some can stay in the castle there, but Wolsey is planning a tented city. He's even having a grand temporary palace built for Henry – and we are to have our own private apartment within it.'

'It will cost Henry a fortune!'

'Henry seems determined to outdo the French – you know how competitive they both are.'

'I was beginning to wonder if I would ever return to France.' She sounded wistful. 'For once we will not make economies, Charles. I must have a new wardrobe.'

Brandon grinned in the darkness. 'Of course. We must show Emperor Charles what he has missed out on!'

He woke to bright sunshine and the calming sound of birdsong drifting through the open window. He heard the shrill voice of one of his daughters calling out to little Harry, warning him to take care, and frowned when he couldn't tell if it was Annie or Mary. He'd seen too little of them to be sure.

Reaching out with his hand, he found the bed empty at his side and realised he must have overslept. Brandon rubbed his eyes and looked around the room. Mary must have taken care not to wake him, as he was usually a light sleeper. He pulled on his clothes and ran his fingers through his tangled hair.

For once he would spend time with Mary and his children, and perhaps take them for a ride in the new carriage. He'd had it made as a surprise for Mary by the wheelwright in the village. The seats were padded with velvet cushions and the wide wheels had springs of hickory to soften the bumps on the rutted roads.

The house seemed deserted and strangely quiet, with no sign of Mary or the children. He rang for a servant and one of Mary's maids appeared from the kitchens, with an anxious face, drying her hands on a cloth.

'Where might I find Lady Mary this morning?'

'I saw her heading for the chapel, my lord, but that was some time ago.' The woman glanced towards the door leading to the inner courtyard. 'Shall I find her, my lord?'

Brandon shook his head. 'I will find her.'

He crossed the courtyard and pushed open the door to their private chapel. Mary kneeled on the cold stones of the chapel floor, her eyes raised to the figure of the Madonna and her hands clasped together in prayer. She hadn't noticed him enter behind her.

His first thought was to respect her privacy. Then he remembered the servant said she'd been there for some time. He placed a hand on her shoulder and felt her start in surprise. When she turned to him there were tears in her eyes. Brandon expected her to be distressed by Henry's treatment of Catherine, but not to shut herself away like this.

'What's the matter?' He reached out a hand to help Mary to her feet and she stood with difficulty, her legs stiff from kneeling for so long.

'I hoped to keep it from you, Charles, but the pain in my side has returned.'

'Why would you wish to keep such a thing from me?'

'I didn't want you to worry about our child.' Her hand went to her middle.

'Last night, you chose not to mention you were in pain?'

'I'm in pain all the time, Charles.'

'I'm sorry, I didn't have any idea...'

'I've learned to live with it.' She forced a smile. 'I've been praying for the Lord's grace and mercy that all will be well. I believe it's all that can be done for my ailment.'

'I trust in the Lord's grace and mercy – but there is always something that can be done.' Even as Brandon said the words he doubted it, and remembered his uncle's sudden death, despite the attentions of his physicians.

'How bad is this pain?' He spoke more softly this time.

'I've had this ache in my side since I was a child,' her hand moved to caress her ribs, 'but now it worsens as the baby grows larger.'

'What has your physician said?'

She frowned. 'I could not bear the thought of his foul-tasting cures. I fear they could harm our child, and they offered little enough help to my poor mother.'

Brandon recalled Mary telling him about her mother's death. Although she'd rarely spoken of it, when she did her face was anguished. He'd been nineteen at the time – a servant in the royal household, watching and gossiping, as servants do.

'Your father hardly appeared in public for almost a year. His court was never the same after your mother...'

Mary looked at him with reddened eyes. 'She died on her thirty-seventh birthday. It seems my mother never recovered from her last child. I was only seven and couldn't understand. My father paid for the best physicians in the land, yet they could do nothing for her.'

'I'm truly sorry about your mother, Mary.' Brandon put his arm around her shoulder.

'The baby would have been my little sister. Father told me she was christened Katherine. Katherine Tudor.'

'I didn't know she'd lived.'

'Barely a week.' Mary shook her head as she remembered. 'My father told me on his deathbed that his faith had been tested by Mother's death. He could never understand why a merciful God should allow her such a cruel fate.'

'I shall stay here with you, Mary. King Henry can do without my services for a while.'

She looked at him in surprise. 'You don't have to—'

He put a finger to her lips to silence her. 'I want to.' His hand moved to her middle. 'I shall pray with you – for you, and our little child.'

Mary looked at him as if bracing herself to ask a favour. 'You might call me superstitious, but when I prayed, the words of Saint Augustine, taught to me as a child, came to mind.'

Brandon saw the sincerity in her eyes. 'You asked for divine guidance, and this is a good omen. We'll return to our sanctuary under the care of the Augustinians at Butley Priory, as guests of Prior Rivers. It's peaceful there, and the monks know more about healing than any physician I've ever met.'

Brandon loosened the tight swaddling which bound his new daughter's arms and watched in wonder as her tiny fingers grasped his thumb. He grinned at Mary. 'What shall we name her?'

Mary, propped up in bed on silk cushions, still looked tired and weak but was relieved he didn't show disappointment the child wasn't the boy they'd wished for. 'I named our last daughter Frances, so this time it must be your choice.'

Brandon thought for a moment. 'I've always liked the name Eleanor.'

'Lady Eleanor Brandon.' Mary smiled at the sight of the two of them together. 'A good name.'

16

MAY 1520

The bells of the magnificent cathedral of Canterbury chimed in melodious welcome as King Henry and Emperor Charles, King of Castile and Aragon and the new King of the Romans, arrived from Dover. The emperor's fleet had been blown off course by violent storms, so he'd been inconveniently late, threatening to delay the court's departure for France.

The king's yeomen held back a noisy throng of common-ers, curious to see their king and the young emperor. Brandon stood at Mary's side. She looked beautiful in her gown of gold embroidered silk, but the mysterious pains were keeping her awake at nights. No one other than him would know, but she was continually tired, finding everything an effort.

He'd written to Wolsey advising that she might be too unwell to make the sea voyage with the king and queen to France. Wolsey's reply was that Mary should make every effort to accompany him, with the veiled threat of consequences if she did not.

Wolsey had sent Master Peter, the king's physician, who'd promptly pronounced Mary to be fit and well enough for the journey. Encouraged, Mary insisted on travelling to France, and reminded Brandon of her motto: *La volenté de Dieu me suffit*. This was God's will, something she had to live with. She said the ache in her side was a small price to pay for their three healthy children.

A fanfare from the king's trumpeters sounded and Brandon felt Mary tense next to him. It must be strange for her to finally meet the man who'd been her fiancé for over six years. On the long ride from Suffolk she confessed to feeling anxious about how to address him, and what she might say.

Brandon followed Mary's gaze and saw the slim figure in a large hat. Nineteen years old, the new emperor had long dark hair, a grave expression and a prominent chin. Four guardsmen carried a cloth-of-gold canopy of estate, emblazoned with the emblem of the Holy Roman Empire, a double-headed black eagle.

The emperor scanned the waiting nobles as he entered, his pale face strangely impassive, reminding Brandon of the late king's lifelike funeral effigy. He bowed graciously to his aunt, Queen Catherine – waiting in ermine-lined cloth of gold, glittering with pearls – but his eyes were on Mary.

Brandon felt a frisson of pride. The young emperor had everything on a golden plate. He'd never gone hungry or borrowed money for a crust of bread. Charles of Burgundy and Castile, heir of three dynasties, was always destined to be a wealthy ruler, yet Brandon smiled at how he'd won the one thing money could never buy – the love of Mary Tudor.

Henry's new barque, the *Katherine Pleasaunce*, sailed through white-crested waves in a fresh breeze on the way to Calais. A dozen royal ships sailed ahead, loaded to the gunnels with men, supplies and horses. More ships than Brandon could count followed in line in their wake, like cygnets following a swan. Henry's fleet looked like an invasion of France, masquerading as a mission of peace.

Brandon took Mary's hand and led her up on deck for some air. They leaned against the wooden rail, watching the grey outline of the French coast becoming more distinct on the horizon. He put his arm around her waist to steady her. There was no need for anyone to know she was unwell, and the sea air might do her good.

She looked into his eyes. 'Something troubles you, Charles?'

'No.' He smiled as she saw through his lie. 'You know me too well, Mary. I confess I'm uneasy about Henry's decision to leave the country in the sole charge of Thomas Howard for so long.'

'I don't like him, but perhaps it's time you stopped seeing him as your enemy.'

Brandon shrugged. 'I've never trusted him. Now he has the chance to turn those who remain in England against me.' He heard the frustration in his voice. It seemed unfair that the old families still resented him, always looking for ways to bring him down.

Mary put a calming hand on his arm. 'Everyone of importance is with us, and Bishop Foxe has come out of retirement to keep an eye on the king's council while we are all in France. He was one of my father's most loyal men and will safeguard our interests.'

'I trust you are right, Mary.' He turned to her. 'Did you see how Emperor Charles embraced Queen Catherine?'

Mary smiled at the memory. 'She looked surprised, although he is her nephew.'

Brandon nodded. 'I thought I saw tears in her eyes.'

'Perhaps she was thinking of her sister. She told me Joanna is confined in a convent in Castile with her daughters.' Mary looked at him with wide eyes. 'She wrote to Catherine, asking for her help, but there is nothing she can do. They say Joanna is mad, because that suits their purpose.'

Mary flinched as the ship plunged through a breaking wave, sending a shower of salty spray into the air. Brandon took off his warm cloak and draped it around her shoulders. 'How is the pain in your side?'

'The motion of the ship makes it ache, but I'll be well enough once we are in France.' She managed a smile. 'You've spent far too much on my new gowns to miss the chance to show them off.'

He grinned. 'They've been worth every penny, Mary. You made quite an impression on Emperor Charles.'

'He hardly spoke to me.' Mary sounded dismissive. 'I think he had more important things on his mind.'

'Like his latest marriage proposal?'

'He cannot marry little Princess Mary. She's been promised to Dauphin François.' Mary sounded certain her brother's plan would fail. 'Whatever would King Francis say?'

Brandon didn't reply but gave her a knowing smile. It seemed everything was a game to Henry. Like his father, he saw his young daughter's marriage as a way to win an ally and keep another in his place. Little Princess Mary would become an empress and the richest woman in the world.

Calais harbour was a noisy confusion of ships moored together in rafts. It was early evening by the time the *Katherine Pleasaunce* joined the melee, and it was a struggle to get the horses ashore before the light failed. Barrels of wine and crates of supplies were piled high on the quayside and the crisp evening air rang with shouted commands.

After a restless night as the guests of a wealthy merchant of the Staple, they woke early for the six-mile ride to the Val d'Or.

Brandon rode with Henry, leading his escort of fifty mounted nobles. Mary, as Queen Dowager of France, rode at the side of Queen Catherine. Behind them followed their ladies-in-waiting, a seemingly endless line of grooms and servants, and a hundred mounted yeomen in royal livery.

As the ramparts of Guines Castle appeared in the distance Henry held up a gloved hand to halt their procession. The open fields between the castle and the town of Ardres were dominated by an impressive encampment of colourful marquees surrounding a grand central palace. The tents of the king's household were in green-and-white striped Tudor colours, while others were cloth of gold and burgundy damask.

Henry beamed with pride as he turned in his saddle. 'Quite a sight, don't you think, Brandon?'

'Wolsey has indeed been busy.'

'Thomas Boleyn informs me King Francis has four hundred tents at Ardres.' Henry gave Brandon a scornful look. 'We have seven times as many.'

As they rode closer, Brandon realised their diplomatic mission had become little more than a contest between Henry and Francis. Men like their ambassador, Thomas Boleyn, spied on the French and doubtless they did the same. Wolsey had excelled himself, encouraging Henry's excess for his own profit. The problem was that, whatever the outcome, a lasting peace between the two seemed unlikely.

Wolsey boasted that the encampment took two thousand skilled craftsmen three months to erect. The centrepiece, which Wolsey called the 'Palace of Illusions', had brick foundations to support the weight and was made from wood and canvas painted to look like stonework. Over a hundred paces square, it was guarded by four golden lions and complete with towers at each corner, a gatehouse, battlements and a chapel.

Red and white wine flowed from an impressive fountain in front of the palace, bearing a sign inscribed in old French –

Faicte bonne chere quy vouldra – inviting visitors to help themselves with silver cups. The royal dining hall had gilded tables and chairs, with a ceiling of green silk decorated with golden Tudor roses and a carpet of richly woven taffeta.

Hung with Henry's finest tapestries, Mary and Brandon's apartment adjoined Wolsey's own. It had a gilded bed with a cloth-of-gold canopy of estate which had travelled by wagon and ship all the way from Greenwich. Mary could be in no doubt of the importance of her role in France. She was there to dazzle King Francis and his nobles, an ornament to Henry's court once more.

With perfect timing, cannons thundered from the ramparts of Guines Castle and the town of Ardres, echoing across the plain in celebration as the kings of England and France set out for their first meeting. As the sound of cannon fire died away a sweeter note carried on the still air. A hundred golden bells sewn to the harness of Henry's warhorse jingled as he rode.

That morning he'd told Brandon that the yeomen riding behind him were hand-picked from the best of his royal body-guard. They'd been warned to be alert for any sign of the French deciding to take this opportunity to attack. Brandon had witnessed Henry's courage often enough at the joust, but now he sensed true bravery as the king rode alone and unarmed at the front.

Henry looked magnificent on his striking bay courser with trappings embroidered in gold. Wearing his golden Garter collar over a doublet of cloth of silver, he had a girdle of cloth of gold studded with rubies, and a black velvet cap, plumed with black feathers and sparkling with jewels in the June sunshine.

French trumpeters announced the arrival of King Francis, resplendent in a cap of black velvet with iridescent feathers.

His doublet was embroidered with gold knots, his shirt and sleeves fashionably slashed and decorated with precious jewels. Over his doublet was a cloak of cloth of gold, fastened over his left shoulder.

The two kings cantered ahead of their mounted escorts and met in the middle of the plain. There was a moment of silence as thousands held their breath, then a rousing cheer rang out as the kings of England and France clasped each other's arms. Henry and Francis dismounted and walked together to the French pavilion. The first step towards peace had been taken.

Brandon cursed as he returned from his work preparing the tournament. The tiltyard was too far from the viewing grandstand and the weather turned for the worse, with brooding rain clouds threatening to turn the tournament field to mud. Worse still, Henry had made a fool of himself, providing encouragement to impudent young French knights who taunted them by calling out traditional insults.

Mary studied his face. 'What's happened?'

He lowered his voice, aware they could be overheard through the thin walls of the temporary palace. 'Henry challenged King Francis to a wrestling match.'

Mary raised an eyebrow. 'Dare I ask the outcome?'

'King Francis threw Henry to the ground – but our honour is hopefully restored, as Henry beat him soon after at the butts in an archery competition.'

'I wonder if Francis let Henry win?'

Brandon looked at her momentarily before he realised she was joking. 'Sometimes, Mary, I forget you are not only a Tudor, but also stepmother of the King of France.'

. . .

The crowd applauded and cheered when Mary took the place of honour on the grandstand under her cloth-of-gold canopy of estate. She'd become the beautiful Queen Dowager of France once more in her shimmering Genoese gown of white silk, the golden coronet over her flowing white veil glinting with jewels. Soon the tiltyard echoed to cries from the French nobles of, '*Vive la Reine!*' and, '*Vive la Reine Blanche!*'

Queen Claude, resplendent in cloth of silver, took her place to Mary's right, along with the French king's sharp-eyed mother, Duchess Louise, who was dressed in a gown of dark velvet. Queen Catherine, her long hair proudly displayed under a jewelled Spanish headdress, sat to Mary's left.

The ladies-in-waiting surrounding them caused heads to turn with their beauty and immodest dress. Lady Mary Boleyn, Catherine's attractive maid of honour, eldest daughter of their ambassador to France, wore a revealing gown and Spanish headdress. The most surprising of Queen Claude's ladies was Françoise de Foix, Comtesse de Châteaubriant. The mistress of King Francis dressed to rival even Mary in an extravagant costume of silks and precious jewels.

Once the ladies were seated, the competitors, English and French, paraded on their fine warhorses, with King Henry and King Francis leading. The English wore gold and royal purple, with the French in gold and white. Henry's destrier was caparisoned in russet damask decorated with golden waves, to show his command of the seas.

As they passed, the shields and crowns of both kings were placed at equal height on a gilded tree with green damask foliage in the centre of the tiltyard. The shields of the other competitors were added below until the tree was covered with the colourful badges of the noble families of England and France.

Brandon cantered to the royal grandstand on his black stallion. He wore shining gilded armour with white ostrich plumes on his helm and a purple cape over his shoulders. He rode up to Mary to seek her favour, as he'd done when she was a young girl.

Raising his lance high in the air, he called out in French so everyone could hear. 'My lady Mary, Dowager Queen of France, I would be honoured to ride as your champion.'

Mary stood and reached out with the favour she pulled from a pocket in her gown. The crowd applauded as Brandon's groom Samuel, who'd been waiting for this moment, stepped forward and tied Mary's purple ribbon to his master's harness. Brandon raised a gauntleted hand in salute before lowering the visor of his helmet.

A trumpet blast signalled the start of the tournament and a herald announced in French and English that King Francis would ride against Sir Henry Courtenay, the Earl of Devonshire. Both riders charged with blunted lances, yet the violence of the clash as King Francis shattered his lance against the earl's buckler made the spectators gasp.

The crowd cheered and applauded as Francis waved in acknowledgement. It reminded Brandon of Henry's masked charades, each playing his part – until the final pass, when the earl's lance accidentally struck the French king's helmet with a juddering crash of wood against metal.

A cry of alarm erupted from the French as their king dropped his lance to the ground and swayed back in his saddle. He was helped to dismount and his supporters led him to his tent. After an anxious moment King Francis emerged, without his helmet, holding a cloth to his nose, the first casualty of the tournament.

At last it was Brandon's turn to ride against the Count of St Pol, who dressed in gleaming armour decorated with gold fleurs-de-lis, his warhorse caparisoned in flowing white. Brandon took care to ensure they both broke an equal number of lances. He could have won an easy victory against the French count, but this was a diplomatic mission, not a contest.

He'd persuaded Henry not to ride against King Francis, and instead matched him with French knights who had the skill to allow an impressive display. Henry shivered more lances than any other, then celebrated by making his horse rear and leap in front of the French crowd, until it collapsed under him from exhaustion.

The jousting continued until night fell, the first of twelve days of tourneying, with archery and contests of arms. Brandon agreed with his friend, the French Admiral Bonnivet, that only blunted swords and lances were used, and they did their best to equally match the English and French contestants each day.

The weather became a constant concern, as jousters complained of the stifling heat. Then a strong breeze blew a fine dust from earth pounded by many hooves on to the spectators. The next day the winds became so blustery several tents were blown down, including the French king's sixty-foot pavilion. When the heavy downpour Brandon had feared finally arrived the tourney was agreed as a draw.

Although King Francis sustained a black eye and a bloodied nose, the only casualties of the jousts were Henry's horse, which had to be put down, and a French knight – the only one of the three hundred contestants to be fatally wounded when he was accidentally struck in the face by his own brother. Brandon and Admiral Bonnivet were commended for a successful tournament by King Henry and King Francis.

A temporary chapel was erected in the tiltyard, decorated with finely embroidered tapestries of the Virgin. Cardinal Wolsey presided over a grand Mass, and Henry and King Francis took turns to sing the refrains. Henry was proud of his fine tenor voice, yet Francis took even this as a competition and sang louder and with more feeling.

There was a surprise waiting for them once they'd retired to an open banqueting gallery beside the chapel. King Francis stood and proposed a toast to lasting peace and friendship, then raised his eyes to the heavens. With perfect timing, a rocket made its thunderous way across the cloudless June sky above them, exploding in a crackling shower of bright sparks. The noise startled several horses but drew cheers and applause from the surprised English.

Brandon leaned across to Mary. 'Once again the French have outdone us, and at significantly less expense.'

Brandon showed Mary the note, worded more like a royal summons than an invitation. 'We are commanded to travel to Gravelines, a day's ride north-east, to welcome the emperor's delegation.'

Mary frowned at the prospect. 'Why does Henry think I would ever wish to see the emperor again? What if King Francis thinks me disloyal and stops my allowance? Is Henry prepared to risk everything we've done?'

'So many questions, yet I have few answers, Mary. I suspect our benefactor Thomas Wolsey might gain from this. Before we sailed from Dover he boasted that Emperor Charles granted him a generous pension – and promised his support in a bid for the papacy, when the time is right.'

'Sometimes I wish my brother could see through Wolsey's scheming...'

Brandon held up his hand to silence her. 'Not so loud, Mary. The walls are thinner than our treaty with the French, and Wolsey never works alone. He has a partner in his plan to support this union.'

She gave him a puzzled look. 'Who else could profit from it?'

'It's Queen Catherine who encourages Henry to meet with the emperor. She wishes Henry to confirm the betrothal of Princess Mary to Charles instead of the dauphin.' Brandon frowned. 'I believe Henry knows exactly what is going on – and that this might be a test of our loyalty. We have to play your brother's games, Mary, or face the consequences.'

17

MAY 1521

Brandon studied the florid, careworn face of his old friend Sir Edward Stafford, Duke of Buckingham, a descendant of Thomas of Woodstock – youngest son of King Edward III – and the senior duke in the kingdom. On trial in the Palace of Westminster by his peers, he was accused of high treason and, but for the grace of God, their roles could have been reversed.

He thought of Edward Stafford as a loyal friend, a fellow Knight of the Order of the Garter. He was popular with the people and had been the first to support the young Henry Tudor. He'd been Lord High Steward at Henry and Catherine's coronation, and was present at Mary's ill-fated marriage to King Louis.

Brandon and Mary had shared a jug of fine wine with Edward Stafford and his wife, Lady Eleanor, at the celebrations on the Field of the Cloth of Gold the previous year. He remembered Edward's indiscretion after he'd had a little too much to drink, calling Wolsey a butcher's cur who encouraged Henry's overspending.

Wolsey kept a close watch on them both, but Edward made the mistake of underestimating the ambitious cardinal, who'd inserted his spies into the Stafford household. He'd waited, like a crimson spider at the centre of a web, for the Staffords to provide the evidence he needed. Brandon knew Henry well enough to be certain Stafford didn't have a chance.

A hush fell over the room as Thomas Wolsey entered and took his seat. He wore new scarlet robes and a heavy gold crucifix hung on his chest, as if anyone needed reminding he was God's representative on earth.

Wolsey's face showed no sign of the satisfaction he must feel, to preside over the trial of his most senior critic, a man who'd treated him with open contempt.

Brandon recalled stories about Sir Edward's father, Henry Stafford, executed for his failed rebellion against King Richard III. Edward's widowed mother, Lady Catherine Stafford, was a Woodville, sister of King Edward IV's queen, Elizabeth. She'd later married King Henry's great-uncle, Jasper Tudor. Such ancestry might help Edward's chances, however slim they might be.

Wolsey's lawyer, a hawkish, self-important man in black robes, saw the nod from Wolsey and read out the charge, that Stafford was accused of treasonable thoughts by repeating the prophesy of Nicholas Hopkins, a Carthusian monk from the Priory of Henton, that the king would have no male heir.

The lawyer turned to Edward Stafford. 'How do you plead?' His tone sounded aggressive and Brandon saw discomfort on the faces of his peers. He wasn't alone in being glad to be spared such a damning accusation.

Stafford looked into the eyes of each of the seventeen lords chosen to sit in judgement upon him. Brandon realised that, apart from Thomas Wolsey, they were all men he'd called friends. The lawyer repeated his question, this time more sharply.

'I am innocent.' Edward Stafford's voice carried a chilling

note, echoing in the old Westminster chamber. 'I am as loyal to King Henry as any man here.'

They waited for him to say more in his defence, but it seemed he was resigned to his fate. It took Brandon a moment to recognise that what troubled him was the hint of fear in Edward Stafford's voice. Anyone who'd witnessed the execution of a traitor would never forget the horror and gross indignity of such a death.

Wolsey waved a gold-ringed hand at the lawyer impatiently, as if he had more important demands on his time. Brandon looked at the cardinal and glimpsed the malicious gleam in his eye. He'd always suspected Wolsey would make a dangerous enemy. Now he was certain of it.

'Do you deny saying that His Grace, King Henry, would have no sons, and you would be made king one day?'

'I deny it.' Edward Stafford sounded less sure of himself.

The lawyer held up a signed parchment and passed it to Wolsey. 'You will see, Your Grace, that the accused's own servants, Charles Knivet and Robert Gilbert; his chaplain, John Dellacourt; and his wife's lady-in-waiting, Margaret Gedding, have all made sworn testimonies before God that they witnessed such remarks.'

Wolsey made a pretence of reading the document as if seeing it for the first time, before handing it across to Brandon. Written in the neat hand of a scribe, the signatures of the witnesses were scrawled across the bottom, as if in haste. He wondered what threats or bribes had encouraged them, and passed the incriminating parchment on as the lawyer continued his questions.

'You have armed some four hundred of your retainers. Why is that?'

'For my own protection, when visiting my estates in Wales.' Stafford looked up at their grim faces. 'As any of you here present would have done.'

'Not in preparation for an attack on His Grace, the King of England?'

'No.'

Again, Stafford failed to defend himself. Brandon guessed his family had been threatened in some way. He knew Sir Edward Stafford as a confident debater at the king's council, often outspoken, yet words seem to fail him now his life was at stake.

The lawyer continued. 'I put it to you, sir, that in the presence of members of your household, you also called His Grace, Cardinal Wolsey,' he glanced back at Wolsey, 'an idolater, and accused him of using magic to retain the king's favour.'

Edward Stafford didn't reply. A defeated man, his downcast eyes showed the stark truth of his situation. Brandon had wanted to say something in defence of his friend but, like all the others, he remained silent.

The lawyer turned to Wolsey and handed him a second parchment. 'This, Your Grace, is a sworn statement of witnesses, examined by the king, testifying that the accused plotted to use a concealed dagger to murder our good sovereign lord, King Henry.'

Brandon shivered as he felt a chill on the back of his neck. He thought it an omen, then remembered that on hearing King Francis had cut his hair short, Henry cut his own and ordered his courtiers to do the same. They later found it was because Francis suffered a head injury, but a new fashion was already established.

Henry also decided to shave off his pale ginger beard, but Brandon had grown too fond of his own. He'd had it so long he couldn't return to the time-consuming business of shaving, and his thick beard, now tinged with grey, helped to hide the jagged scar on his cheek.

He stood in line with Thomas Wolsey and his fellow conspirators to see justice done in the name of the king. Armed yeomen kept the gawping crowds at bay, the sunshine flashing from their sharp halberds, polished silver helmets and breastplates.

They watched in silence as Edward Stafford was led up wooden steps to the raised gallows, where the executioner's block sat, a grim harbinger of death. The king's herald read out the sentence, delivered by Sir Thomas Howard at the trial. Brandon had been surprised to see a single tear roll down Norfolk's face as he sent his friend to such a death.

'Hear this, that the right high and mighty prince, Edward, Duke of Buckingham, Earl of Hereford, Stafford, and Northampton, is sentenced to death by execution for treason against His Grace, King Henry VIII of England.' The herald stood back to allow Stafford to say his last words.

Edward scanned the faces in the crowd and his eyes fixed on Brandon's with a look of unexpected defiance. 'I have offended the king, but only through my own negligence and lack of grace.' He paused to compose himself, and Brandon glimpsed the proud man he'd been. 'I hope my disgrace will provide an example and a warning to the other nobles of England.'

To the surprise of the crowd, he began reciting the penitential psalm in a strong confident voice. 'O Lord, rebuke me not in thine indignation, nor chastise me in thy wrath. Have mercy on me, Lord, for I am weak. Heal me, Lord, for my bones are troubled. My soul is troubled exceedingly but turn to me, Lord, and deliver my soul...'

Sir Edward Stafford, Duke of Buckingham, looked detached as a priest gave his final blessing. He remained composed, but his hands shook as he fumbled to unfasten his cloak. He forgave the masked executioner before being blind-folded and kneeling to place his head on the thick wooden block.

Brandon closed his eyes and held his breath as the axe fell with a heavy thud. He heard a gasp of horror from the crowd and made the mistake of opening them in time to see the executioner curse and chop a second and third time before his work was done.

There was none of the usual cheering at the death of a traitor, only a shocked silence, until some brave woman called out in a shrill voice, 'Shame on you all!'

Brandon lay awake in the dawn light, listening to Mary's gentle breathing. The eerie bark of a fox outside their open window woke her. She looked surprised to find him awake and reached out a pale hand.

'Are you still worrying about Henry?' Her voice sounded sleepy.

Brandon was about to deny it but found he wanted to talk. 'I'm wondering how to regain his trust.' He rubbed his eyes. 'Without it we are lost, Mary. Wolsey might, even now, have spies among our servants, watching and listening...' He forced away the nightmare image that kept returning to his mind.

'Henry loves you like a brother. What makes you think you've lost his trust?'

'I keep thinking about Edward Stafford. His only crime was to be critical of Wolsey. They would have to execute half the members of the king's court if such a thing was high treason.'

'I'm sure Buckingham called you an upstart behind your back. You know what he was like.'

'I don't care if he did – it's not a crime he should have died for. People are saying Wolsey did for him out of spite. I've learned that the witnesses all bore a grudge against him of one kind or another. One of his servants had been dismissed for embezzlement and his wife's lady-in-waiting was one of the worst gossips in London.'

'Buckingham plotted against Henry, Charles. He was raising an army. You should be glad you were not caught up in it all.'

'I confess that I am. I'm sure Norfolk wished it had been me on trial, instead of poor Edward. I told you Wolsey said he'd been told to watch me...'

Mary turned to him and gave his beard a playful tug. 'That doesn't mean you are out of favour. Henry has to be seen to treat you the same as anyone else, even if you happen to be his sister's husband.'

'Edward's estates were forfeited to the Crown. Henry kept the best for himself and shared the rest between his favourites, his trusted men. Norfolk gained the most, but even Thomas Boleyn and Nicholas Carew have been rewarded for their loyalty.' He lay back in the darkness and took her hand in his. 'I've been offered nothing.' He heard the bitterness in his voice.

'Nothing at all?' She spoke softly, her voice serious once more.

'In truth, I've no wish to profit from Edward Stafford's downfall. It saddens me to think Wolsey must have acted on Henry's instruction.' Brandon caressed her long reddish-gold hair. 'He went too far accusing Edward of saying he used magic against the king. I knew him well, Mary. He would never say such a foolish thing.'

'Buckingham was fond of his drink, and I've heard him speak disparagingly of Thomas Wolsey. Who knows what any of us might say in an unguarded moment, in front of trusted servants.'

'We have to find a way to regain your brother's favour, Mary.'

She fell silent for a moment. 'If it suits his purpose, Thomas Wolsey will make sure Henry welcomes you back. I still have some jewels hidden away. You can take him one as a gesture of our good faith.'

'I've set aside the income from my southern estates and will offer repayment of a substantial part of our loan. It will provide a good reason to visit the cardinal, spend some time with him.'

'There is someone else you must find a way to spend time with, Charles. Little Harry is five now. You should get to know him.'

Harry drew back the string of the new bow and aimed an imaginary arrow. 'Will you teach me, Father?'

Brandon ruffled his son's long hair, Tudor red-gold like his mother's. Harry was a sturdy boy, adventurous and already a good rider, a true Brandon. 'Of course.' He smiled at a memory. 'When I was your age we had to practise every day, by order of the king.'

'Why, Father?'

Brandon had to think as they walked together to the rear of the stables, where an old straw target served for archery practice. 'The king wanted everyone to know how to use a bow, in case we had to fight the French.'

'Will I have to fight the French?' Harry's eyes grew wide at the prospect, reminding Brandon of Mary's expression when he told her he was off to attack the town of Thérouanne in Artois.

'No, Harry. Archery is a sport these days. We show our skill with the bow to entertain people, not to hurt them.'

Harry looked relieved, then frowned. 'But you hunt deer with bows.'

Not for the first time, Brandon was surprised at his son.

'We use crossbows now, not bows, for hunting. Once you've mastered your new bow, I shall buy you a crossbow, and we'll go hunting together.'

Brandon led Harry to a grassed area ten paces from the straw target. He'd brought a quiver of arrows and took one, holding it out to show Harry. 'See how this feather is different from the others? It's called the cock fletch. Turn your bow and lay this arrow on the rest with the cock fletch pointing up, then nock the arrow on to the string.'

He watched as Harry fitted the arrow, his face a frown of concentration. It was hard to remember what he'd been like as a five-year-old, but he was pleased to see his son doing so well.

'Good.' He nodded in approval. 'Now stand with your feet the same width apart as your shoulders and put your fingers on the string. This one,' he pointed to Harry's little index finger, 'should be above the arrow, and these two below it. Don't hold the arrow with your fingers. Now draw back the string with your back muscles, not your arm, so the string touches the tip of your nose.'

Harry laughed as he pulled back the bow. 'Like this, Father?'

'That's perfect, Harry. Now look down the arrow and line it up with the middle of the target. When you are ready, let the string slip through your fingers.'

Brandon watched as the arrow flew straight and true, striking the straw target in the centre. He felt a strange mixture of pride and regret. He'd promised himself he'd spend more time with his children but was always too busy with matters in London and at his estates. From now on, that would change.

Thomas Wolsey smiled as he felt the weight of the ruby and held it up to the light to admire its quality. The size of an olive and set in a mount of solid gold, it had been a gift to Mary from King Louis of France. Despite her promise to give Henry all her jewels, she'd kept it hidden where no one would see it – until now.

'A fine jewel, Brandon.' Wolsey nodded as he slipped it into the pocket of his doublet. 'Together with the payment you've made, this will keep the wolf from the door.'

Brandon heard the poorly veiled threat, but forced a smile. 'It's been a good year for my Suffolk estates, Your Grace. There will be more where that came from, rest assured.'

'Good.' Wolsey studied him as if making a judgement. 'Now, I wish to share with you a state secret, which must be disclosed to no one, not even your good lady wife.'

Brandon sat up in his chair. Mary had been right. The cardinal still had the power and influence to make or break them. 'You can rely on my discretion, Your Grace.'

Wolsey crossed to the door and checked there was no one outside. 'We cannot be too careful, as the future of the kingdom sits in the balance.'

'Are you talking of war?' Brandon's mind raced as he thought of the possibilities.

'I'm talking of peace – between England, France and the Empire of Rome.' He poured them both a goblet of claret and handed one to Brandon. He raised his own in the air in a toast. 'To peace.'

Brandon raised his goblet. 'To peace.' He tasted the rich claret. A deep purplish-red, it had a delicate fruity scent and warmed his throat with a mellow aftertaste.

Wolsey paused for a moment, as if wondering where to begin. 'You are probably aware that for some years I've been acting as an honest broker between King Francis and Emperor Charles?'

'Yes.' Brandon took another sip of the claret and made a note to take care to keep a clear head. 'Something of a thankless task.'

'It has been almost impossible to follow events abroad, despite our informers. Loyalties ebb and flow as regularly as the tide on the Thames.' He seemed lost in thought, then looked up at Brandon. 'As brokers of the peace we have the moral high ground – yet we stand the risk of having to defend either one if the other attacks their territory.'

'And be drawn into a war not of our choosing?'

'Exactly.' Wolsey sipped his wine. 'Fortunately, the houses of Hapsburg and Valois both need us if they are to stand any chance of defeating the other, so we play for time while we consider our options.' He swirled his claret and took another sip. 'I told you I wish to share a secret. We cannot wait for events to take us by surprise or end up with no alliance, so we have agreed a pact with Emperor Charles.'

'We are going to war with France?'

'Not yet.' Wolsey smiled. 'I am aware of your reliance on your wife's income from France, so I've ensured that as part of our new treaty Emperor Charles will make restitution of an even greater sum.'

'Thank you, cardinal. I can see you've planned this well.' Brandon could guess what Mary would say, but he liked the irony of the emperor having to pay him.

Wolsey nodded in acknowledgement. 'We have agreed in principle to delay any action until next year.'

'It will be a challenge to be ready for war, even by then.'

'I cannot delay matters further, Brandon. We have until next May, when our ambassador will present King Francis with an ultimatum, setting out our accusations against France, including his support of the Duke of Albany in Scotland. In the meantime, I ask you to help us prepare and, when the time comes, to lead our army against King Francis.'

18

MARCH 1522

Ominous grey clouds gathered over London like a bad omen, threatening to spoil the grand Shrovetide joust to be held in honour of the visiting imperial ambassadors. The rehearsals and preparations had taken a month, but the tourney wouldn't go ahead if the clouds turned to heavy rain.

King Henry glanced up at the sky and frowned as he led out his band of knights, chosen from his favourites. His magnificent black stallion was caparisoned in cloth of silver, embroidered with a pierced heart and, in French, the motto: *She has wounded my heart*. Sir Nicholas Carew, also caparisoned with silver, had an embroidered image of a prisoner peering through iron bars, and the motto: *In prison I am at liberty and at liberty I am in prison*.

Sir Anthony Kingston had a heart bound in blue lace, embroidered on crimson satin, and bearing the words: *My heart is bound*. Sir Nicholas Darrel followed, caparisoned with flowing black satin embroidered with gold broken hearts and: *My heart is broken*. Last came Sir Anthony Brown, in silver with broken spears and hearts, and the words: *Without remedy*.

Brandon raised an eyebrow at the fanciful mottos. The

noticeable absence of the queen suggested the king was playing a game of courtly love with some new young mistress. He wondered what the dour young Emperor Charles would make of it all when his ambassadors reported back.

His own knights were resplendent in russet velvet and cloth of silver, embroidered with golden branches, and their lower armour plated with gold at huge expense to the royal treasury. They cantered into the tournament from the other direction to Henry and his knights, as if they were two great armies about to do battle.

The jousting was arranged by Brandon as a show – entertainment rather than a competition – each rider taking care to make a spectacle of shattering their lances in front of the emperor's delegation. To do so safely required expert horsemanship and skill with the lance. Only the best were chosen, and this was seen as a rehearsal for a show for the emperor's visit in May.

Brandon seemed to be alone in worrying about how these men would fare when the time came for them to be tested against a real enemy. The French would be fighting on their own territory, defending their land with battle-hardened soldiers. The English had few experienced commanders and had not fought a battle for many years. The outcome would be determined by the will of God.

Candles and scented oils in iron cressets lit up the great hall of Wolsey's palace at York Place with a warm, flickering light. The pageant was Henry's idea, created by his pageant master, William Cornish, and organised by Thomas Wolsey to entertain the visiting delegation on Shrove Tuesday evening.

The hall had become an enchanted forest, the walls disguised with impressive tapestries of hunting scenes.

Branches of real trees and bushes painted silver and gold helped to create the illusion of a woodland clearing.

At the far end of the hall a green castle reached to the rafters. With a working drawbridge and high battlements, the central tower was flanked by two smaller ones decorated with embroidered banners of broken hearts, a hand holding a heart, and a hand turning a heart.

Watching through a secret spyhole in the far door, Brandon saw that the high tiers of wooden benches provided for courtiers along both walls were already full. Again, there was no sign of Queen Catherine, but a magnificent cloth-of-gold canopy of estate covered the gilded chairs provided for the imperial ambassadors. It seemed excessive to Brandon, but it was a sign of how important Wolsey's new alliance had become.

He'd been pleased when Henry invited him to take part in the charade. Such things had been fun when he'd been a young man with few responsibilities, but now he felt foolish in his pointed, cloth-of-gold hat and bright-blue satin cloak. He wished he was a spectator – at thirty-eight he was the oldest taking part.

Henry also chose Mary to take a leading role in the pageant. The pains in her side had eased as quickly as they had come, so she was sleeping through the night and had more energy. News of the planned invasion of France had inevitably leaked out and Mary had been saddened, but Brandon managed to conceal his involvement without having to lie to her.

He was pleased to see Mary rehearsing the dances with Queen Catherine's ladies-in-waiting, particularly the vivacious Lady Anne Boleyn. Anne had recently returned to England from Queen Claude's court, and was full of gossip about the latest news from France.

Although she didn't have Mary's natural beauty, Anne

Boleyn had an engaging, attractive confidence that turned men's heads. Like Brandon's daughter, it seemed she'd learned a great deal at the court of Margaret of Savoy, before joining her sister as the French queen's lady-in-waiting.

The minstrels began to play an alluring melody as the ladies emerged from a side door of the wooden castle. Their faces hidden behind golden masks, they all wore diaphanous white satin gowns with Milanese headdresses decorated with gold and diamonds and embroidered with their pageant names.

Brandon felt oddly envious to see the ambassadors eyeing his wife, the curves of her body visible through revealingly translucent silk, then reminded himself it was only a foolish pageant. Wolsey had tipped the delicate balance of power by allying with their guests against France, and this charade was simply another of Henry's games.

As they paraded past the ambassadors, each of the ladies stopped to curtsey and announce their pageant names. Mary was first and attempted to disguise her voice, speaking in French as she said, 'I am the virtue of Beauty.' Lady Mary Boleyn followed, announcing herself as the virtue of Kindness. Lady Anne Boleyn told them her name was Perseverance. The other ladies curtseyed in turn and said they were the virtues of Honour and Constancy, Bounty, Mercy and Pity.

The musicians struck up a sinister note as seven bare-footed maids in black rags, their faces darkened with soot, explained they were the vices of Danger and Disdain, Jealousy, Gossip and Unkindness, Scorn and Strangeness. Their role was to haunt the dark corners of the forest and prevent the lords from besieging the castle.

Stirring music and a staccato drum roll announced the entrance of the swaggering, masked lords, dressed in cloth of gold and bright-blue satin. Their leader, wearing flamboyant crimson satin decorated with golden flames, bowed before the ambassadors and grandly announced himself as the Lord of Ardent Desire.

Brandon stepped forward next and bowed to the audience on both sides of the hall, announcing himself as the Lord of Amorous Love, while the other lords bowed and revealed that they represented Nobleness, Youth and Devotion, Loyalty and Pleasure, Gentleness and Liberty.

On the thumping boom of a drum, supposed to represent cannon fire, Mary called for her ladies to follow her to the safety of the castle. Once they were all inside they raised the wooden drawbridge, securing the door. Brandon, Henry and the other lords besieged the castle, while the maids dressed in black did their best to defend it by throwing sugar-coated comfits.

The disguised leader of the lords called out in a commanding voice. 'As Ardent Desire, I order you to surrender the virtues!'

One of the black-garbed women replied, 'As Scorn, I refuse you.' Another called out, 'As Disdain, I have no fear of you or your lords.'

The lords threw large ripe oranges, brought as gifts by the ambassadors, several striking the green wooden castle with hollow thumps, making the ladies hiding inside call out for mercy. Some of the ladies were armed with cups of rose water, which they threw over the lords, soaking their fine silks.

Brandon was becoming concerned the siege was getting out of hand when the musicians struck up a lively dance, the signal for the ladies to surrender. The black-garbed maids escaped through the side door and the drawbridge lowered, allowing the ladies to emerge from the castle.

The lords each took one of them by the hand and they danced a pavane, changing partners in the formal pattern of steps until each had danced with them all. When the dance was finally over, the lords and ladies pulled off their masks to make the great reveal of the pageant.

The Lord of Ardent Desire was not Henry, but Master William Cornish, cleverly masquerading as the king. Henry then revealed he'd played the part of the Lord of Devotion, to riotous cheering and applause from the ambassadors.

At the lavish banquet which followed, the ambassadors seemed in good spirits and one made a speech. On behalf of the emperor, he thanked King Henry for the hand of his daughter Princess Mary, and raised his goblet, proposing a toast to a new and prosperous alliance between England and Spain.

Brandon threw himself into helping with the preparations for the emperor's visit, determined to show his worth to Henry. The time was drawing close for delivery of Wolsey's ultimatum to King Francis, so the new alliance with Emperor Charles became more important than ever.

Wolsey and Brandon welcomed the emperor, surprised to discover he'd brought not only the senior nobles of Castile, Aragon and Flanders, but an entourage of over two thousand people. These included his own physicians, priests and cooks, as well as more than a thousand Spanish horses.

Wolsey sent for Brandon. 'You must return to London to requisition more accommodation.' He gave Brandon a wry look. 'I don't mind how you do it, but it seems we've been invaded by imperialists!'

Brandon frowned. 'There is hardly enough time, despite all our preparations.'

Wolsey glanced over his shoulder. 'I'll put up as many as I can at York Place – and I expect you to do the same at Suffolk Place. Put them in the Tower if you must. I'll delay the unloading of the emperor's baggage, and I've sent a rider to tell the king in Canterbury. I've suggested it would be timely if the king would take the emperor on a tour of the *Henry Grace à Dieu* and impress him with our navy's readiness for an invasion of France.'

'Has your ultimatum been sent to King Francis?'

Wolsey nodded. 'The Clarenceux King of Arms has delivered the full list of accusations. We will have our war, Brandon, ready or not.'

In a grand flotilla of thirty barges, all flying colourful pennants and led by the king and emperor in the gilded royal barge, they processed up the Thames to Greenwich Palace. Henry ordered all ships not in Dover to be moored on each bank, decked out with royal standards and banners. The emperor flinched as they surprised him with a royal salute of cannon fire as he passed.

Queen Catherine, surrounded by her ladies in all their finery, proudly presented her young daughter to the emperor in the great hall of Greenwich. Although only six years old, Princess Mary had been dressed in a gown and glittering headdress as if she were a fully grown woman.

To everyone's amazement Emperor Charles kneeled before Queen Catherine and asked for her blessing. In that moment, she was transformed from a virtual recluse, kept out of sight in her chambers, to the most important person in Henry's court.

At the grand banquet which followed, Brandon found himself seated next to the emperor's Portuguese ambassador, Charles de Poupet, Seigneur de la Chaux, and discovered it was simply the Spanish tradition when meeting the mother of one's betrothed.

The usually restrained Emperor Charles surprised them all by taking little Princess Mary's hand and trying to dance a galliard with her. He looked uncomfortable doing the athletic dance, with its measured leaps, jumps and hops, although the young princess danced with elegance and grace. She had also become fluent in Spanish, with the help of her mother and her tutors.

Brandon had to extend his loans once more to host a banquet at Suffolk Place, where the sheer number of guests overwhelmed his kitchen staff and drank the entire contents of his wine cellar in one evening. Mary travelled from Westhorpe with Annie for company, and their daughter was presented to both the king and the emperor.

The celebratory joust which followed was the same as that held for the ambassadors in March, except it included all the riders charging at the same time, and the prize was awarded to Brandon's 'army' of knights. The high point of the day was the arrival of the French king's denial of all Wolsey's charges, which Henry took as reason to declare war on France.

Brandon read the terse note from Mary, who'd returned to Westhorpe Hall while he continued his preparations for war in London with Wolsey. Their son Harry had suffered a serious fall and had not risen from his bed for several days. Mary hadn't given any details but begged him to return with the king's physician.

He had a busy day planned – an important meeting with Wolsey, and another with the Master of the Royal Armoury to discuss doubling the production of weapons. The preparations for an invasion of France were taking too long, so Henry had agreed to pay whatever it cost.

Brandon read Mary's letter again, wondering why she hadn't given more information. It was natural for a mother to worry, but boys were resilient and little Harry seemed tougher than most. It would be foolish to make the seventy-five-mile ride to Suffolk only to find his son had made a full recovery.

Mary had no idea how busy Wolsey was keeping him, although the fact he no longer had to make all the preparations in secret made the whole enterprise a little easier. He reached for his quill to reply to her, then recalled his promise to spend more time with his son.

Instead he wrote a short, apologetic note to Wolsey, explaining that an urgent matter in Suffolk demanded his attention and he would return as soon as he could. He wrote another requesting the king's physician to make his way to Westhorpe Hall, then sent a servant to find Samuel and have him prepare the horses.

~

Mary's face was a mask of sadness. 'You're too late.' It sounded like an accusation.

Brandon felt a flicker of annoyance; he hadn't wasted a moment in coming. 'I came as soon as I could...' He frowned at the tears running down her face. 'Too late?'

She nodded but seemed unable to speak, gripping the doorframe with slender, gold-ringed fingers, as if she might collapse. After a long moment of silence, she composed herself and looked at him with cold eyes. 'Our little boy is gone.'

Brandon felt a sudden emptiness, deep in his chest, like a physical wound which took his breath away. He had a sudden image of little Harry's delight at scoring a bullseye with his new bow. He took Mary in his arms and felt her whole body shake as she surrendered to her grief.

His daughters, Annie and Mary, sat with him in the peaceful room he used as a study, with views out over the deer park. At fifteen, Annie had become a beautiful and capable woman, able to run their household without help from Mary, and look after little Frances and Eleanor, now aged five and three.

His wife slept upstairs in her bedchamber, although it was

mid-afternoon. She'd been unable to answer his questions, so it seemed better for her to rest. Brandon's grief turned into guilt as he kept dwelling on how little of his time he'd spared to share his son's short life.

'I want to know what happened.'

His daughter Mary spoke first, with a confidence that made her seem older than her twelve years. 'Harry was shooting arrows at the doves.' She shook her head, just as his first wife Anne used to. 'He said he was hunting them, like Father...' She looked away, unable to say more.

Annie continued. 'We think he climbed the dovecot to recover his arrows and hit his head when he fell on to the cobblestones.' Her voice was matter-of-fact and a little hard, her way of dealing with the grief. 'We sent for the physician from Bury St Edmunds, but he said there was nothing he could do.' Her voice softened and she brushed away a tear. 'He didn't suffer, Father. He just went to sleep and didn't wake up.'

Alone in the privacy of their chapel, Brandon took a taper and lit two votive candles, watching as the tiny flames flickered and took hold. One was for his son, who could one day have become the King of England. The second was lit in memory of his late wife, Anne. Both had been taken before their time.

He'd been spending time with his daughters, both of whom reminded him so powerfully of the first woman he'd truly loved. Brandon could imagine how proud she would have been of her two girls, now both ready to be introduced at court. He'd thought Anne was gone forever, yet her spirit lived on through their daughters.

He kneeled at the altar and prayed for the strength to go on. He'd told no one, even Mary, but he dreaded the prospect of leading an army to invade France. He'd had luck on his side at the capture of Thérouanne and the siege of Tournai. Now he felt his luck deserting him. He was a show jouster, not a warrior knight, and wondered how many good men would die because of it.

Brandon thanked God for his wife and four daughters, the only people in the world who truly mattered to him. He'd put his ambition and concerns for his place at Henry's court before his duty to his family, and now he paid the price.

He looked up at the image of the Virgin Mary, cradling her child, and prayed for the soul of little Harry, his life so cruelly cut short. In a flash of insight, he understood how Henry had been changed by the loss of his children, as had his father before him. At last, he allowed himself to mourn, and wept as he released the pain and sadness deep in his heart.

19

MARCH 1523

Brandon could hardly believe the news. 'We're going to have another child?'

Mary smiled at the surprise in his voice. 'I'm certain of it, and I pray it will be a boy. No child can ever replace Harry, but...' Her voice faltered.

He saw the sadness return to her eyes and took her in his arms. 'Be strong, Mary. This child will help restore your faith, give us hope.'

He'd been worried about how she'd descended into despair, rarely leaving the house. The loss of their son hardened her heart and turned Westhorpe into a place of mourning. A child could offer them hope of a new heir to inherit the Suffolk estates. A fresh start.

'You won't be disappointed if it's a girl?' Her voice was almost a whisper.

'Of course not.' His assurance hung in the air, sounding like the lie it was.

The tragedy brought them closer as a family. He returned from London whenever he could, often riding through the night. He'd promised to be a more attentive husband to Mary and a better father to the girls.

Mary spoke softly, as she did when she wanted something from him. 'I feel the need to restore my faith.' She gave him an imploring look. 'Will you allow me to travel to Butley Priory?'

'I can't think of a better place for your confinement.' Brandon smiled. 'I don't want you riding, though. I'll take you in the new wagon. Annie will look after our girls, and little Mary shall stay with you for company.'

The newborn baby swaddled in white linen was a strong and healthy boy, as Brandon had known it would be. A tear ran down Mary's cheek as she cradled the tiny child in her arms, as if he might be stolen from her at any moment.

The midwife told him it had been an easy enough birth and Mary showed no signs of a fever. Brandon had begun to fear the worst during the long silence, so when at last he heard the sharp sound of a baby's cry it felt as if a great weight had been lifted from him.

He kissed her. 'The two of you remind me of the Madonna and Child.'

Mary looked up at him with wide eyes. 'My faith is restored, Charles.' She held her baby tight. 'God has graced us with a perfect son.'

'We'll name him Henry.' He frowned as she shook her head and lowered his voice so only she could hear. 'He might one day be King of England. There seems little prospect now of Catherine having more children.'

'My sister Margaret has a son, James...'

'Henry would never wish to hand his throne to a Scot.' He smiled as he looked at his new son. 'We must name him Henry. My mind is made up.' He watched for her reaction. Her face was impassive and for a moment he doubted he'd ever understood her.

Mary turned away from him to look into the innocent eyes of her son. 'Welcome to my world, Henry Brandon.'

He held Mary close as they lay awake together, listening to the creaks and noises of the old house in the darkness. They'd argued about a royal summons requiring Mary's presence to entertain Queen Catherine's niece, the emperor's sister Isabella, visiting with her husband the King of Denmark. Mary wanted to plead exhaustion after the birth of their child, but Brandon disagreed.

He ran his fingers through her long, red-gold hair. 'It will be good for you to return to court, and right that you do so if the queen asks for your support.'

'I could be away for weeks...' She sounded unsure.

He tried a different approach. 'I've heard the Queen of Denmark is quite a beauty.'

'What about the children? I would miss our little son...'

'We have nursemaids and servants enough, and it will be good for little Mary to have more responsibility.'

'Annie will travel with us?'

'As your lady-in-waiting. Perhaps this is an opportunity to propose her as a lady-in-waiting to the queen?'

Mary lay back and stared up at the velvet canopy over their bed for a long moment. 'I dread to think what could become of our Annie at Henry's court.'

'You're not ready to part with her?'

'I value Annie's company here at Westhorpe. You won't forget your promise to find her a good husband, someone close to her own age?'

'I'm planning to make Annie a baroness, but don't say anything to her. I don't want her to know until I'm certain.'

'Or me? You keep too many secrets from me, Charles. You've said nothing about my brother's latest mistress. If I'm to visit Queen Catherine I need to know what my brother's up to behind her back. Has he sworn you to secrecy?'

'You must promise not to speak of this to anyone.' He lowered his voice to a whisper. 'Henry sees Mary Boleyn – or Lady Mary Carey, as she is now. They've kept it secret from all but his closest circle.'

'I guessed as much, so I'm sure Catherine knows.' Mary leaned over and kissed him. 'I owe it to Catherine as a friend to support her. Is there nothing you can do to influence my brother?'

'I can't even influence my wife.' He pulled her close to him again. 'For the sake of our family we must take care not to cross the king.' His voice sounded serious. 'Remember what happened to the Duke of Buckingham.'

It took over a week to make the hundred-mile journey to Greenwich. London always seemed noisier and dirtier to Brandon after the serenity of the Suffolk countryside. As they passed through the city gates they were welcomed by a corpse, dangling on a gibbet.

Brandon noted the vigilance of the armed guards at the entrance to Greenwich Palace, a sign the country simmered with unrest. There was opposition to the king's new taxes to fund an army. The people didn't share Henry's ambition to make war on France if it meant they had to pay.

The Danish king seemed pleased with the banquet in his honour, yet was proving a poor companion for Brandon. A sallow-faced man with a pointed black beard and wide-brimmed hat, King Christian's strange accent made him difficult to understand.

The emperor's sister, Queen Isabella, sat between

Catherine and Mary. She had a pale complexion and wore a gown of white silk edged with gold lace, with a starched white coif over her hair in the Danish fashion. She seemed to sense Brandon's stare and smiled at him, revealing crooked teeth.

Cardinal Wolsey, in his scarlet robes, said the grace and formally welcomed their guests on behalf of the king. Once the self-important cardinal was seated, green-and-white liveried servants appeared, to pour wine and set out a bewildering variety of dishes. Brandon thought he should attempt to make conversation with the Danish king.

'What is your first impression of London, Your Grace?'

King Christian thought for a moment. 'The River Thames is like an open sewer – and I wonder why it is necessary to decorate the bridge with severed heads?'

Brandon grinned as he realised the dour king had a dry sense of humour. 'The people of London have short memories, Your Grace. We find it useful to remind them of the consequences if they misbehave.'

Brandon gathered the family together in the spacious new study he'd built at Westhorpe. He glanced at Mary, then turned to his daughters. 'I have to go to France and might be away until next year.'

Annie was the first to speak. 'Are you going to fight the French, Father?'

'I'm in command of fourteen thousand men. It is a great responsibility.'

'But are the French not our friends, Father?' His daughter Mary frowned.

Brandon nodded. 'They are. Our friends and our neighbours.' He looked at their confused faces. 'The king has promised our allies, Emperor Charles and Archduchess Margaret, that England will support a revolt by the Duke of Bourbon against King Francis.' He glanced again at Mary. 'It's my duty to help him keep that promise.'

Annie shook her head. 'There are others who can do that, Father. You haven't been to war for years.'

'Ten years, Annie.' He softened his tone. She was on the brink of tears. 'It's a great honour to be chosen by the king to lead his royal army. If I lead them to victory it will secure the future of our family.'

His mission carried enormous risks. The French were battle-hardened from their foreign wars. The English army were a poor mix of ageing veterans and novices, inexperienced men and adventurers, with little idea what lay ahead of them.

When the time came for him to leave, Brandon gave each of the girls one last embrace and took a long look at little Henry. He kissed Mary and forced a smile, then whispered, so only she could hear, 'I love you. Pray for me.'

Brandon studied her face. He knew she was fighting to remain composed, for the sake of the children. There was so much he wanted to say to her, but now it was too late.

He fastened his gleaming new silver breastplate over his tunic, the badge of his command, and mounted his warhorse. A hundred local yeomen, wearing the blue-and-yellow Suffolk livery, waited for him. Some looked too old to fight; others seemed little more than boys.

Brandon turned to look back at Westhorpe Hall and his family one last time, trying to fix them in his memory, then raised a black-gloved hand in farewell. He led his men over the old stone bridge and on to whatever their destiny might be.

Baron William Sandys, Brandon's second in command and Treasurer of Calais, had a broad barrel chest, a thick grey beard and a liking for rich wine. He'd been a good host and gestured to his serving girl to refill their goblets before he proposed another toast. 'To victory in Paris!'

Brandon responded with less enthusiasm. He'd been kept waiting in Calais for a month for news of Duchess Margaret of Savoy's men. She'd agreed to pay for an army of Dutch soldiers to join them before they advanced into France, but there was still no word.

Sir William sounded a little the worse for drink. A fellow Garter knight, and some fourteen years older than Brandon, they'd served together as Knights of the Body when Henry became king. Sir William helped to arrange the encampment of the Field of the Cloth of Gold and was made Baron Sandys as reward.

Sir William's duties as treasurer kept him in Calais, but he'd been chosen to accompany Brandon's army because of his knowledge of the defences of Paris. He claimed to be experienced in battle and, although Brandon doubted his claim, the baron had somehow earned the respect of the men.

Sir William's servant announced the arrival of the Lieutenant of Guines Castle. Sir Robert Wingfield was Richard's brother and fellow diplomat. He had a reputation as a rough diamond, and more than once the frankness of his dispatches raised eyebrows. Brandon guessed this was why he'd been passed over for the position of Governor of Calais.

Sir Robert carried a well-worn sword at his belt and had battle-scarred armour strapped over his tunic. He gave a nod to Baron Sandys and shook hands with Brandon. 'Good day to you, cousin. I wished to come in person to tell you the good news. Commander Floris van Egmond, Count of Buren, has arrived at Guines Castle with a good number of men.'

Brandon watched as the serving girl, not much older than his daughter Annie, poured Sir Robert a goblet of wine. 'Good news indeed.' He glanced at William Sandys. 'I was wondering if we would ever leave Calais. It's costing a fortune to keep so many men idle, and there's talk of an outbreak of the sweating sickness. Wolsey had to ask the king to find another ten thousand pounds, so we need a result – and soon.'

Sir Robert drained half his wine in one gulp. 'Count Buren seems a good man. He has military experience and hates the French. His Dutch army look an unruly band, but they are well armed.' He emptied his goblet. 'It seems Archduchess Margaret kept her word, despite our misgivings.'

'What news is there of the Duke of Bourbon's rebellion?'

Sir Robert cursed at the mention of the duke. 'None. I don't trust the man, he's a loose cannon.'

Brandon shook his head. 'We're relying on his German mercenaries to open the gates of Paris, Sir Robert, so I hope the duke proves you wrong.'

Brandon turned to Sir William. 'We must send word to our men to be ready to leave at first light – and we should get some sleep, while we can.'

The army looked defeated before they even began the long march to Paris. There'd been an outbreak of a strange fever in the crowded encampment on the outskirts of the town, which some called a plague. Dozens had died in the past week and many more refused to be roused from their tents.

Brandon had to threaten to withhold their pay, and before long his reluctant army began the long march south. He rode at the front with Sir Robert and Sir William. All were wearing armour and carrying their swords, as the French could launch a surprise attack at any time.

Sir Robert scowled up at the brooding autumnal sky. 'I hope we're back in Calais before winter. It's too late in the year for a long campaign – and the last few winters have been cold enough to freeze the gates of hell.'

Brandon agreed. 'I've promised my wife we'll be home in time for Christmas.'

He turned in his saddle and felt a surge of pride as he looked back at the line of over fourteen thousand men, reaching as far as he could see. A third were mounted and some rode supply wagons. Teams of oxen hauled the iron cannons and the rest marched on foot, keeping up a lively pace considering the complaints of illness. 'God willing, we'll prove more than a match for the men left to defend Paris.'

Floris van Egmond, Count of Buren, waited for them as they approached Guines Castle. He wore a flowing black cape over finely engraved silver armour, and a flamboyant ostrich-feather plume on his helmet. Flanked by Spanish knights on black warhorses, he looked older than Brandon expected, with deep lines etched in his tanned face. He called out in French with a Dutch accent.

'Good day, my lord duke.' He held up a gloved hand in welcome.

Brandon raised a hand in acknowledgement and replied in French. 'I am pleased to see you, Buren, and your men. The success of our mission depends on your support.'

'I am honoured.' The count glanced at his men, already mounted and ready to move. 'I suggest we take control of the river crossing at Ancre, and make our camp halfway between here and Paris.'

Brandon smiled, reassured by the count's confidence. 'I agree. Ride with us, Count Buren, so we can discuss tactics.'

Word of Pope Adrian's death travelled like wildfire through France, although it was some days before Brandon had official confirmation from Calais. It seemed a good omen, as Wolsey told him he was confident of being elected now he had the support of Henry and the emperor.

With a victory in Paris and Thomas Wolsey as the new pope, Henry would become the greatest ruler in Christendom. Brandon hoped to be well rewarded on his return, perhaps with the grant of a castle and more estates in the north. At the same time, he dreaded the prospect of failure.

The French defenders of the bridges at Ancre and Bray threw down their weapons in surrender without a fight. Brandon watched as they were forced to swear fealty to King Henry of France, and he began to believe that Paris might also be won without a fight.

They were making better progress than he'd dared to hope and made camp in meadows a mile outside the peaceful French town of Montdidier. Sir Robert led a scouting party ahead to check the defences of Paris, only two days' ride south, and the men had a much-needed break from marching.

As if waiting for a signal, the skies opened with a relentless downpour of freezing rain, turning the green fields to a sea of slippery mud. In no time the rain soaked through the thin canvas of Brandon's tent, dripping on to his papers and bedding, as if Mother Nature was trying to discourage him from reaching Paris.

He wrote a letter home, telling Mary only the good news. It might take some time for his letter to reach Suffolk but it should stop her worrying. He didn't mention there had been a new outbreak of the sweating sickness among his soldiers, or that there seemed no respite from the icy rain, now turning to hail.

To make things worse, the money he needed to pay his men had not arrived, and he was forced to send Baron Sandys back to Calais to discover the reason for the delay. Somehow word had got out, and a militant deputation of the men wished to see him.

Brandon lay awake on his damp bed until dawn as he made one of the hardest decisions of his life. He would have to give his word to his men that every penny owed to them would be paid when they returned to England, even if it had to be from his own purse. If Henry and Wolsey refused to reimburse the money, the promise would ruin him and leave his family deep in debt.

The men stood in the heavy rain, water dripping from helmets and soaking their tunics. They listened to his promises with stony faces. Some shook their heads and muttered before returning to the shelter of their flimsy tents. The Count of Buren stood at Brandon's side for support and turned to him with concern in his narrowed eyes.

'If you cannot pay your men, my lord, it will only be a matter of time before they start vanishing into the night. You should warn them that deserters will be hunted down and executed. Make an example of the first one you catch.' He made a cutting motion with his hand. 'It must be an example none will forget.'

Brandon felt repelled by the suggestion of executing his own men but knew he might have no choice. He must keep discipline, or any chance of success would slip away like the deserters. 'You are right, but I hope it won't come to that. I've given them my word.'

Sir Robert Wingfield returned grim-faced from his scouting expedition, with worrying news. 'The emperor has failed to distract the army of King Francis. The city remains as well defended as ever.' He cursed. 'Worse still, I regret to tell you the Duke of Bourbon's rebellion has come to nothing, as expected.'

The count turned to Brandon. 'We have to change our

plan. Paris is out of the question, so we must choose another objective, where we stand a better chance of success.'

Sir Robert shook his head. 'We have more than enough men between us. Paris is ours for the taking, if we can breach the defences.'

'What do you suggest?' Brandon saw the look of grim determination on Sir Robert's face.

'Send to Guines for battering rams. There are several at the castle. We'll smash open the gates of Paris and show the French what we're made of. I'll not return to Calais without a fight.'

'I agree.' Brandon worried about this turn of events. He'd never had so many lives in his hands and felt poorly prepared for such a burden of responsibility. 'While we wait, we'll keep the men occupied with an attack on Montdidier – and the townspeople shall all swear loyalty to King Henry of France!'

Two weeks passed without news of payment from Sir William in Calais and the men grew restless. The Count of Buren talked of sending his men home if the battering rams didn't arrive in one more week. Sir Robert caught the sweating sickness and hadn't been seen for days.

Now it was Brandon's turn to take to his bed with a fever which left him shivering with the cold one moment, then burning with a heat which made his head ache. He'd neglected to bring a physician on their 'great enterprise', as Wolsey called it, and now he paid the price – the dreaded sweating sickness.

Shivering in the darkness, he opened his eyes to see the count leaning over him. 'How long have I been sleeping?' He saw the frown on the count's face and tried again, this time speaking French.

'Long enough,' the count replied in his heavy accent. He

pulled a thick fur cape around his shoulders and studied Brandon as if arriving at a decision.

Brandon tried to sit. 'Is there news of Baron Sandys?'

'No.' The Count of Buren peered out of the tent flap into the driving rain. 'There is no news of your battering rams, or payment for your soldiers. Many of your men have deserted, and those who remain are eating the horses. Some have died of the fever and several froze to death in this cursed French weather.' He scowled. 'You need to make your way back to Calais, my lord duke.'

Brandon groaned, then remembered he wasn't alone in suffering with the sickness. 'How is Sir Robert?'

'Gone.' The count continued to watch the heavy rain outside.

'He's dead?' Brandon's voice was a croak.

The count shook his head. 'He recovered enough to return to Guines Castle. I regret to tell you, my lord, I've decided to dismiss my men. There is nothing for us to do here.'

Brandon reached out and grabbed him by the arm. 'You must stay – and help me win a victory for King Henry. I can't return to England until I do.' He felt the fever sap his strength and he struggled to continue. 'I will die in France before I surrender.'

Floris van Egmond, Count of Buren, left without replying. Brandon lay back on his bed, damp with sweat, and watched the freezing rain drip from the roof of his tent. He'd failed his men and failed his king. There was no choice: he would have to admit defeat. He shivered in the grip of the sickness and called out, but no one came.

20

MARCH 1525

Brandon returned from Wolsey's great enterprise in France a changed man, with greying hair, his spirit broken. It took over a year for him to recover, and he stayed in Suffolk, returning to the royal court only when he had to. He sometimes woke Mary with his shouting in the middle of the night and confessed to bad dreams about those harrowing months.

His voice sounded cold in the darkness as he spoke. 'I didn't know how long I'd been suffering from the fever, but when I could rise from my bed I found my army and horses were gone. The Count of Buren's men and his own mutineers looted any supplies of value.'

Mary caressed him as he closed his eyes at the memory. 'You've never told me how you made it back.'

'Good men died for no good reason, Mary. You remember Samuel, my groom? No man was ever more loyal to me, yet I led him to a futile death in France...'

She kissed his cheek. 'It was God's will. You cannot blame yourself—'

'It was Wolsey's will.' He took a deep breath before continuing. 'Only a handful of loyal men remained, so we set out on foot to make the long walk back to the coast. We lived off the land, foraging for what we could, but I was soaked by the freezing rain and collapsed from exhaustion. I was ready to surrender.'

'You owe your life to those men who helped you return to Calais.' Mary kissed him again and lay her head against his chest.

'I do. I exercised my right to reward the nobles with knighthoods, and reminded the soldiers of my promise to make sure they were paid, which I have done. We saw no sign of deserters in Calais, but I ordered that if any were caught they were to be hanged.' He heard the bitterness in his voice.

It was rare for Brandon to speak about what happened in France, but he cursed the turncoat Charles, Duke of Bourbon, and the devious emperor, for keeping his Spanish army camped on the frontier at Narbonne. He blamed Archduchess Margaret of Savoy for causing delay. And he blamed the weather, so cold he suffered frostbite in his fingers. He also blamed himself.

He'd done all that was humanly possible, and taken eight French towns in six weeks, without a single English casualty. He could be accused of treason for choosing to ignore the king's orders to proceed to Paris. He had failed to deliver Henry the victory he sought and, as the commander in the field, it was his decision not to attempt a long and costly siege of the city.

Henry might have locked him away in the Tower, for returning home without permission. Instead, he forgave him. He knew Brandon was a man of his word and how greatly he'd suffered in the freezing fields of France. Even after the jousting accident last year, a worrying time for them all, the king refused to blame him.

His vision obscured by his helmet, Brandon's lance struck Henry's visor with a jarring blow and shattered into sharp splinters. Henry was lucky to survive the accident and rode several more courses to show he was uninjured. Brandon was deeply shaken and swore never to ride against the king again. Henry suffered headaches, yet never blamed Brandon.

Instead, he made Brandon the Earl Marshal of England, to the disgust of his rival Sir Thomas Howard, the new Duke of Norfolk, whose father had been the previous Earl Marshal but died the year before. Brandon knew his new title rubbed salt into the wound of the long-standing enmity between their families, but there was nothing he could do.

Thomas Wolsey sat back in his gilded chair, a self-satisfied expression on his face. He'd put on weight from good living and wore the gold chain of the office of Lord Chancellor over his scarlet robes. He waved a parchment at Brandon. 'King Francis has been captured at a battle in Pavia, and is held prisoner by the emperor in Madrid.'

Brandon couldn't conceal his surprise. 'This news changes everything.' He realised Wolsey had chosen to tell him before word spread, as it soon would, and guessed the reason.

Wolsey smiled. 'Indeed it does.' He looked down at the parchment. 'I am informed that a musket ball injured the French king's horse, which fell upon him. It seems our troublesome Yorkist pretender, Richard de la Pole, was also killed in the battle. France is now vulnerable under the regency of the king's mother, Duchess Louise.' The scorn in his voice was evident.

Brandon took a moment to think before he replied. He had no wish to return to another futile war in France. 'We must not underestimate Duchess Louise. She is an ambitious woman, and fiercely loyal to her son.' He frowned. 'We have also learned we cannot trust the emperor's word—'

Wolsey's eyes narrowed as he interrupted. 'He did not only

let you down. He used our money for his own purposes, and forgot his promises to us.'

Brandon understood why Wolsey sounded angry. He'd expected his election to become the new pope to be a formality and everyone, including Henry, had treated him accordingly. Instead, he had suffered a humiliating defeat and now the king's trust in his judgement was undermined.

It had been Wolsey's plan to march on Paris, rather than besiege Boulogne. It was Wolsey who'd failed to ensure they could pay their army and Wolsey who misjudged the commitment of the Duke of Bourbon. Brandon believed if anyone was to blame for the failure of the great enterprise, it was the man who conceived of it – Thomas Wolsey.

Wolsey had also promised payment from Emperor Charles to replace Brandon's French pension and Mary's dowager income. So far, not a penny had been paid. Although Brandon knew better than to mention the fact, the arrears were accumulating and he would have to raise the matter before long.

He looked directly at the self-important cardinal. 'Our army is in disarray. It will take time and money to prepare for a new invasion, and we must learn from the past. We cannot rely on men like the Duke of Bourbon, or on Duchess Margaret. Before we consider returning to France we must have the money to pay and equip our men.'

'Which is why I've called you here.' Wolsey looked pleased with himself. 'His Grace the king has ordered me, as Lord Chancellor, to take advantage of this unexpected opportunity.'

'The council will not be persuaded to support more taxes for another war. The last is too fresh in their memory.'

'I don't need the approval of council.' Wolsey scowled at the thought. 'I am sending out my commissioners to raise a new benevolence, an amicable grant of one sixth on all goods – and one third on ecclesiastical possessions. The king shall have his victory in France, and you will help restore our army.'

. . .

Applause from the small crowd of waiting villagers welcomed the fine carriage, pulled by a team of white horses. Brandon wore an ostrich-plumed hat with his black fur coat and his gold chain of office as Earl Marshal of England. He beamed with pride as he helped Annie step down.

His daughter looked radiant in her shimmering wedding gown, the result of months of embroidering gold thread on the finest silk. She wore the pearl-rimmed French headdress Mary had worn for their wedding in France. Small diamonds set in the filigree border of her gown flashed in the early spring sunlight as she moved.

At eighteen, Annie looked more like her mother than ever. Watching her effortless charm, Brandon felt the deep sense of loss as he remembered how he'd fallen so deeply in love with Anne Browne. She would have been so happy and proud to see how their daughter had grown into a beautiful woman.

All heads turned as they entered the church and he led her on his arm to the handsome Edward, Baron Grey of Powys. Brandon had kept his word. The baron was wealthy, with significant estates in Wales, and only four years older than Annie. One of the few who'd stayed at Brandon's side on the disastrous mission to France, he'd been one of those knighted in Calais before their return.

The choir fell silent and the aging Bishop Foxe began the formal marriage ceremony. He'd come out of retirement as a favour to Mary, despite his failing eyesight. Brandon guessed the elderly archbishop must be close to eighty years old, yet his voice still carried authority in the still air of the abbey church.

Brandon reached out and took Mary's hand in his as he watched his eldest daughter marry. There had been times in France when he believed he'd never live to see this day. Through God's grace he'd been given a second chance, and now he intended to do everything in his power to secure the future of his family.

Wolsey's messenger brought orders for Brandon to take his retainers and disperse rioters in nearby Lavenham with the Duke of Norfolk, in the name of the king. He'd shown the terse note to Mary. In Wolsey's own hand, it looked hastily scratched.

'Have you not done enough for Thomas Wolsey?' There was an edge to her voice.

Brandon frowned. 'It seems fitting work for Thomas Howard's private army of yeomen. They are little more than mercenaries, employed to do his bidding. I can barely muster a hundred local men, poorly armed and of questionable commitment.'

'Is it going to be dangerous?'

Brandon pulled on his riding cape and fastened his sword to his belt. 'I would rather not become involved in enforcing Wolsey's tax but he gives me no choice.' He cursed under his breath. 'Henry's been wishing for another invasion of France ever since King Francis was captured in Italy. Now Wolsey seeks to win his favour by raising the money he needs, regardless of the consequences.'

Mary embraced him. 'Cardinal Wolsey knows it's an impossible task. Too many protest against this amicable grant. While he sits drinking good wine in his fine palace, you risk your life to enforce his unfair taxes.'

Brandon looked at her with a raised eyebrow. 'You sound like the rebels, Mary, but you are right. Parliament never approved Wolsey's amicable grants. It's little wonder people are refusing to pay.'

'I'm concerned for you, Charles. There's no telling what these rioters might do.'

'Norfolk is bound to be heavy-handed if I'm not there to see people are treated fairly. We'll round up the ringleaders and the rest will soon disperse.' He gave her a farewell kiss on the cheek. 'Wish me luck.'

Brandon heard the shouts and jeering before they even reached Lavenham. It was impossible to tell how many had gathered in the town square, but it looked like many thousands. His heavily outnumbered men looked at him with anxious faces.

A well-dressed man, who looked like he might be a wool merchant, stood on a raised platform and spoke passionately about why they should challenge any further taxes on their goods. His words were met by a rousing cheer and applause from the crowd, who seemed united against Wolsey's plan.

Sir Thomas Howard rode to Brandon's side on an impressive black stallion and studied the crowd. 'These so-called rioters look to me like ordinary enough folk, trying to make an honest living.'

Brandon turned to him in surprise. It seemed he'd misjudged Norfolk. 'I agree – but we have our orders, in the king's name.'

Norfolk smiled. 'Do we take orders from cardinals now? Our master is the king, but I didn't see his signature, only that of Thomas Wolsey.'

'What do you suggest?'

'That we give Wolsey a kick up his scheming backside.' He urged his stallion forward and rode alone into the centre of the crowd, which fell silent and parted to make way. 'I am the Duke of Norfolk,' he glanced at Brandon, 'and this is the Duke of Suffolk. Disperse in peace and we will put your case to the king.'

Someone in the crowd called out. 'Will the king listen to us, my lord?'

Norfolk scanned the crowd, looking to see who had shouted the question, and called back his reply. 'Who can know the mind of His Grace the king?' He glanced back at Brandon. 'But I give my word that your concerns will be presented. Now disperse – or face the consequences.' The threat in his voice was clear.

A man who seemed to be one of the ringleaders called out. 'Do as he says. We've achieved what we came here for.'

A ragged cheer came from the crowd and Brandon watched as they began to return to their homes. The few who remained soon ran when Norfolk's armed yeomen rode towards them, unsheathing their swords and seizing a number of the stragglers.

Brandon turned to Thomas Howard. 'I have to congratulate you – although I will be interested to see what the king has to say.'

Howard grinned. 'Our king has been careful to distance himself from this amicable grant, as has his royal council. My guess is he'll be angry with Wolsey. The cardinal's power is on the wane.'

As Brandon rode back he worried about whether he'd been right to support Thomas Howard. If Wolsey was prevented from raising enough money to fund an invasion, he wouldn't have to go war. Preserving the peace might have come at a price though, and he hoped he hadn't just made a dangerous enemy.

Like Wolsey's Hampton Court Palace, the rambling, red-brick Bridewell Palace, on the banks of the River Fleet, had high chimneys and was surrounded by spacious open courtyards. Built by Henry at considerable cost, it served as a replacement for the old Palace of Westminster, which had been gutted by fire.

The grand banqueting hall was crammed with the entire court, who'd come to witness the investiture ceremony. Brandon and Mary watched proudly as their infant Henry was confirmed as the new Earl of Lincoln. As well as securing his son's place in the nobility, the title completed Brandon's control of the former de la Pole legacy.

It would have been the talk of London, but for the investiture which followed. Queen Catherine looked stony-faced as the king's trumpeters sounded a fanfare. Brandon presented the king's son, Henry Fitzroy, now wearing the crimson blue mantle and coronet of a duke, to be made the Earl of Nottingham and Duke of Richmond and Somerset.

Henry had already made his son a Knight of the Garter, and allocated the second stall in St George's Chapel to him. He called his son 'my worldly jewel' and knew what he was doing. His bastard prince now took precedence over his only daughter, Princess Mary.

Brandon liked staying at the peaceful old manor of Ewelme in Oxfordshire, recently granted by Henry as a present to Mary. Henry had used Ewelme as a private retreat, and was still expected to visit when on his progress or for occasional hunting trips.

There was only room for the necessary servants, and the smaller rooms were cool in summer and easy to keep warm in winter. A herb garden flourished under the open window of their bedchamber, and the delicate scent of thyme, lavender and rosemary drifted up to them in the still air.

Brandon lay back in their comfortable bed and listened to the dawn chorus, identifying the tuneful warble of a blackbird and the repeated phrases of a song thrush. The horrors of the futile war seemed a long way away, yet another seemed inevitable if Wolsey had his way.

When Mary woke she turned and put her arms around him in a sleepy embrace. 'Our agents have returned from

France and are visiting today. I pray they bring good news from Duchess Louise about the arrears I'm owed. It's been three years and nine months since we've received any dower payment, thanks to your wars.'

'My wars?' Brandon was about to remind her how he'd been drawn into her brother's plans, then realised she was teasing him. 'Any payment would be timely. I meant to tell you. Wolsey has begun to take his revenge on me.'

She tensed in his arms. 'What has he done now?'

'Ordered a search in the exchequer to itemise my debts to the Crown. He's not missed a thing and seems determined to have repayment of at least a thousand pounds a year. He's also taken my lands in Wales.'

'Can he do that?' She sounded surprised.

Brandon frowned. 'I knew it was a mistake to cross Wolsey over his taxes. He claims to be converting the council of the Welsh Marches for the benefit of Princess Mary, but he's replacing the administrators with his own men.'

'You did nothing wrong in Lavenham, Charles. Your orders were only to *disperse* the people, not to persuade them.' Mary sat up in bed and looked indignant.

Brandon reached out and pulled her back down to his side. 'I think Norfolk implicated me in his plot deliberately, to stop me joining forces with Wolsey against him.'

Francis Hall waited for them when they returned from their morning ride. An experienced negotiator, well versed in the world of the French court, his father Thomas had been a wealthy merchant of the Staple in Calais, which is where he met and married Brandon's cousin, Elizabeth Wingfield.

At his side stood James Denton, wearing a cleric's black gown and cap. Denton had been in Mary's service since her marriage to King Louis and was one of her most trusted intermediaries. Brandon had last seen Denton as the royal chaplain at the Field of the Cloth of Gold. He was now the Dean of Lichfield.

They both removed their hats and bowed as Mary and Brandon dismounted. 'My lord. My lady.'

Brandon greeted them and led them all inside to the great hall, where a servant poured wine. 'I trust you bring us good news, gentlemen?'

Francis Hall smiled. 'We do. Duchess Louise of Savoy has agreed a generous payment on your dower lands, with all the arrears to be paid in twice-yearly instalments.'

Brandon raised his goblet. 'Congratulations, to both of you.' He glanced at Mary. 'That is considerably better than we hoped for, in the present circumstances.'

James Denton raised a hand. 'I regret we cannot take the credit, my lord, although we would of course have done our best.'

'Then who is it we should thank?' Mary looked puzzled.

Denton took a sip of his wine before answering. 'Cardinal Wolsey made the arrangement, before we even arrived at the palace of Duchess Louise. He has also included payment of your French pension, my lord.'

Brandon found it hard to believe that Wolsey had been negotiating on their behalf. 'Are you certain of this?'

Denton nodded. 'The duchess confirmed it.'

Brandon turned to Mary. 'You realise what this means?'

Mary smiled. 'Wolsey has ensured we have the money to repay what we owe him. Perhaps you should write him a letter of thanks.'

21

MAY 1527

Much had changed since the release of King Francis the previous year. Emperor Charles had spurned the young Princess Mary, tired of waiting for her to come of age. He chose instead to marry Queen Catherine's niece – the beautiful, twenty-four-year-old Princess Isabella of Portugal, granddaughter of Queen Isabella of Castile and King Ferdinand of Aragon.

Undeterred, Henry promptly agreed for his daughter to become engaged to Henri, the eight-year-old Duke of Orléans. Although the second son of King Francis, the betrothal would help to bind the new peace between England and France. As well as a generous dowry, Henry had also been promised a pension of fifty thousand gold crowns.

A delegation of ambassadors and dignitaries arrived from Paris to agree a new treaty of eternal peace, to be sealed by the marriage, and a great celebration was to be held at Greenwich. Mindful of the success of Wolsey's 'Palace of Illusions' in France, the king decided to have a temporary banqueting house and a special theatre built at either end of the tournament field.

Brandon went to inspect the work in progress, attracted by the sounds of men hammering and sawing wood, and was surprised at the scale of the buildings. Over a hundred feet long and thirty feet wide, they reminded him of the palace at the Field of the Cloth of Gold, with the same smell of fresh sawdust and paint mingling with grass, damp with the morning dew.

Sir Henry Guildford, who Brandon served under on the fateful voyage of the *Sovereign*, now carried the white staff of Comptroller of the Household. As Master of the Revels, he was responsible for overseeing the arrangements for the royal banquet and masque, as well as making sure the building work was completed on time. He raised a hand in greeting as Brandon approached.

'Impressive, don't you think, Duke Charles?'

'It seems a lot of trouble and expense for a few ambassadors.' Brandon smiled as he studied the huge timber frames, which workmen on ladders were covering with heavy canvas. The hammering he'd heard was the sound of them nailing it in place.

Sir Henry gave him a conspiratorial look. 'The gold fittings are gilded lead, and we've built the whole thing to be dismantled in a few days, to be reused another time.'

Brandon frowned at the large painting on the far wall of their victory at the Battle of Thérouanne by Master Hans Holbein. 'Might that not offend our guests?'

Sir Henry shrugged. 'It's there by the king's order. He said it will serve as a reminder to the French of why they should value this peace treaty.' He pointed to the biblical tapestries showing the story of David, already mounted on the length of one wall. 'The king wanted something more fitting, but there are hundreds of these, stored from the days of his father, so it makes good sense to give them an airing.'

As well as the tapestries, Brandon realised even the

mullioned windows and ornate candelabras – gilded lions, dragons and greyhounds holding candlesticks – had all come from the old king's palaces. Henry had been able to create a grand impression for the ambassadors at little real expense.

A team of carpenters were busy building a gallery for the king's minstrels. Brandon nodded to the king's sergeant-painter, Vincent Vulpe, who he'd known since his early days at court. Vulpe was putting the finishing touches to a colourful painting of the royal arms on the front panel.

'Will your work be dry in time, Master Vulpe?'

Vulpe grinned as he recognised Brandon. 'With luck, my lord.' He pointed with his brush at a series of wyverns, dragons and other mythical beasts. 'We've been kept busy day and night painting that lot.'

Brandon glanced up as more workmen struggled to cover the ceiling with yards of bright red buckram, embroidered with golden roses and pomegranates, the emblem of the queen. As he watched the men at work, a servant appeared to tell him his wife had arrived and was waiting for him in the great hall. Brandon wished the sergeant-painter luck and went to find her.

Since the untimely death of Queen Claude, Mary had resumed her status as Queen Dowager of France. Despite her continuing illness, she'd agreed to come to Greenwich when she was summoned by Henry as guest of honour for the grand banquet. Such prominence also helped Brandon's standing at court, particularly now he was one of the few men of the 'old guard' remaining.

He spotted Mary with a small group of ladies-in-waiting. 'I'm sorry I've been too busy to write.' He kissed her on the cheek. 'You know what it's like on Henry's progresses.' He watched her sharp eyes take in his greying beard and his fine new clothes, and felt conscious of how he'd put on weight since he'd given up jousting.

'You look well, Charles.' She flattered him as she had as a

young girl. Mary glanced around the half-empty great hall, which was usually full of chattering courtiers. 'I understand my brother has done some much-needed pruning since I was last here.'

He smiled. 'There were too many taking advantage of Henry's good nature and draining his coffers. Wolsey saw the chance to remove those who opposed him and, as you see, there is hardly anyone left.'

With a jolt he recognised his daughter, waiting a little behind his wife. 'Mary, it's good to see you again.' Now sixteen, she was the same height as her stepmother and wore one of her fine gowns, with a French-style headdress.

She gave him a confident curtsey, as if meeting him for the first time. 'Good day to you, Father. I am here as lady-in-waiting to the queen.'

He gave her a quizzical look. 'I wasn't aware...'

She smiled at Mary. 'To the Queen of France.'

Brandon sensed a change in his wife's mood when she returned from visiting the queen in her chambers. He led her to a quiet corner. 'What troubles you, Mary?'

'The pain in my side has returned.' Her hand moved to her ribs. 'The roads on the journey here from Westhorpe have not improved.'

'Should I send for the queen's physician?'

Mary held up a doeskin-gloved hand to stop him. 'I shall be well enough to attend the banquet, but first I must tell you something.'

Brandon guessed what it might be. He'd been sworn to absolute secrecy by Henry but, as always, the rumours had already begun to circulate. 'What has the queen said?'

Mary looked to see they could not be overheard, and lowered her voice to a whisper. 'Catherine confided to me that

Henry sent an envoy to Rome, to see if a way could be found for their marriage to be annulled.' She looked saddened for a moment, then composed herself.

'Nothing will come of it, Mary, you may be sure of that.' Brandon recalled Wolsey's warning, that after eighteen years without a legitimate heir, Henry believed he'd broken God's holy law by marrying his brother's wife. The only way to prove their marriage invalid was if Catherine confessed to consummation with Prince Arthur, which she would never do.

Mary gave him a questioning look. 'The queen also informs me that you've purchased the wardship of the daughter of the widowed Baroness Willoughby.'

'Yes, the girl is nine years old and a wealthy heiress. She lives at Parham Hall, a day's ride east of Westhorpe, and young Katherine Willoughby will be a good match for our son—'

'I would like to be consulted about your plans for our son's future.' There was a sharp edge to her voice.

'She is the same age as our Eleanor. They will be company for one another.'

Mary nodded. 'The queen is grateful for our help. Maria Willoughby has always been her favourite lady-in-waiting. I simply wish I'd known of it before—'

A fanfare from the king's trumpeters interrupted her, summoning them to the banquet. Brandon led his wife and daughter through a long, canvas-covered gallery to the new banqueting hall, where a group of musicians with lutes accompanied a man singing of courtly love in a fine tenor voice.

Although Brandon had seen the hasty preparations, he was impressed by the quality of the finished work. The soft light of candles flickered in iron sconces and on the gilded candelabras. Tables had all been set with Henry's golden, gem-studded plate, brought from the Tower of London.

King Henry, dressed in an ermine-fringed cape over cloth of gold with a red-dyed ostrich feather in his cap, greeted them and gave Mary the place of honour, seated at his right hand, as the Queen Dowager of France. Queen Catherine was, again, nowhere to be seen.

Brandon sat with one of the senior French ambassadors, Charles de Solier, Count of Morette. About the same age, they'd first met at the Field of the Cloth of Gold. An impressive figure in furs and slashed sleeves, the count greeted him warmly in accented English.

'My lord, Duke of Suffolk.' He smiled. 'I'm pleased we meet again as friends.'

'So am I, Count Charles.' Brandon shook his hand, relieved to sense no hostility. 'How is King Francis?'

'The king is fully recovered from his ordeal, by God's grace.'

Brandon gave him a wry look. 'It's true he is engaged to marry the emperor's sister, Lady Eleanor of Castile?'

The count nodded. 'It was a condition of his release. I confess to being surprised, particularly as she was engaged to the traitor Bourbon.'

'An unlikely match, although Lady Eleanor was the first choice for King Henry. I'll wager King Francis will delay the marriage for as long as possible.'

'He spends so much time with his new mistress, Lady Anne de Pisseleu, he's taken to referring to her as his wife.' The ambassador raised his goblet of wine. 'To such women, Duke Charles. She is a *bon vivant* and has restored the king's spirits.'

Brandon raised his gilded goblet and returned the toast. 'To such women, Count Charles. Where would we be without them?'

Cardinal Wolsey said an overlong grace, praising King Francis in glowing terms. Brandon marvelled at how completely Wolsey had switched his loyalty. The French delegation would never have believed that this man of God, dressed in scarlet robes, would have destroyed them if his bid for the papacy had been successful.

Servants in Tudor livery brought gilded platters of conger eel and sturgeon, crane and peacock. Then followed plates of rabbit and jugged hare, young lambs and veal. The French ambassador chose a dish of spiced heron, surrounded by small wild birds, all roasted and glazed with sweet honey.

He dipped his bread in the rich sauce and turned to Brandon. 'I confess, my lord, we French make jokes about your English food, yet this is as fine a banquet as any I've attended.'

Brandon used his knife to carve a thick slice from a steaming haunch of venison spiced with ginger. 'Be sure, Count Charles, to report this fully to your king. If this banquet helps secure a lasting peace between us, I shall celebrate every morsel.'

The guests applauded as four strong grooms carried in the centrepiece of the banquet: a manor house, crafted from sugar with a roof of marchpane, and pure white sugar swans, followed by little grey cygnets, swimming in a syrupy moat.

Brandon glanced across at King Henry and saw he'd been distracted. He followed his gaze which rested on a lady talking animatedly with one of the youngest and most handsome ambassadors. It was no mystery why she held the king's attention. Dressed in the latest French fashion, her shapely scarlet gown was cut low at the front, revealing more than most would consider decent.

As Brandon watched, she said something which made the ambassador laugh. Then she turned, calling out to a steward in French to bring the king's best wine. Anyone would be forgiven for thinking she was one of their French guests, but he recognised her as one of Queen Catherine's ladies-in-waiting, Lady Anne Boleyn.

. . .

At the tournament the next day the king wore an impressive jousting costume of purple velvet trimmed with gold. Brandon sat watching in the high grandstand with Mary to one side and his daughter to the other.

Mary placed her hand on his arm. 'I'm not sorry you're not riding, Charles. I heard what happened to your friend, Sir Francis Bryan.'

Brandon agreed. 'He's no friend of mine, but that was an unlucky wound. Bryan will not win any prizes at the joust with only one eye.'

'Are you not taking part because you've sworn never again to ride against my brother?'

'Henry isn't riding today. He says he's sprained his foot playing tennis.' He gave her a knowing look. 'These days, I prefer to leave it to the showmen like Nicholas Carew.'

After the jousting – at which Carew, now Master of the Horse, took the honours – Henry presented a recital in the theatre which he called his 'disguising house'. A carpet of silk embroidered with golden lilies covered the floor, and the proscenium arch over the stage was decorated with terracotta statues.

These would have been enough to impress the ambassadors, but the main feature of the disguising house was the impressive work on the ceiling. Master Hans Holbein had surpassed himself with wonderful paintings of astrological signs. A powerful bull chased a leaping ram, and a roaring lion pursued a crab. A centaur, armed with a bow, took aim at a scorpion as each of the signs of the zodiac ran in a great circle overhead.

Under these was a suspended, transparent silk cloth painted and glittering with silver stars and golden planets. Brandon stared up and realised he was looking at a faithful map of the constellations. Most present had already drunk too much good wine to appreciate it, but he marvelled at how such a thing was possible.

The recital of specially composed poetry in French was too formal for Brandon's taste, but then Henry's musicians struck up a lively dance. Colourfully dressed ladies appeared as if from nowhere, each taking the hand of a different ambassador.

Henry had a surprise he'd been saving for the grand finale. His daughter, Princess Mary, had secretly returned from Ludlow Castle and danced with a silver-netted caul hiding her face. When her dance finished, Henry pulled off her head-dress, letting her long hair cascade over her shoulders, a sign of her purity for the ambassadors to report back to King Francis.

The festivities would have continued all night, but abruptly ended with news that the emperor's Spanish troops and German mercenary soldiers rioted and sacked Rome. It was said their commander, the turncoat Duke Charles of Bourbon, was slain early in the attack. His leaderless army were accused of murdering many men, women and children.

The cardinals had found refuge in Sant'Angelo, but Pope Clement had been taken prisoner. Brandon escorted the French ambassadors back to Dover, content in the knowledge that the Treaty of Greenwich had been signed on behalf of King Francis. He would not have to take another army to war, at least for the foreseeable future.

Suffolk Place looked as grand as any palace. Brandon's improvements, made using borrowed money without Mary's knowledge, were intended as a surprise. The great hall had been converted into a fine chapel for the service, with an altar flanked by tiers of gilded seats with red velvet cushions.

The decorative floor tiles, imported at great expense from Paris, were covered with a scattering of red and white rose petals. Beeswax candles added their warm light and honeyed scent. Brandon wished to show off their wealth and success at the wedding of his daughter.

Mary sat in the place of honour under a canopy of estate with Queen Catherine and Princess Mary. The remaining places were taken by familiar faces from every noble family in England. Sir Thomas Howard, Duke of Norfolk sat alone, without his wife, Duchess Elizabeth, as he'd caused a scandal by leaving her to live with the daughter of his steward.

Also absent was Cardinal Wolsey, sent on a special diplomatic mission by Henry. Brandon heard he'd taken several chests of gold to use as bribes. Although the purpose of his journey was a mystery, Brandon guessed Wolsey's mysterious mission concerned Henry's plans for the annulment of his marriage to Queen Catherine.

The bride, soon to be Duchess Monteagle, had shone at her first visit to Henry's court and now looked magnificent in a gown of silk decorated with pearls. Mary's wedding present, a precious sapphire pendant, once part of the Crown jewels of France, sparkled on a silver chain around her slender neck.

The groom, tall and handsome, wore a silver sword on his belt, a present from the king. Young Thomas Stanley inherited his late father's title of Baron Monteagle and was named after his grandfather, Lady Margaret Beaufort's fourth and last husband, Thomas Stanley, the Earl of Derby.

Bishop John Fisher had been chosen to officiate. Apart from the greying hair showing under his mitre, Bishop Fisher looked almost as he had when the old king had been on the throne, his sharp eyes missing nothing.

Brandon took his daughter's hand and escorted her to where her future husband waited. His other daughters, Frances and Eleanor, now ten and eight years old, followed in silk bridesmaids' gowns. Little Henry, now Earl of Lincoln and next in line to the throne, was dressed like a miniature of his father for his role as his stepsister Mary's page.

Brandon realised how swiftly the years were passing as he heard his daughter repeat her vows in a clear and confident voice. It seemed only a moment ago when he'd held her in his arms as a newborn baby, yet now she would become a duchess, and would soon have children of her own.

22

MAY 1529

Brandon had mixed feelings as he stood alone on the foredeck, watching the familiar outline of Calais slowly emerge from the sea mist, twinkling with lights in the dusk. His memories of his last visit to France still haunted him. It was an honour to be chosen by King Henry for this important mission yet, once again, he'd been caught up in the ebb and flow of Wolsey's scheming.

His task was to encourage King Francis to launch a joint attack on the emperor. Cardinal Wolsey had persuaded Henry that Pope Clement, once free of imperial control, would look more favourably upon what they were all now calling 'the king's great matter'. Brandon doubted it, but had mentioned his concerns to no one, and now it was too late.

Accompanying him was Sir William FitzWilliam. Handsome and likeable, Sir William was a distinguished naval commander and ambassador to the French court. He wore the gold chain and sword of a vice admiral, and was a half-brother to Brandon's late wife Anne, as his widowed mother had married Anne's father, Sir Anthony Browne.

He'd been at Brandon's side at Tournai, and was knighted

after the victory, yet was Wolsey's man, there at the cardinal's insistence. Thomas Wolsey had good reason to be concerned, as Henry had given Brandon a special, secret mission. He was to find an opportunity to privately ask King Francis if he had reason to suspect the cardinal was in any way obstructing the divorce.

As they rode towards Paris, Brandon found himself wondering if Henry planned to use him to bring the cardinal down. It would put him in an impossible position if King Francis had evidence of Wolsey's disloyalty. Brandon owed a great debt to Thomas Wolsey. Without his help and support Brandon's life, and that of his growing family, might have taken a very different course.

Brandon suspected Sir William was charged to keep an eye on him and report back to the cardinal. He decided to put him to the test. 'Wolsey expects King Francis will want to take revenge on the emperor but, as with most things, I believe it is more complicated.'

Sir William rode on in silence for a moment before replying. 'This is our last throw of the dice before a peace treaty is agreed between King Francis and the emperor.'

'You think it's a gamble?'

'The emperor wouldn't accept the king's word that he would not retaliate when he was released, so holds his two sons hostage. If I were King Francis, I wouldn't want to risk taking an army to free them. I would be trying to agree terms.'

Brandon frowned. 'Wolsey has too much invested in the success of our mission. If we prove him wrong...'

'Don't worry about Wolsey, he'll already be thinking at least two moves ahead.'

'You make it sound more like a game of chess than a war between the great kingdoms.'

Sir William grinned. 'I suppose it is, and we are simply two knights being brought into play.'

. . .

King Francis welcomed them both warmly to his palace. His once jet-black hair and beard were turning grey, yet he'd retained his athletic physique and still dressed in distinctive black and silver, with an ornate dagger in a diamond-studded sheath at his belt.

Brandon bowed. 'It is good to see you looking so well, Your Grace.' He spoke in French.

King Francis studied him for a moment. 'Duke Charles, how is my stepmother? I understand she has not been seen at King Henry's court for some time.'

Brandon smiled at the king's witty reference, a good sign he bore no grudge for the attempted attack on Paris. 'Lady Mary is well, Your Grace, and asks me to convey her good wishes. She is troubled by a pain in her side, which makes it difficult for her to travel. I know she would have liked to come to Paris with me.'

King Francis glanced at Sir William and back at Brandon. 'I am intrigued to learn what brings distinguished ambassadors to Paris with such urgency.'

'King Henry is concerned for the safety of His Holiness the pope, Your Grace, and proposes a joint venture to liberate Rome.'

King Francis sat back in his chair. 'There was a time, Duke Charles, when I would have welcomed such an offer, but now I must consider the implications.' He smiled. 'I cannot match the banquet provided for my ambassadors by King Henry, but we will dine, and discuss your proposal further.'

Brandon bowed to the king's young mistress, Lady Anne, and kissed her diamond-ringed hand. Her blonde hair showed under a gold filigree hood, much finer and set further back than the fashion in England. His eyes went to her necklace of sparkling gemstones and the letter 'A' embroidered in gold on the front of her bodice, from which a large pear-shaped pearl shone in the light.

Brandon guessed from their quality that the luminous pearl and gold necklace of rubies, sapphires and emeralds were part of the Crown jewels of France, presents from a grateful king. He made a mental note to ask Mary, who might remember them from her time in Paris.

Like Anne Boleyn in Henry's court, it was easy to see why King Francis had become infatuated with Lady Anne de Pisse-leu. Her warm blue eyes shone with amusement as she explained that the king would join them in good time, and she had been sent ahead to entertain them.

She led them down a long corridor to the sumptuous royal banqueting hall, which had a marble-tiled floor and tall glazed windows with views across the palace gardens. Liveried servants lined one wall and a group of musicians tuned their instruments as they waited for the banquet to begin.

The nobles of the French court stood as a mark of respect as they entered. The high-backed, gilded chairs with cushions of blue velvet at the head of the great table were empty. Lady Anne gestured for Brandon and William to be seated, and took the place next to Brandon.

The musicians took this as a sign to begin playing a tuneful melody, reminding Brandon of the Paris of his youth. A young serving girl washed their hands in rose water and dried them on white linen. Another poured dark-red wine into fine silver goblets, decorated with golden fleurs-de-lis. Brandon took a sip and nodded in approval as he felt the wine's sweet warmth.

A seemingly endless procession of servants in the king's livery began carrying in silver plates of choice delicacies. Whole goslings, roasted chickens and pigeons were served with sugared and spiced fruits. An impressive display of langoustines and small fishes, with a large red lobster sitting proudly at their centre, was placed on the table in front of Brandon.

Lady Anne placed her hand on his, an unexpected and intimate contact. She stared into his eyes, as if able to read his thoughts. 'I've heard the stories of *La Reine Blanche*, and the dashing English knight who won her heart.'

'That was a long time ago, my lady.' He felt conscious of her flirtatious touch. Her hand rested only lightly but he could not move his away without risking offence.

She leaned closer to him, unconcerned by the watching courtiers, her voice almost a whisper. 'I confess to great admiration for a man who risked everything for love.'

'I was lucky. There were those who would have had me executed, but I was forgiven by our gracious king.'

'Would you do it again?'

Brandon looked into her azure-blue eyes, surprised at her question. For a moment he wondered if there was a deeper meaning, then smiled at how easily she'd seduced him. 'I've no regrets, Lady Anne.' He finally removed his hand from hers to take one of the black-eyed langoustines, and pulled off its head. 'Tell me, what has become of King Francis?'

She glanced at the empty chair at her side, as if surprised to see that the king had yet to arrive. 'It seems I will have to ask you to be my dance partner, Duke Charles, as well as my dinner guest.'

Over the next few days, Brandon and Sir William were invited to go hunting with the king, to view his fine horses in the royal stables, and even to see an impressive demonstration of volley fire by the king's arquebusiers. The men stood in two rows, and as their captain shouted commands, one rank took aim and fired while the other reloaded with lead shot. The sound of so many guns was deafening, but when it ended Brandon turned to the king.

'It seems the future of war is changing, Your Grace. A mounted knight armed with lance and sword wouldn't stand a chance against such a volley of lead, however skilled the rider.'

King Francis looked pleased. 'It takes a lifetime to master your English longbow, but my arquebusiers need only a few days of practice.' He produced a lead ball from his pocket and handed it to Brandon. 'And this, Duke Charles, can pierce armour at thirty paces, as I know to my cost.'

Brandon understood why they'd seen this show of military strength. He was enjoying his mission in Paris more than he'd expected, yet each time he tried to raise the reason they were there, King Francis was always courteous but evasive. At last, he summoned Brandon to a meeting in his chambers.

'I regret to say you have had a wasted journey.' The king looked apologetic, as if there was nothing he could do. 'Arrangements are being made for a new peace treaty with the emperor at Cambrai.'

Brandon smiled. 'In truth, I believe that is best for France, Your Grace, and trust that your sons are returned to you safe and well.' He took a deep breath. 'King Henry wishes to know if you have any reason to believe that Cardinal Wolsey stands in the way of his divorce.'

King Francis studied him for a moment before replying. 'I knew the true reason you are here. Wolsey has no love for your Spanish queen but, like all cardinals, he is loyal to the pope of Rome. Tell King Henry to take care who he chooses to trust. Our pope is a timid man, but will never allow him to divorce Queen Catherine.'

Sir William had been right, for by the time Brandon returned to London events had already moved on. It seemed Wolsey had known about the possibility of the Cambrai treaty all along. Brandon was relieved. He'd never wished to be the cause of a war, or to make it possible for Henry to divorce Queen Catherine.

The great chamber of Blackfriars had become a court-room, and Brandon sat on the uncomfortable wooden bench as one of the witnesses to a historic judgement. Henry had tired of the games being played by the papal legate, Cardinal Lorenzo Campeggio, and agreed to the hearing to put his 'great matter' to rest.

Cardinal Wolsey sat at Campeggio's side in a velvet-cushioned chair on a raised platform. A year had passed since the papal bull empowering Wolsey to take cognisance of all matters concerning the king's divorce, and six months since Cardinal Campeggio's arrival in London. The king was running out of patience.

Queen Catherine made the matter more complicated by producing a dispensation from Pope Julius, approving her marriage to Henry. Campeggio's solution was simple. He met with Catherine and urged her to take a vow of celibacy and enter a convent.

When Catherine refused, Henry threatened to prevent her from ever seeing Princess Mary again. He'd even come close to accusing her of treason and of being in league with Emperor Charles, but she had the love and support of the people, who now crowded the courtroom and waited in a large gathering outside.

This hearing was unprecedented. Brandon never imagined he would see Henry being questioned like a commoner by Wolsey. He looked across to where Bishop Fisher and Arch-bishop Warham sat, stony-faced, as they waited. They'd made no secret of the fact they supported the queen, and Brandon wondered what consequences that might have for the bishops.

His own position might be equally perilous if the judgement proved not to be in Henry's favour. Mary was widely recognised as the queen's highest-profile supporter, and even though no one could be more loyal to Henry, his enemies might claim he was Wolsey's man. Brandon saw Thomas Wolsey mop his brow and realised his old benefactor knew his future now hung in the balance.

His reverie was interrupted by the court crier. 'King Henry of England, come into the court!'

Henry was already seated to one side, under a canopy of cloth of gold. 'Here, my lords!' His voice sounded irritated and Brandon saw how he gave Wolsey a warning scowl.

The court crier called out again. 'Queen Catherine of England, come into the court!'

Catherine sat opposite Henry with her loyal maid of honour, Maria Willoughby. 'Here, my lords.' Her voice had a confident note, and Brandon was reminded of the proud Spanish princess he remembered at her coronation.

Brandon watched Cardinal Campeggio's face as the king explained how his conscience was troubled by his marriage to his brother's widow. Those listening no doubt recalled that it would soon be the twentieth anniversary of that marriage. Everyone in the room, and probably in the crowd outside, knew the true reason.

Catherine stood in silence for a moment, as if composing herself, then crossed the room and kneeled at Henry's feet. Brandon heard a gasp of surprise from someone behind him. She began to speak, her voice loud enough for everyone to hear.

'Sir, I beseech you for all the love that hath been between us, and for the love of God, let me have justice. Take of me some pity and compassion, for I am a poor woman, and a stranger born out of your dominion. I have here no assured friends, and much less impartial counsel...'

Henry remained impassive as she continued, her Spanish

accent returning as she reminded him how she had been a true, humble and obedient wife and, as God was her judge, a true maid, without touch of man, when they married.

Queen Catherine remained on her knees, staring up at Henry. 'Would you permit me, as my husband and master, to write to the pope to defend my honour and conscience?'

Brandon realised they had all underestimated the queen. Her question left Henry with no alternative. The king had been checkmated by the queen. He watched her with new respect as she gave Henry a graceful curtsey and swept from the court, the hem of her brocade gown swishing on the tiled floor. The crier shouted for her to return but they all knew the hearing was over. Cardinal Campeggio had the excuse he needed to return to Rome.

Brandon returned from London more tired than usual from his ride. Despite his promises, he'd been detained at court longer than intended, and knew he'd have to explain his reasons. He pulled off his leather gloves and unbuckled his sword, handing it to his servant before embracing Mary. She felt frail in his arms, and he noticed the concern on the faces of his daughters.

Frances had been to Windsor Castle at the invitation of the queen as company for Princess Mary, who was only a little older. The experience had been good for her and she seemed to have a new confidence. Eleanor must be turning eleven, and had the same, enigmatic look as her mother.

His young ward, Katherine Willoughby, standing at Eleanor's side, gave him a welcoming smile. Brandon was pleased at how well she'd become part of his family. Mary liked her and she was inseparable from Eleanor, who was the same age. He'd agreed to pay Henry a substantial sum of over five hundred pounds each year for five years for her wardship, but considered it a good investment for their son's future.

He suspected his wife had made a special effort for his benefit, staying up to welcome him home. He noticed how she held one hand to her ribs. 'How is the pain in your side?' He spoke softly, not wanting her usual dismissive response.

Mary looked up at him with dark circles under her eyes. 'I've been better.' She forced a weak smile. 'It's good to have you home. What news is there from London?'

'All they talk about in London is the king's divorce, and the people seem to side with the queen and blame Cardinal Wolsey.'

'Has Wolsey not done everything my brother commands him?'

Brandon shook his head. 'I fear our benefactor's days are numbered. People would blame him for dry summers and freezing winters if they could. Wolsey has never been short of enemies but he has angered Henry once too often – and I sense the hand of Thomas Boleyn behind this.'

'Thomas Boleyn is back at court?'

'He and most of his scheming family.' Brandon frowned as he thought of it.

Mary reached out a hand. 'Not so loud, Charles, the servants...'

'What of it?'

Mary lowered her voice. 'Frances told me Queen Catherine suspects there are spies within her chambers. I think it is best for us all to be careful now.'

'You think Henry would place spies in his own sister's household?' His tone was scornful.

Mary hesitated to answer. 'Who knows my brother's mind?'

'I once thought I did,' he kept his voice low, 'or at least thought nothing he did would surprise me.'

'We live in challenging times. What word is there of Queen Catherine?'

'She is defiant, which angers Henry still further. Norfolk predictably supports his niece, and others follow, to keep in favour with the king. I counted myself among Wolsey's supporters, but now...'

Mary frowned. 'If we are being forced to take sides, Charles, I would be placed in an impossible position.'

'A few brave souls have spoken out in Queen Catherine's defence, such as Archbishop John Fisher, but most, including me, know to keep our opinions to ourselves.'

'What has Bishop Fisher said?'

Brandon studied her pale face. 'He said he would lay down his life for the queen.'

23

APRIL 1532

Brandon saw the look of distress on the man's face, and recognised him as John Peryent, servant to his friend and retainer Sir William Pennington. William was also a Suffolk neighbour and husband of his cousin, Frances.

'What is it, Master Peryent?' He heard the irritation in his voice. He'd promised Mary he would not be late home but it already grew dark outside.

'It's my master, my lord. He's being assaulted by Richard Southwell and Norfolk's men.' Peryent sounded breathless, as if he'd been running.

Brandon felt his annoyance change to anger. Thomas Howard had been openly goading him ever since Wolsey had been found dead, and could do no wrong now the world rotated around Lady Anne Boleyn. Now it seemed he'd turned his attention to William Pennington, well known for his sense of duty and honour.

'Is he hurt? Where is he now?' His mind raced with questions.

'We were by the bridge at the end of Tothill Street, my

lord, he got in a fight with Southwell but there were too many—'

'Take me there now.' Brandon's hand went to the hilt of his sword.

The bridge was a short distance away, close to the abbey precinct. As they approached Brandon saw the small crowd gathered around a dark shape in the road. There was no sign of Norfolk's men, or anyone in authority. He bent down and lifted the corner of the cape someone had thrown over the body.

'My God!' Brandon had seen dead men in France and passed severed heads on London Bridge most days. He felt the cold dread of shock as William Pennington's unblinking eyes stared at him, but it was the bright blood, puddling from a savage slash deep into the left side of his head that sickened Brandon. He dropped the cape back over Pennington's face and turned to the crowd.

'Who saw what happened here?' He struggled to control the tremor in his voice.

A man stepped forward. 'I saw it all, my lord. They were shouting at each other. The other man cut him,' he pointed down at William Pennington's prostrate body, 'on the face and neck with his sword.'

'The other man, was that Richard Southwell?'

John Peryent answered. 'It was, my lord.'

'Richard Southwell killed him?' Brandon always thought Southwell cowardly and a bully, no match for a man like William Pennington.

Another man in the crowd called out. 'It wasn't Richard Southwell who killed him, my lord. It was his younger brother, Anthony Southwell. I know them both and I'm not mistaken.'

Brandon felt a surge of anger at Norfolk's cowardly men. 'Did anyone see where they went?'

The man pointed to the abbey. 'They ran for the abbey, my lord.'

Brandon turned and ran towards the doors of the great abbey of Westminster. He knew the elderly abbot of Westminster, John Islip, would hesitate to harbour murderers seeking sanctuary. With no thought for his own safety, he burst into the darkness of the silent abbey and called out for Anthony Southwell.

Two men emerged from the shadows and grabbed him from behind. He was too strong for them. Then another punched him hard in the face, making his ears ring with the force of the blow. His arms were grabbed again and he struggled, but this time they held him firm.

'Let go of me, you cowardly bastards!' He managed to free his right arm and his hand gripped the hilt of his sword, but his life might depend on what he did next. Despite all his combat experience he'd never used his sword against another man in anger. Then a familiar voice spoke his name.

'Sir Charles Brandon, Duke of Suffolk. Surrender your sword.' The stern voice carried authority.

Brandon looked up into the dark, intelligent eyes of the king's new right-hand man, Thomas Cromwell. 'Tell these men to unhand me, or they will regret it.'

Cromwell took a step closer. 'Do you know the penalty for striking a man of the king's guard? I ask you to leave the abbey in peace, or I'll have you charged with affray and order you to be detained in the Tower.'

Brandon's head still reeled from the savage punch. He'd heard stories of men who'd died mysteriously while locked up in the Tower of London. He forced himself to focus as a thought occurred to him.

'How did you get here so soon, Master Cromwell?'

'Abbot Islip sent for me to come urgently. Norfolk's men sought sanctuary and he was unsure what to do.' He lowered his voice and looked into Brandon's eyes. 'The matter concerns what the king's sister, your lady wife, has said about Lady Anne Boleyn. I went to find you and heard you'd left in a great hurry.'

'Norfolk's men have murdered Sir William Pennington!' Brandon's accusation echoed in the hallowed abbey, loud enough to wake the sleeping kings.

Cromwell's tone became conciliatory. 'You may leave it to me to see that justice is done, Duke Charles. And now you must go.'

Mary sat up in their grand oak bed, a gold brocade coverlet over her and a single candle, burning in a silver holder, lighting up her concerned face. Brandon sat heavily on the bed and held his head in his hands. He'd expected repercussions after Mary spoke out in defence of Catherine, but had no idea what form they would take and when.

Things had seemed to be going well when Anne Boleyn moved to Greenwich and Suffolk Place returned to him. Now he worried about their future. Even though he'd done nothing wrong, he would have fought Norfolk's thugs if he hadn't been stopped by Cromwell and his guards.

'What's happened?'

'Our good friend and tenant, William Pennington, is dead.'

Mary gasped in disbelief. 'How?'

'Norfolk's men.' Brandon cursed.

She lay back in bed and stared at him. 'How did he die?'

'It seems William was provoked into an argument and chased from Westminster by several of Norfolk's thugs.' He turned to her with anger in his eyes. 'They murdered him, then ran for the sanctuary of Westminster Abbey.' He studied her for a moment, unsure how much to tell. 'William's servant told me he hadn't been defending Queen Catherine's honour – he'd been defending yours.'

'I'm so sorry, Charles.' She put her hand on his arm.

He sat in silence for a moment. 'I don't blame you, Mary. You were only doing your duty to Catherine.' He looked at her pale face and dark eyes. She'd travelled to London to defend the queen despite her illness.

Mary frowned at the sight of the bruise on his face. 'How did this happen?'

'I had to go after the men who murdered William. At the time, I didn't know what I was going to do, but I wasn't going to let Norfolk's thugs get away with it. Somehow Thomas Cromwell found out and stopped me.'

'Thomas Cromwell assaulted you?'

'His men did – and he had the nerve to threaten to charge me with affray.' He stared into the grate of the empty fireplace as he remembered. 'I suppose he was doing me a favour. I wouldn't have stood a chance against so many.'

'All this was because of me, because I spoke out against Anne Boleyn.'

'I think we might be done for after this, Mary. We must not forget what happened to the Duke of Buckingham, and poor Thomas Wolsey.'

'Wolsey died of natural causes, in his sleep at Leicester Abbey.'

'That is what they would have us believe.' Brandon sighed. 'Wolsey was on his way from York to London under guard, to answer charges of high treason. He would not have been afraid to speak the truth if he'd made it to trial at the King's Bench.'

'Are you suggesting my brother had him murdered?'

'Who can know what happened? All I am saying is that his sudden death was too convenient. He might have been murdered, or decided to take his own life, rather than face the indignity of a sham trial. It would have been easy enough for his guards to poison his food. Either way, the king did not mourn his loss.' Brandon shook his head as he remembered. 'Henry couldn't wait to seize York Place and move into Hampton Court.'

'I was told how Bishop Fisher was poisoned by his servant. By the grace of God, the bishop is a devout man and chose to fast that day. He was unharmed but several members of his household succumbed and two died.'

Brandon nodded. 'The bishop's cook was arrested. Henry ordered him to be boiled alive, but it's said even then he refused to reveal who was behind his crime.'

'I've put us all in great danger.'

'Your brother would never raise a hand against you. I think Norfolk saw his chance to bring me down. He knew it was pointless trying to goad *me*, so he had his henchmen taunt poor William...' The memory of his friend's staring eyes returned and he couldn't continue.

Mary stayed silent for a moment. 'Could he have sent that servant to make sure you would go after Southwell? If so, then Cromwell's intervention spoiled his plan.'

Brandon stared at her in surprise. 'John Peryent could have been part of Norfolk's plan, but that changes nothing. The king is displeased with us, Mary, and there will be a price to pay.'

Brandon's bitterness against Norfolk took a new turn when he heard that William Pennington's murderers had been pardoned by the king. It was said they'd been overzealous in defending the honour of Lady Anne Boleyn and were fined a thousand pounds, but Brandon knew it would never be paid.

Mary tried to calm him. 'I suspect you'll find my brother to be greatly displeased to have Anne Boleyn's unchastity being discussed by the King's Bench.'

'I can't ignore this insult, Mary. William's wife Frances is expecting a child, who will never now know its father.' He thumped his fist on the table, startling the serving girl who stood waiting behind him.

'Please, Charles. Anything you do will only make matters worse. We shall invite Frances Pennington and her son to live in our household. William can become part of your retinue when he comes of age.'

Brandon nodded but his fist was clenched at the blatant injustice. 'There are men in London I can call on to defend our honour … for a price.'

'And if they are caught, Norfolk will have you charged with conspiring against the king.'

Brandon scowled. 'It pains me to know Norfolk thinks he's won.'

'You mustn't resort to Norfolk's methods, Charles. Cromwell was Wolsey's man and seems to be taking his place at my brother's side. He might be persuaded to help us—'

'I think not,' Brandon interrupted. 'I've learned that scoundrel Richard Southwell was tutor to Cromwell's son, and they are close friends.'

'You could be locked up in the Tower, or worse, if Cromwell hadn't stopped you.' Mary gave him a stern look. 'You will write to Cromwell. It must be a letter of apology, seeking his support in returning you to the king's favour.'

'No!' Brandon pulled his hand away, struggled to calm himself, and then turned to study her face. 'You are right. I have nothing to lose, and who better as an ally than Thomas Cromwell, who seems to have few friends yet is as close to the king as anyone.'

'Except, perhaps, for Mistress Anne Boleyn?'

He gave her a wry smile. 'I'll need your help with the wording. It's not going to be an easy letter for me to write.'

Cromwell's reply astonished them both. Brandon broke the

wax seal and read it through twice. Written in a neat hand the letter was signed with a confident flourish. Thomas Cromwell had exceeded their expectations. He thanked Brandon for his understanding and said the king would visit them to hunt for stags, arriving in two weeks. Brandon handed the letter to Mary.

'We have some work to do.'

Mary took the parchment and studied it.

'My brother is coming to Westhorpe!' She gave him a look of alarm. 'Do you think he will bring Anne Boleyn?'

'I hope Cromwell has advised him against it. The king's visit can only mean we are forgiven.' Brandon grinned. 'You were right, Mary. It seems Henry has chosen a good man to replace the late cardinal.'

'We only have two weeks to prepare.' She called to Eleanor. 'Tell your brother and sister to meet us in the hall – and assemble as many of the staff as can be spared. We have important news.'

The two weeks passed in a hectic flurry of preparation. Every room in the house was repainted and a magnificent new bed purchased for the king. Mary sold some of her dwindling supply of jewels to buy new Arras tapestries. Their team of gardeners toiled to make her neglected grounds ready for the tented encampment that always followed the king on progress.

The children became increasingly excited as the time for the royal visit approached. The girls sewed new silk gowns and even little Henry helped. Nine years old, he shared his father's love of horses and rode out with Brandon and the foresters to scout for stags.

At last the yeoman posted as lookout announced the royal party was approaching. King Henry rode at the front with Thomas Cromwell, followed by his mounted royal guard and wagons carrying his luggage and servants. Mary thanked the Lord there was no sign of Lady Anne Boleyn.

The family stood in a row in the July sunshine as they waited to welcome the king. Brandon removed his hat, stepped forward and bowed.

'Welcome, Your Grace. It is a great honour you do us.'

Henry beamed and embraced him warmly. 'It is good to see you again, my lord Suffolk. We've missed you at court,' he turned to Mary, 'and you, dearest sister, we are most sorry to hear you've been unwell.'

Mary smiled. 'It warms my heart, Your Grace, that you travel here to see our modest home. May I present our son, Henry Brandon, Earl of Lincoln?'

Little Henry stepped forward and bowed. 'Your Grace.'

The king studied him for a moment. 'You take after your father.' He grinned. 'Would you like to ride with us in the hunt?'

'I would be honoured, Your Grace.'

Mary introduced her daughters who each stepped forward in turn and curtseyed to the king. They had decided Katherine Willoughby should remain out of sight, as her mother, Maria Willoughby, had also been vocal in her support for Queen Catherine, and was punished by being banned from seeing her.

Henry and Brandon returned from a successful hunt with a handsome stag. Little Henry was rewarded for his help with a gold angel. The one moment of tension during the king's short visit was when King Henry cursed the lack of progress in persuading the pope to grant a divorce from Catherine. He told them he planned a visit to France to secure the support of King Francis and wished them both to attend.

Brandon gave Mary a warning glance to remain silent. She would be second in importance to Anne Boleyn. It would be

humiliating to attend her former lady-in-waiting, but he understood Henry wanted to use her to send a signal to King Francis
and, most importantly, to Queen Catherine.

Mary smiled at Henry. 'My physicians advise me against
travel, dear brother, although I would ask you to convey my
warmest regards to King Francis.'

Henry stared at her for a moment, a questioning look in his
eyes. 'That is a great shame sister. We sail in October, so you
will reconsider, if your health improves. In the meantime, you
will lend Lady Anne your French jewels.' It seemed he'd known
all along she'd kept them back, and it was a command, not a
request. It sounded like a punishment.

Brandon rode with Thomas Howard behind King Henry
and King Francis as they returned to Calais after visiting the
French court at Boulogne. Behind them followed an army of
retainers, as King Francis had brought over a thousand men
and horses, servants and wagons and mules laden with everything he might need.

Not to be outdone, Henry arranged for a welcome by his
son, Henry Fitzroy, Duke of Richmond, two miles outside
Calais. Accompanied by a hundred armoured knights, the
king's son reminded Brandon of his father at the same age.
Henry Fitzroy was already tall and broad-chested, making him
look older than his thirteen years.

The streets of the town were lined with soldiers in coats of
red and blue, armed with halberds, holding back the cheering
crowds. On the other side of the road were the men of Calais
all dressed in brown coats with scarlet caps adorned with white
feathers.

Brandon patted his borrowed French stallion to settle it as
the cannons of Guines Castle boomed their salute in the
distance, and were replied to by those in the Rysebank Tower.
The harbour was crammed with the royal fleet decked out with

flags and pennants. The town had never looked more prosperous.

He raised a hand and waved to the cheering crowds as their grand procession rode to the great hall of the merchants of the Staple. The only building in Calais with room for so many guests, it had been converted into a temporary chapel for a thanksgiving Mass.

Henry then escorted King Francis to his lodgings, where his chambers were carpeted with cloth of gold and damask, and the walls hung with silks embroidered with realistic-looking roses, which seemed to grow up to the vaulted ceiling.

Brandon found himself missing Mary. She'd been tearful when he left, and would have travelled with him had it not been for Anne Boleyn. So far, he'd managed to avoid the woman who'd caused him and his family so much hardship. She'd not accompanied Henry to the French court at Boulogne, but King Francis had sent the Provost of Paris to Anne Boleyn with a gift of a precious diamond. It seemed he would have no choice but to accept that she had replaced Queen Catherine.

24

MAY 1533

Brandon wore a blue velvet doublet and a feather in his hat as he waited outside the great hall of Suffolk Place, once again converted into a magnificent wedding chapel. His daughter Frances, now a grown woman, laughed happily as she gossiped with Eleanor and Katherine Willoughby, her bridesmaids. Young Henry, acting as her page, looked nervous, although little was expected of him.

Mary had made the long journey from Suffolk, determined not to miss her daughter's wedding. Despite her ill health, she never complained. The pains in her side had moved to her chest, and she was often short of breath. Her overcautious physicians advised against the journey, and Brandon worried about the toll the rutted country roads took on her already frail health. Mary's absence would have brought her illness to public attention, but for far greater news in London.

Henry declared himself head of the Church of England, finally making the long-threatened break with Rome. The previous month he'd summoned the council to inform them that his marriage to Catherine of Aragon had been pronounced invalid by Archbishop Cranmer.

He wasted little time, privately marrying Anne Boleyn and proudly boasting that she already carried his heir. Brandon had to accept that the Boleyns and Norfolk had won, and preparations for Lady Anne's coronation began. Henry made him Lord High Steward and sent him with Norfolk to tell Catherine she could no longer use the title of Queen of England.

It was a difficult duty to be the bearer of such news and, as expected, Catherine reacted badly. She shrieked in dismay, called him a disloyal traitor and locked herself in her chambers, refusing to come out.

Frances reminded him of Mary when he'd first married her. She looked beautiful in her wedding gown with her Tudor red-gold hair unplaited and combed until it shone, worn long as a sign of her purity. She turned to him as they waited to enter, and placed her hand on his arm with unexpected affection.

'Thank you, Father, for everything.'

Brandon smiled back in acknowledgement, yet felt a sting of guilt that he'd spent so little time with Frances he hardly knew her. Despite his promises, he'd become preoccupied with matters at court and his Suffolk estates. Now it was too late.

'I couldn't be prouder of you, Frances.' He saw his daughter's cheeks blush. It was the first time he'd told her.

Two liveried servants pulled open the doors and everyone turned to see the bride. Thomas Howard, seated at the back, was closest to them. Brandon hadn't wanted to invite him, but Mary argued the wedding was a time for reconciliation. Brandon was pleased to see Thomas Cromwell had also come, although he suspected both were only there because of the king.

Henry surprised them all by declaring he would attend the wedding, although without his new wife. He'd arrived in good spirits, accepting congratulations as he passed through the guests to the gilded chair reserved for him.

The choir began singing as Frances and Brandon made their short walk to the altar. Brandon smiled at Mary, looking as beautiful as ever in her new satin gown. After much deliberation she'd chosen to wear her glittering diamond necklace. Henry would be asking how many more jewels she'd kept secret from him, but Mary said she no longer cared.

Brandon's eldest daughters, Anne and Mary, sat with their husbands behind her. Both evoked memories of their mother, helping to make sure he could never forget her. Anne had inherited her mother's attractive looks and Mary shared something of her character.

He was proud of his two baronesses, both dressed in fine silks and wearing precious jewels. Brandon had been saddened to hear that, after eight years of their childless marriage, Anne's errant husband, Baron Edward Grey, had a mistress. Anne responded by openly taking a lover of her own, causing an even greater scandal.

His daughter Mary's husband, Sir Thomas Stanley, Baron Monteagle, had become a favourite of the king, chosen to carry Henry's sword at the forthcoming coronation. They had given Brandon two healthy grandchildren – a boy named William, after Brandon's father, and a daughter they'd named after Frances – but they were hopelessly in debt.

Young Henry Grey stood waiting at the altar and smiled as he turned and saw his bride approaching. Brandon had kept his promise to Mary, as his handsome new son-in-law was only six months older than Frances. The great-grandson of Elizabeth Woodville by her first marriage to Sir John Grey, he'd inherited his late father's title of Marquess of Dorset.

Despite his youth, he'd shown the courage to speak out in support of Queen Catherine. He'd been banished from court, but Mary said it was proof he'd made the right choice for her eldest daughter. Henry had privately promised Brandon that Henry Grey would be allowed to return once he'd learned his lesson.

Frances looked back at him as she stood at the altar, and Brandon once more felt the years passing too quickly. He glanced at his wife. A tear glistened on her cheek. Her white-gloved hand felt frail in his, but it was good for her to be there to see their daughter saying her vows in a clear and confident voice.

Brandon climbed the familiar narrow stairs to see Mary, excuses already forming in his mind. He'd not been able to return to Westhorpe since their daughter's wedding, and he would have to return to London as soon as he could. He forgot his excuses as he saw the change in her. Mary's face looked thin and her voice sounded weak as she reached out her hand.

'I'm so happy you're back.'

'You should have stayed in London, Mary.' He crossed to the window and threw it open, taking a deep breath of the fresh Suffolk air. 'The journey back here is too much for you.' He returned to sit in the chair at her bedside and loosened the front of his doublet. 'I've been speaking to our physicians. They despair of you.'

'I couldn't miss our daughter's wedding, but I wanted to come home, and I'm not sorry to miss the coronation.' Her hand went to her chest as she fought off the pain of speaking.

'The people are still shouting "Whore!" and cursing as her carriage passes.' He didn't add that several had been arrested and charged with treason.

Mary managed a weak smile. 'My former lady-in-waiting has won my brother's heart but not the affection of the people.' She lay back and closed her eyes, a sign she needed to rest.

Brandon took Mary's hand. Once her gold rings were so tight

she couldn't take them off, but now they felt loose on her slender fingers. He was glad to see her open her eyes, as he thought he'd have to wake her. He sat looking at her for a moment, knowing that what he had to tell her could only add to her pain.

'I have to return to London, Mary, there is much I have to do.'

'You've only just come home.' She sounded tired.

'Eleanor and Katherine have promised to care for you until I return,' he smiled, 'and Henry will be the master of the household.'

He kissed her. 'I love you, Mary Tudor.'

She called out as he turned to go. 'I need you here, Charles. Please, stay with me a little longer.'

He forced a smile. 'I promise to return as soon as I can.'

He said his farewells to Henry and the girls, then went outside and mounted his waiting horse. He took one last look up at Mary's window, hoping to see her face there, or a wave of her hand as she'd always done, but realised she'd been too unwell to rise from her bed.

He'd told her the truth. There was much to do before the day of Anne Boleyn's coronation. Although he could have used Mary's illness as an excuse, people would interpret his absence as lack of support for the king. He urged his horse forward and began the seventy-five-mile ride back to London.

Brandon travelled with the lords behind the queen's barge as their procession made its way from Greenwich up a choppy, grey River Thames. He could see where the queen's badge had been stripped from the stern of her royal barge and the grasping white falcon of Anne Boleyn fixed in its place, a sign of things to come.

He watched the oarsmen straining against the outgoing tide and silently cursed the Boleyns and all they stood for. He hated the pretence he saw all around him and the injustice shown to Queen Catherine, and to Mary for supporting her. Anne Boleyn brought out the worst in Henry, and men like himself had no choice but to play along with her relentless ambition.

A crowd of curious onlookers waited to greet them at the Tower of London, where King Henry, dressed in cloth of gold, welcomed Anne Boleyn and kissed her hand. Cannons roared in celebration from the Tower and the ships of the king's fleet until no one could be left in any doubt. The coronation of a new queen had begun.

Lady Anne rode from the Tower for her procession through the city in a silver carriage pulled by two white palfreys. Four lords dressed in scarlet held a canopy of silver over her head. More carriages followed with her ladies-in-waiting, then her gentlewomen riding white horses caparisoned with silver.

Brandon rode behind, leading the lords, ahead of the king's yeomen, all wearing crimson velvet. Thomas Howard, who would have been riding at his side, had somehow managed to be away in France on a mission for the king. Brandon envied him. He would rather be anywhere than riding behind the king's mistress.

All the guilds lined the route in their liveries, and at Cheapside the mayor and aldermen assembled to present Anne with a heavy purse of cloth of gold containing a thousand gold angels. Brandon could imagine what they said in private about such a generous gift from the city. He had no doubt many of them felt the same as him, but could never take the risk of speaking out.

Under a clear blue sky on Whit Sunday, the grand procession left Westminster Hall with the abbots, bishops and archbishops, and all the lords in their parliamentary robes. Brandon led the way, carrying the heavy crown of St Edward, the first time it had been used by a queen consort.

Anne Boleyn followed under a canopy of cloth of gold and wore a kirtle of crimson velvet trimmed with ermine and a robe of purple velvet. The old Duchess of Norfolk struggled to carry her long train, and they were followed by ten of Anne's ladies-in-waiting, all in robes of scarlet trimmed with ermine and wearing gold coronets.

Brandon felt his arms begin to ache under the weight of the ancient, holy crown. His reversal of loyalty had secured his place in the new court, yet it created a strange mix of pride and defeat to have such a prominent role. As the people cheered and applauded and called out, 'God save the queen!', he wondered if they'd been paid to do so.

He watched as Anne Boleyn, who'd once helped his wife to dress, sat in the royal throne on a high platform before the altar and was anointed and crowned Queen of England by the arch-bishops of Canterbury and York. It felt like the end of an era as the choir sang a *Te Deum*, and Brandon wondered what changes the new one would bring.

He woke Mary with a tender kiss on the cheek. She opened her eyes and stared at him. 'You've returned.' Her voice was a whisper.

'I promised I would. I bring good news, Mary. Thanks to Master Thomas Cromwell, the king is reconciled with you again.'

Her eyes went to the jewel in the silver-handled dagger at his belt as it caught the light of her candle.

'A gift from the king?' There was a note of disapproval.

He glanced down at the dagger. 'Your brother is grateful for my support. He made me High Constable for the corona-tion day.'

'That means he recognises you as the senior earl.'

'It might, but Norfolk was away in France, and has demanded to be made Earl Marshal in my place.'

Mary frowned. 'Thomas Howard? The man is a rogue, who beats his wife.'

'Henry has agreed. He thanked me for taking it so well and offered me the royal forests.' He scowled. 'I could have refused but no longer care.' It was the truth. He'd been used by her brother, and forced to declare his loyalty to the new queen.

'How long can you stay this time?'

'Only one night. This is a busy time at court.'

'But now Anne Boleyn is crowned—'

'There is even more for me to do.' He sat at the side of her bed. 'I know how unwell you are, Mary. You hide it well, but I've spoken with your physicians. I wish I could stay here. In truth, I'm concerned my enemies might poison the king's mind against me if I stay away from court. I will return as soon as I can.'

'Will you spend your one night with me, my lord the Duke of Suffolk?'

'I would be honoured, my lady, Queen of France.'

A shaft of bright sunshine woke Brandon early and he was washing in a bowl of cold water as Mary woke. He dried his face and hands then turned and saw her as he pulled on the clean linen shirt she'd spent hours sewing for him.

'I must leave now, Mary.'

'When will you return?'

'A week, perhaps two. Then I will stay and care for you.'

'Do you give me your promise?'

He fastened the front of his doublet and strapped on his sword, then leaned over to kiss her. 'You have my word.'

Brandon heard muffled voices in the corridor outside his

rooms in Westminster, followed by a knock at the door. His servant looked apologetic. 'Begging your pardon, my lord, but a messenger has arrived from Suffolk. He has travelled a long way, my lord. Shall I tell him he must wait until morning?'

'No, I'm nearly finished here. I'll see him now.'

The black-garbed messenger entered, removed his hat and bowed his head. He smelled of horse sweat and his cape was spattered with mud from the road.

'What brings you to London?' It was unusual to have a messenger ride so far, but Brandon was more curious than concerned.

'I have to tell you, my lord, your wife, Lady Mary, is ill, and you are requested to return home to Westhorpe.'

Brandon had become used to the concerns of Mary's physicians. They cost him a small fortune and tended to over-react when she was weakening, then claim the credit when she recovered, which she always did. He reached into his pocket and handed the messenger a gold coin.

'Are you returning to Suffolk now?'

The messenger nodded. 'I shall be leaving at first light, my lord.'

'Please tell my wife I shall return when I can. This has been a busy time...' He was about to dismiss the man when a thought occurred to him. 'Who sent you to me with this message?'

'Your daughter, my lord. Lady Eleanor.'

'Eleanor?' Brandon still thought of his youngest daughter as a child, but she was fourteen now, a grown woman, and well able to run the household at Westhorpe when Mary was away or unwell.

He remembered how frail Mary looked the last time he saw her, and his promise to return as soon as he could. Eleanor would only send for him if it was truly necessary. He decided to put his family first, for once, and return home straight away.

. . .

It was late, and the house was in near darkness when he arrived after riding as fast as his horse could take him. He was surprised to be welcomed not by his daughter, but by the young priest from St Margaret's in Westhorpe. The priest looked grim-faced and ushered Brandon into his study before closing the door behind them.

The priest took a deep breath. 'I am the bearer of the saddest news, my lord. Your wife, Lady Mary, has finally found her peace with God.'

Brandon stared in disbelief. 'I'm too late? Mary is dead?' It felt like a bad dream to even say the words.

'Your daughter, Lady Eleanor, summoned me and I administered the last rites. I can tell you, my lord, your wife did not suffer at the end.'

Brandon slumped into his chair, his mind numbed by the news and an overpowering feeling of guilt. Mary's pains in her chest had been worse than ever last time he saw her but, as usual, he'd been torn between his duty to his family and the need to return to London.

'Did she say anything … at the end?' His voice wavered with emotion.

The priest nodded. 'She spoke of her love for you, my lord, and of her children.'

Brandon fought back tears. He should have stayed at Westhorpe. Henry was so preoccupied with his new queen he wouldn't even have noticed. He'd planned to return soon with the king's physician, who'd spoken of a new potion that might help Mary's chest. Now it was too late. Mary was gone and he felt the cold pain of grief in his heart.

'I would like you to hear my confession in the morning, if you will...' His voice faltered.

The priest nodded and looked at Brandon with sadness in his eyes. 'I am sorry for your loss, my lord.'

As the door closed behind the priest, Brandon surrendered to his grief. He held his head in his hands, unable to contain his composure any longer. He'd failed his wife, sister of the king, and Queen of France, who'd given so freely of her love.

He remembered the sparkle in her eyes as she handed him her favour at a tournament. He recalled the excitement as they risked Henry's anger by deciding to marry, and the passion of their first night together. He saw her beaming with delight as she held little Harry in her arms, and her devastation when he died so young. She had never been quite the same again, but he'd truly loved her, with all his heart.

The sobbing began deep inside him and grew until he wept as he had never done before, the tears streaming down his face and his whole body shaking. He sat alone, long after the candle burned away, plunging his world to darkness, and prayed for forgiveness.

Katherine Willoughby wore mourning dress, although it was two full months since Mary's passing. Brandon felt awkward as he greeted his ward. What he had to tell her was going to be difficult. He looked at her as if seeing her for the first time, and saw something of her mother's Spanish spirit in the determined gleam in her dark brown eyes.

She had a natural presence, an elegance rare in one so young. As he struggled to find the right words, he studied her perfect, unblemished skin and the small gold crucifix on a chain around her neck. Katherine had the same self-confident innocence which had attracted him to Mary at the same age.

'You understand why I could not attend my wife's funeral?'

'Of course, my lord.' She spoke softly, never taking her eyes from his.

Brandon hoped she wasn't judging him. He wanted to tell her to call him Charles, but it was too soon for that. 'I arranged a memorial service at Westminster Abbey, and paid for prayers to be said for her soul each day.' It sounded like an apology.

Katherine looked as if she had many questions, yet said nothing, holding the silence and forcing him to speak. He could imagine such a talent would serve her well at Henry's court, or when faced by the self-opinionated ambassadors of France and Spain.

'How old are you, Katherine?'

'Fourteen, my lord.' She gave him a modest look. 'I shall be fifteen on the twenty-second of March.'

'You have been told I planned for you to become betrothed to my son when he comes of age?'

'I have, my lord.'

Brandon waited for her to continue. She must have views on such a commitment, and wondered if she noticed his use of the past tense, but again she held the silence. It seemed this was something he would have to get used to.

'Well, the thing is...' He wished he'd prepared better. He would like to tell her how he longed for a woman's touch to comfort him, help him overcome the despair of loss which made his life feel so empty. Well-chosen words would have served his purpose, yet now they eluded him. He saw she waited for him to continue.

'I've decided it's best for both of us if I marry you myself. You will become the Duchess of Suffolk, one of the most senior ladies of the court.' He watched the faintest trace of a smile appear on her face. 'Are you ... content with such an arrangement?'

'Yes, my lord, I am.'

25

FEBRUARY 1534

Brandon's marriage to Katherine caused few tongues to wag, despite it being less than three months after Mary's funeral. The thirty-four-year age difference between them was unusual but the men of court gave him a knowing look. They understood his new wife's income of fifteen thousand ducats a year solved his financial problems and made him a wealthy man.

On the day of their wedding at Greenwich, Henry's court buzzed like a hive with more important news. People had been taking bets on whether the king would name his son Edward or Henry. Then the royal heralds proclaimed the child a daughter. Henry promptly cancelled the tournament he'd planned to celebrate the birth of a prince.

Instead, he made the christening a great event, with five hundred torchbearers lining the route to the Church of the Observant Friars. The red-haired child was wrapped in a robe of royal purple velvet, trimmed with ermine, and carried by the old Duchess of Norfolk under a canopy of estate.

Brandon and Katherine, at their first public appearance as husband and wife, watched as the child was christened over the silver font, brought from Canterbury. Named Princess Elizabeth, after her grandmother, Elizabeth of York, the king's new daughter would take precedence over Princess Mary.

The early months of Brandon's new life passed in a whirl of change. Katherine inherited thirty manors in Lincolnshire and over fifty in Norfolk and Suffolk but, as always, her legacy was far from settled. There were challenges from her scheming uncle, Sir Christopher Willoughby, and disputes with tenants to resolve. Brandon also had to deal with the reversion of Mary's properties to the Crown, as well as the French incomes.

It kept him busy, but his new income enabled him to settle debts and make improvements to Suffolk Place, which became their main residence. Westhorpe held too many memories for him, although his children still lived there and Brandon planned to visit them whenever he had business in the north.

Katherine made him feel young again with her girlish sense of fun, although he'd put on weight and his beard had turned white. After such sadness in his life, it was good to be able to laugh again. As they lay together in the privacy of their velvet-canopied, four-poster bed he enjoyed completing her education. Her lively, enquiring mind meant she was always asking questions he struggled to answer.

'Why do you have to obey the king, even when you don't agree?' There was a hint of mischief in her voice.

'We must all obey the king, Katherine.' Even as he said the words, he smiled as he remembered the times he hadn't done so. 'Those who do not will face the consequences.'

'Why can my mother not visit Queen Catherine?' She played with the grey hairs on his chest, as Mary used to do when she wanted something.

Brandon suspected Katherine's mother had told her to secure his help. Henry banned anyone from meeting his former wife, but Maria, Baroness Willoughby, was a determined woman. 'I see no good reason, but you must remember not to call her the queen in front of the servants.'

'Why not? Is she not a queen?' Katherine turned to stare into his eyes.

He glanced at the closed door and lowered his voice. 'I suspect some members of our household might be in Cromwell's pay.'

'Why would Master Cromwell wish to spy on us, Charles? He knows your loyalty to the king.'

He was pleased to hear her use his first name. It had taken her a while. He often had to remind her to stop calling him 'my lord' and stop curtseying to him. 'Cromwell's job is to be the king's eyes and ears, Katherine. There are,' he struggled to find the right words, 'harsh punishments for those who speak ill of Queen Anne.'

'They cannot punish me for telling the truth.'

Brandon wondered whether to tell her of the two women who'd been stripped naked to the waist and publicly beaten, their ears nailed to a post, for daring to call Catherine the true Queen of England. He decided not to worry her unduly, and instead smiled at her youthful innocence.

'It took me many years to understand, but life at court is much like a game of chess. Men like Thomas Cromwell make it their business to always think at least one move ahead.' He frowned. 'Sometimes, sacrifices must be made to protect the king.'

Katherine swept her long dark hair from her face and gave him a knowing look. 'Sometimes, even a queen might be sacrificed.'

The arrival of Eleanor and young Henry with their servants from Westhorpe ended this idyllic time and changed everything at Suffolk Place. Eleanor had written to Brandon, explaining her brother was unwell and refusing to eat, so he sent for them both to come to London.

Katherine began spending much of her time with Eleanor, who was excited at the prospect of her marriage to Henry Clifford. Only two years older than Eleanor, Clifford was heir to the title Earl of Cumberland and stood to inherit a great fortune, as well as Skipton Castle and vast estates in Yorkshire.

Brandon felt left out when he heard his wife and daughter giggling and gossiping, and wondered if they talked about him. He had more important things to worry about, though, as his son Henry caused him great concern. Although eleven, he seemed small for his age, and was prone to bouts of a strange malaise.

Their physicians were at a loss to explain what was wrong, and tried everything from leeches and noxious potions to daily bleeding. Now young Henry had a fever and took to his bed, once again refusing to eat his meals. This made him pale and weak, reminding Brandon of Mary.

Eleanor and Katherine decided to care for Henry them-selves and dismissed his nurse, taking turns to feed him with a small silver spoon. Brandon worried they might catch his fever, but was encouraged to see a little colour return to his son's face.

He held a hand to Henry's forehead. 'How are you feeling, Henry?'

His son seemed listless, and made no effort to sit up until Brandon helped him, using a velvet cushion to support his back. 'I'm tired, Father.' His eyes went to the bowl of stew. 'I'm not hungry.'

'I shall consult the king's physician, William Butts. He's a Suffolk man, and his wife Margaret...' He was going to say she had been friends with Mary, then stopped himself. 'He has cared for the king's son and daughter, Henry Fitzroy and Princess Mary.'

Doctor William Butts arrived later that afternoon. A kindly looking man, clean-shaven with grey hair and a brown fur collar to his doublet, the physician wore his gold chain of office. He studied Brandon's face for a moment, as if wondering whether he might be the patient.

'What can I do for you, my lord?'

'I need your help, Doctor Butts. My son, Henry, grows weak with some illness, and my own physicians seem at a loss.'

He led William Butts to Henry's chamber and watched as the physician examined his son, checking for signs of a fever and looking into his mouth. The physician turned to Brandon.

'Has he been bled?'

'Often – but, it seems, to little effect.'

'It might be an imbalance of the humours. The right balance and purity of humours is essential for maintaining good health, but an excess of phlegm is associated with this type of apathetic behaviour. How long has he been like this?'

'My son has always been a sickly child, but never quite as bad as he is now. He refuses to eat and is now too weak to rise from his bed.'

The doctor nodded. 'I shall do what I can.'

Brandon returned from Greenwich Palace with new orders from the king. Katherine would struggle to understand what he must do, so he decided to explain to her. He had no choice, but couldn't allow the king's wishes to come between them.

He waited until late evening, when they were alone together in their bedchamber. Katherine sat at her dressing table in her cotton shift, unplaiting and combing her long hair, a nightly ritual. Brandon lay back on their comfortable bed watching her, as he often did. It seemed a shame to spoil her good mood.

She stopped her combing and turned to him, her eyes shining in the candlelight. 'Doctor Butts persuaded Henry to eat bread soaked with warmed milk today.' She smiled. 'He says Henry must soon walk in the fresh air with Eleanor and I in the gardens.'

'Doctor Butts is a good man.' Brandon sat up. 'I confess to being worried about Henry, so that's encouraging.' He realised his own news could wait no longer. 'The king has given me a new commission, but I'm afraid it might upset your mother.'

'What has he asked this time?' There was an edge to her young voice. 'Does it involve Queen Catherine?'

He frowned at her tone. 'I have to take my men to Buckden Palace and dismiss any of Catherine's servants who refuse to refer to her as princess, rather than queen.'

'Why has he chosen you, Charles?' She crossed the room and sat on the bed next to him. 'The king must know how difficult it will be for you.'

'It's better that I do it than someone like Norfolk. He gives me no choice, Katherine.' He stroked his hand through her long hair. It ran like fine silk through his fingers. 'I think it might be a test of my loyalty.'

'Anne Boleyn put him up to this. Mother says—'

'Stop.' He held up his hand to her lips to silence her. 'I know what your mother says, and it helps no one to repeat it.' He kissed her on the cheek. 'I want you to understand that I will do what I have to with proper respect for Catherine.'

She seemed to sense there was more, and looked deep into his eyes as she read his thoughts. 'What else has he asked you to do?'

Brandon took a deep breath. 'I've been ordered to remove

Catherine and her household from Buckden and escort her to the bishop's palace in Somersham … by force if necessary.'

'You cannot.' She stared at him as if her words carried more weight than the king's.

He ignored her protest. 'I visited Somersham once. The former Bishop of Ely, Nicholas West, was a good friend. It's no further from London than Westhorpe.'

'Can't you reason with the king? You could offer her Westhorpe. It's a peaceful enough place and as far from London as Somersham.'

'I shall see what can be done, Katherine, but make no promises. King Henry seems in no mood to be challenged over this.' He decided to tell her his plan. 'I must do as the king commands but if, as I suspect, Catherine objects too strongly, I shall not use force. I'll buy her as much time as I can until King Henry is ready to discuss the matter.'

Brandon felt in no hurry to reach Buckden in Huntingdonshire, and stopped his men several times at taverns on the way to rest the horses. A mournful church bell chimed noon as they finally rode into the sleepy village, dominated by the high towers and battlemented walls of the palace.

Brandon remembered his last visit to Buckden Palace, home to the bishops of Lincoln since the twelfth century. He'd once lent money he could ill-afford to spare to Nicholas West. His friend became one of the wealthiest bishops in the north, and helped Mary when their daughter Frances was born. He'd visited Nicholas on his deathbed the previous year, and had his blessing.

Henry took the bishop's palace for the Crown, and it was where Catherine had lived since the previous July. Although visitors had been banned by order of the king, Catherine had kept most of her ladies and over a hundred members of her household.

These now gathered in the great hall on Brandon's orders, to hear what he had to say. They looked warily at his armed yeomen, although he intended to keep his promise not to use force. Brandon scanned their faces, recognising some from happier times.

'Where is your mistress?' His voice sounded louder and sterner than he intended.

One of Catherine's ladies spoke out. 'Her Grace is resting in her chambers, my lord.'

'Kindly inform Her Grace that I wish to see her, with a message from the king. I cannot leave until it has been delivered.'

He watched as the lady curtseyed and left through a side door, and then turned to face those who remained. 'I have orders from the king to dismiss any of you who refuse to swear you will no longer refer to the princess dowager as the queen.'

He saw a look of defiance on several faces, but also some of the women weeping. An elderly servant, dressed in Catherine's livery, stepped forward. He stood looking at Brandon, no doubt knowing what he was about to say could have terrible consequences.

'My lord, Queen Catherine will always be the true and rightful Queen of England.'

There were mutterings of agreement from the assembled household. Brandon had to admire the man's courage, but he had his orders and had to be seen to follow them. 'Then you are dismissed. Leave immediately or I shall have you arrested.'

The old man gave Brandon a dark look but said no more and left, the door closing behind him. He hadn't bothered to collect his possessions, although Brandon guessed he would return for them when it was safe, and be welcomed as a hero.

'Are there any others I need to dismiss?' Brandon tried to sound firm, although his task left a bitter taste.

'No, my lord.' They spoke as one, perhaps realising that, like them, he had a job to do.

'Good.' He turned to one of Catherine's ladies. 'Please escort me to Her Grace's chambers.'

Catherine stared at him from her canopied bed, where she lay propped up on a pillow of cloth of gold, her ladies standing to each side as if to protect her. She wore an old-fashioned gable hood which covered her hair, which was said to have turned grey. Although a year younger than him, she looked much older.

A pomander of perforated gold openwork hung from a gold chain around her neck, to freshen the air. In her hands she held a leather-bound prayer book, gripping it as if he might take it from her. Her dark eyes studied him, as if making a judgement.

'Duke Charles. I was saddened to learn of Mary's passing. She was a good friend.' Her voice sounded hoarse. 'I understand you have married the daughter of Baroness Willoughby.'

Brandon bowed out of courtesy and ignored the hint of disapproval. 'I have, Your Grace.' He'd decided deference would make his difficult task easier. 'My wife asked me to send you her best wishes.'

Catherine nodded. 'And my bigamous husband – does he also send his best wishes?' She coughed, and the dry, hacking sound echoed in the bare room. 'Does he know His Holiness the pope has declared his marriage illegal?'

Brandon knew better than to respond, but realised that while the strain of the past year had not diminished her Aragon spirit, it had taken its toll on her health. He doubted Henry knew or cared if she was unwell and it occurred to him that she might have been poisoned. First Bishop Fisher, then Wolsey. He dismissed the idea. Henry was not a murderer.

Catherine held a folded white linen cloth to her mouth as she coughed again. 'Does Henry not have a care for his soul if he is excommunicated?' She spoke quickly, not caring about his silence, her Spanish accent returning. Catherine coughed again, holding the linen cloth to her mouth.

'You are unwell, Your Grace?' Brandon frowned with concern but saw a chance to escape his duty to remove her.

Catherine nodded. 'God knows, my treatment by him is enough to shorten ten strong lives, much more mine.'

'I have orders to escort you to the bishop's palace in Somersham—'

'That damp, miserable place?' She scowled. 'To agree would be suicide, a mortal sin. Henry hopes I will die there, but I shall deny him that satisfaction.'

Brandon bowed. 'I will inform the king you are too unwell to travel, Your Grace.' He was about to leave when he decided, for Mary's sake, to tell her. 'You are loved by the people, Your Grace. They cheer your daughter, Princess Mary, and you are not forgotten.'

Catherine dismissed him with a wave of her hand, yet he'd seen the glint in her eye. She was too proud to ever say, but she'd understood he remained loyal to her.

As soon as Brandon returned to Suffolk Place he sensed something was wrong. The stable boy who took his horse avoided his eye, and he felt a familiar feeling of dread. Katherine and Eleanor met him in the hall, wearing mourning dress once more. The sadness in their faces told him what he needed to know before either of them said a word.

'Henry?' In his heart he'd known, although he'd hoped and prayed he was wrong.

Katherine took his hand. 'We went to wake him, and found he'd died in his sleep.' A tear ran down her face. 'I'm so sorry.'

Brandon reached out and embraced them both. They stood in silence while he came to terms with the news. Once again, he felt a sense of guilt that he'd not been there, but he'd had no choice. At least Mary had been spared the pain of losing another son.

26

FEBRUARY 1535

Brandon wrote a long and carefully worded letter to the king, explaining how he'd found Catherine on her sickbed, too ill to be moved. He confirmed he'd dismissed those members of her household who refused to swear to refer to her as the princess dowager. He'd added that the former queen would only be removed if bound with ropes and carried out, in the hope the king would reconsider.

He had also placed Catherine's chaplain, Thomas Abel, under arrest and locked him up for his refusal to follow the king's orders. The rebellious priest had encouraged Mary to speak out against Anne Boleyn, and Brandon found it impossible to forgive the trouble he'd caused them all.

Abel had been imprisoned in the Tower of London, charged with encouraging the queen to persist in her wilful opposition to the divorce. It was a mystery to Brandon how the cleric had come to be released and at Catherine's side in Buckden.

His son's funeral meant it was some weeks before Brandon returned to court, and by then it seemed the king had forgotten his original orders. Keen to uncover the true wealth of the

Church of which he was now head, he'd tasked Thomas Cromwell to arrange commissioners to record anything of value.

Cromwell promised to make Henry the richest king in Christendom. Brandon thought Cromwell might regret his boast, as King Francis was known to be five times richer than Henry. Like all of them, by his silence Brandon became part of the conspiracy to rob the Church of its property. To oppose the policy could endanger his life, yet to support it could lead to a share of the spoils.

He watched as the old world unravelled before his eyes, all because an indecisive pope had not allowed the king's divorce. Brandon worried in the past about making an enemy of Thomas Wolsey, but his successor would make an infinitely more dangerous enemy. Unlike Wolsey, Cromwell was ruthlessly effective and not encumbered by any allegiance to Rome. People were right to live in fear of crossing Thomas Cromwell.

Katherine's spirits seemed restored when she welcomed Brandon home after a long day at court. She had changed from her mourning dress into an attractive gown of cornflower-blue silk, one of his favourites. She poured wine into two of their best goblets, and handed one to him.

'It seems you have some good news for me, Katherine.' He sipped the rich red wine and recognised it as one of the best in their cellar. 'Tell me, why have you sent our servants away – and where is my daughter?'

Katherine smiled at his questions. 'Eleanor has gone to stay at Willoughby House with my mother, who visited here today.' She glanced around the room as if surprised to see the servants had all retired early. 'I wish to speak to you in private, without our words being reported to the king.'

Brandon frowned. 'I regret to say I think your mother is a

dangerous influence on you. I hope she hasn't been speaking out against our queen?' He took another sip of wine and wondered what Maria Willoughby was up to.

'Mother told me Anne Boleyn is out of favour with King Henry, who has taken a new mistress!'

'That is supposed to be a great secret, Katherine. You must never mention it again, do you understand?' His voice became stern. 'Lady Courtenay, Marchioness of Exeter, was nearly imprisoned in the Tower with Bishop John Fisher and Sir Thomas More for her indiscretion.'

'What was her crime? Speaking the truth?' Katherine looked at him with wide eyes.

'Lady Courtenay spoke out against Thomas Cromwell's religious reforms, and in support of Bishop John Fisher. It's a dangerous game, Katherine. She only escaped by writing a grovelling letter to the king.' Brandon shook his head. 'She was lucky to find him in a good mood.'

Katherine glanced towards the closed door. 'We are alone now, Charles, and I've taken care to make sure no one listens.' A thought seemed to occur to her. 'You already knew about the king's new mistress?'

'The king has always had mistresses.' Brandon relented. He could forgive Katherine anything, as long as she didn't endanger them with her girlish enthusiasm for the truth. 'I will tell you what I know, but you must promise not to repeat a word of it – particularly to your mother.'

She hesitated for a moment. 'I promise.'

'His mistress is Lady Margaret Shelton. He calls her 'Madge'. She's the youngest daughter of Sir John Shelton, comptroller of Princess Elizabeth's household, and Anne Boleyn's uncle.'

Katherine raised an eyebrow. 'I think I've seen her. A pretty girl, not much older than me, with fair hair?'

Brandon nodded. 'She's a cousin of Anne Boleyn – and not

only one of her ladies-in-waiting, but her closest companion. I hope you understand why this must be kept secret?'

'I do, although I've no doubt some mischief-maker has already let the secret out.'

He was surprised at her insight into the workings of court, then remembered her mother was Catherine's confidante, who'd been watching Henry since he was a child. 'You are probably right. I've sensed a different atmosphere at court of late, and it doesn't end there. Another of Sir John's daughters, Mary, is also a great favourite of our king – if you take my meaning.' He drained his goblet of wine, feeling its warmth improve his mood.

'Not both of them, at the same time?' She sounded shocked.

Brandon smiled at her innocence. 'Three, if you count Anne Boleyn.'

'Mother takes some comfort from knowing Anne Boleyn is out of favour, but now I understand why that is of little help to Catherine.'

'Anne Boleyn must provide King Henry with an heir, or her days as queen might be numbered.'

Katherine gave him a coy look and took his hand to lead him up the stairs. 'I'm sixteen next month and ready to become the mother of your child.'

Once in their bedchamber, she began to unfasten his doublet. He took her in his arms and returned her kiss, then helped her to undress until she stood before him naked.

She gave him a shy look, as if it was their first time together, then took off the rest of his clothes and led him to their bed. He held her close as they lay together, and felt her respond to his touch. Katherine was right. It was time for a new beginning.

John Fisher looked like a hollow-eyed scarecrow, deathly pale after a year of imprisonment in the Tower of London.

Brandon heard he'd been kept in solitary confinement, without any visitors, not even allowed a priest to hear his confession. He looked painfully thin and needed help to stand.

The elderly bishop stumbled and nearly fell as he walked between two yeomen warders, and had to be helped to climb the wooden steps to the scaffold. He looked out at the unusually silent crowd gathered at Tower Hill to see him die, and his lips moved in a prayer.

Brandon knew him as a proud, honourable man – Lady Margaret Beaufort's confessor, Henry's own chaplain, and Bishop of Rochester. He'd been a comfort to Mary when her grandmother died, and visited her at Westhorpe. It had been Fisher who gave a passionate speech at the funeral of the last king, yet he'd suffered greatly under the present one.

Always forthright, the bluff northern bishop opposed the annulment of the king's marriage. He could have followed the lead of other bishops and looked the other way, but chose to speak out on behalf of Queen Catherine. No one was surprised when he refused to swear an oath accepting the king as Supreme Head of the Church of England.

Brandon frowned at how his world had been turned upside down. John Fisher was an honest man, the champion of the Catholic cause. The pope announced he would make him a cardinal, the official representative of Rome. The people began calling Bishop Fisher a martyr, comparing him to St John the Baptist, and Henry had heard enough.

The problem of what to do with Bishop Fisher was solved by Thomas Cromwell, who had him sentenced to be hanged, drawn and quartered at Tyburn, a traitor's death. Henry heard the public outcry and showed the king's great mercy by commuting the sentence to beheading. Brandon would not have chosen to attend, but was there on orders from the king.

In a drunken moment Henry told him he would have liked to attend in person, and joked he would place the scarlet cardinal's hat on John Fisher's severed head. Brandon made the mistake of disapproving of the king's gallows humour, and had been sent to witness the sentence being carried out as a punishment.

He watched as the executioner hefted his axe and examined the blade, as if concerned about its sharpness. This wasn't the first such execution of Catholic dissenters, and Brandon was sure it wouldn't be the last. The previous week the king's executioner had hanged, drawn and quartered the Prior of Charterhouse, John Houghton.

Cromwell arrested the unfortunate prior for the crime of pleading to the king for exemption for the monks of Charterhouse from the oath. Brandon knew John Houghton as a devout man, but lacking in judgement, who deserved better than to have his dismembered limbs nailed above the city gates.

It was rumoured that John Fisher had been warned not to make a final speech mentioning the king or to preach his treasonable views, so an expectant hush fell over the crowd as he turned to face his last congregation. Brandon admired the bishop's courage, although he was a man with little to lose. As he began to speak, Fisher's voice rang out as clearly as it had so often in the great cathedrals.

'I thank God that I have not feared death, but I desire you all to assist with your prayers, that, at the instant of death's stroke,' Fisher looked back at the waiting executioner, 'I may in that moment stand steadfast without fainting in any one point of the Catholic faith, free from any fear.'

There was a muttering in the crowd and the king's yeomen gripped their weapons, under orders to arrest any protestors or dissenters. Bishop John Fisher refused a blindfold and kneeled at the wooden block, still saying a prayer as the axe fell with a sickening thud.

The crowd groaned at the sight of the bishop's staring eyes, as his head rolled across the scaffold. Cromwell had misjudged the mood of the people, and had made the bishop a martyr for his cause. Brandon turned and walked away, struggling to control the anger in his heart that he'd been part of the murder of an innocent man.

God had saved Bishop Fisher from their attempt to use poison to silence him, so they'd used an axe. He cursed Thomas Cromwell for leading the king down such a path, and was glad Mary had not lived to see her brother become so cruel.

He later heard that the bishop's body had been stripped naked and displayed on the scaffold until evensong, by order of the king. John Fisher's severed head was placed on a spike on London Bridge, as was the custom, but people found his contorted face disturbing and it was thrown into the River Thames.

Brandon paced the tiled floor of Willoughby House, trying to think of anything other than the cries of pain. He could hear Katherine calling out his name, but the midwife had banned him from seeing his young wife. 'It could bring bad luck, my lord, and there will be time enough after.' He'd cursed the old woman but had to respect tradition.

Now he worried about the long silence. He stopped pacing and listened, but heard nothing. He said a prayer for Katherine, not asking for a son, simply that she would not suffer unduly. He would never forgive himself. He'd married his ward for her inheritance and, if honest with himself, desire had played its part. Yet now, that same desire had become a love he thought he'd never feel again.

Katherine chose to spend her confinement at her mother's house in the Barbican, while Eleanor had kept him company at Suffolk Place. Then the long-awaited message arrived. The child would be born soon. Brandon threw on his coat and galloped through the crowded London streets as fast as he dared. He needn't have hurried, as he'd been made to wait for hours.

Willoughby House was a fine old mansion, part of Katherine's inheritance, but it suited them for her mother to be in London, rather than distant Parham in Suffolk. Brandon liked his mother-in-law's spirit, although he worried her support for the former queen could give the Boleyn faction the excuse they needed to bring him down.

The sharp squeal of a baby's cry suddenly echoed through the house, a sound that made his heart race. He ran up the narrow stairs, but then hesitated at Katherine's door. When he was younger he would have kicked the old oak door open, but now he waited in the dark corridor. He was a guest in this house, and must wait a little longer.

After what seemed like an eternity the door opened and the midwife appeared. She seemed surprised to see him waiting outside.

'Good news, my lord.' A smile broke through her professional detachment. 'You have a healthy son.'

Brandon could wait no longer. He pushed the door open. Katherine sat propped up in bed, her mother on one side and his daughter Eleanor on the other. Katherine's long hair looked damp and her face flushed, but her eyes shone with happiness.

'A boy.' Tears ran down her face. 'We have a boy.'

He sat on the edge of her bed. 'You should be the one to name him.' He smiled at the joy on her face. 'After all, you are the one who has done all the hard work.'

'I choose Henry Brandon.'

He frowned. It was the custom to name a child after one recently lost, yet it seemed to be tempting fate. 'We could name him William, after our fathers.'

'You can't say the choice is mine, then disagree.' She looked defiant, and turned to her mother and Eleanor for support.

Brandon crossed the room to where the nurse swaddled the child in fresh white linen. He looked into the bright eyes of his new son, and agreed. 'You are right, as ever. This is a fresh start, a time to put my differences with the king behind me. We shall name him Henry, and the king will be his godfather.'

27

JANUARY 1536

Brandon found Katherine in tears, her eyes red from grief. 'What is it?' His first concern was for little Harry. 'What's happened?' He doubted he could bear the loss of another son.

Katherine shook her head and wrapped her arms around him as she sobbed. 'Mother sent a messenger.' She handed the scrap of parchment to Brandon.

Written in haste, the blunt message was in Maria Willough-by's own hand. Catherine of Aragon, once Queen of England, had died from her illness. The news was no great surprise to Brandon, although Ambassador Chapuys had reported to the king that Catherine's health was improved.

Katherine looked up at him. 'I'm concerned for my mother. She defied the king and left London to see Queen Catherine.'

Brandon tried to comfort her. 'I'm sorry, Katherine. This will be difficult for your mother, and for Princess Mary.'

'The king stopped Princess Mary from visiting her mother, even when he knew she was dying. This will break her heart – and must have made the end more difficult for poor Catherine.'

'The king didn't know she was going to die.' Although he found himself defending Henry, Brandon struggled to understand why he'd felt it necessary to keep Princess Mary from her mother.

Katherine pulled back from his embrace. 'You must help make sure Mother isn't punished.'

'Of course.' He kissed her on the cheek. 'In truth, I have no idea how Henry will react, but I'll do whatever I can.'

Katherine held him close. 'My mother dedicated thirty-five years of her life to the queen.'

'I well remember the excitement of the Spanish princess's arrival. She was fifteen years old – and I was the same age as you are now.' He smiled at the memory. 'They called her Princess Catarina. We all thought she was a great beauty.'

'Will you permit me to attend her funeral? It would be a comfort to my mother.' She looked at him with pleading in her eyes.

Brandon hesitated. 'There is a risk, but it is one I'm prepared to take. You may go with my blessing, and Eleanor will travel with you for company.'

As he said the words a shadow passed over his thoughts. Thomas Cromwell would be watching, ready to note the names of those who supported the late queen. His daughter Eleanor, Katherine, and her mother would be prominent among the mourners, and he prayed Henry would show understanding, for once.

Brandon felt a chill in the air and was glad of the thick fur collar of his cloak. The King's Hall in the Tower of London had become a courtroom, with seats for the lords and benches along the walls of the hall, already thronged with eager spectators. In the centre of the room stood a single chair on a raised platform.

He sat at the side of Thomas Howard, and was troubled by his conscience. He'd escaped the trials of Mark Smeaton,

Henry Norris, Sir Francis Weston and William Brereton, four innocent young men, who at some time or another had made an enemy of Thomas Cromwell.

It was rumoured that torture on the rack persuaded Smeaton, the queen's handsome young musician, to plead guilty to the charge of the violation of Anne Boleyn. The rest professed their innocence yet, without evidence or confessions, the jury declared them all guilty of treason, and they were sentenced to be hanged and drawn, their heads cut off and their bodies quartered at Tyburn.

He glanced at Thomas Howard and was glad he'd relinquished the post of Lord High Steward to him. As the king's representative, Norfolk sat grim-faced, clutching his white staff of office, under a canopy of estate. Brandon didn't envy him the task of presiding over the trials of his own niece and nephew.

Sir Thomas Audley, the Lord Chancellor, sat on the other side of Thomas Howard. Brandon could not forgive the self-important lawyer, now the king's serjeant-at-law, for presiding over the trial of Bishop John Fisher. His legal skills would not be needed at *this* trial, as the king required only one outcome.

Brandon studied the faces of the other peers waiting to pass judgement. Henry Percy, slighted by Anne Boleyn, and Henry Pole, a supporter of Princess Mary, were deep in private conversation. Also there was Baron Edward Clinton, the husband of the king's former mistress Bessie Blount. He had never liked Anne Boleyn.

Brandon raised an eyebrow to see the anxious face of Thomas Boleyn half-hidden among the peers, his hands clasped in prayer. Brandon had never liked him, but felt sympathy for the man, a father forced to watch the humiliation of his daughter. Boleyn made many enemies during his rapid rise, and would now know his fall was imminent.

Brandon saw his two sons-in-law, Anne and Mary's

husbands – Baron Edward Grey and Thomas Stanley, Baron Monteagle. Except for Anne Boleyn's father, all twenty-six peers present had been chosen because they had reason to dislike the Boleyns, himself included.

He had cursed her insolence when she'd said he had murdered one son to beget another. Then it got back to him that she'd joked with her ladies about his relationship with Katherine being like incest with his own daughter. Now she was to be accused of incest with her brother, and all he felt for her was pity.

The usher called the court to order and a hushed silence fell over the hall as Anne Boleyn entered with her head high. Brandon was surprised to see her wearing a black velvet gown with a bright scarlet damask petticoat and a feather in her hat. She curtseyed to the assembled peers, as if this was a social gathering, and showed no fear of what was to come.

He studied her face as the litany of charges of incest and adultery were read out. She didn't frown when accused of conspiring to bring about the king's death. She didn't flinch, even when charged with being a disciple of Satan, who had bewitched the king with sorcery. Anne Boleyn pleaded not guilty in a clear and confident voice.

Each of them had rehearsed questions, written by Cromwell, but when it was Brandon's turn he hesitated, unhappy to take such a prominent part in the charade. He cleared his throat. 'Do you deny that you lay with your brother to conceive a son, contrary to all human laws?'

Anne looked Brandon directly in the eye. 'As God is my judge, I deny it.' Her voice sounded calm and assured, and he believed her.

Thomas Howard struggled to compose himself as he read the verdict, also written by Cromwell before the trial. 'Because you have offended against our sovereign the king in committing treason against his person, and are here attainted of the same, the law of the realm is this,' he took a deep breath, 'you deserve death, and the judgement is that you shall be burned here within the Tower of London, on the Green, or else have your head smitten off, as the king's pleasure shall be further known.'

It was small consolation to Brandon that he'd not had to watch Anne Boleyn burned at the stake. The king showed mercy to the convicted men, permitting them to be beheaded, rather than face the nightmare of a traitor's death. He'd decided Anne would be executed by the swordsman, brought from Calais, who now waited in the Tower Green.

She wore a grey damask robe over her crimson kirtle, and needed help to climb the steep steps of the scaffold. The crowd fell silent as Anne Boleyn turned to face them, and Brandon again felt pity for this proud woman, much the same age as his own daughter, Anne.

He tried not to listen as she gave her final speech, for fear her words might trouble his conscience, yet he couldn't help himself. She said Henry was a good, gentle, and sovereign lord, and asked them to pray for her. He watched as Anne's ladies removed her gable hood and tucked her hair under a linen coif with unnecessary care, as if trying to prolong her last moments.

The only sound was Anne's voice, softly repeating, 'Lord have mercy on me, to God I commend my soul. To Jesus Christ I commend my soul. Lord Jesu receive my soul.'

Brandon had planned to close his eyes when the blow came, but the swordsman was too quick, his blade flashing in the early morning sunshine as it scythed through the air. He might never have accepted her as Queen of England, but the horrific sight of her headless body would haunt his dreams for many years to come.

. . .

Katherine looked shocked. 'I should not be surprised, but I confess I am.'

Brandon shook his head. 'It's the truth. The king was betrothed to Lady Jane Seymour the day after Anne Boleyn's execution.'

'Jane was a maid of honour to Queen Catherine, and lady-in-waiting to Anne Boleyn. Was she also the king's mistress?'

Brandon shrugged. 'Who can know? All I hope is that she will bring a little calm to court. People are frightened to speak their opinions about anything now.'

'Well, I think Jane Seymour will be kind towards Princess Mary – and to my mother.'

'Lady Jane knows your mother well, so the king's choice takes one more worry from my shoulders. The Seymours will surely treat us better than the Boleyns ever did, and Jane's brother Edward was in my household, a good man.'

Katherine embraced him. 'I know how difficult the past months have been for you, but it seems some good might have come from it after all.'

He kissed her. 'I forgot to tell you. The king has granted me Anne Boleyn's de la Pole estates, an income of at least a hundred pounds a year.' He smiled. 'I think we've weathered the storm.'

Brandon rode into the teeth of an October breeze that made his eyes water. He turned and looked behind at a thousand men following on the narrow, winding road, and had a sudden recollection of his failed mission to capture Paris.

Rumours trickled down from the north, slowly at first, then building into a flood Henry could no longer ignore. It seemed Cromwell's commissioners had been overzealous and had begun robbing the wealth of parish churches as well as the monasteries. The king had summoned Brandon.

'A band of rioters have marched on Lincoln, and occupied the town. This is a rebellion.' Henry scowled. 'One of the ringleaders is William Willoughby, son of your wife's uncle – so you are to ride north without delay and put an end to it.'

Brandon cursed under his breath. Katherine's uncle, Sir Christopher Willoughby, fought hard over her inheritance, and almost won. It seemed unfair that he should be associated with that side of Katherine's family.

If Sir Christopher's son had the same adversarial temperament, this could be a challenging mission. Somewhere among the men now following him north were his old friends, Sir William Parr and Sir William Fitzwilliam, who'd been with him on his last visit to France, as well as Sir Francis Bryan, in charge of their sixteen fine cannons.

At Brandon's side rode Sir George Talbot, the battle-hardened old Earl of Shrewsbury, who'd mustered their army on his own initiative. Sir George fought at the Battle of Stoke under the last king and, although close to seventy years old, Brandon was glad to ride with a man of his experience.

Sir George saw him looking back. 'We could make camp outside Lincoln. Rest the men, then march on the town at first light and seize the ringleaders.'

Brandon hesitated. 'I was told there could be as many as forty thousand gathered in Lincoln, and they've occupied the cathedral...'

'I believe they'll be quick enough to surrender when they see armed men. We act in the king's name, my lord, so anyone who assaults us commits an act of treason.'

'These rebels believe they have God on their side.'

Sir George gave Brandon a questioning look. 'Do you know what this is really about? I suspect there's more to this rebellion than protesting against Cromwell's heavy-handedness.'

Brandon frowned. 'If the rumours are true, this is a rebellion by Catholics against the establishment of the Church of England. We must not fail to end this, or it could turn into a civil war.'

Sir George nodded. 'It might be necessary to make an example of the ringleaders. It's what the king would expect.'

Their plan worked even better than Brandon hoped, as they caught the rebels off guard, and many woke to find the town of Lincoln back under control of the king. All that remained was to uncover the leaders, who were soon brought before Brandon in the town hall.

He was relieved to see William Willoughby wasn't among them, but recognised Sir John Hussey, Baron of Sleaford. Sir John had been one of the lords carrying the canopy of estate over the infant Princess Elizabeth at her christening, and was also Princess Mary's chamberlain before her household was dissolved.

'You don't seem to be the sort of man to be leading a rebellion, Sir John. What is your grievance against the king?'

Sir John looked at Brandon with undisguised contempt. 'I've taken no part in any rebellion, and you well know our grievances. I am steward to the Bishop of Lincoln, and we stand against the pillaging of our holy churches by Cromwell's men.'

'Cromwell acts on orders from the king.' Brandon raised his voice so that everyone could hear. He glanced at Sir George Talbot, who nodded in agreement. 'Those who challenge the king's reforms will be arrested, and you, Sir John, have condemned yourself by your words and your actions, by inciting the people to dissent.' He gestured to the guards. 'Take Sir John Hussey to Lincoln Castle jail.'

He'd been disappointed to see such open hostility towards him by a fellow lord but, then, he acted as the king's lieutenant in the north. Brandon took little pleasure in jailing the abbot of Barlings Abbey, Matthew Mackerel, and six of his canons, for their vocal opposition. He pardoned several lords and commoners, in return for their oath to return home in peace.

A plan formed in his mind as Brandon rode back to London. His mission in the north had been a complete success. The rebellion in Lincoln had been crushed by his decisive action and both Henry and Cromwell would be grateful. He could expect to be rewarded for his loyalty, and knew what he would ask.

His many holdings in Lincolnshire provided the basis for a new life in the north. He would transfer Westhorpe and Suffolk Place, with their sad memories, to the king. In good time, he would make Katherine's inheritance, Grimsthorpe Castle, into a grand country home in Lincolnshire for his new family.

Before he'd left London, Katherine told him she was expecting their second child. This time he would learn from the mistakes of the past, and make time to be a good father to his children, and a better husband to his young and beautiful wife.

28

APRIL 1537

Queen Jane sat at the king's side, silently observing. She dressed richly, but in muted colours, only spoke when asked a direct question, and could not have been more different from her predecessor. There was speculation about the reason she had yet to be crowned. Brandon guessed that Henry waited to see if she would provide him with his longed-for heir.

Now the demure queen was said to be two months pregnant, and although the bulge could not be seen under her brocade gown, the change in Henry's mood was unmistakable. He welcomed Brandon with a beaming grin and called for good wine to celebrate.

Brandon took a sip and nodded appreciatively. 'What do we celebrate now, Your Grace?'

'News from the north. You did well, Brandon. The rebels you arrested were all tried and found guilty. They've been hanged as traitors in Lincoln town square.'

'All of them?' Brandon felt a sinking feeling in his heart, and the celebratory wine left a bitter taste in his throat. He should have released them with a warning.

Henry grinned. 'Thomas Cromwell wished to make an example of the dissenters, but it didn't stop them at York.'

Brandon had been relieved when Thomas Howard was sent to deal with what they called the Pilgrimage of Grace. Thousands had occupied the city of York, but Norfolk promised a general pardon. It was being said he sympathised with the rebels, so when the riots continued he'd arrested the ringleaders.

'I think they shall learn their lesson now, Your Grace.'

'Indeed they will, Brandon.' Henry leaned forward in his chair, a glint in his eye. 'I've ordered that Sir Thomas Percy must suffer a traitor's death, and that troublesome lawyer Aske is to be hanged in chains from the walls of York Castle, to remind the good people of that city what happens to traitors.'

Eleanor kissed Brandon on the cheek and he escorted the last of his daughters to her waiting bridegroom. He spared a thought for Mary and wondered if she watched over them. He'd kept his promise to see her girls married well, to men close to their own age.

The last time, at Frances' wedding, they'd worried whether Mary would be well enough to attend. Now it was Katherine who caused them concern, although not from ill health. Katherine had given him another son, christened Charles Brandon.

Mindful of what happened to Mary, he'd told her to stay at home, but with typical Willoughby stubbornness she refused. Eleanor was her best friend, as well as her stepdaughter, and she was determined to be at the wedding at Brandon House in Bridewell.

Another guest who surprised them by his attendance was the king, who appeared in a jovial and charming mood. He congratulated the bride and groom, as well as Brandon and Katherine on the birth of little Charles. He seemed more like a favourite uncle than the tyrannical king Brandon had begun to fear.

The dashing Henry Clifford would make Eleanor a countess, and they planned to live at Skipton Castle, his ancestral home in Yorkshire. Brandon stood at Katherine's side as they waved his daughter farewell. Eleanor had been a great comfort to them both since her mother's death. They would miss her.

The city of London rejoiced with bonfires and constant ringing of church bells, as cannons blasted in endless salute from the Tower. Queen Jane had given birth to a son and the king's succession was secure. At last he had the legitimate male heir he'd longed for, and Henry celebrated with a grand torchlight procession at Hampton Court.

At the midnight christening Brandon wore a long cape of dark-blue velvet over a doublet with fashionably slashed sleeves showing gleaming white silk underneath. Katherine looked magnificent in a crimson gown of rich brocade trimmed with gold lace. A diamond necklace, part of the legacy of Brandon's last wife, glittered at her neck.

Cardinal Wolsey's former chapel at Hampton Court was lit up by a thousand candles, and a scented carpet of white rose petals and scattered herbs covered their path. Henry wished the christening of the infant prince to impress the ambassadors of France and Spain, and show the world the Tudor line was secure at last.

Brandon, Thomas Howard and Archbishop Cranmer were chosen as godfathers, and the prince's half-sister, Princess Mary, as his godmother. The Marchioness of Exeter helped the four-year-old Princess Elizabeth carry the rich christening robe.

Every noble of the court, bishops, clergymen of the Chapel Royal and officers of government followed in the procession from the queen's apartments. Brandon was surprised to see Thomas Boleyn carrying a taper. The once-proud earl seemed to have aged ten years, and people shunned him as he passed.

Queen Jane, recovering from two days and three nights of her long ordeal of childbirth, remained in her bed, but was said to be in good spirits. The queen was able to sit and greet the christening guests who called to wish her well.

Brandon held the golden pole of one corner of the cloth-of-gold canopy of estate over the prince, with the Marquess of Exeter, the Earl of Arundel, and Lord William Howard holding the others. The king's choristers sang the *Te Deum* as Archbishop Cranmer named the prince Edward, Duke of Cornwall and Earl of Chester.

After he'd been taken to the royal bedchamber for blessing by the king and queen, Katherine had the honour of carrying the precious child back to his nursery. She later told Brandon the king had tears of joy in his eyes at the sight of his new son.

Queen Jane, who suffered with a difficult birth, died nine days after the christening, with the king at her bedside. Brandon joined the sad procession of twenty-nine mourners at her funeral in St George's Chapel at Windsor Castle. Jane's step-daughter, Princess Mary, whom the queen had helped to restore to the king's great affection, was the chief mourner.

Henry, by tradition, remained with his grief, shut away from the world, and Brandon sensed the king might never be quite the same again. The only consolation was that the infant Prince Edward seemed a strong enough child, in good health.

Brandon finished his business in Suffolk and decided to make one last visit to Westhorpe Hall, a place of so much happiness – and sadness. Soon to be handed over to the king, the rooms had been stripped of his personal possessions, and much of the furniture sold.

He stood for a moment in his former study, where he'd learned of his beloved Mary's death. He pictured her now, not as the thin woman on her deathbed, but as the joyous and beautiful young Queen of France. He wished her peace.

Stepping out into the cobblestoned courtyard, he stopped to look at the ill-fated dovecot. The white paint was peeling and the fluttering doves were long gone, but he thought of his son Harry as he crossed to the private chapel.

The hinges squealed in protest as he pushed open the door, and cobwebs glistened in the light. He remembered Mary's gasp at her first sight of the magnificent stained-glass windows, a surprise he'd planned for her. It warmed his heart to see they were as bright and translucent as ever.

Brandon bent to his knees before the altar and clasped his hands in prayer. He thanked the Lord for the great good fortune of his life, for Anne, Mary, and Katherine, the wives he loved with all his heart. He gave thanks for all his children, Anne and Mary, Frances and Eleanor, Harry and Henry, whose lives were cut short, and Henry and little Charles, his heirs and successors.

He looked up at the centre window, where the vibrant image of the Madonna and Child glowed in the evening sunlight. To the left was Mary's golden fleur-de-lis and crown as Queen Dowager of France, and to the right shone his gold-crowned arms and Order of the Garter – the badge of a Tudor knight.

Brandon said his final prayer for the future, that his sons would have a life with as much adventure and opportunity as his, and that his wonderful wife Katherine would be at his side forever. He prayed for his daughters, that they would remember their mothers and have long and happy lives. 'O Lord, I pray I have lived a life that is good.' He smiled to himself. 'Amen.'

AUTHOR'S NOTE

Charles Brandon lived a full and active life right up to the day he died on 22 August 1545. He attended a meeting of the Privy Council in Guildford the day before his death, and Katherine was at his bedside with Frances and Eleanor to comfort his last hours.

Thomas Cromwell's reforms to the royal household created the new position of Lord Great Master to oversee everything. Charles Brandon was the first to hold this post until his death, when King Henry said that in all their long friendship Charles Brandon had never knowingly betrayed a friend or taken advantage of an enemy. He is reported to have asked his council, 'Is there any of you who can say as much?'

Brandon departed this life owing a considerable sum of money. His widow Katherine and the executors of his will spent many hours trying to understand how a man of great wealth managed to have such complicated debts with so many creditors.

Sadly, Brandon's two sons, Henry and Charles, both died within an hour of each other of the sweating sickness on the 14 July 1551. They had been at university in Cambridge but moved to the bishop's palace in Buckden (where Brandon visited Catherine of Aragon) to avoid the epidemic.

I was surprised to discover Brandon's widow Katherine was reported by Ambassador Eustace Chapuys to have been 'masking and visiting' with the king, starting rumours he might marry her. Katherine became one of Anne of Cleves's ladies, and in 1543 was lady-in-waiting to Queen Catherine Parr and they became close friends. She married a courtier, Richard Bertie, her Master of the Horse, for love in 1553.

Brandon's daughter Frances was the mother of Lady Jane Grey, who at sixteen became Queen of England after the death of her cousin, King Edward VI. Edward's half-sister, Princess Mary, was next in line for the throne but, as a Catholic, was out of favour. Mary overthrew Jane after nine days as queen, and she was found guilty of treason and beheaded on 12 February 1554.

Brandon wished to be buried in the college yard at Tattershall in Lincolnshire, 'without any pomp or outward pride.' Henry VIII insisted his oldest friend was laid to rest with full honours in St George's Chapel at Windsor Castle, where he had been made a Tudor knight. King Henry was buried less than two years later in the quire, only a few yards away.

Charles Brandon has been part of my life for the last two years, so I felt quite moved as I stood at his modest tomb in St George's Chapel. Set into the floor in the south transit of the chapel, it is adjacent to the tomb of King Henry VI and strangely inscribed: 'Charles Brandon, Duke of Suffolk KG. Died 24 August 1545. Married Mary daughter of Henry VII, Widow of Louis XII King of France.' (I believe it was at four o'clock in the afternoon, on 22 August, by chance the same date his father died at the Battle of Bosworth.)

All the names, places and events in this book are real and as accurately researched as possible, with the one exception of Brandon's groom Samuel, who I included to represent his many servants. Their names are lost to history but some members of Brandon's household followed him for most of his life.

I would like to thank my wife, Liz, and my editor, Nikki Brice, for their support during the research and writing of this book. I would also like to take this opportunity to thank the many readers around the world who have encouraged me to explore the real stories behind the Tudor dynasty.

If you enjoyed reading this book, please consider leaving a short review. It would mean a lot to me. Details of all my books can be found at my author website **www.tonyriches.com**.

Tony Riches
Pembrokeshire

MARY ~ Tudor Princess

Midsummer's Day 1509: The true story of the Tudor dynasty
continues with the daughter of King Henry VII. Mary Tudor
watches her elder brother become King of England and wonders
what the future holds for her.

Born into great privilege, Mary has beauty and intelligence beyond
her years. Her brother Henry plans to use her marriage to build a
powerful alliance against his enemies – but will she dare to risk his
anger by marrying for love?

Meticulously researched and based on actual events, this 'sequel'
follows Mary's story from book three of the Tudor Trilogy and is set
during the reign of King Henry VIII.

Available in paperback, audiobook and eBook

Katherine - Tudor Duchess

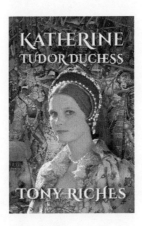

Attractive, wealthy and influential, Katherine Willoughby is one of the most unusual ladies of the Tudor court. A favourite of Henry VIII, Katherine knows all his six wives, his daughters Mary and Elizabeth and his son Edward.

She marries Tudor knight, Sir Charles Brandon, and becomes Duchess of Suffolk at the age of fourteen. Her Spanish mother, Maria de Salinas, is Catherine of Aragon's lady in waiting, so it is a challenging time for them all when King Henry marries the enigmatic Anne Boleyn.

Katherine's remarkable true story continues the epic tale of the rise of the Tudors, which began with the best-selling Tudor trilogy and concludes with the reign of Queen Elizabeth I.

Available as paperback and eBook

OWEN - Book One of the Tudor Trilogy

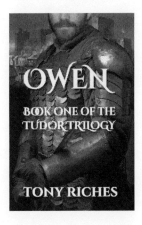

England 1422: Owen Tudor, a Welsh servant, waits in Windsor Castle to meet his new mistress, the beautiful and lonely Queen Catherine of Valois, widow of the warrior king, Henry V. Her infant son is crowned King of England and France, and while the country simmers on the brink of civil war, Owen becomes her protector.

They fall in love, risking Owen's life and Queen Catherine's reputation, but how do they found the dynasty which changes British history – the Tudors?

This is the first historical novel to fully explore the amazing life of Owen Tudor, grandfather of King Henry VII and the great-grandfather of King Henry VIII. Set against a background of the conflict between the Houses of Lancaster and York, which develops into what have become known as the Wars of the Roses, Owen's story deserves to be told.

Available as paperback, audiobook and eBook

JASPER - Book Two of the Tudor Trilogy

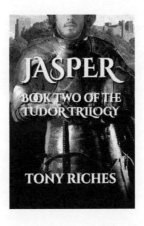

England 1461: The young King Edward of York has taken the country by force from King Henry VI of Lancaster. Sir Jasper Tudor, Earl of Pembroke, flees the massacre of his Welsh army at the Battle of Mortimer's Cross.

When King Henry is imprisoned by Edward in the Tower of London and murdered, Jasper escapes to Brittany with his young nephew, Henry Tudor. With nothing but his wits and charm, Jasper sees his chance to make young Henry Tudor king with a daring and reckless invasion of England.

Set in the often brutal world of fifteenth-century England, Wales, Scotland, France, Burgundy and Brittany, during the Wars of the Roses, this fast-paced story is one of courage and adventure, love and belief in the destiny of the Tudors.

Available as paperback, audiobook and eBook

HENRY - Book Three of the Tudor Trilogy

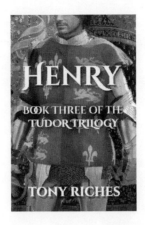

Bosworth 1485: After victory against King Richard III, Henry Tudor becomes King of England. Rebels and pretenders plot to seize his throne. The barons resent his plans to curb their power and he wonders who he can trust. He hopes to unite Lancaster and York through marriage to the beautiful Elizabeth of York.

With help from his mother, Lady Margaret Beaufort, he learns to keep a fragile peace. He chooses a Spanish Princess, Catherine of Aragon, as a wife for his son Prince Arthur.

His daughters will marry the King of Scotland and the son of the Emperor of Rome. It seems his prayers are answered, then disaster strikes and Henry must ensure the future of the Tudors.

Available in paperback, eBook and audiobook

Made in the USA
Middletown, DE
26 June 2020